The Winding

Ali Ives

Literary Wanderlust | Denver, Colorado

Published in the United States by Literary Wanderlust LLC, Denver, Colorado. www.LiteraryWanderlust.com

ISBN print: 978-1-956615-10-4
ISBN digital: 978-1-956615-11-1

Cover design: Craig Terlson
Printed in the United States of America

Dedication

For Dad. This one's for you. I'm keeping the line where I use the word "chiaroscuro," to which you said, "Oh brother!"
Love always.

The Missing God

There is a place, somewhere in the imponderable depths of the universe, where time does not exist. This is the Crossroads.

Philosophers, of course, may argue that this timeless place is everywhere, time itself being a relative and man-made concept. This is their prerogative and a wise person knows not to argue with philosophers unless you have an awful lot of time to spare.

Place without time is an odd thing. It has no boundaries, for there is no time existing to take to travel to them. Instead the place stretches on and on toward endless horizons.

It does have a middle, though, and there lies the Crossing of the Ways.

Were mortals to gaze upon it, they would likely find themselves unimpressed with this strange world all its own. For all the grandeur of its impossibility, the view isn't anything especially awe-inspiring. Two narrow dirt roads, long and dusty, flee their crossing toward the boundless edges of perception. They never twist, never turn, and never cross another path. Only here, at the Crossroads.

It's the place of a lonely god, and he isn't home.

The sky above, as endless as the horizons, was once blue and cloudless. Now towering pillars of storm clouds gather, rumbling like the thousand voices of an army awaiting its general.

There is no time here, but there is in other places. Somewhere far away from the Crossroads it is a very important time indeed.

It is a beginning.

Chapter 1

The Burning Car

It started off, as so many things do, with a bang.

The pleasant pink-orange hue of the morning sky above the ancient city-state of Frettchen was interrupted by an intrusion of blasting light, accompanied by the deafening sound of an explosion. Smoke plumed upward, further marring the sunrise.

Since the fall of the old empire more than a thousand years ago, Frettchen had been the jewel of the Lower Lands. More temperate and stable than the Nordlands and more of a technological hub than the South Cities, the city-state lay nestled between the desert to the east and the ocean to the west, a bustling metropolis that had long garnered what its citizens considered to be a well-earned respect and healthy amount of wariness from the neighboring regions.

The actual site of the explosion was just outside the city limits, on a wooded hill overlooking its far-flung streets, at the very top of which sat a majestic mansion. The smoke was black and heavy, clogging air that had until seconds previously been sweet with the scent of flowers and the freshness of spring. Birds, startled from their perches, ascended from the canopy of the forest surrounding the mansion in a cacophony of alarm.

Down on the ground, the high minister, lord of the city-state, watched the burning wreckage of what had very recently been his favorite car from under the sudden cover of several black-clad security agents. A lot of shouting filled the smoky air, but he was having a rather difficult time making out any specifics between the ringing in his ears and the fact that someone's arms were braced over his head and muffling everything. He could hazard a guess, though. A car exploding into a ball of fiery death seconds before the city's topmost official stepped into it was cause for concern, after all. If he hadn't turned back halfway between the front steps and the car, intent on summoning one of his aides for a last-minute request, he wouldn't still be alive.

"Get off me," he said, the demand as muffled as his hearing. He struggled a bit and tried again, raising his voice. "Get off me! That's an order."

The agents shielding his body were reluctant but eventually complied, disentangling themselves from their protective cocoon of limbs. They shuffled around him as he got unsteadily to his feet, a be-suited wall that blocked him from the still-burning car and any lingering danger.

The minister swept a hand through his graying hair, trying to catch his breath. He wasn't a tall man, and he had to crane his neck to see past the shoulders of his guards, who all wore the stern expression of professionals trying not to panic. Behind them, the burning car coughed another billow of smoke and fire. The noise sounded like the death rattle of some giant beast suffering through its final breath.

"Well damn," the minister said faintly, eyes watering in the smoky air. "I loved that car." A gift from one of the lords of the South Cities, it had been one of a kind, a vintage body powered by the latest and most advanced model of the perpetual engine.

He'd been quite determined to keep it maintained and running well into his retirement. So much for that. He sighed, brows lowering as he did his best to clear his mind and throat. There would be time later to mourn expensive automobiles. Right now there were more important things to deal with. Namely the fact that someone had just tried to kill him.

It wasn't unexpected in his line of work. As high minister of Frettchen, he'd been in charge of religious affairs in the city for the past decade, and when he won the post of lord of the city-state four years ago, he became the chief of secular matters as well. He possessed an intoxicating amount of power, but with it came more than his fair share of enemies in Frettchen and the outlying regions alike. It would seem someone had finally found the courage and foolhardiness to act on their dislike of him. A mistake they would come to regret dearly, he vowed, eyes narrowed as the smell of burning rubber filled his nostrils.

Hearing a fresh cry of dismay, he stopped trying to see over his guards and turned instead to the harried man who dashed down the front steps of the mansion, hastening toward him. Toby Mulligan, his chief adviser, looked horror-struck, the flames from the burning car reflected in the lenses of his horn-rimmed glasses, painting the glass orange and yellow. He gaped at the scene before him.

"What—What happened?" he managed in a strangled voice. He looked from the fiery wreckage to the minister, hands raking through his short brown hair, making it stand on end. The effect made him look quite mad and would have been comical in different circumstances.

The minister, in contrast, looked very serious. Though his eyes were red and his throat raw from the smoke, his brain had banished the shock to the back of his mind with a proficiency that always worked in his favor during crises.

"Obvious, isn't it?" he said. He thought he sounded admirably gruff and authoritative for someone covered head to toe in ash. "Someone's trying to kill me."

He caught the look Mulligan sent him, panic and confusion pinching his features, but he offered only a determined scowl in return. The wordless warning silenced his adviser. The high minister straightened his lapels in a matter-of-fact way. "Now. I'd rather like to do something about it before they realize they've failed."

—

An hour passed in a rush of clamor and kerfuffle, and the minister found himself increasingly peeved with the fact that very little was being done in the aftermath of his near-demise.

Perhaps this was ungenerous. The car had been extinguished, its skeletal remains were being worked over by security agents who searched diligently for evidence, and the press was being waylaid by his very best team of public relations experts. He supposed it was unrealistic to hope they would have progressed any further in the span of a mere hour. Assassination attempts had a way of making a person impatient, however. Besides the urgency of finding out who and how and why, he had to deal with the additional irritation of his schedule being so unceremoniously disrupted. Leading an independent city as old and influential as Frettchen didn't leave a lot of time free. He would have to reschedule half a dozen meetings, at least. Still, those obvious questions were the ones at the forefront of his concerns.

"That's all very well and good," he said, shooing another medic away like a bothersome mosquito and glaring at his chief adviser. "But who is it, Mulligan? Who's behind it?"

"Hard to say." Mulligan scratched his chin.

He'd calmed down a lot in the past hour. The minister wasn't sure whether he ought to be pleased that his adviser was being so professional in a crisis or miffed that he had so quickly shaken off his concern for his life.

"You do have more than a few enemies, sir," Mulligan added.

"Quite," the minister grunted, frowning even more. Another

unrealistic expectation had been thinking Mulligan would have any better idea as to the culprit's identity than he did. Yet the question was chasing its tail in his head, around and around endlessly. "But it's the first time someone's gotten this close to blowing me up, and I can't say I'm much pleased with it." He gazed around the room, trying to sort through his thoughts. Through the open door of his office he could see his staff and security detail hurrying hither and thither like distressed sheep. A dozen worried voices blended together into a hectic buzz that did nothing to calm his nerves.

Again it, grudgingly, occurred to him that his irritation with his people was unfair. They were working hard to figure this out. He just wasn't convinced it would be enough. He made a point of trusting no one completely and suspecting everyone to varying degrees. While this approach played well to politics, it left him with a long line of suspects and not a lot of surefire allies.

"We'll get to the bottom of this, sir," Mulligan said, as if reading his mind. He had a knack for it, just as he did for stating such things in an earnest tone that made it sound like he had no idea he was doing anything of the sort. It was at once comforting and disconcerting, an oxymoron of a sensation that only Mulligan seemed capable of instilling. "Trust me."

The minister regarded him seriously. Trust no one, he told himself. Every seeming friend was an enemy waiting to happen, especially at a time like this. And yet, on the other hand, he knew he couldn't do this alone. Power and connections were his weapons, but the former wasn't enough on its own to find and deal with an assassin, and the latter was negated entirely if he cut himself off from the people around him. He certainly couldn't trust anyone, but he would just as certainly need to use them.

What he needed was the *right* help.

"I want to talk to Gloucester."

—

Another fifteen minutes passed and the minister's sympathy for his staff was eroding dramatically. No longer was the reminder that they were doing their best working to dissuade his impatience. From where he sat behind his desk, suit still gray with ash, he glared at his adviser, watching Mulligan shift his weight from foot to foot and feeling extremely annoyed when his intimidating glower didn't change the answer he was getting. He knew the expression was a good one. One of the best in his arsenal of displeased faces, its furious effect was only increased by the angry red in his eyes left behind by the smoke. Clearly he used the glare too liberally when it came to Mulligan; the man was gaining immunity or something.

"How many times do I have to say this?" he demanded, pointing an accusatory finger at the other man. "Bring me Gloucester."

"It's not that easy, sir," Mulligan insisted, as he'd been doing for the last quarter of an hour. "He *is* in prison, after all."

"Which should make fetching him quite easy! You know right where to find him."

The minister sensed Mulligan was resisting the urge to wring his hands. He was a slow one to temper but always quick to start fretting. A quality that made him very good at his job, the minister mused, the best adviser being the sort who quickly spotted problems other people might miss. Still, it probably wasn't the best for Mulligan's own sake. He'd worry himself into an early grave, no doubt.

Or I'll bloody kill him for not obeying orders. The minister's fingers drummed an uneven beat against the smooth surface of his desk. His thoughts still chased each other in his mind, possible answers and solutions intermingling with potential pitfalls of each course of action that occurred to him. The future had become perilous waters to navigate the moment that bomb went off. No matter how he considered the situation, though, one plan stood out to him as the least terrible.

If only his chief adviser saw things the same way.

"I just don't think he's someone we ought to be turning to with this," Mulligan said. The minister looked up from the desktop, where he'd been absently staring at his own reflection on the polished wood. Mulligan met his gaze with worried eyes. "Protecting you and all. I mean, you were the one who *put* him in prison. That sort of thing doesn't really make people feel all that inclined to be helpful." He glanced over his shoulder to check no one else was within earshot, then added, "Think about what happened." His voice dropped to a whisper. "What we saw. I don't think he'll—"

"Oh, he'll help," the minister said. "If it means his freedom. Now, enough waffling. This is an order. Bring me Gloucester."

Chapter 2

Gloucester

Mikalai Gloucester stared up at the blank ceiling of his cell. The white-painted tiles were cracked: long, thin fissures spider-webbing across the expanse of the surface above his head. He knew none of these cracks ran deep enough to be of any use to him; he'd tested them all months ago in search of a weak spot, just as he'd tested the walls and the door. There were eighty-one cracks in the ceiling in total. He knew that too. He'd counted each and every one of them, every day for the past six months.

Gloucester was not a criminal. He'd told himself that as often as he'd counted the cracks on the ceiling. He wasn't a criminal and he didn't deserve to be here.

Unfortunately, knowing this didn't change the fact that here was where he was. He'd shouted his innocence—at the walls, at the ceiling, at the guards who brought him his food twice a day and a change of clothes twice a week. For the whole first month he'd shouted, his voice growing rough and his words desperate.

Finally, he'd given up. Not in his own belief of his innocence or his desire for freedom, but in his efforts to convince people he now knew weren't listening. The realization of *why* had settled in with clarity after the loud anger and panic passed, and allowed his mind to grow quiet. He knew why he was here. Not for something he'd done, but for something he knew. This wasn't punishment, it was protection. Just not his own.

Therein lay the problem, though. One atop a mountain of others.

He didn't know what it was that he *knew*.

Whatever damnable piece of information he'd happened upon or secret he'd unintentionally stolen, he had no idea what it was. Yet his insistence of this had fallen on deaf ears, even as it turned to pleading. And then months passed, and more and more he wondered if maybe he'd simply lost his mind. Had he somehow forgotten? Misunderstood something? Sometimes he wondered if this wasn't just all in his head, some torture his broken mind had conjured up for him, a prison of his own making. From day to day and week to week, he teeter-tottered between a simmering anger, panic, and despair, and the nuance of each particular mindset shifted him between existential crisis, crushing fear, and bleak curiosity.

As he stared up at the ceiling now, he felt no great sense that things would soon be changing for him. He didn't sense the dawning of some great new adventure. Mostly he just felt bored.

Gloucester had a youthful face, the scruffy beard incarceration had granted him barely making him look his twenty-six years of age. Beneath a mop of curly black hair, his eyes were equally dark, unfocused at the moment as his mind wandered. His fingers tapped a quiet rhythm against the flat mattress of his bed. He'd long since given up wondering what day it was. Days of the week held little meaning in this place. Time was marked instead by meals, laundry day and, whenever he was feeling particularly bored, escape attempts.

The lock clicking in the door made him blink, and it took a few seconds to chase away his idle thoughts. By the time the door swung open, he was sitting upright, alert and wary.

The men and women who filled the open doorway weren't dressed like soldiers, but Gloucester could tell from the way they carried themselves and the steely looks in their eyes that these were people trained not to take any fuss. They wore well-tailored black suits over crisp white shirts, and though not a single pair was in sight, he felt each of them was wearing sunglasses in spirit.

"I used to have a suit like that," he said, surreptitiously rolling his shoulders, limbering up his muscles. "What do you want?"

One of the men, a brawny, bald fellow of towering height, carried restraints. Bad sign. Gloucester watched him until another stepped forward, brandishing a syringe. Worse sign.

"Please hold still, sir," the man said. He was, if possible, even brawnier and balder than the first man and had a deep, calming voice to which Gloucester immediately took umbrage. He narrowed his eyes. Polite tones from someone wielding a needle was never a good thing unless they were a doctor. Even then there were more than a few exceptions.

"What do you *want*?" he asked again, an edge creeping into his voice as he stood. He took a few steps back, the floor cold beneath his bare feet. He couldn't avoid getting cornered, but he wasn't about to make things easy for them.

It came as no real surprise when his question wasn't graced with an answer. Instead, the man with the syringe moved forward, flanked on either side by a man and a woman with matching expressions of stolid disinterest. Each held a heavy cudgel. Gloucester shifted his footing, hands curling into fists. A fight against these people was doubtlessly doomed, but it would be better than no fight at all. He wasn't naive enough to believe that things, even as bad as they were here, couldn't get worse. He had, after all, the misfortune of possessing an active imagination. And one aspect of an active imagination is being able to comprehend that others might have one too.

Taking note of his defensiveness, the man with the syringe retreated a few steps, but Gloucester didn't think for a moment that this was a good thing. Indeed, it made room for the other two to step forward, their weapons raised menacingly. Gloucester could guess how this was going to go. The logical part of his brain despairingly considered his plans for the immediate future pointless and ridiculous. The rest of him ignored it. If he couldn't fight in the name of escape, he sure as hell would do so in the name of pride.

Not wasting any time, he made the first definitive move, abruptly pushing forward from where he'd backed himself against the wall of the cell opposite the door. Though the guards had clearly been expecting trouble, instinct was difficult to fight, and they halted in their steps, the man on the left even flinching a little. The woman did better at keeping her composure but raised her cudgel just an instant too late—Gloucester's fist barrelled through the air and collided with her jaw with a resounding thud.

Ignoring the pain in his knuckles, Gloucester shifted his stance fluidly and struck again, this time aiming lower, and delivered a solid punch to the security agent's abdomen. The breath whooshed from her lungs in a wheezing gasp, and she collapsed to her knees. Before she was even down, Gloucester was pivoting to face her partner, fists raised—

But he'd run out of time. He managed a single sharp kick to the man's shin before two more agents crowded into the now-cramped cell, grabbing his arms and pulling them roughly back to an awkward angle that made movement impossible. A hand on the back of his neck forced his head down, until he was staring at his feet. He swore. The harsh words came out in Nordish, his mother's first language. Raising his gaze as much as he was able, he took in the damage he'd managed to inflict in his brief moment of control.

The man with the syringe had stepped forward again. Behind him, the two unfortunate agents were picking themselves up and being helped from the room, both limping. Gloucester allowed himself a moment of bitter satisfaction at the sight. It was short-lived, however, as his attention was soon pulled back to the man with the needle.

"This could have been a lot easier, Mr. Gloucester," the man said with a touch of reproach. His smooth face was as frustratingly calm as his words.

"Dunno," panted Gloucester. Caught between the two men holding his arms, he had to crane his neck to look up at the other man, further hindered by the hand still pressing down on the base of his skull. "Seems like it'd be about the same for me either way."

Perhaps the needle man had no retort for that, or maybe he'd simply run out of patience; either way, he didn't reply as he stepped up beside Gloucester and nodded to one of his subduers. Gloucester's shirt sleeve was pushed up his arm, out of the way. Then came the sharp prick of the needle, like the bite of an insect injecting him with some unknown venom. Though he struggled to keep his thoughts clear, it quickly became a lost cause. The room blurred at the edges and skewed oddly, as if he were looking at it through curved glass. Darkness wormed its way into the cracks of his consciousness, spreading until all the world was black.

—

The waking world was slow to return, pieced together in a haze of blurred confusion. Gloucester's head spun, vision dancing drunkenly even as his sluggish mind began to clear. He shook his head, trying to dislodge the lingering effects of the drug. Even with clarity returning, he felt bogged down, his very bones lined with lead. Probably an intentional side effect. Keep him slow. Easy to control.

Coughing quietly, he raised his eyes to take in his

surroundings. It wasn't a shock to find himself no longer in his cell. The familiar four walls he hated so much had been replaced by a room that was equally sparse, if differing in contents. He took in a table, two chairs—the one he was sitting on and another on the opposite side of the table, awaiting an occupant—and a stern-faced guard in the corner. She stared straight ahead, her eye-line about two feet up and over to Gloucester's right. He peered at her warily, but she seemed intent on ignoring him. After a moment, he left her to it and turned his attention to the rest of the room.

There wasn't much more to see. A door stood closed in the corner to the guard's right—his left—and that was about it. The off-white walls were blank and his companion in the corner silent, giving no clue as to where he was or why.

That was, beyond the educated guess he could make from past experience. Its appearance was that of a fairly standard interrogation room. But after six months of nothing but the inside of a cell to look at, what were they intending to interrogate him about? And who were "they"?

The latter was a question soon answered, but it brought on its heels a dozen new mysteries to replace it. The door opened soundlessly and another man stepped into the room. He was of middling age as well as height, and Gloucester knew that were they both standing, they would meet each other almost exactly eye to eye. Once upon a time, he had spent hours a day standing at this man's shoulder.

After all these months, and everything he'd been put through, what more could the high minister of Frettchen possibly want with him?

"I apologize for the, ah, less than polite manner of your coming here," said the high minister as he sat in the chair across the table, sounding entirely unapologetic. Gloucester didn't grace him with a reply, merely eyed him and waited, in the same way he had with the agents back in his cell.

"Forgive me," the minister continued, unfazed by the lack

of a greeting, "but I'm sure you understand that I cannot expect you to be the most . . . trustworthy, given the circumstances."

Gloucester broke his silence with a laugh, still trying to blink away the blurred edges of his vision. "Given the circumstances, you're talking an awful lot about apologies, forgiveness, and understanding."

There hadn't been much opportunity for conversation in the last several months, and his voice sounded alien in his own ears, at once too loud and too quiet. Though his speech seemed unimpeded by the effects of the drug, his bout of forced sleep hadn't helped matters, leaving his mouth dry and throat raspy. He wanted to shout, to snarl and snap, but his own voice protested the notion, and even if it hadn't, he doubted he could summon the effort for it. If anyone deserved his rage-filled shouts, it was the gentleman sitting across from him, with his dapper suit, neat graying hair, and cold politeness. But Gloucester had long since lost the energy for that sort of heated anger. It had tempered into a quieter, resigned fury that burned cold. He glared at the minister.

"You've yet to give me a good reason to accept or offer any of it."

"Indeed," the minister said, infuriatingly lackadaisical. Before everything had gone wrong, it had been Gloucester's job to watch discreetly from the sidelines as the lord of the city-state used this calmness against belligerents and adversaries. Though he'd never been altogether fond of the man, he'd admired the strategy and the talent he possessed. Now that he was the one bearing the brunt of it, the minister's imperturbability only made Gloucester loathe him all the more.

"What do you want?" he ground out. He felt like the question was becoming his motto. The after-effects of the drug were starting to wane and he moved his arms experimentally, only to blink and look down at them when they were stopped short with clinking resistance. His wrists were secured to the arms of the chair with handcuffs, the metal cool against his skin. He blamed the drug-induced daze for not noticing earlier. They certainly weren't underestimating him this time, he mused; he couldn't move his hands more than two inches in any direction.

"I'm assuming there's some point to this," he added waspishly. The cold anger was heating up again, as if coming out of hibernation.

The minister spread his hands in a magnanimous gesture, though Gloucester suspected it was an intentional reminder of his own inhibited movements. "I want to give you your job back."

Whatever Gloucester had expected to hear, it wasn't this. For a moment, he was so surprised he forgot to be angry. His surliness blinked away, replaced by wide-eyed confusion. "What?"

The minister nodded patiently. Yet Gloucester noticed, as he eyed him with renewed keenness, a tightness around his eyes that suggested he wasn't as calm and collected as he was presenting himself to be.

"I want to give you your old job back," he repeated. "With full compensation for the past six months, of course—"

"You mean the six months of being locked up in solitary confinement for no bloody reason?" Now that Gloucester's anger had begun to thaw, he found it more and more difficult to keep it in check. But despite his increasingly hot temper, his attention was divided. What had the high minister so worried? So concerned that he would renounce Gloucester's sentence with so little reason or to-do?

He's desperate. Or scared. Or both.

He'd never known the lord of the city-state to be either. Something was happening. Something bad. At least, bad for the politician. And while Gloucester was pleased at the notion of bad things happening to the man, he knew things were never so simple. Bad things rarely happened to just one person; they affected anyone and everyone around them. Getting involved would be foolhardy—

Yet it could mean freedom. A way out of the four walls of his cell and the confinement that had been his life for half a year now.

Provided the high minister was telling the truth. He was a politician, so this didn't seem terribly likely. And not just any politician, either. This was the person who'd ordered Gloucester's imprisonment in the first place. Trusting *anything* he said would be idiotic.

The minister's voice broke through his conflicted thoughts. "Yes, those six months. Mr. Gloucester, I know it's too much to ask for your forgiveness or even your understanding. But you're not a stupid man. If you were, you'd never have been working for me in the first place. I have no use for stupid people. At least not on my payroll," he amended with a quiet chuckle. "You're smart and resourceful. And so I'll appeal to your logic. Agree to hear me out and you may just win your freedom. Otherwise . . . Well, that cell you've been in can always be . . . downgraded." He shrugged with an admirable imitation of nonchalance. "It's your choice."

Gloucester's stare was flat, his fists clenched against the cold metal arms of the chair. "Not really." What choice was there? Jump in bed with those who had hurt him or suffer even more at their hands. Some decision. The minister had backed him into a corner, with no way out but through cooperation. It tempted him to turn the offer down just to spite the bastard. Still, he gritted his teeth. "Fine. I'm listening."

"Excellent," the minister said. He spread his hands again, but this time the gesture had lost its smug humor. His eyes were serious, the taut line of his mouth grim. "Someone's trying to kill me."

"Congratulations to them," said Gloucester, sitting back as comfortably as he could in his restraints and turning his face away from his captor in favor of surveying the room again. The drugs had left him with a nasty headache. "Sounds like I should just choose the cell for a little longer, then."

"Yes, I figured you'd say something to that effect. Look, Mr. Gloucester—or do you prefer Mikalai?"

"No."

His taciturn reply earned a shrug. "Mr. Gloucester, I know you bear me nothing but ill will. I don't expect anything else, all considering. But if I die, it's not just me who loses."

"Though arguably you lose the most," Gloucester muttered.

The minister pretended not to hear. "It would be bad for everyone, for the whole city."

Surprised by his earnest tone, Gloucester reluctantly turned to meet his gaze.

"I'm the high minister of Frettchen, Gloucester," he said slowly, clearly determined to ensure the words sank in. "And the lord of the city-state. Hate me all you want, but I protect our citizens, and my death would have repercussions for everyone. In fact," he added with a dry huff of laughter, "when you think about it, I'd be the only one *not* suffering them. Arguably, I'd lose the *least*."

Not terribly appreciative of his own mockery being used against him, Gloucester stared down at the tabletop in silence as he gathered his thoughts. Unfortunately, the man was talking sense. High minister and lord of the city-state were two of the most vital positions in Frettchen's hierarchy and, unlike anyone before him, he held both. He'd managed, through a long career of bullying, weaseling, and cleverness, to make himself indispensable to anyone who didn't want to see the city fall into civil unrest at best and war at worst. His followers in the church were devoutly loyal and would surely be in an uproar were anything to happen to him, and tensions with the Nordlands and the South Cities grew with each passing year. A sudden power vacuum would present dangerous opportunities for these outside forces.

Gloucester sighed, a long sharp breath through his nose. "Yeah, okay. Fine." Drumming his fingers on the arm of the chair, he cocked his head. "That explains why I should help.

Hypothetically. But why should you *want* me to help?"

"Well, I'm not very fond of dying—"

Gloucester rolled his eyes. "No. Why do *you* want *me* to help?" He raised his hands enough to make the slim chains of the handcuffs clink. "I'm not exactly 'employee of the month.' And even before you locked me up and left me to rot, there were other agents more qualified."

The minister wagged a finger at him, clicking his tongue like a teacher admonishing a pupil. Gloucester hated him even more. "Don't undersell yourself. But yes, there are others who are better. More talented, more experienced, more intelligent—"

"Wow, don't go flattering me too much," Gloucester grumbled. "I'm supposed to be mad at you."

"But you are the man for the job," the minister said, once again ignoring him. "You're resourceful, careful, smart. And there's no way you're involved in the assassination attempt."

"And there it is." Gloucester nodded, smiling with no real humor. "There's the real reason. You don't trust your people. You're afraid someone's been compromised."

"Corrupted," the minister said, with a faint chuckle. "But yes. You have to admit, you have one hell of a solid alibi."

Gloucester's laughter was as humorless as his smile. "Lucky me. So you want me to come back to work, like nothing's happened, and find out who the assassin and their associates are."

The minister's own smile vanished, chased away by the return of steely determination. The expression looked much more at home on the man's face than something as benevolent as a smile. "Find out who, find out how, and most importantly, find *them*." He dipped a hand into his jacket and pulled out something small and silver. A key. The minister set it down on the table between them with a quiet sound that nonetheless echoed like thunder in Gloucester's ears. A cold gaze met his. "And then I want you to kill them."

Gloucester looked down at the key. Such a simple thing,

small and unadorned. Nothing about it looked special. And yet it represented everything. It meant freedom.

Or, he thought, raising his gaze back to the man across the table, as close to freedom as he could hope for right now. He wasn't foolish enough to think he'd be going from solitary confinement to free citizen just like that. Life wasn't that easy, and it certainly wasn't that fair. But it would be a step closer. It would get him out of the damned cell that had been his waking nightmare for months.

"I'll help you," he said, matching the minister's even tone. "Whatever it takes. Just let me go."

Chapter 3

Shaky Ground

The next few days passed in a blur. After the sense of urgency the high minister had given him, Gloucester had expected to get right to work solving the mystery of the would-be assassin, but as was often the case, life wasn't so simple.

What he hadn't been expecting—though in hindsight he knew he should have—was a whirlwind of suit-fittings, aptitude tests, and pointed questions about his physical and mental well-being.

The last was broached by a shrewd-faced doctor who sat across from him in a sterile interrogation room and asked him questions in an innocent tone rarely adopted by anyone without an agenda. Gloucester answered the questions carefully and with as much frank honesty as he could fabricate. It was more conversation than he'd had in months, and he felt strangely out of his depth. He'd never been very fond of talking to strangers, but now it felt like a skill he'd left untouched for too long and allowed to get rusty. The result was an awkwardness that ground at his nerves as much as the doctor's questions. Eventually, the doctor seemed satisfied, or at least had gotten what he came for, and Gloucester was led back to his rooms.

It didn't take him long to reach the conclusion that he and the high minister had vastly different notions of what constituted his freedom. True, he was no longer drugged, handcuffed, or locked in a cell, but he wasn't convinced his new circumstances were the dramatic step up he was supposed to believe them to be.

For one, they wouldn't let him go home. Though after all these months, he wasn't sure he had a home to go to. He didn't want to think about that; doing so only made things worse. Life had been good before his arrest. Despite his job, his day-to-day existence was mostly uneventful, which was the way he preferred it. He was happy. As he'd done for the duration of his solitary confinement, he tried not to wonder what his family had been told, where his parents thought he was or what Jeb believed had happened to him.

The latter haunted him the most. The thought of his boyfriend was a painful twist in his chest, a stab of emotion that hadn't dulled over time. Had they told him Gloucester was arrested? A criminal? Or had some other lie been concocted? Did the man he loved and everyone else in his life think he was dead? No one would answer his questions on the matter, rebuffing every attempt he made to get in contact with his old life. Instead, he'd been set up with rooms in the minister's massive mansion, under the rather weak justification that it would make his job of protecting the man more convenient, and with several none-too-subtle threats about what would happen should he talk to anyone to whom he wasn't given permission.

The rooms were pleasant enough at first glance. They were generous in size, the bathroom alone as big as the cell he'd left behind. The furniture was expensive and well-made, the bed soft and the shower hot. He even had a small balcony overlooking the gardens below, though he noticed anything that might have helped him climb down to the ground had been removed. There also always seemed to be a security agent loitering in the shrubbery below or sitting on one of the benches, their neat black suit decidedly out-of-place among the colorful peonies and lilacs.

He'd discovered a similarly dressed figure on the other side of his door when, the first night of his stay, he tried to leave his room after being dismissed to it. As he was herded back inside by the impatient agent, the realization had properly sunk in: pretty furnishings aside, he was still a prisoner.

At the moment, he was pacing his room. The view outside the sliding glass door to the balcony was painted in darkness, a bare sliver of moon casting a pale silver glow over the silhouettes of the trees surrounding the high minister's gardens. Beyond them, only the tallest buildings of the city were visible: the twin spires of the Old Cathedral and the less majestic shapes of skyscrapers over in the financial district.

The night's peacefulness went unnoticed by Gloucester, caught up as he was in the chaos of his own thoughts.

Every now and then, he halted his pacing in front of the desk against one wall, to glance over the documents spread across an open case file. Photographs of a smoldering wreck of a car, reports on the attack, documented bomb fragments. He'd been over it all a dozen times in the last few days, in moments like these when he was left alone to his own devices. But only so much could be learned from studying pictures and paperwork. He needed to get out there. Talk to people, investigate.

For the fourth time that night, he strode to the door and stood with his hand on the doorknob, about to push it open and demand the agent on the other side let him see the high minister. But he knew he'd have no chance of an audience with the man at this hour. He'd have to wait until the morning and hope he could convince the minister that he was of no more use to him locked up in here than in prison.

He was just so antsy. He'd have thought after six months locked up, he'd be used to confinement. Maybe the change of environment or the promise of freedom, false or not, had given him the hope that was so absent in his cell. Whatever the cause, ever since the minister unlocked his handcuffs in the interrogation room, Gloucester had found it nearly impossible to relax. Each night, when he finally grew too tired to keep reading over the case, he'd lie awake in bed, staring up at the ceiling until exhaustion allowed sleep to take hold. It was strange to lie under a different ceiling. There were no cracks in this one. It was pristine. Too perfect, like everything else here. In the darkest moments, right before sleep, he found himself wondering if he missed his cell. There, at least, he knew who he could trust. Himself and no one else.

But that was crazy, as he told himself each time. He didn't miss the prison. He ought to miss the life he'd had before it. Those memories of happier, simpler times were what he wanted to cling to. To return to. Yet even the most recent ones, the ones from right before his imprisonment, felt oddly disjointed and distant. It was another reason to not think about them for now. And anyway, being here now didn't change the fact that he couldn't trust anyone beyond himself. It was a change of setting, nothing more. An improvement. It wasn't freedom, but it was one step closer. All that stood between him and liberty was the case. Find who had tried to kill the high minister and he was a free man.

Or so he was told. This thought haunted his mind in the shadowy moments of oncoming sleep each night as well. He had only the assurance of the very man who'd locked him away that this would lead to his freedom. For all he knew, the moment he solved this case, he'd be right back in that cell.

Only if they catch me. He cast another glance at the case files before returning to his pacing. He knew the exact number of steps it took to cross from one side of the room to the other. Seven paces to the window, seven back to the door. And back and forth and back again.

Was escape possible?

Not if he didn't solve this case. Until he did, he would always be watched. The minister might not trust his men enough to give them the job of finding his assailant, but obviously he didn't mind putting several to the task of keeping an eye on Gloucester.

But maybe if he solved it, he could slip away in the aftermath. The chance was slim, but it felt like the only one he had.

Which meant being patient. He breathed a quiet huff of laughter at the thought. He'd waited this long for freedom, he could manage to wait a bit longer.

And how long do I wait for justice? He stopped by the window, sourly searching the darkness outside, staring past his own reflection. Was he just supposed to *help* this man who had torn him away from everything he knew and everyone he loved and put him through months of solitary confinement? All to *maybe* gain his freedom, *if* he was lucky? Or escape and live the rest of his life looking over his shoulder? It wasn't fair.

Nothing ever is. The reminder was cold as winter wind. He turned sharply away from the window. He'd do what he had to.

—

The next morning dawned crisp and clear, as if in deliberate contrast to Gloucester's murky thoughts the night before. He was still far from accustomed to the natural light from the windows, and he rose from bed early, unable to sleep with the slanting rays of sun falling across his face. As the sky outside grew brighter, he passed the time stretching, then moved onto sit-ups and push-ups. This exercise routine required little in the way of space and had thus become an ingrained part of his mornings all those months in his cell. Once that was done, he showered, shaved, and dressed, forsaking the jacket and tie he'd been provided and rolling up his sleeves haphazardly before settling down at the desk to look over the case yet again.

By the time the distant bells of the cathedral struck seven

o'clock, however, he'd lost patience with the exercise in redundancy. Getting to his feet with a muttered oath, he strode to the door and swung it open.

He immediately came face to face with the agents standing guard on the other side. There were two of them; it must have been the morning switch-off, night shift for day shift. They both stared at him, clearly not expecting his sudden appearance in the doorway.

"I need to talk to the high minister," he told them, not bothering with a greeting, and jerking his wrist away when one of them stepped forward to snatch at it. He flashed a glare at the offender, holding his ground but instinctively shifting his footing into a defensive stance.

"It's seven in the morning," the agent who'd made a grab for him protested. Gloucester guessed she was the night shift. She looked tired and ill-tempered, her once-tidy braid fraying with flyaway strands and dark bags under her eyes from a sleepless night. Gloucester didn't feel much sympathy for her, considering said sleepless night had been spent ensuring his continued imprisonment.

"Sorry," he said, putting very little effort into sounding very sorry at all. He'd never had a good face for sneering, but he made up for it in tone. "I didn't realize the high minister's beauty sleep was more important than finding the person trying to blow him up. I'll just leave him to it, then."

The tired agent looked affronted, but before she could say anything, her replacement stepped forward, shaking her head. "Don't worry about it, Amelia. I'll take him to His Lordship."

Amelia's glare faded to a faint smile as she cast a glance at the other woman. "Thanks, Jess." Clapping her on the shoulder, she spared a quick disapproving look Gloucester's way, then turned on her heel and trudged away down the hall and out of sight.

The other agent, Jess, frowned at Gloucester. "Right, you," she said, with significantly less friendliness. "C'mon, then. And don't try anything." She gestured for him to follow her and started down the hall in the opposite direction as Amelia.

Gloucester watched her out of the corner of his eye as they walked. She was a tall, solemn-faced woman, though he couldn't say whether the latter was a result of her professionalism or her personality. He'd never seen her before a few days ago, which raised a question he'd been pondering for a while: "How come I don't know any of you?"

Jess gave him a questioning look, and Gloucester went on to explain. "The agents. You're all security detail for the high minister. So was I. But I've yet to see a single face I know. I wasn't gone *that* long. Despite what it feels like." The last bit was mostly to himself, grumbled in the breath of a sigh as he glanced down the length of a perpendicular corridor. Another black-suited agent was walking in their direction, carrying a thick stack of paperwork. Aptly proving Gloucester's point, it wasn't anyone he recognized. The agent offered Jess a polite nod and Gloucester a curious glance as he passed them. Gloucester slowed his steps to watch him go for a moment, before turning back to Jess.

"You can't all be new. That'd be a bit harsh in the way of spring cleaning, even for *him*," he said, wrinkling his nose and nodding indicatively in the direction they were headed.

Jess snorted. "Nah, it's not that. We've just had all our shifts switched around." Despite the dislike in her gaze when she'd eyed him before, she didn't seem opposed to answering his questions. "Bit of a nuisance, really. But at least we all know each other."

"Just not me." Gloucester hummed thoughtfully. So the minister wanted him without potential allies. Not a very encouraging sign. Nothing since his so-called release had shaken his suspicion that the moment he solved this mystery for the minister, he was going right back in that cell again. Or worse.

Returning his attention to the woman walking beside

him, he caught the guarded curiosity in her eyes. He raised his eyebrows questioningly, but Jess didn't ask whatever was on her mind, instead looking ahead again, as if the glance had never happened. Gloucester remained silent for a moment, then decided to continue with his own line of questioning.

"What did he tell you about me?"

This time, Jess didn't bother pretending not to look at him. Her gaze was guarded still, but less hostile. Gloucester had a feeling he was a puzzle she was trying to work out.

"Him?" she said after a moment. She scoffed. "Nothing. Just to keep you in your room and make sure you behave yourself. Wouldn't know you from the celestial voice herself if it were just His Lordship's information we were going on."

"Flattering as it is to be compared to the divine leader of an entire religion, I think she's taller," Gloucester quipped. "By 'we,' you mean you and the rest of the security detail?"

Jess nodded. "He might have jumbled us around enough that no one who knows you is on duty anywhere near you, but you know how this place is. Word has a way of getting around. Your old detail knows you're back. Rumors are all abuzz." She waggled her fingers airily and offered him a smile for the first time. It was so small and fleeting he almost missed it. "Makes things interesting. Even if you can't be trusted."

Gloucester's brows rose again. "Oh, can't I? What exactly were you told I did?" He did his best to keep the question lightly sardonic, hoping Jess wouldn't realize just how much he needed the answer. He doubted whatever rumors were being whispered amongst the security personnel would be the true reason he'd been locked up, but it would still be something. A clue.

Unfortunately, he'd pushed his luck. Jess's good humor vanished. She regarded him stonily for a long moment, pausing in her steps and holding out a hand to stop him walking too. Then she shook her head. "Don't try to play me, Gloucester. I won't buy it. You're here to do a job. So am I. Let's both just do them and not make trouble for each other, all right? Now come on." She took him by the arm, giving him a light push as they started walking again.

Gloucester shrugged away from her hand but didn't offer a protest. Clearly he wouldn't be getting anything more from this conversation.

They walked in silence for the length of several more corridors and two flights of stairs. Gloucester had forgotten just how big the high minister's house was. He made note of their surroundings as they went, re-familiarizing himself with a layout he'd once been able to navigate in his sleep.

Finally, they reached a pair of elaborate double doors that he remembered as the entrance to the minister's private quarters. Jess slid another sideways glance his way, then knocked. They fell back into silence for another long minute. No sound came from the other side of the doors. Gloucester and Jess exchanged a look, the former shrugging.

Before he could suggest knocking again, the sound of footsteps reached their ears, and a moment later one of the doors swung inward, just enough to reveal a robed and grumpy high minister. Gloucester was pleased to see him appear so ruffled, not bothering to hide his amusement as he looked the minister over.

"You better actually have something, Gloucester," the minister grumbled, glaring at him through eyes bleary with sleep.

"I do," Gloucester replied firmly. "I need to talk to you." It was his turn to slew a sideways look at Jess, before adding, "Alone."

The minister frowned at him, then sighed. "Yes, all right. Off you go, Riggs." He waved a hand when Jess opened her mouth to argue. "It's fine. If I was worried he'd kill me, I wouldn't have hired him to find an assassin, now would I?"

Jess looked dubious but retreated without voicing an argument. Once she'd turned away, the minister beckoned Gloucester into the room.

"Close the door behind you," he ordered as he moved away from the entrance, stifling a yawn.

Gloucester did so, the door closing with a quiet click. Walking further into the room, he looked around. Unsurprisingly, the room was a great deal nicer than the one he'd been given. He remembered it from the few times he'd been called in to attend the minister back before everything went wrong.

The double doors led into an impressive entry hall, with doors on either side. If memory served, the one on his left led to the minister's bedchamber, from which he'd clearly just come. The door on the right led to a study and small but impressive library. Gloucester recalled admiring the handsome wood-panelled walls and the tall shelves stacked with hundreds of books. Dotted intermittently amongst the books were interesting artifacts: gilded globes of the ancient world, figurines carved of stone and metal, and delicate glass instruments.

Directly across the room, large bay windows and doors wrought in a clever marriage of steel and glass opened to a balcony that put the one in his own room to shame. Two stories higher, the minister's balcony provided a much better view: the gardens far below transitioned into thick forest, the trees a wild tangle of greens that eventually surrendered in turn to the city skyline.

Frettchen was an old city, harkening back to a time before the cities of the Lower Lands fought for and won their independence and the city-states were born. The urban landscape was still densely populated by surviving remnants of that time, ancient architecture standing alongside the sleeker buildings of present day. Even from where he stood in the middle of the room, several meters from the glass, Gloucester could see the Old Cathedral, its rose window a shining spot of color in the morning sunlight.

The minister stepped into his line of vision, interrupting the pleasant sight. Everything from his stormy frown to his arms crossed over his chest exuded grouchy impatience. "So?" he demanded. "What's so urgent that it couldn't wait until a decent hour?"

"Seven is decent," Gloucester said. Another easily recalled fact from his life prior to captivity was his employer's hatred of morning hours. "And I want out."

"Oh, come now. I've already made it clear—"

"I want *out of this building*," Gloucester clarified, directing a scornful look the minister's way before stepping past him toward the wide windows. "I can't do you or anyone any good locked up in here reading over the same damn files again and again. I need to see the scene of the crime, for starters. And I should go with you wherever you go." Glancing over his shoulder, he caught the look on the minister's face and snorted. "I'm not exactly tickled by the idea either, s—"

He cut himself off before the unthinking *sir* could be voiced. The high minister had lost his right to that particular honorific. Gloucester was done calling anyone *sir*.

"How do I know you won't try to escape?" the minister asked. Gloucester suspected he'd been expecting this confrontation, just perhaps not so early in the day.

Why do you care so much? He sorely wanted to shout the question in the minister's face, to demand answers for his arrest and imprisonment. But he knew this man well enough to know he wouldn't get anything but grief for asking. He certainly wouldn't get answers. Whatever the high minister was convinced he'd seen or knew, it was enough to justify locking him up and throwing away the key. It wouldn't be something he'd willingly discuss. He would need to be forced, and Gloucester wasn't in any position to do that. Yet.

With a sigh, he turned back to face the window. Down in the garden below, black-furred squirrels darted about as they chased one another through the flower beds. "What would be the point?" he said quietly. "I don't have anywhere to run to." On the other side of the garden, the woods were still dark, sunlight not yet pervading the thick canopy. "Running's not freedom."

The bright blue of a jaybird flitted around the forest's edge.

Suddenly, it veered into the sky, spooked by some unseen predator hidden in the trees. A faint line creased Gloucester's brow.

"Too true," the minister said. "I suppose you're right. Though I think you know this could have waited until—"

Watching the trees where the jay got startled, Gloucester saw the rising sun glint off of something in the branches—

The window shattered with a sharp crack, followed an instant later by the delayed blast of a gunshot.

The floor was hard, and Gloucester hissed in pain as he hit it, his elbow rebounding off the floorboards and sending a lancing pain down the length of his arm. His fall was only partially cushioned by the high minister's body, who voiced similar sounds of discomfort at his collision with the floor and Gloucester's weight on top of him.

"What the—"

The minister's alarmed cry fell on deaf ears. Gloucester shoved him down as he went to sit up, eyes never leaving the shattered window. Keeping low, he scrambled toward the cover of the wall next to the balcony doors, out of any line of fire, dragging the minister roughly along with him.

"Stay out of sight," he snapped. Across the room, one side of the beautiful double doors was splintered, where the bullet meant for the minister had struck. "Do you have any weapons here? Any guns?"

The minister was still pale with shock, but his wits seemed to be returning. "In the study," he said, clutching his chest. "Top right drawer of the desk."

Gloucester nodded. "Right. Stay where you are. You have any way of contacting security on you? Get them down in the grounds *now*. We need to get to the sniper before they have a chance to escape." With a final glance at the broken window, he pushed away from the wall and dashed for the door to the study.

It was impossible to say whether the shooter was still watching or not. Were it him, he would be on the move already, mission accomplished or not. The shot had been heard and security would be on the move, even without the minister's orders. If the assassin was smart, they'd be running.

The gun was where the minister said it would be. Gloucester snatched it out of the drawer, its weight in his hand and the act of loading it a grounding familiarity, even after all this time.

Now it's just a question of whether I can still shoot the damn thing.

Not that he thought it would make much of a difference either way. Whoever had taken the shot had done so from the forest. They had to be armed with a long-distance rifle. The weapon in his hand would never be able to make a shot that could even come close to matching it. The gun was more for his own comfort than anything, a reassurance that he wasn't completely helpless.

Shut up. Thoughts like that were dangerous. Gun in hand, he slipped back through the doorway into the entry hall at a crouched run. The minister was where he'd left him, growling into his phone.

"Let me know the *moment* you get anything," he said as Gloucester crouched beside him. The minister hung up the phone with a cursory goodbye. "Security's on the ground. They'll be searching the forest any minute now."

Gloucester gave a single mute nod. The drawn-back curtains swayed gently in the breeze through the broken glass. He leaned to the side just enough to peer around the corner of the window frame. It took only a few seconds to locate the spot on the forest's edge where he'd seen the flash of light. It had been high off the ground; the shooter must have had a perch in the trees. *Good.* Trees made excellent hiding spots, but they took time to get down from.

As expected, he could make out no visible sign of the shooter from where he was, just the thick foliage. He needed to get the minister out of the room and away from any potential line of fire. Without knowing who the assassin was, Gloucester had no way to know if he or she was the sort to run after a failed attempt or risk everything to try again if the target presented itself.

"C'mon." Gloucester grabbed hold of the minister's sleeve and pulled him away from their hiding spot. They stayed tight to the edges of the room, hugging the wall to keep from the open space at the center of the entry hall. "Keep low," he said when they reached the doors to the hallway. It was the only part of their short trek in the sniper's sight line, judging from the bullet's trajectory, and he darted forward to pull the door open as quickly as he could. Grabbing the minister again, he threw him through the doorway before hurriedly following. The heavy door swung shut behind them, its solid wood providing thick cover if the shooter was of any mind to try again.

Leaning back against the wall, Gloucester shot the minister a look, both to gauge his well-being and to judge his reaction to the whole thing. "Well, I definitely believe someone's trying to kill you," he said.

The minister's brows rose. His robe was mussed, his hair in disarray, and despite his relative composure, he was still wide-eyed and panting in shock. "Oh, good! I'm glad my near-death experience has convinced you."

The sound of hastening steps made both of them look up. A bevy of security agents rounded the corner of the corridor. Jess was among them, and they were led by one of the few familiar faces Gloucester had seen since his return, the minister's chief adviser, Mulligan. Mulligan wasn't a security agent, but at the moment he wore such a fierce expression that he looked right at home with them.

"Sir! Sir, are you all right?" Mulligan demanded, rushing forward to help the minister to his feet, before stepping back to regard him with worried eyes. He didn't spare more than a glance Gloucester's way.

The minister brushed aside his concern with an impatient wave of his hand. "I'm fine. Not a scratch on me. What about the shooter? Did you get him?"

"Shot dead, I'm afraid," Mulligan said. "Tried to fire on the security team. Should we bring in the police?"

"No," the minister said firmly. "I want this taken care of in-house. No word gets out about this, are we clear?" He cast a sharp look around at everyone assembled, the security agents and Mulligan all nodding. "Bring the body in. Let's find out who the hell's behind all this."

Chapter 4

Chasing the Lead

"This is ridiculous. Sir, you almost died. Again!"

"That hasn't escaped my notice, Mulligan, shocking as that may seem. And it doesn't change anything."

"He can't be trusted. I've said it right from the start—"

"Another detail I managed to pick up on, yes."

"He—"

"He saved my life."

Outside in the corridor, Gloucester considered how people always seemed to think walls made their conversations inaudible to anyone but themselves. The high minister and Mulligan had relocated to an office in the inner corridors of the mansion, far away from any windows, and ordered Gloucester to wait outside under the watchful eye of a security agent.

"Funny how he just happened to be there at exactly the right moment," said the high minister's chief adviser. Though the conversation was muffled by the closed door, Gloucester could easily hear exactly what was being said. He reckoned he would have a lot more trouble eavesdropping if either man put any sort of effort into lowering his voice. As it stood, he much preferred to listen than to point this out.

"Oh, come now. You really think he had anything to do with it? The sniper was probably waiting for hours—days, even—for the perfect shot." The minister's scoff cut through the walls. "A shot that Gloucester ruined, I should remind you. What's your theory? That Gloucester planned the attack and then, what? Got cold feet? And how would he plan it? He's been in our custody for months."

A long moment of silence followed. Gloucester imagined Mulligan's mouth opening and closing like a fish as he worked out his reply.

"It just seems like too much of a coincidence," came his eventual counterpoint.

Though Gloucester couldn't hear anything in the seconds that followed, he guessed the high minister was sighing. From what he knew of the man, he was definitely giving Mulligan a Look.

"Despite what people say, there are such things as coincidences. They're not mermaids."

"I—I know that." Mulligan sounded indignant. "But I've read the reports on him. I've watched the surveillance videos. He's not as okay as he's pretending to be."

"Are any of us, I wonder . . ."

The rhetorical question was quiet, Gloucester straining his ears to catch it.

"The psychiatrist says it's hard to say at this point what effect imprisonment might have had on him, but there's no way he's not been affected at all. He could be—" Mulligan cut off suddenly, and Gloucester, who'd gone very still, imagined the minister holding up a hand to silence his adviser.

"Enough." The single word had an edge to it that brooked

no argument.

Footsteps approached the door beside which Gloucester was seated, and a moment later it opened, Mulligan holding it for the minister as they stepped out into the corridor. They were both grim-faced. The minister offered him a curt nod, while Mulligan shot him a much darker look.

Getting to his feet, Gloucester raked a hand through his hair, pushing the dark curls back from his brow. "You said the sniper was shot," he said to Mulligan, without preamble. Mulligan had shown no interest in offering him any real courtesy, so he wasn't about to put in the effort to be polite to him. Especially not with the conversation he'd just heard echoing in his thoughts. "Where's the body? Did you get an ID off of it?"

Mulligan looked like he was going to protest rather than answer. Before Gloucester could do more than square his shoulders in preparation for an argument, the minister cleared his throat. The disapproval in his eye as he glanced between them hinted that he'd also foreseen what was coming and was having none of it.

Mulligan glowered but backed down. "They should be bringing the body in now. You can see for yourselves."

—

An elegant marble staircase led the way down into the front foyer of the mansion, its many steps skirting the walls, beginning at a third floor corridor and descending opposite the front doors before reaching the ground floor on the right side of the spacious room. The high minister, Mulligan, and Gloucester made their way down the final few steps just in time to watch the sniper's body be brought in on a stretcher.

The security agents carrying it laid the stretcher down in the middle of the room and stepped back, giving the three men room to move forward and inspect the body. Mulligan hung back, face pinched in distaste, but both Gloucester and the minister approached. Gloucester crouched next to the body, examining its lifeless face.

The corpse was a young man, perhaps a handful of years older than Gloucester himself. His gray eyes stared up at the ceiling overhead, his face pale in death. There was something familiar about him, though Gloucester couldn't place where he might have seen him before. He glanced over his shoulder at the minister, who was standing a step or two behind him and staring down at the body with an unreadable frown.

"Do you know him?" Gloucester asked.

The minister didn't answer immediately, and Gloucester could almost see the lie forming in his head. Then he appeared to change his mind.

"Yes. He looks familiar, at least." He hesitated, then crouched beside Gloucester to inspect the dead man's face more closely. "I think . . . Yes, he used to work for me. Mulligan, I'm not wrong, am I? Do you recognize him?"

The prospect of getting anywhere near the dead body didn't seem to agree with Mulligan. Grimacing, he took a step closer with great reluctance. His disgust shifted to surprise after a moment's inspection.

"I do," he said. "Name's escaping me, but I know the face." He turned toward a tall, dark man who Gloucester belatedly realized was the man with the syringe from the day he'd been taken from his cell. Tension crept into his muscles, tightening his shoulders. Mulligan beckoned the man over. "Harrison!"

"Yes, sir?" the agent asked, stepping forward from where he'd been standing quietly by the wall.

"Go to my office and pull up employee records for the mansion. Security detail, house staff, everything. For the past few years. If this man's face shows up, let me know immediately."

After Harrison nodded and walked away, Gloucester turned his attention back to the corpse over which he was crouched. A search of his pockets revealed nothing of use: no wallet, no ID, no handy note explaining his motives. Gloucester sighed.

Then paused. Something in the man's jacket pocket, tucked

so deeply away as to almost be missed, grazed his fingertips. A slip of paper, crumpled into the lining of the pocket. It felt thin and weathered. He slowly worked it free, careful not to tear it, and pulled it out to take a look. Holding up his new find, he ignored the curious questions of the other two as they noticed his discovery.

A receipt, crinkled and creased, but the ink not yet very faded. A recent purchase, then? He read it over, brow furrowing. The name of the business printed at the top of the receipt read Zephyr Clocks. Was it simply unrelated? It was reasonable to assume it had nothing to do with anything. Assassins used clocks, just like everyone else. Just because the man had it in his pocket didn't mean it was relevant.

Except maybe it was. His eyes traveled down from the name of the shop to the listed purchases.

"*Gloucester.*" The distinct edge to the minister's voice hinted he'd been trying to get his attention for a while now. "What is that?"

"Maybe something. Maybe nothing." Gloucester lowered the receipt and looked back up at the other two. From his angle, they loomed over him, their expressions impatient. "I think the real question's why a clock shop would be selling parts for long-distance rifles."

The high minister snatched the receipt from his hand and squinted down at it, Mulligan peering over his shoulder in keen interest.

"That *is* odd," muttered the minister, frowning down at the slip of paper, his brows knitted. "And not, I think, a coincidence." He exchanged a quick glance with Mulligan that Gloucester pretended not to notice.

"Worth looking into, at least," he agreed, getting to his feet. Feeling crowded by the other two men so close at his back, he stepped over the body to stand on the other side of it. The newfound space wasn't much of a comfort, but it was an improvement. Arms crossed, he eyed the corpse speculatively.

"Might be he was working alone and the clock shop happens to sell more than just, well, clocks. Could be with him dead"—he nodded down at the body—"this is the end of it. I don't think so, though."

Mulligan squinted at him. "Oh? Why's that?" His narrowed eyes and pursed lips said a lot more than his question, and Gloucester imagined Mulligan was following a train of thought similar to his own: If all *was* said and done, did that mean he was free?

Gloucester shook his head. "Two assassination attempts, two totally different approaches. The bomb in that car was powerful, but it was an amateur's work. This guy tries to take him down with a high-powered rifle, with a shot only a trained marksman could make. Why start with the sloppier attack if you're good with a gun? And most people wouldn't switch MOs so dramatically like that." He dragged a hand through his hair again. "No, I reckon it's two different people."

Mulligan didn't look convinced. "Two different people try to kill His Lordship within days of each other? What, you think this one's a copycat?" He nudged the corpse with the toe of his polished shoe, his disdain for Gloucester's opinion apparently outweighing his disgust at the dead body. "The first attack was buried in the press. How would this fellow even hear about it? Unless you think . . . you think they were working together?"

Gloucester shook his head again, chewing absently on the nail of his thumb as he considered the dead man's face. "Not quite. I think they were working for the same person."

The high minister had been silent throughout this exchange, seemingly lost in thought as he stared at the receipt in his hand. He looked up now, meeting Gloucester's eyes. His steady gaze made it clear he had been thinking the same thing.

"Someone has a problem with me and doesn't want to do their own dirty work," he mused coldly.

A throat cleared, and they all turned as one toward the source of the noise. Harrison had returned, entering the hall from a corridor that branched away from the corner of the room behind Gloucester. He looked a little short of breath, as if he'd run the whole way there from Mulligan's office. A bounce to his step and the faintest of smiles playing across his lips gave his appearance an undeniably victorious air.

"I found him, sirs," he said, crossing the room to stand beside Gloucester as he addressed the minister and his adviser. Gloucester took a deliberate step to one side to put some distance between them.

"So he did work here," said the minister. "Who was he?"

Harrison handed him a printed piece of paper. Though Gloucester got only a brief glimpse before the minister took it, he could see the familiar format of a personnel file.

"Jeremy Wall," Harrison said. "He was a security agent here three years ago. Until he was terminated for allowing civilians access to the house. Lost his pension, everything."

"That'll do it," Gloucester said under his breath. He adopted an innocent expression when Harrison glanced at him.

The minister read over Jeremy Wall's profile. "A man with an axe to grind. If your theory's correct, Gloucester, he probably didn't need much convincing to go after me."

Gloucester hummed in agreement, deeming it more polite than pointing out that a lot of people could probably be easily convinced to kill the minister. Politicians just brought that out in people. And Frettchen's high minister had a particular flair for it. Many were unhappy with his increasingly isolationist policies, for starters, as he pushed for harsher trade restrictions with the Nordlands and South Cities alike. More and more people were also displeased with the integration of the high minister's religion into previously secular politics. The high minister might still have the love of his flock in the church, but his popularity outside of the religious sphere had diminished significantly over the years, as he'd proven to be conniving, elitist, and self-serving. The charisma and grand campaign promises that had won him the election four years ago were no longer enough to keep him in favor.

Mulligan frowned around at all of them. "So now what? If there's some person pulling the strings, how do we find him?"

The minister waved the receipt like a tiny flag. "We have a place to start, at least. Gloucester, I want you to find this Zephyr Clocks place. Talk to whomever sold Wall the gun parts, see if there's anything to learn."

"Is that really a—"

Before Mulligan could finish, the minister held up a hand for silence. "Harrison can go with him. Keep him out of trouble."

Gloucester glanced at Harrison, who offered him a bland, unreadable look in return. He resisted grimacing. "Just try not to drug me again," he said.

Harrison smiled. "I'll do my best."

Chapter 5

Complications

The sky above Frettchen was a pale blue on the horizon, darkening to a more vivid cerulean overhead. A pleasant warmth in the air still held the freshness that came of a long winter's end.

The energized spring day had put a fever in people's blood, bringing them to life after the plodding days of winter gray, and driving them outdoors to enjoy the weather and inescapable feeling of rejuvenation. The city streets bustled with activity, filled with chattering shoppers, friends out for a day on the town, and people taking what time they could away from their work to be outside in the sun. While summers in Frettchen brought with them oppressive heat and sand-filled winds from the Great Desert to the east, spring days like this were ideal for being outdoors.

To Gloucester, it was overwhelming. It had been autumn the last time he was outdoors—not counting standing on the balcony of his room back at the minister's mansion—and it felt bogglingly over-stimulating to be surrounded by so much space and activity after so long. Everything dragged at his attention, from the passing traffic to the talk-show buzzing on the car radio to the pedestrians at every street corner. He wanted both to look at everything and to push it all away. Everything felt too loud, too chaotic, too much.

"You're not a very chatty one, are you, Mr. Gloucester?" Harrison said. He was behind the wheel, and he took his eyes off the road just long enough to glance at Gloucester in the passenger seat.

"Not much to chat about," was Gloucester's terse reply. A car ahead of them honked, the driver apparently averse to the notion of advance greens. Gloucester's eyes narrowed. He was getting a headache.

Harrison shrugged and returned to driving. For all his ill will toward the man for drugging him, Gloucester found Harrison's company preferable to most of the other people he'd met since being brought from his cell. He was quiet, mild-mannered, and for the most part he left Gloucester to his thoughts. Or, as the present case may be, his efforts to keep the world at bay.

The best way to do so seemed to be focusing on something else, so he turned what they knew so far over and over in his mind. Was this excursion to the clock shop worth anything? Chances were the proprietor simply sold more than the title of their shop described. He had no proof this lead was anything more than a waste of time.

But neither did he have proof it wasn't. Could they afford not to chase all possible leads? If someone out there was hiring killers to go after the high minister, how long would it be until the next attack? And who knew if the next time wouldn't be successful?

"Now that we know who the sniper was, do we have any leads on the bomber?" he asked, turning away from the passing scenery to flick a questioning glance at Harrison.

The agent shrugged his broad shoulders again as he navigated around a puttering car, whose driver turned out to be a wizened old lady so small she could scarcely see over the top of her steering wheel. "Sort of. Mr. Mulligan's back at the mansion, going over every file and bit of information he can get his hands on to build up a list of suspects. Both for the bomber and any other potential assassin-types."

It didn't sound much like a job for the chief adviser, but Mulligan seemed to be taking this whole situation personally. He might have been a pain in the ass, but he wasn't short on loyalty. In fact, the more Gloucester thought about it, the more he suspected Mulligan was the only person besides himself that the minister didn't suspect of complicity. And *he'd* only made the cut because of his incarceration. Mulligan made it in on sheer trustworthiness. That was almost admirable, he had to admit. It made sense, then, that the minister would task him with jobs not strictly in his field of expertise. When you had who knew how many grudge-holders gunning for you, it was best to keep things to the few people you could trust.

" . . . something to look forward to when we get back," Harrison was saying. Gloucester stirred from his thoughts in time to catch the tail-end of the comment.

"Hm?" He blinked owlishly at Harrison. He'd gotten so lost in his musings that he couldn't say how long the other man might have been talking.

Harrison didn't appear fazed by his lack of attention. Ever patient, he offered another of his hard-to-read smiles. "I said that it'd be something to look forward to when we get back from this errand, hearing what Mr. Mulligan might've found out."

"Maybe *we'll* find something," Gloucester suggested dryly.

Harrison nodded, but he didn't appear very convinced of the idea.

Their brief foray into conversation seemed to have reached an end; Harrison returned his full attention to the road, while Gloucester looked to the passenger-side window, watching the people and buildings as they passed them by.

—

Zephyr Clocks turned out to be a small shop, tucked away at the north end of Frettchen's shopping district. It had the quaint and singular appearance of an independently owned business, its front window showing off a vast display of clocks in every shape and size, while overhead a wooden sign proclaiming the name swung idly in the breeze.

Gloucester tilted his head back to watch the sign's lazy movements, while behind him Harrison locked up the car.

The place certainly didn't look suspicious. Then again, that could be the point. Few dens of thieves—or assassins—tended to present themselves as such. Lowering his eyes from the sign, he looked at Harrison as the taller man stepped up next to him.

"After you," he said, gesturing to the door. He wasn't sure himself if it was a joking quip or a more legitimate reticence to be the first one stepping into an uncertain situation. For long months, he hadn't had much use for his emotions, and he found he was having more trouble sorting them out than he cared to admit.

Harrison didn't argue, at least, nor even comment on the words. He stepped forward and pushed the front door of the shop open. A delicate tinkling sound accompanied the action, and Gloucester, following Harrison through the door after a moment's hesitation, looked upward to find the source. A wind chime hung over the threshold, placed so as to be struck by the movement of the door. A gentle alarm for whomever was on duty. A small business like this, he wondered if that would be the owner or an employee.

Once inside, he quickly felt that something was off-putting about the place. Gloucester looked around, trepidation building in the back of his mind. The shop's many shelves were laden not only with clocks but a thousand other delicate pieces and parts wrought in brass and steel and clay. It took him a minute to realize what was prickling at his nerves: his ears weren't filled with silence, but rather the quiet, rhythmic ticking of countless time pieces. They covered the walls, clocks of all shapes and sizes, from the smallest, most ornate cuckoo to the massive grandfather with its long swinging pendulum. Watches were on display beneath glass counters, from elaborate wristwatches surely costing thousands to humble trainmen's pocket-watches.

But the clocks on the walls drew the most attention. Their ticking hands were a hundred different volumes and tones, and seemingly as many different rhythms. Gloucester wondered if they'd been set deliberately out-of-sync with each other, their ticks and tocks at once blending together and disparate, creating a white noise that buzzed in his ears.

"Hello."

The word broke through the trance into which the murmuring clocks had been threatening to pull Gloucester. Blinking, he spotted a young woman approaching them from the back of the shop.

"How can I help you?" she asked, in the politely charming tone of a seasoned retail worker.

She was curvaceous and round-faced, with dark skin and full lips pulled into a smile of greeting. Gloucester estimated she was about the same age as himself. Her hair was her most striking feature at first glance, a mass of dark curls, far wilder than his own, swathing her head like a storm cloud. Harrison made a quiet noise beside him, and Gloucester looked over, amused by the stunned expression the other man wore for an instant before he regained his composure. Gloucester guessed that Harrison, like himself, had been expecting someone more along the lines of *portly old man*.

"Hello," he said, stepping forward and hesitating a moment before offering his hand. She eyed him, brows faintly creased in speculation, then shook it. She probably thought his hesitation was rude or odd, but handshakes were high on the list of things he'd rather fallen out of practice with. "We're from the high minister's security detail. We'd like a moment of your time to ask you a few questions. I'm Agent Gloucester and this is Agent Harrison."

Harrison murmured a polite greeting, offering his hand to shake in turn.

Now the woman's frown lines were anything but faint. "I . . . I don't think I've done anything wrong," she said, a note of worry in her voice. For now, Gloucester didn't think that necessarily made her suspicious. Most people felt nervous when official folk came nosing around asking questions, whether they were guilty of something or not.

"Do you own this shop, Miss . . . ?" Harrison's question trailed off in expectation of a name.

"Zephyr," the woman supplied. "Zane Zephyr. And yeah, I do."

"A family business?"

"Yes. My grandfather started it when he was young, and then my father passed it on to me when he moved to the South Cities a few years ago." Zane cocked her head, arms crossing her chest. "Sorry, I'm still not sure what this is about. I've never even met the high minister."

Gloucester pulled a small, clear plastic bag from his pocket. Inside was the receipt he'd found in the shooter's jacket. He held it out for Zane to see. "Do you remember this sale?" he asked.

Zane took the bagged receipt. "This is dated a week ago . . . Yeah. Yeah, I think I remember. It's not often I sell parts like that. Young-ish guy. Really stone-faced, you know?" She emphasized her frown to a comical level in demonstration.

Gloucester chuckled. "I imagine so. Tell us, why does a clock shop sell gun parts?"

The humor left Zane's face. "Is that what this is about? It's all perfectly legal. I sell a lot of things that aren't for clocks. If it's small and finicky and mechanical, it's probably crossed my desk at some point."

"Fair enough. What about the man who bought the parts?

Can you tell us anything else about him? Was he alone?"

Zane nodded. "I don't remember anyone with him. It seemed like he knew exactly what he was looking for—Oh, bloody hell, he went and shot someone, didn't he? He had a firearms license—I always check when I'm selling things like that. Did he shoot someone?"

She bounced a little on the balls of her feet, her nerves clearly making it difficult to stand still. Again, Gloucester knew her anxiety wasn't a surefire sign of guilt. She was fretting over an understandable concern. He shook his head, hoping to assuage some of her worry. "He didn't shoot anybody. Just not for lack of trying."

He caught Harrison's sideways glance out of the corner of his eye. The car ride back to the mansion would probably now include a lecture on discretion when it came to interviewing civilians. Gloucester ignored the glance, just as he intended to ignore the lecture. They'd bullied him into this job—he didn't care about following all their rules.

"Oh," Zane said, sounding both relieved and intrigued. "That's good, at least." Between this news and the fact that they were making no moves to arrest her, she seemed quite cheered up. "Was there anything else you needed to know?"

Gloucester opened his mouth to reply, but Harrison spoke up. "I think that's everything for the moment, Miss Zephyr. Or is it Mrs.?"

Zane gave an emphatic shake of her head. "Just me. I'm not interested in any of that. Happy as can be just tinkering with my clocks."

Gloucester resisted the urge to laugh at the look on Harrison's face, a conflict of relief and disappointment all at once. He doubted that particular question had much to do with their investigation. Not exactly professional, but he wasn't about to give Harrison a hard time for straying from the point. This lead had been a long shot and it seemed to end here. He hadn't really expected Wall to have taken his mysterious employer with him to pick up the supplies. Better to search his home now that they knew who he was and hope to find some clue there.

"We'll be on our way, then," he said. "If you can think of anything else about the man, call—" He paused, then jabbed a thumb in Harrison's direction. "Well, call Agent Harrison, because I don't have a phone." Harrison shot him another warning look, but Gloucester pretended not to notice again.

"Er, right," said Zane, apparently choosing not to question this. She accepted the card Harrison held out to her in exchange for the receipt and rolled back on her heels, eyeing them both with an expression no longer apprehensive so much as curious. "If anything, uh, occurs, I'll let you know."

"Thanks very much, Miss," Harrison said. If the tall agent were wearing a hat, Gloucester imagined he would be tipping it. "We'll let you get back to your business. We appreciate you taking the time to talk to us."

With that and a nod, he turned on his heel and made for the door. Gloucester offered Zane a wave and followed in his wake, his footsteps accompanied by the ever-ticking clocks.

Without the shop's ambient noise, the sounds of the city seemed strangely quiet. Gloucester turned to Harrison, who was blinking in the sunlight. "Well, that was a colossal waste of our time."

"Seems that way," Harrison agreed. "We'll run a background check on her, just in case, but I don't think she has anything to do with anything." He glanced over his shoulder at the shopfront as he spoke, brow creased thoughtfully. Gloucester wondered if he'd thought of something or was merely wishing he'd asked Zane Zephyr out for a drink, no matter her disinterest in romance.

He was about to ask as much when someone jostled his shoulder. Gloucester jumped, startled. He hadn't even noticed anyone else there. Turning quickly toward the clumsy passerby, his eyes met ones even darker than his own, black as spilled ink. A smile, razor sharp. And whispered words for only his ears to hear—

"Gloucester!"

Harrison calling his name, as close to emotional as he'd yet heard from the man, pulled Gloucester's attention back to the other security agent. The big man was staring down at him, something akin to wary alarm in his eyes. Gloucester blinked. His head felt oddly heavy, like he'd just woken up.

"Are you all right?" Harrison asked. "You looked sort of . . . funny there. Like you were somewhere else."

Watching Harrison's face, Gloucester thought back to the conversation he'd overheard between the high minister and his chief adviser earlier that morning. Mulligan thought he'd lost it. How many others did too? Jess had been right when she said the security staff liked to gossip. What would they be saying about him now?

Maybe the gossip was justified. Maybe he *was* losing it. He knuckled his forehead distractedly. He had the strangest feeling that something lurked just beyond the edge of his memory. He felt as if he were trying to recall a dream he'd had, but with nothing more to go on than the nagging sensation that somewhere in the shadows of his own mind there was a story to tell.

"I'm fine," he muttered. It sounded unconvincing even to his own ears, so he hastened on before Harrison could get any ideas about running off to the high minister or Mulligan with his concerns. "Just thinking."

Harrison still looked dubious, and Gloucester's patience grew strained. "Look," he said. "I've not been out and about in the city for half a bloody year. Forgive me if it's a little overwhelming."

Harrison, apparently determined to prove his decency when needles weren't involved, looked abashed. "Of course," he said. It was quite impossible to gauge whether the sentiment behind the assurance was kindness, condescension, or meaningless appeasement. Whatever it was, at least it meant an end to the questioning, which Gloucester told himself was all he cared about.

"Right." He shifted on the spot, still trying to shake off the feeling of discombobulation. Instead of fading, it was developing into a headache. "We . . . we should get back. See what Mulligan's found. And we should search Wall's house. It's a better lead than this place, anyway."

He glanced over his shoulder at the clock shop. He had the eerie feeling he was being watched from behind the wide front window, but he couldn't see any sign of Zane through the glass. Shaking his head at his own paranoia, he turned away again. As far as he was concerned, the paranoia was well-earned, but that didn't mean it was always indicative of an actual threat.

Or maybe I am going mad.

Well, the first step toward madness would probably be listening to himself when he thought things like "Maybe I am going mad." Better to simply live in denial, he decided. That was all sanity really was, wasn't it? Everyone's denial of their own unique madness.

Harrison was side-eyeing him again, and Gloucester realized he'd allowed himself to fall back into deep thought. This whole "fake it 'til you make it" approach to mental well-being wasn't off to the best start. Pretending not to notice Harrison's look, he held his head high and crossed the sidewalk to the car, waiting by the passenger-side door until Harrison unlocked it.

"Hopefully Mulligan will have found something," Harrison said, getting in the driver's side. Gloucester nodded as he opened the door and climbed in after him. The engine clicked and whirred to life, and then they were pulling back out onto the busy streets of Frettchen, leaving the quiet clock shop behind in the rear-view mirror.

Chapter 6

Dangerous Thoughts

As it turned out, Mulligan had found plenty.

"This," he said, holding up a sheet of paper triumphantly, "is our list of suspects."

Gloucester wasn't sure the victorious tone was all that warranted. The page was covered top to bottom with names. Clearly Frettchen contained no shortage of people the high minister had rubbed the wrong way.

They were standing in the minister's study. Several tasteful lamps filled the room with artificial light. A large window stood behind the desk, its panes stretching up to the high ceiling, but thick shutters had been drawn across it, in case any other assassins thought to follow Wall's example. The minister himself was seated at the desk, his back to the shutters and Mulligan standing beside him, hovering over his employer like an overbearing mother hen.

"This is everyone who's been tagged as a potential threat

since His Lordship took up the titles of high minister and lord of the city-state," he said. "And anyone who might have cause for a grudge. Former employees like Wall, political rivals, foreign leaders, concerned citizens, activists, anyone who seemed at all capable."

Gloucester, who was still feeling poorly, fought back the urge to point out that maybe the high minister ought to invest in being a bit more decent to people. If even half the people on that list were there out of fault only their own, he'd be much surprised.

"Have you got an address on Wall?" he asked instead, gritting his teeth. His headache, which he'd hoped would fade once they were away from the noise and constant activity of the city, had only grown worse.

"We do," Mulligan confirmed. "Though it's from a year ago, so whether it's current or not is anyone's guess."

Gloucester rubbed his temples, trying to think. The ache pounded against the inside of his skull, making it difficult to focus. "I should take a look at it. If there's anything pointing toward who might've hired Wall, chances are it'll be there."

Still, they would be lucky to find anything anywhere. Wall might have been disgraced, but he was still a trained security agent. Besides that, they would be wise to assume whoever hired him wasn't stupid either. They would have been careful to avoid leaving a trail that could lead back to them.

Even careful people make mistakes. They'd just have to hope that someone involved had slipped up. And that they'd be there to catch the mistake before another attack happened. Gloucester felt like he was still in Zane Zephyr's shop, an invisible clock ticking away in the back of his mind, counting down the time they had before another assassin made an attempt.

Emerging from his train of thought, it dawned on Gloucester that his words had gone unanswered. He looked around at the others and found them all staring back at him. Harrison's brow was furrowed in concern and Mulligan's eyes were narrowed suspiciously, while the minister's look was more difficult to read. Gloucester thought it might be speculation. Or maybe just impatience.

"What?" he asked irritably.

"Perhaps it can wait a few hours," the high minister said, steepling his hands in front of him and resting his chin on his fingertips. "You look like you could use a rest, Mr. Gloucester."

Gloucester shook his head emphatically, then immediately regretted the action. "I'm fine." At the unanimous expressions of disbelief this statement garnered, he amended it to "It's just a headache. From all the noise in the city. Nothing serious."

The high minister clicked his tongue. "You're of no use if you can't think straight. The search can wait until this afternoon. Harrison will escort you back to your room. Get some rest."

His tone left no room for arguing, though Gloucester opened his mouth to do so anyway. Harrison took hold of his arm before he had a chance.

"Come along, Mr. Gloucester," he said, before leading him gently but firmly away from the desk and out of the room.

"We're wasting time," Gloucester grumbled as he was marched out of the high minister's quarters and back down the corridor.

Harrison shook his head. "His Lordship's got a point. He needs you at the top of your game, and you're clearly not there right now. A nice lie-down will do you good."

Gloucester was tempted to tell Harrison just what he could do with his nice lie-down, but he knew in the back of his mind that he and the minister were right. His head felt heavy, and thinking was growing more and more difficult as the ache grew stronger.

Still, he didn't want to give Harrison the satisfaction of agreement, so the rest of the walk to his room was completed in silence: surly on his part and amiable on Harrison's. The other security agent held the door open for him when they arrived.

"I'll be just outside the door," he said, though Gloucester

wasn't sure if this was meant as a reassurance or a warning. "Feel better, Mr. Gloucester."

—

He didn't feel better. No matter how long Gloucester lay on his soft bed, staring up at that perfect ceiling darkened by the drawn curtains, his mind couldn't find rest. His headache was no longer worsening, but neither did it relinquish its vice-like grip on his skull.

He felt fine earlier; what had brought this on? He'd never been prone to migraines. Was it really just the stress of being out in the city after such prolonged solitude? The idea rankled him. He ought to at least be capable of handling a couple hours out and about. If he was this easily affected, what would full-fledged freedom be like?

An unexpected surge of anger rushed through him. *If* he ever got his freedom. Chances were the minister and his cronies were fully prepared to dump him right back in that cell again the moment they didn't need him anymore.

It was their fault he'd been there in the first place. If it weren't for the damned high minister, he never would have been locked away, never would have been alone and forgotten for months, left to struggle in the aftermath with aspects of day-to-day life that had once been easy. Everything was the high minister's fault.

He deserves what's coming to him.

As soon as the thought crossed his mind, he pushed it away. As tempting as it was to relish such vindictive sentiments, he knew they were useless. For all he loathed the high minister, the fallout of his death wouldn't be worth it. A nation without a leader was a target, and both the Nordlands and the South Cities had preyed upon vulnerable city-states in the past. Both regions were made up of a network of once-independent cities, now united under one flag. Frettchen was the last of the city-states, and though it was a strong nation in heritage and industry, no one could say what its future might hold with the high minister suddenly gone.

His headache spiked and he closed his eyes, pressing the heels of his hands against his eyelids. *Gods*, what was wrong with him? He hoped to distract himself with thoughts on the case, as he had in the car earlier, but the pounding in his temples made it impossible. Every time he tried to latch onto an idea or train of thought, it escaped him, like a butterfly evading a child's net. Frustrated, he groaned and squeezed his eyes shut tighter.

He didn't know how much time had passed when there came a knock on the door and Harrison's voice rang through the silence. "Gloucester, I'm coming in."

If he was worrying he might wake Gloucester or catch him in some state of undress, he needn't have. Gloucester was lying fully clothed on top of his bedspread, in the same spot he'd collapsed when he was led back to his room however many hours earlier. Sleep had never come. He eyed Harrison in bleary misery as the other agent walked into the room.

"Feeling any better?" Harrison asked.

Rolling his eyes felt too painful to attempt, so Gloucester settled with rubbing them instead and sat up with a groan. "What d'you want?"

Harrison proved immune to his grumpiness, but he didn't persist with his question either. "His Lordship wants to see you before we head over to Wall's home." He hesitated. "If you want me to tell him you're still feeling ill—"

Gloucester shook his head, hissing a breath as the motion disagreed with him. "No, no, it's fine."

He didn't know what had caused this headache, but he wasn't about to spend another useless day cooped up in his room because of it. Gloucester dragged himself up from the bed, setting his feet down on the floor as he tried to ignore the pain in his temples. He needed to be able to focus, to *think*. "I don't suppose you have any painkillers," he grumbled, pinching the bridge of his nose.

"I'll send someone to fetch some for you and meet us at His Lordship's rooms," Harrison said. Gloucester spared him a grateful look, too distracted by the headache to be miffed by how difficult Harrison was making it to continue disliking him.

"Thanks." He shrugged back into his jacket and moved toward the door. "All right, lead on."

Harrison spoke into his radio for a moment, requesting the medicine, then nodded and led the way out into the corridor. He didn't seem to mind slowing his long stride for Gloucester, who was finding it a challenge to manage anything beyond a moderate trudge.

"What does he want me for?" he asked, but Harrison merely shrugged. Either he didn't know or he deemed it unnecessary to tell Gloucester. Either way, even his helpfulness had its limits.

The rest of the walk through the mansion's tastefully decorated hallways was done in silence. As annoyed as he was about being summoned without explanation, Gloucester had to admit he was grateful for the quiet. He concentrated on clearing his head. It didn't make much sense to him, but the headache reminded him of the clock shop; the ache was akin to the ambient noise there, a hundred different clocks all vying to be heard. His thoughts felt similarly cluttered, loud and whispering all at once, creating a chaos that made his head throb. If only he could sort through all of these thoughts, he would feel better, but focusing on any one thing was too much.

Soon they were standing in front of the double doors of the high minister's quarters. Jess was waiting for them. When they approached, she pulled a small pill bottle from her pocket and held it out to Gloucester. He muttered his thanks and accepted the medicine, wasting no time before unscrewing the lid and tapping a couple of pills onto his palm. He didn't bother asking for a glass of water and instead just dry-swallowed the painkillers. At least if they gave him heartburn it would be a distraction from his head.

Jess eyed him curiously, but a pointed cough from Harrison

had her excusing herself and retreating down the hall in haste. Gloucester watched her for a moment before turning away. He couldn't help but wonder if he was disappointing the staff's rumor mill or living up to whatever they were saying about him.

Harrison knocked on the door. The minister's voice, muffled by solid wood and distance, rang out to invite them in.

"I'll wait out here," Harrison informed Gloucester, moving to stand against the wall of the hallway, hands clasped in front of him. He radiated such calm patience that Gloucester couldn't help but think he'd been born to do work like this. Trying to imagine Harrison any other way was a challenge. Surely he'd been a child once. Yet even imagining that, Gloucester just pictured a shorter version of the man in front of him, solemnly standing on the sidelines of the schoolyard at recess, happy to watch the others play and step in to mediate any brawls between the other children.

The comical thought wasn't much easier to focus on than anything else, but it worked to cheer him up a little, at least. He swung the door open and stepped into the high minister's quarters.

The minister's voice issued from one of the ajar doors leading off of the entry hall. "I'm in the study."

Gloucester crossed the room. The windowed doors to the balcony had been covered over with plywood, blocking the view of the gardens and woods, and obstructing the wind that would have swirled into the room through the broken glass. What had been a beautiful view just that morning now looked messy and marred. It was odd, knowing that only hours ago a gunshot shattered the window and interrupted the conversation they'd been having in almost exactly the spot he was standing now. It felt both like days had passed and no time at all.

Shaking his head at his own pointless contemplation, he pushed the study door further open and entered the room. Why were the only thoughts managing to make it over the wall of his headache dumb imaginings and pointless musings? Neither were of any use to him right now. He hoped the medicine would kick in soon.

The minister was seated behind his desk again. Maybe he simply hadn't moved since Gloucester left the room hours ago, but somehow he doubted it. The minister wasn't the type to sit around when there were things to be done. Especially not when he was in the state of mind to trust no one.

"You don't look like you're feeling much better," the minister said in lieu of a greeting.

Gloucester sighed. "So I keep being told." If this was just going to be the high minister checking up on him, then they were wasting both their time.

"Hm," said the minister. As replies went, this was a difficult one to read. He was holding something, turning it over and over in his hands. It was the gun he'd pulled from the desk drawer that morning. They'd taken it away from him the moment security was assured of the minister's safety, and it had clearly found its way back to its rightful owner.

The minister's gaze was downcast, his eyes focused on the weapon. From the angle of Gloucester's view, he couldn't see the man's expression, but his voice was thoughtful when he spoke next.

"You saved my life this morning."

Gloucester crossed his arms, unsure where this was going. "Just doing my job."

The minister laughed. "That sounds like the old you. Before . . ." He trailed off with an unapologetic shrug, setting the gun down in the middle of the desk.

"Before you arrested me for nothing and ruined my life," Gloucester finished helpfully. His eyes were on the gun, and though the comment was meant as bitter humor, his heart wasn't in it. His head throbbed.

The minister was silent. When Gloucester dragged his gaze away from the gun, he found the minister staring at him with an odd look in his eyes, one foreign to the politician's features:

incomprehension.

"I know you resent me," he said, "but I don't see the point in playing this game. This pretending you don't know—"

"Don't know what?" Gloucester demanded. The pain in his head was worse than ever, making his ears ring with each word he spoke. Darkness crept into the edges of his vision, and he stepped closer to the desk, bracing a hand against it to stay upright.

The minister didn't seem to care about the state of Gloucester's head anymore. He rose to his feet, glowering. "Enough of this. All this playing innocent. After what you saw— What are you doing?"

He stared at the gun in Gloucester's hand. Gloucester stared at it too. He hadn't even noticed he'd picked it up off the desk. Now it pointed at the minister's shocked face, and though Gloucester felt his whole body shaking, his hand was steady.

The gun felt right in his hand. Justified. *I should shoot him,* his thoughts whispered, sounding clear for the first time in hours. *He deserves it. I should kill him.* For a moment his headache lessened, the thoughts a cold comfort, like a balm for his mind. *He deserves it. He deserves to die. I want to kill him.*

But I shouldn't.

No comfort came with that thought. It didn't soothe the headache. If anything, it brought it raging back to full strength. With a groan of pain, Gloucester staggered, but still the gun remained steady.

"What the hell is wrong with you?" The minister's voice had shed all traces of calm. He didn't move from where he stood behind his desk, staring wide-eyed down the barrel of the gun. It was the most honest look Gloucester could ever remember seeing on him.

His headache was doing something odd. It intensified, blood thudding like an angry drum in his ears, pressure squeezing his skull. He shook his head, face pinched in distress, trying to dislodge the feeling. The only part of him that didn't feel like it was coming apart at the seams was the hand holding the gun.

Shoot him.

Though the thought was in his voice, it felt foreign and not his own. He flinched. The minister was still snapping furious words at him, reaching for the phone on his desk—

The gunshot cracked like cannon-fire, and Gloucester gasped like he was the one who had been shot. Sweat ran into his eyes and he blinked it away, staring at the destroyed telephone. Without conscious thought to direct it, the gun was pointed once more at the high minister's head.

Shoot him. Do it now. Do it now and it will all be over. Do it now and I'll be free.

I'll be dead.

Shoot him!

No!

The sound of the gun hitting the floor was nearly as loud as the shot fired seconds earlier. He leapt back from it as if it were some vicious creature that had bitten his hand. His head gave another wrenching throb, enough that, for a moment, he thought he was about to faint—

And then the headache was gone, the sudden absence of pain leaving him gasping again, in mixed alarm and relief. The murderous urges that had felt so dire and all-encompassing an instant before vanished.

He met the high minister's eyes. The older man wasn't yelling anymore. He wasn't saying anything. But the look on his face said everything his silence didn't.

"I didn't want to do this." Gloucester's protest sounded ragged in his own ears. He didn't bother pleading for the minister to understand. There was no time. And anyway, it seemed hypocritical. *He* didn't know what had just happened.

He sure as hell was going to find out, though.

The minister reached into his jacket. For a phone or a weapon, Gloucester didn't know. Either way, if he stayed there, he was dead. Or he was going to wish he was. It was a miracle

Harrison hadn't already burst through the door, alerted by the gunshot obliterating the phone.

"I didn't want to do this," he repeated urgently. "Whatever this is, whoever's behind it, I've got nothing to do with it."

The minister spoke, shock clearing into fury in his voice, but it wasn't to Gloucester. "Security," he shouted into the radio he'd pulled from his jacket. "My study, now."

Snatching the gun up from the floor, Gloucester did the only thing he could do.

He ran.

Chapter 7

Running

Gloucester's escape nearly ended before it even began. He'd scarcely made it out the study door when he collided with Harrison, whose calm demeanor had shattered into confused alarm. Behind him, the door to the hallway stood open, beckoning escape.

"I just left for a moment to go to the washroom," Harrison said. "What happened? Was that another shot? Hey!"

Despite his brawn, he stumbled back as Gloucester shoved past him, the stagger powered more by surprise than a show of superior strength on Gloucester's part. The shock swiftly gave way to reflexes, and Gloucester saw Harrison's expression harden. Seizing his split-second opportunity, he lunged toward the other man and slammed the butt of the gun against his jaw.

Harrison dropped like a felled tree. Whether he was unconscious or merely stunned would take more time to determine than Gloucester had to spare, and so he didn't waste it, not looking back as he barrelled toward the door.

—

He had almost made it to the first floor when the sound of raised voices and running feet reached him. Ducking into an alcove at the end of a corridor, Gloucester strained his hearing, catching his breath as silently as he could while he listened.

From the sounds of it, they were still a floor above him. That was something, at least. But he knew how protocol for something like this worked. They'd be sealing off all exits, nobody in or out. The front door would already be locked and guarded. Chances were all other doors were already blocked off too. Gloucester guessed he had five minutes at best until the grounds were flooded with agents as well. Better to tread on the pessimistic side and say two. He had to get outside *now*.

Footsteps, made loud by haste, came from the direction of the stairs to the first floor. Gloucester swore under his breath. *Okay, think. Options, options . . .*

A window. It was the only way. He'd just passed one further up the corridor. It would be a bit of a jump and possibly a painful landing, but still better than being caught.

He had no time to waste on weighing pros and cons. Leaving the cover of the alcove, he made a dash back up the corridor, heading for the window.

The glass was sturdy, but a few strikes from the butt of the gun shattered it. Gloucester pulled off his jacket and wrapped it around his hand to knock the remaining glass from the window frame. Throwing the jacket aside, he risked a look down at the ground below.

It was distressingly far. A path followed the wall directly below the window, but no one was anywhere along it yet. This was his chance, now or never. He clambered onto the window ledge.

A door at one end of the corridor burst open, agents flooding through. Gloucester could hear them yelling for him to stop, to freeze.

He jumped.

Landing clumsily, but for the most part unscathed, he broke his fall with a roll across the rough gravel of the path. Glass littered the ground, and shards of it sliced across his forearms and knees, but he paid it no mind beyond a hiss of pain as he forced himself to his feet and started running again.

Woods or garage? Both were risks. The woods could provide cover, but would also slow him down. The garage could mean a car and quick escape, but only if he found keys and if there were no guards already there.

For the time being, he settled for a compromise, running down the path in the direction of the garage, but ready to make a sudden change in course toward the forest at the first sign of trouble.

That sign came a minute later, as Gloucester approached the corner of the mansion wall. The expansive garage housing all the minister's cars would come into view just across the lane the moment he rounded the corner. When he was just a few meters away, however, a nearby voice ground him to a halt. He flattened himself against the wall, holding his breath as he listened.

The voice was female and, from the sound of her clipped tone as she alerted someone she'd found nothing, belonged to a security agent. Her words were answered by a crackly response on the other end of a radio. From the sounds of it, she was alone, speaking to others via remote communication.

Good. One on one he could manage.

The idea of just changing course and making a break for the woods crossed his mind, but he dismissed it as quickly as it occurred. She'd have a gun; she could take him down before he ever reached the trees. Right now he had nothing useful on him but the gun he'd nearly shot the minister with. One gun against an army of security agents wasn't going to get him very far. What he needed was a way out of there and a place to hide.

The agent was getting closer. Her footsteps crunched on the

gravel with each nearing step. He waited until he could hear the quiet sounds of her breathing, then struck.

Swinging around the corner of the mansion, he kept himself low, a small target, and bowled the surprised security agent off her feet. She wasn't anyone he recognized, but she clearly knew who he was, her shock switching to anger in an instant as Gloucester grappled with her. She hadn't raised her gun in time, and now he had the hand clutching it pinned to the ground with his knee against her wrist. The barrel of his own gun nestled under her chin.

"Don't move," he said, voice low and dangerous. Instinct had kicked in the moment he fled the minister's study, keeping panic and confusion at bay. He'd been trained to keep his head in dangerous situations, and he knew how to think on the fly. He just used to be one of the people *catching* the fleeing criminal, not the one doing the fleeing. "Don't say a word."

Careful to keep his weight on her wrist and his gun steady against her throat, he sifted through her pockets with his free hand. He pulled out a portable phone and pocketed it. It could prove useful. "Sorry," he muttered as he continued his search. Something jangled in the depths of her jacket pocket, and Gloucester pulled his hand free, a set of car keys in his fingers. "Are these yours or for one of the high minister's cars?"

The agent glared up at him. Gritting his teeth, Gloucester shoved the gun harder against her neck, pressing her head against the path. "Yours or his?"

"Mine."

Gloucester pocketed the keys. "Then I'm sorry about this too. Where is it?"

"You won't get away with this," said the woman, baring her teeth at him. Gloucester gave a near-silent scoff of laughter. He didn't have time for this.

"*Where . . . is . . . it?*" He shifted his weight to apply a painful amount of pressure on the wrist beneath his knee. There would be time later to feel bad about hurting her. Provided he actually managed to escape.

The agent winced, biting her lip to keep from crying out in pain. "The staff garage," she ground out. "Parking spot nineteen."

"Thank you," Gloucester said. "And sorry again." He pulled back and struck her across the jaw with the butt of the gun. Then he snatched the weapon from her now limp hand and leapt to his feet. Leaving the stunned agent prone on the gravel path, he dashed in the direction of the staff garage.

Larger but less impressive than the minister's private garage, staff parking was located in a separate building, mostly hidden from the mansion by a thick patch of woodland with a well-maintained path cutting through it. Luckily, it was in the direction Gloucester had already been heading, saving him the trouble and time of doubling back.

Which was for the best, judging from the sounds of agents approaching from behind him. Gloucester picked up his pace, a gun in each hand and the stolen keys jingling in his pocket. The mansion would be swarming with black suits searching for him now, like an anthill that had been disturbed. He stuck close to the walls, out of easy view of the windows above him for as long as possible. Once he reached the point where he would have to break away from the walls in order to reach the path through the trees, he slowed for a moment, taking a deep breath.

Everything about this was crazy. Half an hour before, he'd been desperate to get out of his room. Now he wished he'd never left.

No time to think about that now. Survive first, fret later. Stowing the spare gun in the back of his belt, he drew one more deep breath and charged away from the mansion, making a beeline for the garage.

He expected at any moment to hear angry voices shouting his name. Or worse, the crack of gunfire and the fatal pain of bullets in his back. Yet he reached the trees unharmed. No one was calling after him, not yet at least, but he didn't risk looking back as he careened down the path.

—

The garage came into sight after a few minutes, but so too did the pair of agents standing outside it. Gloucester wasn't sure if they were patrolling or had simply been lounging there on their break when the alert of his escape reached them. They certainly were on their guard now, stances wary and weapons drawn, though lowered in such a way that he knew they must not be expecting him there. They probably assumed he would go for one of the high minister's cars, since they were closer, or try to escape into the forest.

The guards were speaking to each other, heads ducked close, too quiet for Gloucester to hear. After a moment, one stepped away, heading toward the far side of the garage. Walking the perimeter of the building, Gloucester presumed. The other guard, who looked barely old enough to have the job, stayed at his post by the door, glancing around nervously. Gloucester watched him, deciding what to do. He could try to take him by surprise before the other agent returned, but he'd have to be quick.

Fortunately, it turned out not to be necessary. A shout of alarm sounded from the direction of the mansion, making Gloucester and the young guard both jump. Someone must have come across the agent he'd laid out on the path. After a moment of apparent waffling, the guard broke into a jog toward the house.

Which also meant toward Gloucester. He hastily jumped behind the thick trunk of an oak tree, holding his breath as the guard ran past. He waited until the man's footsteps faded in the distance, then darted out from behind the tree and made a break for the entrance to the garage. The wide wall of doors was entirely open, giving the staff easy access to their cars. He was lucky, at least in this regard. Another hour or so and the night shift would have started, the doors shut and locked until morning.

He managed to pass through the doors undetected and, thanking whoever had decided to go with a simple numerical system for the parking spaces, headed as quickly and quietly as he could in the direction of parking space 19.

It didn't take long to find. The unfortunate agent's car was a slate-blue sedan, small and practical. An unremarkable vehicle all around, but he made a mental note to take as good care of it as possible. The poor woman had only been doing her job.

He'd just stuck the key in the lock when the first shout reached him. Out of time. He ducked into the car. Not bothering with the seat belt, he jammed the key into the starter port and shifted sharply into reverse. The perpetual engine whirred, the complicated clockwork under the hood spinning to life. Looking over his shoulder as he backed speedily out of the parking space, Gloucester spotted the agent who had been walking the perimeter. He was running toward Gloucester, gun in hand.

Catch me if you can.

Not the most productive of thoughts, and one that would feel idiotic if the man did indeed catch him, but he was running on instinct and adrenaline, so he wasn't about to judge his own taste in split-second challenges. Especially when they were only in his own head.

With a screech of tires and a loud rev of the engine, Gloucester shifted into drive and slammed his foot down on the accelerator.

He winced at the car's clumsy lurch. An oddly calm voice in the back of his mind posited that driving was something a bit difficult to jump right back into after six months. He told the voice to shut up and roared around the corner at the end of the line of parked cars. The exit was straight ahead, with only the agent standing between him and it.

Here goes nothing.

There would be time later to ponder how cliché his thoughts became in a pinch, he decided in the scant instant before he pressed the pedal to the floor, ducked his head, and *hoped.*

The car leapt forward like a pouncing jungle cat, barrelling toward the exit. A gunshot cracked through the air, and the driver's side mirror shattered. Gloucester ducked down further, the car swerving as his hands jerked on the wheel, but he managed to straighten it out and it shot past the agent, who threw himself out of the way at the last moment.

The way was clear. Gloucester risked sitting up a little so he could see where he was going. He sped down the drive, foot still heavy on the accelerator. Trees whizzed by, the perpetual engine roared, and soon the front gates loomed up ahead of him.

They were still open.

Not for long; the wrought-iron bars were swinging closed, controlled electronically from the guard house on the right-hand side of the lane. Gloucester swore, putting more weight on the pedal, one last-ditch attempt to gain more speed—

And it worked. There was an ugly grinding of metal on metal as one of the gates scraped along the side of the car, but he was through. The lights of the city lay ahead, even mostly hidden as they were by the forest, and the minister's mansion fell farther and farther away behind him.

Chapter 8

Shelter From the Storm

Sunsets were beautiful in Frettchen. The sun sank low over the ocean beyond the harbor, fiery colors spread out across the endless water. Boats became silhouettes, dabs of black paint against the impressionist kaleidoscope of hues. The day had been a warm one, and the streets remained busy even as night approached. Restaurants and clubs were packed to capacity, and evening traffic had yet to show any sign of slowing.

Gloucester paid little mind to the pleasantness of the weather, nor the good cheer of passersby out enjoying the day's end. His thoughts were locked on an old red brick apartment building, across the street from where he lurked in the gathering shadows of an alley. After escaping the high minister's property, he'd driven cautiously through the city for the better part of an hour, heart skipping every time he glimpsed a suspicious car or black suit. Once he managed to convince himself he'd gotten away without a tail, he parked the stolen car a couple streets away and made the rest of the trip on foot, sticking to side streets and alleyways his feet memorized long ago. The high minister's agents would be on the lookout for the vehicle.

Gloucester was glad he'd taken the precaution. He'd scarcely been there two minutes before he spotted the first black-suited figure. A security agent, standing discreetly outside the front window of a coffee shop three doors down the street. Then he caught sight of another, almost hidden by a tree near the entrance to the building. If there were two, there were surely more. He drew back further into the shadows. He shouldn't have come here.

And yet he lingered. Though his eyes flickered warily to the security agents at their posts, he couldn't stop himself from finding the right window, counting up the stories until he was looking at the one he sought.

Home.

Was Jeb inside? Gloucester squinted in the dimming sunlight, searching for some indication of movement on the other side of the glass. Between the distance and the reflection of the sky, he couldn't see into the apartment that had once been his. Did Jeb even still live there?

No way to find out now. Gloucester's eyes strayed back to the security agent by the door. They were waiting for him. Hoping he would do exactly what he'd done: try to go home. He wasn't even certain why he had. It was stupid. *Obviously* they would look for him there. What had he been thinking?

The truth was, he hadn't been. After escaping the mansion, he'd driven more on autopilot than with any sort of plan. His mind was buzzing, thoughts too chaotic and conflicting to follow. If it hadn't been for the precautionary instincts that led him on such an indirect route, he would have arrived in his old neighborhood even sooner. He'd followed his heart, not his head.

And if he wasn't careful, it would lead him right into disaster. Not just him, either. What would happen to Jeb if Gloucester got him mixed up in all of this? Gloucester leaned back against the rough brick of the alley wall and allowed himself the briefest of moments to close his eyes. In his mind, he could see Jeb's face. That brilliant smile carving mischievous dimples into his cheeks. His glasses sliding down his nose as he concentrated on his photography, long dark braids falling around his shoulders. The warmth in his laughter. Perfect memories of a happy past.

But no longer with a safe future. Gloucester opened his eyes again. The agents still lay in wait across the street, and Gloucester knew. Knew what he had to do. And what he couldn't.

He couldn't go home. Jeb had been a huge part of his life here in Frettchen. Gloucester hadn't known if they would last forever, had never been that much of a romantic, but he'd been happy. They'd been happy together. But now, were he to cross that street and try to sneak his way past the security agents, he'd only bring trouble with him. Jeb didn't deserve to have his life tangled up in the mess that Gloucester's had become. He had to let him go.

—

The sky was fully dark by the time Gloucester finally made use of the stolen phone. He'd left it turned off since his escape, not wanting to risk it being traced. The technological side of security had never been his forte, but he'd been trained in the basics and knew not to use the device until he absolutely needed to. Like now.

Frettchen's shopping district was still wide awake despite the late hour, pubs and other restaurants keeping longer hours than the boutiques that attracted the daytime crowds. Lights were strung through the branches of small trees lining the streets, adding an air of whimsy between the more practical streetlamps and illuminated storefronts. Gloucester watched everyone who walked by, searching for any sign they were coming for him. He'd found another shadow-filled alley to hunker down in. The car was a few blocks away, parked in one of the dimly lit rear lots of a particularly boisterous club. After leaving his old neighborhood behind, an idea had stirred in his mind. Not a plan, really, but the closest thing he had to one.

Dropping his gaze away from the passersby, Gloucester stared down at the dark screen of the phone in his hand. How much time would he have once it was turned on? His training told him thirty seconds, give or take, but technology had a pesky way of improving dramatically while he wasn't paying attention. On the other hand, he had no way of knowing if they were even tracing the phone.

Better safe than sorry. He'd have to make the call as quickly as he could. Digging in his pocket with his free hand, he pulled free the only piece of the puzzle he had in his possession.

The receipt was more crumpled than ever, even protected as it was by the plastic evidence bag. He smoothed it out as well as he could one-handed and squinted down at the phone number printed on it, hoping this wasn't all for nothing. He turned the phone on and dialed.

Ringing reached his ears and he held his breath, waiting. Another ring. And another.

And then the soft click of someone picking up.

"H'lo?" a sleepy voice said. Gloucester nearly laughed in relief.

"Zane Zephyr?" A gaggle of teenagers tromped past the mouth of the alleyway, and Gloucester leaned back against the brick wall, deeper in the shadows.

"Yeah, that's me," said the voice, sounding more awake. An edge to the words implied, *This better be good.*

"This is Agent Gloucester," he said, talking fast. "We spoke this morning. You live above your shop, right?" He recalled a second story above the clock shop, but no indication that the second floor was open to customers. He was making a guess, but one that seemed confirmed by the fact she'd answered the number on the receipt at this hour.

A long pause stretched out before Zane spoke again. "Yeah."

Even through the phone, her confusion was clear. "You're the short one, right? I thought you didn't have a phone."

"Borrowed a friend's. Listen, I need to talk to you. Face to face."

"Right now?" Zane's voice gained a plaintive note. "It's really . . . oh, it's not actually that late. Huh. Look, I'm really tired. Can't this wait until tomorrow?"

A large sedan, its windows as dark as its paint job, cruised past the alley, and Gloucester turned to hide his face. "Not really. This is important."

"Fine, fine." Beneath her grumpiness, he could hear curiosity. Worry relinquished some of its iron hold on his stomach. "Where are you? I don't need to go anywhere, do I?"

Gloucester shook his head, then remembered she couldn't see him. "No, I'll come to you. Just unlock the door. Thank you." Without waiting for a reply, he hung up. He'd probably already spoken for too long. He needed to ditch the phone and get as far from it as he could.

—

Ten minutes later, Gloucester stood outside the now dark shopfront of Zephyr Clocks. Some sleight-of-hand involving a taxi letting out a passenger near the alley had gotten the phone off his hands. If the high minister's security force was tracking it, it would lead them on a merry chase all through the night-time streets of the city.

At first, he couldn't see any lights on inside the shop as he warily approached. But as he neared the wide window, he detected a faint glow emanating from the back of the building, muted by the shadows of all the shelves and the reflections on the window itself, which cast a ghostly image of his own face back at him.

He looked haggard. He'd lost his jacket before the jump from the mansion window, and his previously pristine white shirt was now stained with sweat, blood, and dirt. His hair was a tangle of disarrayed curls, and he saw nothing but tired confusion in the stare beneath it.

Remembering the chimes above the door, he turned the knob carefully, leery of making any unnecessary commotion. Zane had done as he'd asked; the door opened without protest, the wind chimes quieted by Gloucester's slow motions.

The ticking of clocks enveloped him as he stepped inside. It muffled the noise of the door closing behind him and his footsteps as he crossed the threshold, headed in the direction of the light. Beyond the clocks, no other sound could be heard. He brushed one hand over the gun stowed in his waistband. With no holster or even a sizable enough pocket to store a weapon, he'd had to leave one of the guns behind in the stolen car. He'd decided to leave the one belonging to the car's owner, figuring she'd do well to have at least two of her stolen possessions returned to her together. It was the high minister's gun his fingertips ghosted over now. The one with which he'd almost killed the man.

The light was coming from a room off the back of the shop floor, its doorway nearly hidden between the shelves. Two massive grandfather clocks stood on either side like ancient pillars, their ticking voices loud in the still air. Gloucester approached on silent feet, peering past the ajar door when he got close enough.

He found a small break room, complete with a couch, kitchenette, and a table and chairs. Zane Zephyr was collapsed in one of the chairs, her head and chest prone on the tabletop, face hidden by crossed arms and copious amounts of wild, curly hair. She wasn't moving.

Swearing under his breath, Gloucester hurried forward. He held the gun half-raised and reached out with his free hand to check for a pulse—

Only to leap back in alarm when Zane sat up with a gasp.

"I wasn't—Ahh!" She spotted him and jolted back, nearly falling off her chair. "You scared the shit out of me."

Gloucester, meanwhile, clutched his chest as surreptitiously as possible, trying to remember how to breathe. "*Me* scare *you*?" he said, the stress of the day really starting to catch up with him. "I thought you were dead."

"Dead?" Zane repeated, sounding both curious and unnerved. "I was asleep. It's what people do at nighttime. Especially when weird agent-people call them in the middle of the night and drag them out of bed."

"It's not actually that late . . ." Gloucester knew he was getting side-tracked, yet he couldn't help but point this out.

A sleepy Zane glowered up at him. "It's been a long day."

Gloucester sighed. "You have no idea."

—

Five minutes later, they stood on the sidewalk outside the clock shop, bathed in the orange glow of a street lamp. The warm light reflected off the shop's window and sparkled off the misting of rain in the air. Gloucester had summarized the night's events as best as he could. He watched Zane as she knuckled her brow. She was looking more awake now, but not any less grouchy.

"Let me get this straight . . ."

Gloucester resisted the urge to groan. When people you were trying to convince of something said things like *Let me get this straight*, it generally meant *I still don't believe you.*

"So you left my shop, met someone, and then tried to kill your boss? The one you were trying to *stop* from being assassinated?" She'd thrown on a thick woollen sweater before stepping outdoors and kept picking at the hem of one sleeve, clearly antsy.

Gloucester shook his head impatiently. "Something happened. I wasn't . . . I wasn't in control. I had this headache . . ."

Zane didn't look any more convinced. "A headache made you do it?"

"*No.*" Gloucester bit the inside of his cheek to keep from shouting the word. "Something happened, okay? Something . . .

someone got to me. It all went wrong when we left your shop."

Looking away from Zane's dubious expression, he turned in a slow circle, searching the dark street for some clue, some hint of who or what might have caused all this. He was trying to remember. Something had happened here.

"There was someone," he said. "Someone here. Right here." He stopped turning, facing down the sidewalk. He'd been standing right in this spot that morning. Eyes closed, he searched his memory. The image was hazy, more like a dream than real life. "I . . . Someone bumped into me. They were smiling . . ." There had been something about the smile, something unnerving. And the eyes . . . Dark and deep, with almost no whites around irises as inky as the pupils. "Like a shark," he finished aloud. The comparison had finally clicked in his head.

He turned back toward Zane, expecting her look of disbelief to have only intensified. He couldn't really blame her; if someone he'd met only that day woke him up in the middle of the night, dragged him out of bed, and ranted at him about a shark-person giving them a magic headache to murder a major political figure . . . well, he wouldn't be buying into it either.

Except that Zane's expression was no longer disbelieving. She didn't scoff or gape or back slowly away from him. She looked troubled but thoughtful, her eyebrows scrunched together in a frown like she'd just thought of something important.

"What?" he asked. "Does that actually make sense to you?"

She didn't answer right away, and for a moment Gloucester wasn't sure she'd even heard him. Her fingers curled around strands of her hair, which she tugged on in an absent manner, clearly thinking hard about something. He was about to repeat the question when she shook her head and spoke, her tone vague.

"No. Uh, no, not to me. But I think I know someone who might be able to help. Provided you're not, you know, just crazy."

"I'm not crazy," Gloucester said, firmly enough that he

hoped to convince both of them. "Something got into me. Got into my head."

Zane's look was difficult to read, especially in the shadows of the nighttime street. "I suppose no one really knows that but you, eh?" She jerked a thumb in the direction of the shop. "Come on. You can sleep on the sofa. We can figure out your next move in the morning. As long as big men with guns haven't burst in to kill us both because of you."

Gloucester shook his head. "You were dismissed as a lead. They won't think to come back here for a while, if they even bother to at all." He hesitated, watching Zane as she moved toward the door. "Why are you helping me?"

Zane glanced back at him. "Dunno," she said after a moment's pause. "'Cause you seem nice enough, long as you're telling the truth about not actually wanting to murder someone. From your own story, you had the high minister dead to rights and you didn't take the shot. Reckon that means something." She held the door open, gesturing for him to come inside. "And because I think that if you're telling the truth, something big might be going on. Something bad."

Gloucester hesitated a moment longer. He hadn't had a clue what was happening in his life for a long time now, but since that morning, whatever sanity was left in his world had fled. Choosing the next move forward was like walking a cliff's edge in the dark: any wrong step could find nothing but doom underfoot. But what choice did he have but to keep pressing onward, no matter where it might lead?

"Thank you," he said, and followed Zane inside.

Chapter 9

The Hidden Truths

Waking up the next morning, the first thing to cross Gloucester's mind was that he wasn't lying on the soft bed in his room at the high minister's mansion. It was too narrow, too short, and the pillow was small and flat. He must be back in his cell. They'd captured him. Or maybe he'd dreamed the whole thing, the lonely frustration of so many months in solitude making him live out a bizarre fantasy of escape.

Yet as he rolled onto his back to stare hopelessly up at the ceiling, he blinked the haze of sleep out of his eyes and both the world and his thoughts came into focus. He hadn't imagined the headache that gripped him and urged him to murder, nor the angry look on the high minister's face, nor the sting of glass shards as he landed two stories below the window, nor the panic and adrenaline of his escape. That had been no dream.

Which raised the question of where he was now. Sitting up slowly, he held in a groan as the aches of the day before rushed back. He looked around.

He was lying on a sofa in a small room. Pleasant, light green walls decorated with paintings of birds and coastal scenes surrounded him, and the dark orange cushions beneath him were slightly threadbare, but friendlier than the bare cot in his old cell. It all struck him as vaguely familiar, and after a moment of sleepy memory-sorting, he came to the conclusion it was the break room in Zephyr Clocks, where he'd found Zane sleeping at the table the night before.

Of course. That was it: Zane had given him permission to sleep on the sofa, a place to stay until morning came and she took him to see . . .

Whoever it was she thought might have answers. Gloucester had no idea what sort of person could help in this situation. He knew he was grasping at straws, but he also knew if there was the slimmest chance he hadn't completely lost his mind, he had to investigate it. He was tired of worrying that he was crazy.

Dragging tired hands over his face, he rubbed any lingering sleep from his eyes and groaned. Adrenaline was no longer keeping the aches and pains of his escape at bay. As a result, he felt a little like he'd been hit by a car rather than escaped in one. He tugged his shirt sleeves up to his elbows and assessed what he could of the damage.

His arms hosted an assortment of small cuts, doubtlessly from his landing after leaping from the mansion window. His knees stung when he moved them, hinting at similar injuries there too. Luckily they all appeared to be minor, already scabbing over. The skin was taut and red, and he guessed it would itch like mad over the next few days as it healed. There were more than a few bruises to accompany the cuts, but for the most part, he was in surprisingly good condition.

"Oh good, you're up."

Zane stood in the doorway, holding two steaming mugs and looking almost as bleary with sleep as she had the night before. "I made tea," she said, stumping into the room and holding out one of the mugs. "Roasted almond."

Gloucester accepted the tea, cupping the mug between his hands and breathing in the steam. It smelled good. He'd never really been one for tea or coffee, but his stomach was protesting the unintentional fasting he'd put it through, and he was eager to get something into him.

"Thanks," he said around a yawn, before nodding appreciatively and taking a sip.

Zane perched on the arm of the sofa, near Gloucester's feet. She wore a fluffy orange housecoat loosely tied over a T-shirt and semi-fitted sweatpants. The outfit didn't exactly scream *work clothes.*

"I take it you have the day off?" Gloucester asked, watching her over the rim of his mug.

Zane chuckled dryly. "I know I'm a small business owner, but I am allowed to have time off, you know. Might as well go with the standard." At Gloucester's nonplussed frown, she added, "It's Sunday." She raised her eyebrows as if this ought to have been self-explanatory. Gloucester supposed it probably should have been, if only he'd had any idea what day of the week it was. Sundays were considered the day of rest for religious institutions and secular businesses alike in Frettchen.

But he wasn't even sure what the date was. Not that he was about to say so.

"Of course," he said instead, nodding. He took another sip of tea. Though not a four-star breakfast, he was enjoying the rich flavor.

Zane's tea, on the other hand, was going mostly untouched, nestled between her hands in her lap while she eyed him intently. After a moment, she blinked and shook her head, giving a quiet breath of laughter. "You know what? I've just realized. I don't even know your name."

"Yeah you do," Gloucester said. Perhaps it had slipped her mind. He could hardly blame her for not committing it to memory. She wouldn't have expected to ever see him again. "It's

Gloucester."

"No way that's your first name, Agent Gloucester. Unless 'Agent' is your first name. In which case, wow, your parents must've really hated you."

Gloucester snorted. "It's Mikalai."

Zane made a face, scratching her chin. "Marginally better than 'Agent,' at least. Do I call you Mikalai? Mika? Mik? Mickey?"

"Gloucester is good," he said, cutting her off as politely as he could.

"Just the last name, eh? Classy. All right, then." She held out a hand. "Nice to re-meet you, Gloucester. In the light of day and all."

Shifting his mug to his left hand, Gloucester reached across the couch to shake the proffered hand. "And you, Zane." He sat back again. "So what now?"

Zane echoed Gloucester's earlier amused snort. "Shouldn't you be the one deciding that? You're the one all fugitive-y and on the run. Not to mention some kind of secret agent."

"And you're the one who said you know someone with answers," Gloucester pointed out.

Zane held up a finger. "Maybe. *Maybe* has answers."

"Who are they?" This was only the first of a thousand questions bubbling to the surface of his mind, demanding attention. But he knew enough about questioning people to know not to rush things. Ask too many questions at once and you ended up with fewer answers than if you employed enough patience to ask them one at a time.

"She," Zane said. "Her name's Antimony Jones. She's a scientist . . . of sorts. I worked with her a few years back. She needed someone to help her with some clockwork mechanics. Dad was still running things here at the time—he and my sister moved down to Pesk when he retired—so I could spare the time away from the shop. Antimony's a bit of an odd duck, but dead clever." She saw the look on Gloucester's face and shook her head before he could say anything. "It's not her science we need to talk to her about. Like I said, she's an odd one, and she knows people who are even weirder. That person . . . thing, whatever it was you say you saw, the one who caused all this, I think she might know something about it."

Gloucester eyed her dubiously, but he didn't argue. It wasn't like he had anywhere else to go or any other leads to follow. Not ones that were accessible, at least. His thoughts swirled with as many speculations as questions. His bizarre mind control headache the day before had to be linked to the attempts on the high minister's life. Had whoever got to him done the same to the other would-be assassins? Or had their actions been encouraged by more mundane incentives? Either seemed possible, though the former struck him as a more reasonable assumption than he ever would have thought had he not experienced the headache himself. Certainly something to ponder. But if the bomber and the shooter had been affected in the same way he was, how come it hadn't worked on him? It was like Zane said: he'd had the minister dead to rights. If he'd been under someone else's control, why hadn't he pulled the trigger? How had he been able to resist?

Questions for this Antimony person, if she did indeed know anything. "Where can we find her?" he asked, finishing off his tea and sitting up straighter now that he was feeling more awake.

"She has a house on the other side of Uptown. She spends most of her time there, last I checked. Works out of a lab in her basement," Zane said. "Give me a chance to get dressed properly, and we can head over there."

—

Half an hour later, they pulled out of the narrow lane beside the clock shop in Zane's car. When he'd seen the shop yesterday, Gloucester had mistaken the driveway for a simple alley, albeit a wider-than-usual one. As it turned out, a small parking lot was hidden behind the building, just big enough for Zane's car and perhaps one on either side of it, provided the drivers didn't mind a tight fit.

Zane's car itself made the one Gloucester had stolen look big. She must have seen something in his expression as they climbed into it, since she was quick to state that she'd never had need for a bigger one, her tone distinctly defensive. Gloucester refrained from commenting, though sitting in the small space felt cramped and claustrophobic.

The hour was still quite early and the city hadn't properly awoken yet, even the sounds of traffic oddly muffled as they navigated their way through the streets of the shopping district. It soon became apparent that Zane, sleepily nonchalant as she hummed along to the radio, knew the less-used side streets like the back of her hand. She didn't press Gloucester for conversation, for which he was grateful. The excitement of the past twenty-four hours had taken a toll that couldn't really be counteracted in full by just a few hours' sleep on a sofa and one cup of tea. On top of that, the close quarters of the little car continued to play on his nerves. He attempted to calm his mind enough to snooze as they drove, but the combination of anxiety, confusion, and nagging speculation kept any relaxation at bay. He stared out the window, as he had during the car ride with Harrison, mulling over his thoughts.

Unfortunately, no matter how hard he thought, no answers were forthcoming to the million mysteries teeming in his mind. By the time Zane pulled the car over to a stop at the side of the road some fifteen minutes later, things were no more clear to him than when he'd first clicked his seat belt into place.

They parked on a quiet residential street, the sidewalk lined with a row of tall brick homes that all had the old but well-looked-after appearance of moderately expensive townhouses. Whatever this scientist did, she seemed fairly well-off for it.

He let Zane take the lead as they made their way up the short path to the front steps of a house. Flowering gardens filled the small front yard with color. Gloucester eyed the dark wood of the door as he and Zane approached it. He wasn't sure what to expect on the other side. What would someone who knew about mind control look like? It struck him as formidable knowledge to hold and conjured to mind someone equally so. Someone big and imposing and perhaps even dangerous.

Certainly not the person who answered the door a few moments after Zane rapped her knuckles against it.

She was a young woman, perhaps a few years older than Zane and himself. Beneath a bob of walnut hair, her face was open and honest, though a natural downturn to her eyebrows gave her a perpetually mournful expression. Nothing about her could be described as imposing or dangerous.

"Hello?" she said. "Can I help you?"

Zane glanced over her shoulder at Gloucester, then back to the woman in the doorway. "Hi. It's, uh, it's Murphy, right? I dunno if you remember me. Zane Zephyr? I worked with Antimony a while back. I think you'd just moved in at the time."

Murphy's sad brows drew together for a moment, but recollection came quickly and the contemplative look was soon replaced with a friendly smile.

"Zane, hi. The mechanic, right?" Zane nodded and Murphy brightened even further. "Long time no see." The door opened wider, revealing Murphy to be wearing a long tartan housecoat, her feet bare where they poked out from the hem.

"Is Antimony around?" Zane asked.

Murphy shook her head. "Not at the moment. She went out for the morning. You know her, early riser." She noticed Gloucester for the first time and blinked in surprise, then adjusted her housecoat, as if suddenly realizing how she was dressed. "Oh! Hi. I didn't even notice you there. I'm Murphy."

Gloucester offered her a wave, but no name. He hadn't forgotten there were security agents all over the city searching for him and that dropping his name to anyone who asked for it wasn't a good idea.

Zane realized this as well, apparently, as she hurried to step in. "Do you know where Antimony was going?" she asked, tentative hope in her smile.

The other woman scratched her chin in thought. "She wanted a word with Orange Ianto, I think. You know, the psychic over on Miller Street? But she left pretty early. She's probably done there by now, unless they had a lot to talk about. My guess is she's at Purpurrot's." She shrugged. "It's still generally where she is if she's not here. You remember?"

Zane nodded again. "Yeah, I do. Thanks, Murphy, we'll check it out."

"No problem," Murphy said, yawning. "Good luck."

—

"What's Per-per-oh's?" Gloucester asked as they pulled away from the curb and headed in the direction of the city center.

"Purpurrot's," Zane corrected, squinting in the morning sunlight. "It's a bakery. Purpurrot is the owner's name. Can you pass me the sunglasses in the glove compartment?"

A quick search of the glove box revealed a pair of orange sunglasses, which Gloucester handed to Zane. She took them with a murmur of thanks.

"Anyway," she continued after slipping them on. "It's a restaurant sort of thing. A pie shop. Antimony's been going there for ages. When I worked with her, she spent almost as much time there as in her lab. She's friends with the owner and staff. Murphy back there? She works at Purpurrot's as a server."

Yesterday Gloucester had stopped the assassination of a major political figure, then nearly murdered the same man and gone on the run, all after being locked up for months on end for something he couldn't remember doing. Today he was looking for a scientist in a pie shop. He marveled at the universe and what a strange place it could be.

"I really hope this is worth it," he said, pinching the bridge of his nose. Without his own pair of sunglasses, the sun was giving him a headache. The sensation stirred his anxiety, but it felt nothing like the pain from the day before. A mundane headache, nothing more.

Out of the corner of his eye, he saw Zane glance at him before returning her gaze to the road ahead. "Do you have any better ideas? I mean, you could just run. From what you told me, I'm kind of surprised you haven't. What's keeping you here if everyone is out for your blood? Why don't you just leave Frettchen?"

The notion was tempting. Just not a good one in the long run. Gloucester shook his head, dropping his hand back to his lap with a sigh. "The thought's crossed my mind, believe me. My family's up north, far away from this whole mess. I don't want trouble following me to their doorstep, though." He hesitated, heart clenching as his thoughts turned to Jeb, here in the city yet still out of reach. In his mind's eye, he saw the black-suited agents lurking in the shadow of the apartment building, waiting for him to go home. His words were bitter as he continued on. "But the high minister's right, that rat bastard. If he dies, everything goes down like a house of cards. Look at the way things have been with the Nordlands lately. Not to mention how mad his followers in the church would be, especially if it was obviously an assassination. They already think he's god-sent. They'd riot in the streets."

Zane didn't look away from the road again, but her eyes narrowed in surprise. "All good points, but . . . You want to save the life of the guy you tried to kill . . . who probably wants you dead . . . who you talk about like thinking of him leaves a bad taste in your mouth. Gloucester, has anyone ever told you that you're a little weird?"

"It's been mentioned," Gloucester said as jauntily as he could manage, though the moment of humor was short-lived. His smile faded as he considered Zane's point.

"I'm not really thinking of him," he admitted after a while. "Honestly I'm not even thinking of the city, at least not as much as I probably should be." He shrugged a shoulder, watching the city streets through the window as they drove. They passed by a park, its paths populated with morning joggers and early risers out for walks beneath the trees. "Mostly I think I'm doing it for me. Something happened to me and it involves the high minister. I want answers."

Maybe something in his voice, some edge to his tone he hadn't meant to inject, betrayed the turmoil in his mind, because Zane sounded a little apologetic when she said, "Hopefully we'll get some today."

"Hopefully," Gloucester agreed. He didn't only mean answers about what had happened the day before, though that was certainly a priority. He was thinking back, recalling the fateful moment in the minister's office before the gun found its way into his hand. The look on the minister's face had been angry even before Gloucester involuntarily betrayed him. He'd almost forgotten amidst everything that happened afterward, but the minister had been warning him of something, angry at him for "playing this game," whatever that meant. He'd thought Gloucester was pretending not to know something . . . What was it he was supposed to remember? Whatever it was, it had to be the reason he'd been locked up. He suspected the mystery of the day before was only one piece of the puzzle.

—

There was no missing Purpurrot's Pies, its large sign proclaiming the name in purple block lettering from above the long front window. The view inside was of a room filled with quaint tables and booths furnished in tasteful violet fabric. Most were empty at the moment, but here and there sleepy families were gathered around tables, laughing and chatting as they shared their baked goods.

Gloucester and Zane pushed through the door and were met with the pleasant smell of baking pastries. Gloucester's stomach was quick to remind him that the cup of tea earlier hadn't been nearly enough, grumbling loudly in protest.

"Hungry, are we?" said Zane, chuckling. Then she returned

her attention to the room at large, sweeping her gaze across it, eyes searching. At the far side of the shop, a counter displayed a wide variety of pies. A long line of blackboards was mounted on the wall above it, listing the menu. A door swung on its hinges as a waiter made his way through, carrying a plate of pie. He stopped briefly in the doorway, holding it open with his free hand as he spoke with a woman in the kitchens wearing a long white apron. Was that the mysterious Purpurrot?

Gloucester asked Zane as much, but she shook her head. "That's Bleifrei, the chef. Trust me, you'd know Purpurrot if you saw her. She tends to stand out from the crowd." She didn't explain what she meant by this, however, and went back to searching the customers' faces. Her gaze stopped on the furthest window booth from the door. A woman sat there alone, only the top of her blonde head visible from where they were standing.

"There she is." Zane nodded in her direction. "That's Antimony. Come on." She led the way toward the woman's booth.

Antimony didn't look up until they were almost upon her, and the reason for this became clear when they rounded the edge of her booth and saw she had a book in her hands. Bound in dark leather, no visible title declared what it might be about. She appeared entirely engrossed in it.

Despite this, she wasn't startled by their approach, setting the book aside without missing a beat when they came to a stop beside her table. Turning her gaze onto them, she regarded them both with a solemn but curious look.

"Hi, Zane," she said. "Who's your friend?"

Zane smiled, looking a bit uncertain. Gloucester wondered how long it had been since the two women spoke last.

"Hey, Antimony. This is—" She glanced over her shoulder at him, and he nodded his acquiescence after a moment's hesitation. "This is Gloucester," Zane finished, dropping her voice to a whisper.

There seemed little point in lying about his name. With

Murphy, giving his name hadn't been necessary, but they were here for Antimony's help, so he didn't think it would be so easy with her. At least the connection between where he'd been yesterday and where he was now was so obscure that it was unlikely the high minister's people would sniff it out.

"Hello," he said, nodding stiffly in greeting. Little risk or not, he couldn't help the feeling of hyper-awareness tugging on his nerves. His gaze kept straying to the window and the street outside.

Antimony eyed him for a moment, her face so unreadable that she'd give the minister a run for his money. It was difficult to tell if she was bored or angry or merely contemplative. "Hi," she said after a moment, then flicked her eyes back to Zane. They were a clear blue-green, half-hidden by her glasses and the hooded cast of her eyelids. "What brings you here? I haven't seen you in a while. The shop's doing well?"

Zane nodded. "Same as always. Good days and bad days. Antimony, Gloucester here has a problem that I think you might be able to help with. Something . . . weird happened to him. I'm, uh, I'm not really sure how to explain it . . ." She trailed off, turning to Gloucester again. She looked expectant this time. Antimony was watching him too, and Gloucester resisted the urge to stare down at his feet. A job where he stood invisibly on the sidelines had suited him well; he hated being the center of attention.

"I met someone . . . I think," he said. The night before, driven by adrenaline and desperation, he'd been eager to share his story with Zane, but retelling it now, in the light of day, he realized how mad it must sound. He pressed on anyway. "I don't . . . I don't remember. I remember dark eyes and a smile. A shark's smile. Then I got a headache. Worst I've had in my life. Then I almost . . . did something. Something that I shouldn't do."

He spoke quickly, the brief story tumbling out of him as if the words were eager to escape. Antimony, in contrast, said nothing at all for a few moments after he finished. Then she tilted her head to the side and asked, "What did you almost do?"

Now Gloucester did drop his gaze. Not from shame, nor even from discomfort. He was weighing his options, deciding how much to divulge. Finally, he looked up to meet her eyes again. "I nearly killed someone. I *wanted* to kill him."

"But you didn't," Antimony said.

"No. Does that mean something to you?" He still didn't understand how the scientist tied into this. What was it she was supposed to know?

"It means you're not a killer," she said simply. She tapped a long finger on her book, then looked at Zane. "You're thinking it's one of them," she said. It didn't sound like a question.

Zane shrugged and twiddled her thumbs. "The way you used to talk about them, the way the Gambler was . . . It sounded like they could have something to do with it."

"The Gambler?" Gloucester asked.

"I think you'd better sit down," Antimony said. "And tell me the whole story."

It wasn't the whole story that Gloucester told. That would take too long, and there were too many parts he didn't even understand or know himself. Not to mention the two women sitting in the pie shop booth with him were still essentially strangers to him. He remembered what he'd been telling himself ever since Harrison and the other agents came to his cell: He couldn't trust anyone but himself.

He told Antimony what he'd told Zane. The truth, just not all of it. He'd been recruited to investigate an attempted assassination. Though he'd had severe differences of opinion with the lord of the city-state, he'd taken the case anyway. He told her about the shooter and about following the lead to Zane's shop. He described, as well as he could, the strange encounter outside Zephyr Clocks and the headache it had heralded. Finally, he detailed the way the pain in his head urged him toward murder, whispering thoughts that weren't his own and only vanishing when he dropped the gun.

It was more talking than he'd done in a long time, and by the end of it his throat felt raw and dry. He finished the story off with a cursory mention of his escape, glad to be done. He coughed to clear his throat, then fell silent as he watched Antimony for her reaction.

She'd listened in silence as the tale unfolded, her only responses the rise and fall of her eyebrows and the occasional ambiguous hum. Now she frowned, tracing invisible patterns on the tabletop with her fingertips.

Finally she nodded. "It's quite the story. If it's true"—she ignored his scandalized protest and instead exchanged a look with Zane—"then Zane's right, I might be able to help you. Point you in the right direction, at least. But more than me believing *you*, you're going to have to believe *me*." For the first time since Gloucester and Zane approached her, Antimony smiled. "And trust me, it's going to feel like I'm asking a lot."

She waved the waiter over and requested a jug of water for the table. As Gloucester's stomach gave another loud growl, Zane pitched in to request a couple slices of pie. Once their order had been delivered, Antimony launched into her story.

"People often talk of how strange the world is," she said. "How bizarre this little planet can be, spinning through space, everything on it some weird cosmic anomaly. And it is. Life's crazy and unbelievable. Only, most people don't even know the half of it."

"But you do."

Antimony waved aside Gloucester's interruption. "Just eat your pie and listen, all right? You can be all judge-y and skeptical afterwards." She took a long drink from her glass, then cleared her throat. "I'm not all that good at explaining things at the best of times, so bear with me.

"Some years back, something happened. It was a bad time in my life, and like all bad times, big decisions had to be made. Scary ones. Keep going or give up, that sort of thing. Sink or swim. And then, when things were at their worst, I met the

Gambler."

Zane hushed Gloucester before he could do more than open his mouth, a question on his tongue, and Antimony held up a hand. "Not a gambler. *The* Gambler. It's what he calls himself."

"Who is he?"

Antimony's mouth pulled into a lopsided smile. "'What' might be the better word for that question. He's a . . . well, 'god' doesn't seem like exactly the right way to put it, but maybe it's the closest thing. Or maybe 'force of nature.' Personification. The Gambler is the personification of Choice. He embodies the essence of it."

Gloucester stared at her flatly, waiting for the punchline. It wasn't a very funny joke. But as the silence stretched into the territory of uncomfortable, he started to think there wasn't a punchline at all. Neither Antimony nor Zane were looking the least bit mischievous or amused.

"Wait," he said, eyes narrowing in disbelief. "You're trying to tell me that there are . . . gods of some sort? Ones you've met personally?" He'd never considered himself a person who would question other people's faith, but this sounded pretty far-fetched.

Antimony raised her eyebrows. "Just now you were telling me that a magical headache tried to make you commit murder."

Gloucester threw up his hands. "I thought it was . . . I dunno! Drugs or something. I thought someone must have drugged me." Antimony made a fair point, though, and even as he protested, Gloucester knew there was no way he could've been dosed with anything without Harrison noticing. Lowering his head to his hands, Gloucester chewed his lip, wondering if they were all crazy. "So you think this Gambler thing is behind it? Behind what happened to me yesterday?"

Pale strands of flyaway hair swayed against the sides of Antimony's narrow face as she shook her head. "No. Mischief's not his style. He's a lot of things, but he's not a troublemaker."

A frustrated frown knitted Gloucester's brow. "So what's

the point of this story?" He ignored Zane when she hushed him again, glaring across the table at Antimony.

The scientist wasn't perturbed by his annoyance. "The point is that he's not the only one."

"What?"

"There are others like him. Gods, demigods, whatever you want to call them," she explained. "His brothers, you could say."

"Exactly what I was thinking," Zane chipped in, sounding pleased.

Unlike when Gloucester had spoken, Zane's interruption only earned her an approving nod from Antimony. "They're only personifications, so they're not exactly all-powerful, but that doesn't mean they're not forces to be reckoned with if you get on their bad sides. If one of them is involved with your mess, Mr. Gloucester, I think I know which one."

"Which god," said Gloucester, unsure if he was asking for clarification or just trying to wrap his head around the impossible idea. Either Zane and Antimony were completely mad, or things had just gotten a lot more complicated.

"Do you want the high minister dead?" Antimony asked abruptly.

Gloucester stared. "What? No!"

His indignation did nothing to faze her. She had a piercing gaze that made him want to look away. "Are you sure? Do you like him? Do you think he's a good man?"

After all this talk of supernatural beings, the blunt questions struck him. "I . . ." Gloucester hesitated. "No. I don't like him."

"Did any part of you, no matter how small, wish you could kill him?" Antimony leaned forward, her stare unblinking. "Even if you knew you shouldn't. Knew you *wouldn't*. Did part of you *want* to?"

Gloucester was silent as he mulled this over. He thought of the doctor he'd been faced with after agreeing to work the case, the one who'd stared at him intently and asked meaning-laden questions. He'd said what he thought he was expected to say, what he thought were the "right" answers. The answers that would get him out of there. He wasn't sure there were any right answers now. Just the truth.

"Yes," he said. "I wanted to kill him."

He could feel Zane's eyes on him. Was she thinking she'd made the wrong choice in helping him? She didn't know the whole story; he could only imagine what he must sound like to her.

Antimony's gaze softened, like she understood. Nodding, she sat back in her seat again, all the intensity that had emanated from her moments before gone. "Thought so. It makes sense, though he obviously misjudged you."

"*Who* did?" Gloucester demanded.

"Denken. The Gambler's brother. The personification of Thought."

Chapter 10

Losing Home

This was madness. No, it was beyond madness, it was *stupidity*. Every logical thought in Gloucester's head was telling him to walk out of Purpurrot's Pies right then and there and leave all this behind. He still had a chance to get away. He could get out of the city and far from all the plots and machinations he ought to have nothing to do with. He could return to the Nordlands, where his parents lived, safe in the wilderness of the northern mountains. Without his job or his home or the man he had loved, he didn't have anything to keep him here. Let the high minister fend for himself, and best of luck to the next sorry bastard who tried to take his life. It would be the logical thing to do. The easy thing.

But life was rarely logical, and it certainly wasn't easy.

"Are you all right?"

Antimony's question pulled Gloucester from his thoughts. He looked up from his crumb-covered plate and regarded her carefully. He was trying—hoping, maybe—to find some trace of a lie in her features. There was none to be found.

"Why?" he asked. "Why would a . . . a creature like that do this?" The question sounded strangely hollow in his own ears, like he was listening to someone else ask it. He felt dazed.

Antimony's mouth twisted into a grimace as she shrugged. Her shoulders were as narrow as her face. Everything about her could be described with the word *slight*. Slightly built, slightly featured, slightly interested. But her guarded expression was fading, revealing something more animated behind her eyes.

"It's hard to know for sure," she said slowly. "Denken's always been a bit . . . out of control, I suppose you could say. Still, I don't think he'd be up to something like this just out of boredom. Now *he* is a troublemaker, but he's not a killer. None of them are. It's not just against their nature, it's something they are incapable of. Divine rules. There must be some bigger reason behind him acting up like this."

Gloucester rubbed his temples, still trying to assimilate all this new information. It was a lot to take in. "Why would these things even be here? In this city, out of everywhere in the world?"

"I wondered the same thing for a long time," Antimony said. "They're personifications, so they're sort of everywhere, you know, in spirit. But there's something here in Frettchen that keeps them coming back."

"What's that?"

Antimony's smile was enigmatic. "It's a long story. One I'm pretty certain you're not up to hearing right now. You look like your head's about to explode."

Gloucester wanted to argue, but at the same time knew she was right. He wasn't sure how much more of this he could handle. "So now what?" he asked wearily. "Do you know where we can find this . . . this Denken? Or if he's too dangerous to get near, what about his brother? The one you said you knew."

Zane, who had been silent for several minutes now, leaned

forward. "Would the Gambler be willing to talk to him?"

"Probably," said Antimony, but her smile had fled, a more serious look taking up residence in its place. "It's odd, though. I haven't seen him around in ages."

"Is that unusual?" Gloucester mirrored her frown, though his was dosed with a healthy sprinkling of incomprehension. "Does he usually hang around or something?" He'd have thought the personification of Choice would have better things to do with his time than loiter around one single city.

"Not exactly." Antimony drummed her fingers lightly on the tabletop. "He comes and goes as he likes. Vanishes off to wherever it is he calls home. But it's sort of weird for him to be absent for this long. I don't think I've seen him for . . ." She trailed off, apparently doing some figuring in her head. " . . . about a year. Wow, I hadn't really thought about it until now."

"Do you think you could try to reach him?" Zane asked. "Maybe Purpurrot can—"

"I can try," Antimony said. "I'll get back to you with whatever I can find out. In the meantime, you might want to think about finding some new clothes, Mr. Gloucester. You're not exactly inconspicuous, looking like you've been in a brawl."

Gloucester looked down at himself. He was still wearing his clothes from the day before. The shirt in particular showed the highlights of the action-packed series of events: blood from his leap through the window, dirt from his scuffle with the security agent on the path, and countless wrinkles and tears from a night on the run.

"Not really sure where I'll find a change," he said. "It's not like I can go home."

"We'll figure something out," Zane assured him. The words held a deliberate heartiness, and though he wanted to resent it as condescension, he suspected she was just being kind. "No worries."

"No worries," he echoed with a hollow laugh. If only.

—

They left Antimony at the pie shop, with her assurance that she'd let them know the moment she learned anything new. Though she never showed more than reserved impressions of emotion, Gloucester got the feeling she was troubled by their conversation. The last they saw of her before they stepped back out into the morning sunshine, Antimony was staring down at her book, but the volume was closed and she looked lost in thought.

The drive was quiet, the natural cacophony of the city muted by the car and the white noise of its engine. Zane kept the radio switched off, leaving them both to listen to their own thoughts instead. After several long minutes, Zane finally broke the silence.

"So where is home?" she asked. When Gloucester didn't answer, she spared a quick glance his way. "I mean, I know you can't go there. First place they'd look and all that, but I was just sort of wondering . . ." She trailed off uncertainly.

Gloucester remained silent as he contemplated the question. Homesickness, suspicion, confusion, and no small amount of anger roiled through his head and his heart. Not anger at Zane, who had no way of knowing her seemingly simple question was anything but, of course. The storm of emotions had been building for days, for weeks, for *months*, battened down behind the safeguards of necessity and self-control. The floodgates rattled, and he closed his eyes with a sigh.

When he opened them, Zane was glancing at him again, looking like she regretted asking her question. Gloucester felt a twinge of guilt; Zane had been nothing but helpful and kind since he'd embroiled her in this whole mess. He owed her the courtesy of a response.

"I don't really know," he admitted, looking back out at the passing scenery. "Things have been sort of complicated. I've been away."

"On assignment?"

"Something like that."

He liked Zane, for all he'd only met her the day before. She was smart and unnecessarily willing to help him despite the brevity of their acquaintance, but some things took too much explaining. And anyway, announcing he'd spent the last several months in solitary confinement didn't feel like the best move at this point.

"Where were you living before you were away?" Zane caught Gloucester's look and raised one hand from the steering wheel in a placating gesture. "I'm not trying to be nosy. Just trying to make conversation. Though, you know, if I'm putting myself out on a limb for you like this, it seems only fair you answer some of my questions."

Gloucester eyed her for a moment longer, then nodded in defeat. "I lived here in Frettchen." It felt like a lifetime ago. "I had an apartment with my boyfriend."

Zane blinked. "Your boyfriend? Does he know you're in trouble? Did you—" She cut herself off when Gloucester shook his head emphatically.

"No. Trust me. They've already been there. Probably still are. Hoping I'll be stupid enough to try and go back." He didn't elaborate, didn't want to admit that he almost *had* been that stupid. There was no going back. He sighed. "No point in putting anyone in danger who doesn't need to be."

Zane pulled a face, but left the subject alone beyond a semi-joking mutter of "Gee thanks, I feel so special."

The months Gloucester had been locked up felt like an impenetrable wall between his present and his past. He remembered happiness and simplicity and the comforts of home, but they seemed like distant things, unreachable. He remembered love, marred now by the cruel taste of bitterness. Jeb's laugh from behind the lens of his camera as he cheerfully ordered Gloucester to smile, the petals of Frettchen's Flower Festival cascading around them. Kisses in the morning, sunshine cast across their bedroom. The first time they'd exchanged *I love you's*, in the shadowy confines of Jeb's car, parked outside of Sweetpea, a romantic restaurant they'd had to save up for in order to afford the meal. The last time they'd said those words, as Gloucester left the apartment one autumn day, with no idea that he might never return.

The more he thought about it, the more it struck him as likely that Jeb believed he was dead. Or maybe an envoy of the high minister had told Jeb some tale of his fall from grace to explain away his disappearance. And what about his parents? Had word reached them up north? Surely they would have wondered why they hadn't heard from their son for months. What had they been told? Again the questions clamored in his skull. Was he a criminal in the eyes of the people he loved? Dead or hated, it was hard to say which would be worse.

One thing he knew for sure, however, was that now wasn't the time for these thoughts. He had the mystery of the attempted assassination to contend with, as well as the frankly earth-shattering revelations about gods and the role they seemed to play in the whole mess. There was too much to do and far too much on the line to distract himself with useless thoughts of home.

"What do you think he wants?" he asked abruptly, shoving back the longing for his old life in favor of these more pressing matters. "This Denken or whatever?"

It was Zane's turn to take a moment to reply, though Gloucester didn't know if this was because the question was a difficult one or because she was concentrating on driving. A motorcyclist had pulled out in front of them and was now meandering along at a speed highly disproportionate to the sleekness of the vehicle.

"You said someone was trying to kill your boss, right?" Zane said, frowning through the windshield at the motorcycle. "Someone other than you, I mean."

Gloucester's quiet laughter was devoid of humor, but also

lacked venom. "Yeah. A few different people, we reckoned, actually."

"So what if—"

"What if he was behind them all," he finished. The thought had been bouncing around his head from the moment Antimony confirmed that a person—or something like one—could be behind the disaster of the day before. "He's making people go after the high minister. But if he can do that . . . there goes the theory about the attacks being by people holding grudges against him."

"Not necessarily," Zane said, prompting Gloucester to look at her in surprise. She shook her head. "From what I know about the Gambler, his power's not boundless. It has limits. I'm betting his brother's the same way. You already admitted you don't like the high minister, right? You said so to Antimony."

Gloucester frowned, but nodded.

"Did the guy you stopped yesterday, the one you came to ask me about, did he hate the high minister too?"

Gloucester was starting to see her point. "We were pretty sure he had reason for a grudge, yeah. So, what? This thing has the power to make us act on our desires? Even ones we know we should resist?"

Zane shrugged. "That'd be my guess. Makes sense, doesn't it?"

The car rounded the corner onto Zane's street. It wasn't yet mid-morning and the shopping district, especially the far end of it where Zephyr Clocks was located, was still mostly deserted.

"Hey . . . what's going on?" said Zane.

The lack of traffic made the large black sedan parked in front of the clock shop all the more conspicuous. Its nondescript appearance was immediately familiar to Gloucester. After all, it was only yesterday he'd been riding in it.

Swearing quietly, Gloucester sank lower in his seat, leaning away from the window. "That's Harrison's car. Drive past. They're waiting for you."

"For *me*?" Zane slowed down, staring nervously at the vehicle parked outside her shop.

"Speed up," Gloucester urged in a low hiss, ducking further back in his seat. "Just drive past."

Zane's swearing was distinctly less restrained than Gloucester's, but she obliged, picking up speed again. She continued down the street past her driveway, muttering to herself, " . . . not how I wanted to spend today. It's my day off! I should be sleeping in. Catching up on reading. Grocery shopping. Not bloody playing spy because some sad-faced stray comes barging into my life. *No point putting anyone in danger who doesn't need to be, Zane.* Bah! Now I can't even go home. This is ridiculous."

Gloucester didn't reply. He held his breath as they passed the clock shop, waiting for someone to shout out his name or demand Zane stop the car. At long last, they reached the far end of the street and turned the corner. Gloucester twisted around in his seat to look over his shoulder, half-expecting to see Harrison's car peel away from the sidewalk to speed after them in pursuit.

When he and Harrison went to investigate Zephyr Clocks the day before, they'd had next to no idea what they would find there. They hadn't known who the owner was, nor the state of the shop, nor what it might have to do with the attempted assassinations. Now, luckily, it would appear whatever information they had gained in the time since Gloucester's escape didn't include the make and model of Zane Zephyr's car. No vehicles rushed around the street corner to chase them. Gloucester faced forward and sighed in relief, some of the tension easing from his shoulders.

Zane, on the other hand, wasn't at all put at ease. "Why are they there?" she demanded, shrill with alarm. "You said they wouldn't come looking for you there for ages, *if they came at all.* That's what you said. If they came at all."

Gloucester offered her an apologetic look before turning in his seat to stare over his shoulder at the road behind them again. The coast was still clear. "It must be Harrison," he said. "He was with me when that Denken thing ran into me outside your shop."

"Do you think he saw him too?"

"Definitely not. He acted like nothing had happened. But he's smart. Apparently smart enough to put together that it was then I started acting differently." *Dammit, Harrison. Why do you have to be so good at your job?*

"So now what?" The alarm in Zane's voice took on a dangerously annoyed edge. "Now I just can't go home? It's my *home.*"

Gloucester hushed her, only to be met with an affronted glare. "Sorry," he muttered. "Just let me think."

Zane looked like she wanted to argue, mouth opening and closing several times, but she stopped herself, biting her tongue with a sour grimace. They turned down another street, heading away from the shopping district and into the shadows of more modern buildings, tall skyscrapers inside of which Frettchen's business men and women worked. Towers of glass and steel gleamed in the sun, and the streets buzzed with industry that hadn't yet awoken in the quieter shopping streets. Pedestrians in tidy suits hurried to and fro, toting briefcases and nursing disposable coffee cups. Day-to-day business, Gloucester mused, watching them. Nothing amiss.

They weren't driving anywhere in particular. Zane turned onto streets at random, still muttering under her breath every now and then. Gloucester felt a pang of sympathy for her. She hadn't asked to be involved in any of this.

"If you drop me off somewhere, you can go home. I doubt they suspect you of anything," he said. "My guess is they came back because Harrison's retracing my steps. Whatever Denken did, it happened outside your shop. Harrison probably thought I might go back there."

"Smart man," said Zane.

Gloucester clicked his tongue in reluctant agreement.

Things would be easier for him if the minister's men were more incompetent. "Point is," he pressed on, "they didn't find me there. They've nothing that proves I ever returned. You can play dumb. Just tell them you went out to visit a friend or for a morning walk in the park. They don't have any reason not to believe you."

His words had the desired effect, and some of the tension in Zane's demeanor drained away. "But where should I drop you off?" she asked. "Where's safe?"

Good question. Gloucester was eyeing a chessboard in his mind, the pieces scattered and at odds, pondering his next move.

The best thing to do was wait for Antimony to get back to them with anything she found out, but he had no idea how long that might take. It could be longer than they had to spare. Somewhere out there, someone—or something—lurked, murder on their mind. Despite all of his pressing problems, each vying for his focus and deliberation, what nagged most at Gloucester's mind wasn't really about himself at all:

The high minister was still in danger.

Zane took his silence as a lack of ideas, which he had to admit was fair. "How about back at Antimony's? Seems pretty damn unlikely they'd ever work out that connection. 'Specially if they're not really looking at me as an accomplice. What?"

Gloucester realized he was staring at her. With a short laugh, he dragged his hand through his hair in a jerky motion that gave away his nerves more than he intended. "What must you be like when you're helping a friend, if this is how helpful you are for a stranger?" Though he said the words like a joke, he didn't try to keep the honest gratitude from bleeding through.

This got him a laugh in return. Zane's smile was crooked, still edged in anxiety of her own. "I'm a gem, what can I say?"

Chapter 11

The Wait

It took nearly half an hour to circle back through the city to the home of Antimony Jones. Though there was little chance they were being followed, Gloucester still directed Zane to stick to back streets and not stray too close to the clock shop on their return trip. Zane seemed uncomfortable with breaking away from her familiar paths and grumbled to herself in a barely audible undertone. Having grown used to silence in his time of enforced solitude, Gloucester found the noise odd, like a tickling in his ears. He did his best to ignore it.

They ventured away from the bustle of downtown, driving through quiet residential neighborhoods, the hubbub of the city center replaced by tree-lined sidewalks and children on bicycles. Gloucester's anxiety drifted to the back of his mind. It was difficult to feel the encroaching shadow of his enemies in such a place.

Morning was steadily waning, the sun high in the sky. It

was another clear spring day, crisp unending blue stretching above the city's architecture, interrupted only by feather-light brushstrokes of white clouds that hung lazy and unmoving high above them.

Finally, they turned onto a street Gloucester recognized as the one they'd visited earlier that morning. Zane pulled over into the same spot she'd parked before. Their car doors closing as they got out sounded loud in the serenity of their surroundings. Gloucester glanced around, some of his nerves returning now that they were no longer on the move, but there were no signs of anything amiss. He was being paranoid. They'd never find him here.

What about Denken? The mysterious god-like creature had found him before. Somehow he had zeroed in on Gloucester's grudge against the high minister like a shark scenting blood in the water. Had their encounter been coincidence? Or had he known Gloucester would be there? If he truly was some kind of god, who knew how he might find people or what he might be capable of?

Too many questions. Gloucester had always been someone who over-analyzed, who couldn't help but turn every difficult situation over and over in his head like a puzzle he could solve if only he looked at it from all angles. *You ask too many questions. You think too much.* His parents had always told him that. His teachers. His trainers. Jeb. *You worry too much, Mikalai. Why do you ask all these questions?*

Because these ones needed answers. The high minister's life depended on it, and by extension, the well-being of the entire city-state. Gloucester's freedom hung in the balance too. Not to mention the lives of whomever else might be compelled to do the bidding of this petty, vengeful god.

His worries accompanied him up the path to Antimony's front stoop. Murphy answered the door again, now dressed and properly awake, and showed Gloucester into a cluttered sitting room after bidding Zane a quick goodbye. The shopkeeper promised to be back as soon as possible, looking almost hesitant to leave him as she turned away from the door. Gloucester wondered what she was reading in his eyes to make her worry so. He did his best to purge his features of any emotion, to restore the calm composure he'd once so easily been able to adopt as a default of his job. He wasn't sure it worked, since in his final glimpse of Zane before she slipped out the door, she didn't look very comforted.

Morning passed into afternoon. Gloucester was left mostly on his own, except for the handful of times Murphy stuck her head through the sitting room door to ask if he needed anything. As far as he could tell, she was the only other person in the house. She was cheerful and polite, but seemed to catch on quickly that he didn't feel like chatting, and amiably left him to his own devices. Every now and then, he thought he heard sounds from somewhere beneath his feet, but no voices reached his ears, and the noises were infrequent enough that they could be nothing. Perhaps Antimony or her friendly roommate owned a cat.

He gave up sitting after a while and took to pacing instead, bleeding out through movement what he could of the nervousness simmering within him. After the storm of questions that had raged so furiously in his mind all morning, he was now trying to think as little as possible. He needed to clear his head, to make room for answers and to figure out just what he was going to do when he got them.

Antimony's sitting room was smaller than the quarters Gloucester had been given at the high minister's mansion. Five long strides from the door to the floral-printed armchair against the opposite wall. Three between the blue sofa under the front window and the bookshelf across the room. His pacing was also impeded by the clutter of the space: a coffee table buried under stacks of books and half-finished knitting, boxes by the bookshelf filled with what appeared to be photo albums and old journals, and a towering and odd-shaped object in one corner that, upon his curious closer inspection, turned out to be a covered harp.

At a quarter after two, he heard the front door open. Grown tired of pacing, he'd started working out his stress through sit-ups instead, and he froze at the sound, lying on the floor in the middle of the sitting room. He rose slowly off his back and into a loose cross-legged sit, silent, ready to leap to his feet at any sign of trouble.

Relief washed away the worst of the worry when Zane rounded the corner of the doorway a moment later. Antimony followed a few steps behind her.

"Hey again," said Zane. "Just bumped into Antimony right on the doorstep. Talk about perfect timing, eh? I—What in the world are you doing down there?"

Zane stared down at him. Gloucester stared back.

"Sit-ups," he replied, unsure what else to say on the matter.

For some reason Zane didn't seem satisfied by this answer, but after a moment's longer look of confusion, she let it go. Stepping to the side, she gave space for Antimony to enter the room.

Antimony looked almost as unfazed as she had that morning, only a faint twist at the corner of her lips hinting that she wasn't completely unconcerned. Her long blonde hair, which had been piled atop her head in a bun when they'd met her in the bakery, was now in a ponytail that cascaded down her back in a straight golden sheet.

"What did you find out?" Gloucester asked, picking himself up off the floor with an eager bounce.

"Not much." Antimony's tiny frown deepened to become more evident. "And that could mean nothing. Or a lot." She caught the looks on Gloucester's and Zane's faces and actually smiled. "I'm not trying to be enigmatic, honest. I'm just . . . thinking. I couldn't find him."

"Denken?" Zane asked. Unlike Antimony, there was no hint of amusement on her face.

"No, the Gambler. I don't see the other ones often enough to know how to find them. But the Gambler is usually somewhere around. He likes this city. But he wasn't at any of his normal haunts. And none of the usuals have seen him."

"The usuals?" This time it was Gloucester who raised the question.

Antimony waved a hand airily. "He has a few friends around here other than myself. None of them have seen him in a while, though. It's weird. Even Purpurrot doesn't have any idea where he might be, and she always seems to know where any of them are if she really needs to."

"Why—" Gloucester started to ask, but Antimony's hand waved again, cutting him off. She took up pacing the room, treading the same path Gloucester had an hour before.

"I'm starting to think something really is wrong. If something's happened with the Gambler, it could explain why Denken's acting up. They couldn't be more different, but they're still family."

The afternoon sun had begun its slow descent toward the horizon, and though it still had a long journey ahead, it was shining at a low enough angle to cast light through the window, bathing them all in the warmth of a sunbeam. Gloucester fought his instincts and turned his back on the glass, arms crossed and eyes downcast as he turned things over in his mind.

"So what does this Gambler have to do with the high minister? There's got to be a connection, if Denken's focusing his anger on him."

Somehow it didn't surprise him that the lord of the city-state had even managed to anger a god. That was taking things to a whole new level, but the man had never been one to shy away from a challenge.

"Has he ever said anything that could hint at him knowing about beings like the Gambler and his brothers?" Antimony asked.

Gloucester shook his head. "He's one of the most pragmatic

people I've ever met. I wouldn't ever have thought he'd believe in things like magic."

Zane smiled as she crossed the room and sat down on the couch, a halo of sunlight glowing around the curly mass of her hair. "Magic's all around. Most people just don't ever notice. You kind of have to be . . . shown, I guess. Then suddenly you start seeing it everywhere."

"So what now?" Antimony asked. She sat down next to Zane, perching daintily on one of the couch's arms. Both women watched Gloucester. He blinked in the metaphorical spotlight.

Clearing his throat, he did his best to disguise his discomfort and his uncertainty. "I need answers about the high minister. I need to get close to him again."

Zane was less than impressed with the dramatic reveal of this plan. "Sorry, what? You need to get close to him? The man you were *running* from—literally running from—yesterday? And now you want to go back? Are you insane?"

Possibly. Gloucester kept this thought to himself. Out loud, he said, "The fact that he's wrong about me being in on this whole conspiracy doesn't change the fact that it exists. He's in danger. And as long as he's in danger, the whole city is."

"So, what? You want to watch him from the shadows and stop any more attempts on his life? Gonna be a bit difficult, what with all his people out looking for you."

"Nothing in life is easy," Gloucester quipped, voice lighter than his actual mood. Zane was right, this could very well be a disaster. Maybe it *would* be better to just get out of town. Leave Frettchen to take care of itself, for better or for worse . . .

No. Too much was at stake. Frettchen was filled with innocent people who didn't deserve to be abandoned. People like Zane, helping a stranger out of the goodness of her heart. People like Murphy and Antimony, sheltering him with so few questions asked. People like Jeb. Gloucester's heart hurt at the thought of him, but if he couldn't return to the life they'd had together, he could at least do everything possible to protect him from afar.

"All right, here's what we need to do," he said, hoping his determined tone didn't waver and give away that he was coming up with the plan on the spot. "One, keep an eye on the high minister." He ticked off a finger as he spoke. "Two, find out why Denken wants him dead." A second finger flicked out to join the first. "Three, stop him. Possibly both of them, depending on what the high minister's up to." A third and final finger.

Until Antimony raised one of her own, the digit as pale and slender as the rest of her. "Four, find the Gambler. I'm not joking, something's wrong about him being missing. I'm sure of it."

"Right, right," Gloucester agreed. If the disappearance of Denken's brother had to do with the so-called god's wrath, then finding him probably was for the best. From everything he'd experienced and heard so far, he just wasn't sure he was so keen on meeting either of them. "If there's a connection, investigating the high minister seems like our best bet for finding him."

Chapter 12

The Rendezvous

Night hung heavy over the city and heavier still over the woods blanketing the hills to the north, where there were no streetlamps or lights from houses to infiltrate the darkness. The only lights were the ghostly flicker of fireflies at the forest's edge and the distant glow of the moon overhead.

Gloucester sat unmoving between the roots of a massive oak tree, its rough bark catching on his sweater each time he shifted position. He'd been there for hours, long enough for his eyes to accommodate to the minimal lighting and make out the silhouetted shapes of his surroundings. In any case, what he was keeping an eye out for would be difficult to miss. Even if they turned their headlights off, any car traveling by on the narrow road that threaded through the forest toward the high minister's mansion would not be able to pass Gloucester's hiding spot undetected.

A notebook sat open in his lap, a pen clutched between his

cold fingers. He'd come prepared each day to make note of any important movements on the part of the high minister or any of his associates. Antimony had advised him to write down a description and the license number of any vehicle he spotted, citing a connection at the DMV who would be able to help them identify anyone coming and going. When he'd raised his brows, surprised by this unexpected announcement, Antimony simply shrugged and claimed that she had friends in many walks of life. Which was certainly useful, as long as he was able to garner some information to bring to her. Beyond this meager reconnaissance, there wasn't much more he could do, but at least he would have some idea of what the high minister was up to. And who might be trying to get to him.

So far no one had come. Or left, for that matter. Gloucester had spent the better part of three days there, making his way up and down the stretch of country road, and had seen little more than squirrels and birds, who chittered and called to one another from the trees. Normally there would be the comings and goings of staff headed to and from their shifts, but apparently no one was getting to go home at the moment.

Lockdown. But even the high minister, with all of his well-founded paranoia, couldn't stay hidden away for long. He would have to let his employees change over at some point and, as the city's leader on not just one but two fronts, his own list of duties was nigh on endless, ranging from banal conferences to deeply influential matters of diplomacy. Some of that work could be postponed or done from the safety of his guarded home, but not all of his responsibilities would be so easily shirked or manipulated. Sooner or later he would have to leave the mansion, and Gloucester was betting on sooner.

As plans went, he knew this one wouldn't be winning any awards. What could he do, even if the high minister—or worse, his assailant—made a move? Without direct access to the minister, he was stuck watching from a distance, trying to ignore the whispers at the back of his mind saying this was a hopeless endeavor. Days had passed since he'd stood in Antimony Jones's sun-filled sitting room and proclaimed with false confidence what needed to be done. If only actually doing it was so easy. It was one thing to say he needed to find out more about what the high minister was up to, it was another entirely to figure out how in the world to do that.

It was a slight comfort to know Antimony was down in the city, on the hunt for answers as well. Her concern seemed mostly to revolve around the mysterious Gambler, but she'd promised to find out anything she could involving the high minister. Gloucester was beginning to suspect that she was some sort of information peddler, though Zane had rebuffed his curiosity when he asked her about it. Antimony, she told him, was a firm believer in the idea of "knowledge is power." Though she hadn't said more on the matter, this felt like a confirmation of his suspicions. Perhaps, then, she would have more luck than he. They would both play their parts in their imperfect plan and hope for the best.

So here he sat, for the third day in a row, hidden by the trees and waiting for some sign of activity from the mansion on the other side of the woods. Every now and then, when he was certain no one else was around to hear, he'd turn on the small radio he'd brought with him, hoping to catch any news that might hint at what the leader of Frettchen was up to. So far nothing.

In the dim moonlight, he squinted down at the watch on his wrist. Zane would be coming to pick him up soon. He'd lost track of the time, staring into the darkness and listening to the night sounds of the forest. If he didn't head for their rendezvous point now, she'd be kept waiting. Considering she'd been letting him sleep on the sofa in her breakroom, on top of all the other help she had offered so far, he at least owed her punctuality.

He tucked the notebook and radio into a canvas tote and got to his feet silently, though his body was stiff from being still so long and protested the action. He pulled his sweater closer around him as he straightened up, shivering in the night air. Despite the warmth of the days, the nights still had a lingering chill that came with the spring season. The sweater, along with the rest of the clothes Gloucester was wearing, had been provided by Antimony. She didn't say where they'd come from, nor had Gloucester seen any sign of a man living with the scientist, but there had been a closed look in her eyes and a warning in Zane's that kept him from saying anything other than "Thank you." The clothes smelled strongly of mothballs, like they'd been in storage for a long time.

The trek back through the woods to their rendezvous spot on the road was uneventful, the loudest noises an owl's call somewhere deeper in the forest and the distant sounds of city traffic. The streets of Frettchen would be visible from the minister's mansion, but were hidden from Gloucester's sight where he walked now. Surrounded by the dark trees, he may as well have been in the middle of nowhere, alone in the wild.

Zane's tiny car was parked by the shoulder when he arrived, and he could see the clockmaker's anxious face through the driver's side window as she watched him approach. Though she was quick with a joke and even quicker with a smile, Gloucester had come to find Zane Zephyr was far from immune to worrying. She had a pragmatic side that coupled well with her cheery demeanor, giving her a keen eye for potential problems, without being too much of a downer about them. It made her a refreshing person to be around.

There wasn't much optimism in her eyes now, however.

"Anything?" she asked once Gloucester joined her in the car.

Gloucester shook his head, tossing the tote bag into the back seat and carefully removing the high minister's gun from his waistband so he could sit. Zane eyed the weapon unhappily and gave a loud sigh.

"Maybe this isn't the way to go about it," she said.

Gloucester—frustrated, cold, and stiff after his day of fruitless surveillance—bristled. "What other way do we have?"

he demanded. "Maybe you think I should just walk up to the mansion and knock on the door? Request an audience?"

Zane wasn't cowed, flashing him a scandalized look before turning her gaze pointedly to the road as she pulled away from the shoulder. "Of course not. Don't bite my head off. I've been worrying about you all day, you know. I barely got any work done, picturing you out here all on your own. This plan is so risky, and you have to admit it isn't really getting us anywhere."

Gloucester grunted. Much as he hated to admit it, he knew the plan wasn't great, it was just the only one he had. He muttered a sour apology to Zane, surly gaze turned away from her.

"I don't know if maybe—Oh shit!" Zane's voice decrescendoed into a hiss, the alarm enough to make Gloucester whip his head around. Zane was staring into the rear-view mirror, face stricken with panic. "There are headlights. Someone's coming down from the high minister's place." She seemed unable to tear her eyes away from the mirror. "What do I do?"

Gloucester's heart hammered in his chest. If they were found here on this private road, they would be chased down as suspicious. Even if they turned their headlights off, they had nowhere to pull over to hide the car, as deep ditches lined both sides of the road. They'd taken a risk having Zane pick Gloucester up here instead of on the main road further down the way. Now they'd be sitting ducks for whomever was making their way down from the mansion.

"They're getting closer," Zane said. "I can see their lights on the trees. They'll be around the bend soon!"

Gloucester could hear the rising panic in her voice, and his mind raced to come up with some safe way out of this. "Turn the headlights off. The main road's not far ahead," he said. He made his voice as calm and encouraging as he could. "If we get to it, they'll never know we were here. Can you get to it?"

Zane didn't need telling twice. Muttering a curse under her breath, she switched the headlights off, gripped the steering wheel in both hands, and accelerated down the dark road.

"I can't see a thing," she whispered, as if their unknowing pursuers might hear them if they spoke too loudly.

"You're fine," Gloucester assured her, squinting into the darkness up ahead. He realized after he spoke that he too had lowered his voice to a murmur. His heart was still racing, a prickle between his shoulder blades as he thought of the car getting closer behind them. "We're almost there. Just a bit further. Just a bit—"

"If I didn't know better, I'd say you were as scared as I am." Zane checked her rear-view with frightened eyes.

"If only." Gloucester's eyes were locked on their path forward. "I'm probably *twice* as scared as you are. There!"

In the moonlight up ahead, he could see the main road, running perpendicular to the one they were on now, its surface paved instead of packed gravel. Zane's gasp of relief was audible as she turned the car onto it. Out of the woods, the darkness lessened, the stars and moon casting silver light from up above and the lights from the city stretching out below.

"Wait until we're a ways away from the turn-off before turning the headlights back on," Gloucester warned her. Though they were no longer in immediate danger, his whole body still felt taut with tension and he had to force himself to slow his breathing, easing the tightness from his shoulders and the whispering fear in his mind. "And drive slowly."

"Drive slowly?" repeated Zane, surprised.

She took an obvious deep breath, glancing into the mirror again before switching the headlights back on. Following her gaze, Gloucester watched the lights of the car behind them turn onto the main road. Out of the corner of his eye, he saw Zane look his way in confusion before she returned her eyes to the road.

"Shouldn't we go faster? Try to stay ahead of them?"

"No," Gloucester said firmly. "We want them to pass us. So we can follow them."

"Ah." Zane sounded resigned. "Following creepy secret agents in the dead of night. Fun!"

After a few minutes, Gloucester saw the headlights behind them shift sideways as the car moved over on the road to pass them. He lowered himself in his seat, not wanting anyone in the mysterious vehicle to catch a glimpse of him as they went by. Zane hummed under her breath, an anxious noise that was more whine than tune. The car, a sleek black sedan, drove past them. After another tense moment, Zane let out a long breath. He did the same, trying to smooth out the nervous pounding of his heart.

Trailing the taillights of the car, they left the quiet darkness of the forest behind and entered the lights of Frettchen. From the bright colors of traffic lights to the distant pinpricks of lit windows in skyscrapers high above, the city was alive in a chiaroscuro of light and darkness. The daytime crowds had retreated, replaced by the young and adventurous, the rowdy and the rushed. None of the bustling activity that came with diurnal city life remained. Instead, the citizens of Frettchen who braved the dark flitted and meandered in equal measure, all either eager to get where they were going or enjoying nothing more than the night itself.

Gloucester had eyes for none of it. Scarcely remembering to blink, he watched the car ahead of them. Zane had enough common sense to know without being told not to stay too close to their quarry; she'd allowed the distance of a few cars to come between them, but never enough to risk losing them entirely. She, too, was silent, though in the small space of the car, her tension felt almost palpable.

"You know . . ." she said after a while, as they turned a corner and left the bright lights of one of the busier streets and entered the darker warehouse district on the harbor side of the city. "You can be . . . intense." She looked away from the road long enough to offer Gloucester an apologetic grimace. "I just mean, you're sort of . . ." Eyes back on the road, she relied on her facial expression to take the place of eloquent description, arranging her features into an exaggerated look of stern concentration.

Gloucester snorted. "Sorry," he said, gaze already dragged back to the car they were following. "Just thinking."

"Do you think it's him in the car? The high minister?"

Gloucester had a feeling Zane was mostly talking to keep her nerves at bay. He shrugged, the action little more than a miniscule jerk of his shoulders. "I think it's the only car that's left the property in more than a day. It's got to be something."

—

Even in the warehouse district, the lights of Frettchen shone. They were fewer and farther between, but never so much as to allow more than brief patches of darkness to shroud the quiet streets; the occasional streetlamp cast its yellow glow over the pavement, a security light above the threshold of a door flickered to life at the passing of a stray cat, and the more distant twenty-four hour illumination of cargo areas could be seen from the road, past the tall walls that guarded the properties. There were no cavorting pedestrians here, just the infrequent sound of a slamming car door or footstep of a nightwatchman. Further away, out past the harbor, a lighthouse turned its searching glow back and forth.

Not wanting to risk the blatancy of following the minister's car into such a desolate part of the city, Zane and Gloucester didn't stop when they watched the mysterious car finally park. Its destination was an empty lot sandwiched between lofty warehouses that would no doubt be converted into apartments for rent the moment their current businesses failed. Zane circled her car around the block and parked a safe distance away. They approached the parking lot on foot, anxiety clutching at Gloucester's stomach with increasing zeal as he pictured finding the parking lot empty, their quarry lost, and with it their best— and maybe *only*—chance at some answers.

As they neared the lot, Gloucester was relieved to see the car still there. He didn't want to consider the fact that this might be nothing, that they might have just spent the last half hour tailing some weary security agent or house staff on their way home from work after days of lockdown.

Except, this car, with its smooth lines and expensive build, wasn't the type to be owned by a mere employee. And this didn't look like anyone's home.

A light in one of the warehouses illuminated a long rectangle of the parking lot's pavement, stretching out from the open doorway like a welcome carpet. The light reached far enough to filter through the windows of the parked car. It was empty.

Beside Gloucester, Zane looked as on edge as he felt. Though she trod as soundlessly as he did, he could see her fear in the sharp angle of her shoulders, the stiffness of her back, and the way her fingers tugged on the hems of her sleeves as she walked. Even distracted as he was by what they were heading into, Gloucester's heart went out to her for willingly walking alongside him. He wondered if she realized how brave she was.

Though he knew it was an unnecessary warning, he raised a finger to his lips as they passed the parked car and drew closer to the door of the warehouse, both he and Zane careful to stay out of the light. Sure enough, Zane rolled her eyes and mouthed what could only be a very emphatic, if silent, *Duh*. Gloucester offered her an instant's smile before refocusing on the situation at hand.

They pressed their backs against the wall on either side of the door, out of sight of whomever was inside.

"They're late," said a familiar voice. Gloucester would know it anywhere. The high minister. "Bloody typical. They never miss an opportunity to be dramatic. Even if it makes them a walking cliché."

Gloucester fought the urge to peek around the corner of the door.

"They could be here already," said another voice. Mulligan. "I've never actually seen them in a car. Maybe they walked.

Seems like them to lurk in the shadows, waiting to step out when we're least expecting them." Unlike the minister, he sounded more nervous than annoyed.

Gloucester stood very still as he decided what to do. If someone else was due to arrive, he and Zane could very well be stuck right between them and the high minister and Mulligan inside, with nowhere to hide. Yet there was nowhere else to go now, short of abandoning this entirely. On the other side of the doorway, Zane looked petrified.

"Your friend knows us well," a new voice crowed.

Gloucester's heart skipped a beat, and he reached around his back for the gun in his waistband, but the newcomer was already inside the warehouse, hidden from view. Which meant he and Zane were still out of sight of enemy eyes. Some of the thundering pressure in his chest lessened its grip. Nonetheless, his hand came back around holding the gun.

The new voice wasn't one he recognized. Cheerful and confident, it echoed off the high walls and ceiling of the warehouse. It belonged to a man, and again Gloucester fought the urge to peek around the corner and put faces to the conversation he was overhearing.

"Where's your son?" the minister asked with a note of suspicion.

"Just me tonight. He's a busy lad, you know how it is. But what can I do for you, my High Minister Lordship, sir?" A lilt in the unknown man's voice made him sound all the more unconcerned.

It was in sharp contrast with the minister's tone. "You can answer my questions. I find I have quite a few that require explanations."

The other man laughed heartily. "Don't we all, Mister Minister, don't we all. What questions are these that call for dragging a poor old man out of bed in the middle of the night?" He made no mention of their peculiar location, a fact that Gloucester was quick to make note of. Had the high minister and this man met here before? Why?

"It's about the Gambler," the minister said.

Zane gave a start, visibly surprised. Gloucester leaned closer to the door, barely daring to breathe lest he miss anything.

"Big surprise there," said the other voice, still sounding amused.

"When you told me of his powers . . . when you explained to me what they could do, did you tell me about all of them?"

"All of them?"

"Does he have any others?" the minister said with increasing impatience. "Telepathy, mind control, anything like that."

"Oh my god," whispered Zane. "We were right. Gloucester, we were right. It all comes back to the Gambler."

Gloucester didn't reply. Something cold and metallic had just pressed itself against the back of his head. The click of the safety rang in his ears.

"Evening, friends," said a voice behind him. "Nice night, don't you think?"

Chapter 13

Answers

Gloucester and Zane were shepherded into the warehouse, and he blinked in the fluorescent light. Judging from the emptiness of the space, it wasn't in commercial use. The owner was probably the high minister himself, which would explain why it would be a safe place to meet with his conspirators. Their captor walked alongside them, his gun pressed to Gloucester's temple. Gloucester's own gun was out of sight and reach, stowed away in the man's coat pocket.

He was a grinning man who looked to be in his early thirties, with dark red hair and a few days' worth of stubble. A sun, or at least half of one, was tattooed across the left side of his brow, stretching in a semi-circle from his hairline to his temple. He spoke with the same lilting accent and jaunty tone as the mystery voice to which Gloucester and Zane had been listening.

They entered with their hands raised. Three men stood in the warehouse, dwarfed by the stark emptiness of the large room. Two of them Gloucester instantly recognized, as he had known he would: the high minister and Mulligan wore matching expressions for once, both facing the doorway with surprised stares. The third man had to be the owner of the unfamiliar voice. He was in his middling years, fast approaching the end of them, with a round face and rounder body. His hair receded from the top of his head into a semi-circle of gray, ringing from his ears around the back of his skull. He, too, looked surprised, though the smile never left his face.

"What's this?" he cried, as if the sight of them was a welcome bit of interest, and they were just unexpected house guests showing up at his front door. "Visitors!"

Mulligan shared none of his good cheer. He gasped, then the shock hardened into anger. "*Gloucester*. What in the world?"

"They were listening at the door," said the man holding a gun to Gloucester's head. "You know them? Something tells me they aren't friends of yours."

Mulligan pointed an accusing finger. "He's a murderer!"

"No, I'm not," Gloucester said, nettled. Zane shot him a look that clearly told him to shut up. His heart pounded in his chest, but his training was kicking in, holding his panic at bay.

"Oh, sorry," said Mulligan snidely. "Just an *attempted* murderer. A shining example of—"

"Quiet."

The minister's order wasn't loud, but it stopped his adviser's words immediately. Mulligan snapped his mouth shut, glaring at Gloucester in silence.

"We've been looking for you, Mr. Gloucester," the minister said. Unlike Mulligan, he didn't sound angry. If anything, cautious curiosity colored his voice. "How nice of you to save us the trouble."

This time Gloucester followed Zane's nonverbal advice and remained silent.

"Oho! A fugitive, eh?" said his captor. "Not doing the best job of running away, are you?" Like the other stranger, he sounded more amused than anything else.

"It would seem that way," the minister said, when Gloucester again offered no response. "Except that isn't you. If you were really running, you wouldn't be here. So I wonder, what brought you back? You must have followed us practically from my front door."

The man with the gun gave Gloucester a none-too-gentle prod to the side of his head when he didn't answer right away. "Not a chatty fellow, this one. Maybe we should ask his friend." The gun swung away from Gloucester's temple to point instead at Zane.

The instant it wasn't against his head, Gloucester struck, whipping to face the other man and snatching at the gun.

The gunman had been overconfident in his holding of the upper hand; Gloucester saw his expression change from smirking to surprised in the blink of an eye, and then the gun was in Gloucester's hand. The panic slipped away.

"Back up," he ordered, his breathing harsh but steady. "All of you, hands where I can see them. Not *you*," he added to Zane.

She lowered her hands, looking a little dazed. "Sorry. Got caught up in the moment."

"This again?" the high minister cut in. He was doing his best to sound bored, but his expression gave him away. Mouth drawn in a tight line, his eyes flickered between the gun and Gloucester's face. Beside him, Mulligan managed to look both scared and furious. "Think how this ended last time, Gloucester."

"This isn't the same," Gloucester said shortly. He might have a gun in his hand, but this time it wasn't some supernatural compulsion steering it, steering *him*. He was certain of that, at least. He was making his own choice. He pointed the weapon at its owner, the redheaded stranger. "You took my gun before. Slide it over to me."

The last thing they needed now was a shoot-out. Not with Zane there. And not when answers were so close at hand.

The redheaded man had nothing to say for once, merely

grimacing as he pulled Gloucester's confiscated gun from his jacket and crouched to set it down on the concrete floor, then slid it toward Gloucester like a bizarre shuffleboard biscuit.

"Pick that up, please," Gloucester said to Zane, who complied, still looking dazed and scared. Gloucester didn't waste time thinking about that now. Though he kept the gun pointed at the redheaded man, he addressed the older stranger. "Who are you?" he demanded.

"Could ask the same of you, lad." While levity still buoyed the man's voice, he was no longer smiling. "You're the interloper, not us. Mr. Gloucester, was it?"

"You know my name. Let's have yours."

"They're none of your concern," said the minister. "What are you doing here? Does your friend know how much danger you've put her in by not just running away?"

Zane gave a harsh laugh. "Danger? Really? Here I thought we were just driving around in the dead of night following strange cars and listening at doors for fun." Her voice shook.

"Indeed," the minister said tightly. "Who are you, then, anyway?"

"*I'm* asking the questions here." Gloucester hastened on before anyone could cut in again with a smart comment. "What do you know about the Gambler?"

Silence fell. The air in the warehouse grew still, and though all eyes had been on Gloucester since he'd grabbed the gun, the focus of their attention seemed more intense than ever, boring into him.

"Now then," the minister said. "What do *you* know about the Gambler?"

"Answer the question!"

The minister's piercing gaze was familiar, the same angry look he'd worn back in his office, right before Gloucester pointed the gun at him.

"So much for not remembering," the minister said coldly, voice as smooth and edged as a sword.

The remainder of Gloucester's patience peeled away like old paint. "Four of you—that's eight kneecaps in all. Between both guns I've got, I can make life *very* painful for you before I even get serious. Now *talk*."

Zane was staring at him. He wished she wouldn't. He could only hope this would work out well enough that he'd have a chance to explain things to her later. If it meant she was alive and well, he'd accept her not wanting to have anything to do with him.

"Charming fellow, you are," said the gray-haired stranger. "Sorry, Lordship, but if you won't talk about it, I will. My son and I have better things to do than get shot full of holes by your enemies. What is it you want to know about the Gambler, Mr. Gloucester?"

What *didn't* he want to know? He sorted through the flood of questions in his mind as quickly as he could, searching for the most vital. "Where is he?"

The old man glanced the high minister's way. A clear warning sparked in the politician's eyes, but it was in vain: the old man turned back to Gloucester with a knowing smile. "Ah, that *is* the question. And one I think more people than just you are asking."

"*What*?" said the high minister. For once, no one paid him any mind. All eyes were now on the gray-haired man, who looked pleased to be the focus of attention, even with the gun pointing at him.

"I can't say for certain where he is, though," he said. "Only His Lordship there can answer that."

"Finch, say nothing more." It wasn't a request. The old stranger—Finch, it would seem—glanced his way again, and for the first time Gloucester thought he saw uncertainty in his eyes.

"Shut up, unless you're planning on saying something useful," Gloucester told the high minister curtly. Beneath the cool calm of the training to which he clung, his heart raced. The minister knew where the Gambler was? *How? Why?* "What's the Gambler got to do with all this? What was this meeting about?"

Finch gave an incredulous laugh. "Oh, mate, I dunno if you know too much or nothing at all. The Gambler's got to do with *everything*."

The warehouse went deadly quiet in the wake of this statement. Zane was still silent in stunned fear, Mulligan and the minister staring at Finch in mute fury. Finch's son stood motionless a few feet from his father, face difficult to read. Finch himself preened in the effect he'd managed to achieve.

"Why?" Zane's question seemed as loud as a shout in the air laden with silence.

"Don't you dare, Finch," the minister said, his voice more menacing than Gloucester remembered ever hearing it before. "If you speak another word—"

Tink.

Had it not been for the rapt quiet of almost everyone in the room, Gloucester never would have heard it. It sounded like a cup being dropped, something small and hard clattering lightly on the floor. He looked toward the source of the noise.

A grenade, small enough to fit in his palm, rolled to a stop several meters away from where they all stood. No pin was in sight.

The world seemed to fall away. Gloucester distantly heard himself shouting, yelling for the others to take cover, for Mulligan to get the minister out of there. He grabbed the two nearest people, Zane and the younger Finch, and threw them and himself toward the open doorway. They needed to get to cover. They had seconds at most—

BOOM.

—

Movement. Gloucester groaned as the world returned with the vague sensation of motion. He kept his eyes closed, dizzy even in the darkness, and slowly regained his bearings.

Judging from the rumble of wheels and the slight jostling of the uneven road beneath them, he was in a vehicle of some sort. Judging from the bite of metal pinning his hands behind his back, it wasn't by choice.

He opened his eyes, lifting his head groggily and squinting around. He was in the backseat of a car, bodies slumped on either side of him and his hands cuffed, wedged uncomfortably between his back and the seat of the car. It was still nighttime, but there weren't any city lights lining the road. They were outside of the city again.

"What happened?" he asked no one in particular, voice slurring a little. The body on his left was that of the younger Finch, his face hidden from view by the angle of his limp head and shoulders. Though he wasn't moving enough to indicate consciousness, Gloucester could feel the rise and fall of his chest against his side.

"This is the last time I help you," Zane's voice hissed to his right. Gloucester turned his head and, sure enough, the other person next to him was the clockmaker. Her face was also mostly hidden, though in her case it was by the chaotic disarray of her curly hair. What he could see of her expression was wide-eyed and furious. Like Gloucester, her hands were cuffed behind her.

"I'm never helping anyone ever again," she continued, her voice barely audible but shaking with emotion. "No more Nice Zane. I'm gonna be the most self-centered, reclusive asshole ever. Unless I spend the rest of my life in prison, of course. Because of *you*."

Gloucester wished there was something he could say. But his head ached, his ears were ringing, and guilt swarmed in his chest like angry bees in a hive. Zane was right. He'd known how much danger he was putting her in, and he'd let her be a part of it anyway. Whatever happened to her now was his fault.

Chapter 14

Frying Pan to Fire

"Who threw the grenade?"

Gloucester didn't bother looking up from the tabletop. Whether this was the same interrogation room he'd woken up in after being taken from solitary confinement was hard to say. That felt like eons ago now. It *looked* the same, but then again, it was so lacking in distinguishing features that it could have been one of many identical rooms. Same blank walls, same unadorned table, same metal chair—though this time his hands were cuffed behind his back instead of secured to the arms of the chair itself.

The other notable difference was the stern face staring at him from across the table.

"Gloucester, where did the grenade come from?" Harrison repeated, a new edge to his voice.

"I don't know," Gloucester ground out, not for the first time since he'd been pulled out of the backseat of the car and marched into this place with a bag over his head. The last thing he'd seen before the fabric fell over his eyes was Zane's frightened face. When the bag was removed, he'd been here, Harrison's glare boring a hole in his head and that question being asked, again and again.

Telling the truth didn't appear to be helping matters, unfortunately.

"Probably the same person who blew up the high minister's car," he said. It seemed the most reasonable conclusion. That, or Denken had found someone else with an axe to grind with the high minister and a proclivity for explosives.

"Give me a name."

"I don't have one to give." Gloucester leaned forward in his chair, ignoring the discomfort of his bound wrists. "Where's Zane? What have you done with her?"

If anything, Harrison's expression soured even further. "She's secure," he grunted, sounding nothing like the calm and collected man who appeared in Gloucester's cell less than a fortnight before. "And in a hell of a lot of trouble because of you. Just tell us what we need to know and maybe we can cut her a deal."

"You could have just *not* arrested her," Gloucester pointed out, in what he felt was a reasonable tone given the circumstances.

One could cut stone with its edge.

"You got her tangled up in something way above any of our pay grades." A muscle in Harrison's jaw kept twitching, as if he were forcibly keeping angry words from spilling out of his mouth. It was alarming to see so much emotion from the usually imperturbable man. The last several days were obviously wearing him thin.

"Oh, am I being paid now?"

Harrison shifted suddenly in his seat, and Gloucester flinched away, for a moment convinced Harrison was about to strike him.

"Don't be smart."

"Have there been any more attempts on the high minister's life? Other than tonight?" Gloucester asked, deciding that if he was going to push his luck, it might as well be in a useful way.

Harrison's already towering height seemed somehow to increase, his shoulders rising, stiff with anger. He looked as though resisting violence was physically costing him. Gloucester braced himself for the explosion. Slow-tempered people often made for the most frightening furies. After a moment, however, Harrison managed to rein in his anger, his glare tempering to one of annoyance rather than outrage.

"I'm the one asking the questions, Mr. Gloucester. Now, who threw the grenade? What is their name? You can't expect us to believe you showed up *coincidentally* at the same time as yet *another* attack."

"I followed the car from the high minister's private road," Gloucester said through clenched teeth. "Maybe they did too, whoever they are. As coincidences go, it's not all that unbelievable. What happened after the explosion?"

He asked the question quickly, not giving Harrison the chance to cut him off. Still, he'd expected the security agent to brush the question aside, so it came as a surprise when he answered, even if his voice was uncharacteristically heavy with snide derision.

"Mulligan signaled for back-up the moment you two were caught spying. We arrived after the grenade went off, before the police could get there."

"And the high minister's not dead?"

Harrison slammed his hand down on the tabletop, the sharp sound making Gloucester jump. "Dammit, *I'm* asking the questions here. Cooperate, Gloucester, or you'll be dealing with someone a lot less friendly than I am. And a lot less patient." He glowered across the table, and Gloucester met the angry look with one of his own.

"I don't have any answers," he said hotly. "I was bloody following that car in hopes of finding some."

Harrison had made no mention so far of the Gambler, and Gloucester wondered if he even knew anything about it. Difficult to say, and it was clear that his opportunity for asking Harrison questions was waning fast.

"This is your final chance with me, Gloucester," Harrison said. "Just tell the truth. Who threw the grenade? Who told you to kill the high minister? Did they offer you money? Freedom? How did they contact you?"

"That's an awful lot of questions."

The slap shouldn't have caught him by surprise. He'd seen it building up, the anger, glowing hotter and hotter behind the man's eyes. Yet he'd been held back by memories of Harrison's gentle tone and patient demeanor, by what had almost felt like camaraderie—the first of its kind since his incarceration—as they'd chased down the lead of the receipt together. Memories that dulled common sense. He couldn't help the gasp of pain as his head was knocked to the side, his cheek stinging. He swore in Nordish, blinking away stars.

By the time he raised his head, Harrison was gone. Empty space stared back at him, and Gloucester listened to the only sound in the room, his own uneven breathing.

—

For all the questions Harrison had asked, the man who took his place had very few. He asked them with gruff detachment in between flurries of violence, one hand latched onto Gloucester's hair, forcing him to meet his gaze, while around them the room spun and his voice echoed in Gloucester's ringing ears.

"Who hired you to kill His Lordship?"

Silence. Pain.

"Who do you work for?"

More silence. More pain.

"Who threw the grenade?"

Gloucester didn't bother with the pithy replies he'd had for Harrison. He doubted they would make a difference now. And anyway, he hurt too much to dwell on things like sarcasm or wit. He only hoped his interrogator would grow bored of this when it became apparent he wasn't as useful to them as they'd expected.

You know what happens to useless things.

The thought rang clear in his mind, even amidst the chaos and clamoring of pain. He spat a mouthful of blood, most of it not making it far past his lips, dribbling red lines down his chin. "I'll talk to the high minister," he mumbled, the words slurring off his tongue.

"What?" said the man. He'd offered no name upon his arrival in the interrogation room.

"The high minister," Gloucester repeated, voice thick with the blood filling his mouth again. He resisted the urge to lean forward and spit it out onto the shining stainless steel of the tabletop. "I want to speak to him."

The man snorted. "Too bad, sunshine. You've only got me." He reached forward, fingers tangling in the front of Gloucester's sweater, pulling him half out of his chair.

"I know about the Gambler," Gloucester said, throwing caution to the winds. "I know about Denken."

For a moment, nothing changed. The man drew his fist back again, knuckles already torn and red from previous encounters with Gloucester's face. There was no change in his demeanor to give Gloucester hope that his words had meant anything—

And then he froze. His hand relaxed out of the fist, rising instead to touch his left ear—the telltale sign of an earpiece. Someone on the other end of the line clearly had something to say. His eyes never left Gloucester's face, but the angry determination in them faded, like a flame shrinking down to embers. A dangerous state, where the fire could go out entirely or be swept back to full strength at the slightest gust of wind.

"What did you say?" he asked after a moment. Gloucester had the feeling he was repeating someone else's question.

Gloucester coughed, wincing at the twinge of pain it brought to his aching ribs, and spoke as clearly as he could. "I know about the Gambler and Denken."

The man stared at him in silence. Then, as abruptly as he'd arrived, he let go of Gloucester and straightened up, turning away without a word. He disappeared through the door, which shut behind him with a click.

A few minutes later, the door swung open again. Mulligan crossed the space between the doorway and the table in two strides and glowered down at Gloucester. He'd never looked as intense and, frankly, intimidating as he did in that moment.

"Who the *hell* is Denken?"

Gloucester's head was pounding, nothing magical whatsoever about the headache that thudded through his skull like an angry marching band. The epicenter of the pain was where his interrogator's fists had landed, mostly against his jaw and cheekbones. Whoever the man was, he'd been more careful than he'd seemed with his strikes; despite the aching pain and bloody lip, Gloucester didn't think any serious damage had been done. Mulligan's voice grated against his senses, though.

"Bring the high minister here and I'll tell *him*," he said, giving up on dignity and spitting a mouthful of blood onto the table. He was relieved to find no teeth had been knocked loose. Thank heaven for small miracles.

Mulligan's nose wrinkled in disgust, though Gloucester couldn't say whether it was at the blood on the table or the audacity of his demand.

"Listen here! You'll bloody well *tell* me. Who is Denken?"

But Gloucester kept his mouth shut, returning Mulligan's glare. His knowledge about Denken wasn't so much an ace up his sleeve as the only hope he had left; he wasn't about to give it up to the chief adviser. If he wasn't *very* careful, he knew he would end up back in the cell in which he'd spent so many months.

Never again.

After several long moments of a furious staring match, Mulligan swore and looked away. "You're a real pain in my ass, you know that? Fine. I'll see what I can do." He turned to meet Gloucester's gaze again, and his face was deadly serious. "This had better be worth it."

Without waiting for a reply, he stormed out of the room, leaving Gloucester alone once more.

—

His head felt fuzzy. Even besides the ache and heaviness left in the wake of his interrogation and the tumbling stress of the explosion, Gloucester was running on fumes. His brief stint of unconsciousness hadn't exactly been restful, but it was the closest he'd gotten to relaxing since waking from a fitful sleep early that morning. Or yesterday morning, maybe. He wasn't sure what time it was, nor how many hours might have passed since the explosion in the warehouse. With no windows or clocks in the room, time seemed to stand still.

The hard surface of the table, spattered with his blood, was becoming more and more inviting as a pillow. It wouldn't make for a comfortable place to lay his head while his hands were cuffed behind his back, but at that moment it was still tempting. His chin lowered, bumping against his collarbone as he fought to keep exhaustion at bay.

The sound of footsteps almost wasn't enough to stir him. He hadn't heard the door open. His eyes fluttered open, alerting him for the first time that they'd even fallen closed, and he shook his head slowly from side to side, clearing it as best he could. "You took your time," he muttered.

"Always," replied a smug voice that most definitely did not belong to the high minister.

Gloucester's head shot up. He stared wide-eyed at the newcomer.

"I think it's time we talked face to face again," said the creature called Denken, his wide grin shining with teeth too pointed to be human.

A memory returned with all the gentleness of a freight train.

Gloucester was standing outside Zephyr Clocks, getting ready to leave with Harrison, when someone bumped into him. Someone black-haired, slim, and grinning. He remembered Denken's face, dark eyes almost too large in his thin face, the irises wide and black beneath curved eyelids. But for the sharpness of it, his smile would have seemed joyous. And Gloucester remembered his voice, smooth and alluring and impossible to ignore, even when he spoke quietly. How had he ever forgotten? He remembered, now, that soft, commanding voice murmuring in his ear, a hand on his face, whispers urging him to act on what he already longed to do, what he *needed* to do.

"*Fuck,*" he gasped, reeling. The force of the memory threatened to overwhelm him.

"Maybe later. Talk first," Denken said happily. His smile twisted in mock sympathy. "Dearie me, you've looked better, haven't you? What did they hit you with, a truck?"

Gloucester took several deep breaths, too busy trying not to throw up to muster more than a half-hearted grimace. "You're him. Denken. How—Why do I remember you *now*?"

Denken shrugged, lounging back in the chair across the table from Gloucester and casting a lazy glance around the room. A tattoo stretched along the length of his neck, a simple weaving pattern of curved lines that traced a path in ink from the shadow of his jaw to the neckline of his dark shirt. When he raised a hand to scratch his chin, Gloucester saw the pattern continued all the way down to the base of his thumb.

"Memory's a funny thing," he said. "I'm a lot to take in." He smiled again, smug. "Sometimes your silly human brains just go '*Whaaaaa?*' and repress things."

He had an animated way of speaking, his hands swirling in emphatic gestures as he talked. Gloucester followed the movements with his eyes, mesmerized in spite of himself. He wasn't sure what he'd expected when it came to the strange demigods Antimony had spoken of, but it certainly wasn't this. Denken barely appeared older than Gloucester himself, a smiling young man beneath tousled hair and a carefree attitude. He was hardly what one imagined when picturing the personification of something as powerful as Thought.

"What do you want?" he asked. It was only one of a thousand questions clamoring to be voiced.

Denken smiled his shark's grin up at the ceiling. Arms crossed over his narrow chest, he looked perfectly at ease. "I want my brother," he said idly. "And I want the man who took him dead."

Gloucester stared. "So the high minister *does* have the Gambler."

"Got it in one!" Denken snapped his fingers under Gloucester's nose, suddenly leaning into his personal space. Gloucester hadn't even seen him move. He reared back in alarm and almost toppled his chair, his bound arms useless for balance. A slim brown hand snaked forward, snatching his shirtfront, and Denken pulled him forward onto his seat.

"They'll be listening," Gloucester said, staring into the face now mere inches from his own.

"All the boring lads and ladies in suits in the other room, you mean?" Denken snorted. "Doubtful. They're . . . thinking of other things at the moment." His good humor returned to full strength and he released Gloucester, sitting back down on the other side of the table.

"What do you want from *me*?" demanded Gloucester. He had no idea what to expect from the bizarre being sitting across from him, nor what Denken meant by "thinking of other things." His imagination, always eager to jump to the worst possible scenario, was having a field day.

Denken cocked his head to the side, like a curious bird. "I'm not quite sure yet," he said, tapping a finger on his chin. "You didn't do as you were told. Naughty. But I think you might still be of use." He clapped his hands together suddenly, making Gloucester jump. "Which means I need to get you out of here before they lock you back up in the slammer 'til you're old and gray."

"I—What?" Gloucester gaped, caught off-guard by this announcement. He wondered if it was even possible to predict what a creature like Denken would do at any given time.

At the moment, Denken was rolling his eyes with all the condescending expertise of a sixteen-year-old. "I . . . am . . . going . . . to . . . get . . . *you* . . ." He pointed emphatically at Gloucester, speaking each word with exaggerated slowness, as if talking to someone quite thick. " . . . out . . . of . . . here."

Gloucester bristled. "Yeah? How do you plan on doing that? And why should I help you with anything? You're some sort of loony god or something."

Denken made a face. "*Wellll*, here's the thing. I'm not asking."

He surged forward with the swiftness of a striking snake and pulled Gloucester out of his seat. He'd somehow gotten around the barrier of the table, which clattered against the wall to Gloucester's right. With his hands still bound and his head spinning, Gloucester could do little as he was half-marched, half-dragged toward the door. Denken hummed under his breath as he kicked it open and pulled Gloucester into the hallway.

"Wait," Gloucester said, digging in his heels. "Zane."

Denken squinted sideways at him. His thin, arched eyebrows lowered in consternation. "Nooo, I'm *Denken*. Wow, you're bad at this. Those don't even sound alike."

Gloucester tried to wrench his arm free, to no avail. "No. My friend Zane, she was taken alongside me. I'm not going anywhere without her."

For a moment it looked like his argument had fallen on deaf ears. Denken continued dragging him along, but Gloucester made it as difficult as possible, throwing all of his weight into slowing their progress. Finally Denken stopped, growling in frustration. It was the closest to anger Gloucester had seen from him yet.

"You know, I could just *make* you cooperate. Or bonk you on the head and carry you out over my shoulder."

"You can try," Gloucester said grimly, very much hoping he didn't. "Or you can help me rescue Zane and get my cooperation without force. I don't *want* to leave here without her." He hoped he and Zane were right in their hypothesis about the creature and his powers. If he could only influence people to do something they already wanted to do, then perhaps Gloucester had a chance.

Denken stared at him, huge inky eyes unreadable. Then he threw back his head with exasperation, huffing a dramatic sigh. "Okay, fine. So, where is your precious Zane?"

Gloucester hesitated. "I don't know."

"Bit rich asking for a favor then, isn't it?" Denken boxed him lightly around the ears. Even relatively playful as the action was, it made Gloucester's tender head throb, and he hissed in pained annoyance.

"I'm not going without her," he said. "Not willingly. And if you think I'm going to help you if you don't—"

Denken clapped a hand over his mouth, paying no mind to the furious, indignant look sent his way. "Here I thought you were a quiet one! Fine. We'll check the room with the boring people, it was full of camera feeds and the like."

Hand still firmly over Gloucester's mouth, the other keeping a vice-like hold on his arm, Denken led the way down the hall and around the corner. The corridors were as plain and windowless as the interrogation room, giving Gloucester no hint as to where they were. Denken seemed confident in where they were going, however.

Up ahead, a door stood ajar, light leaking out into the more dimly lit corridor. Denken shouldered it open and stuck his head into the room. "Don't mind us," he called out jauntily. "Just looking for a lady-friend, you know how it is."

No reply. Gloucester stared past Denken into the room. It was clearly a control room of some sort, overseeing various other rooms and areas in whatever compound they'd been brought to.

Gloucester recognized his own interrogation room on one of the screens, familiar from the blood splattered across the table. But it was difficult to pay much attention to the screens when his eyes kept straying back to the security agents seated at desks in front of the monitors.

Each and every one of them sat motionless. Their faces were cast in varying expressions of puzzlement, hazy interest, and even enjoyment, though none of them seemed the slightest bit aware of their surroundings, let alone the two intruders in the doorway.

"*Mmmph*—What have you *done* to them?" Gloucester demanded, as he finally succeeded in pulling his head away from Denken's smothering hand. He gaped, horror-struck, from the eerie scene before them to the man-shaped thing holding onto his arm.

Denken shrugged. "Oh, they're *fine*. Just thinking of other things. I'm good at distractions. Now, is your friend on any of the screens?"

Too uncomfortable to look closely at the hypnotized agents, Gloucester refocused on the closed-circuit televisions set up throughout the room. "There," he said after a minute. Without his hands free to point, he made do with jabbing his chin in the direction of the right screen. "The one labeled Interview Room Three." Through the camera feed, he could see Zane sitting glumly in an otherwise deserted room identical to the one he'd been in. She wasn't handcuffed anymore, and as far as he could tell, she looked unharmed, though she was fidgeting with the hem of her sweater in a way he'd learned meant she was extremely anxious.

Denken cocked his head to the side, eyeing the indicated screen. "Pretty thing. Hm. She looks vaguely familiar . . . Right! On to Interview Room 3."

"Wait," Gloucester interrupted again, still staring at the wall of screens.

Denken made an impatient noise. "Look, this isn't a day trip.

I'm not here on vacation. Bloody hell, you're one of the most annoying people I've ever kidnapped." He pulled Gloucester toward the door, but Gloucester resisted, glaring at him.

"That man on the other screen, he's a part of this."

He nodded emphatically at the screen beside Zane's; the red-haired man from the warehouse, Finch, was seated in another interrogation room. It was hard to say if he was also a prisoner, as his hands weren't bound, but he was sitting alone and motionless, his face hidden as he stared down at the tabletop in front of him.

Denken didn't look convinced. Gloucester fought the childish urge to stamp his foot in impatience, nerves shot after the events of the day.

"He knows about the Gambler," he said. This got Denken's attention, the demigod's eyes narrowing. "I think he and his father might have been the ones who delivered him to the high minister."

"Oh really?" Denken's eyes gleamed with dark interest as he examined the tiny figure onscreen.

"He's worth more to you alive," Gloucester said quickly, sensing the shift in Denken's mood. "If you're thinking of trying anything—"

He was rudely interrupted by a finger pressed to his lips.

"Yeah, uh-huh, duly noted. This has been fun, Mik, but I think it's your bedtime."

Gloucester jerked away from the hand at his mouth, with an angry "What—"

But the question died on his lips as he met Denken's gaze. The demigod's eyes were bigger and darker than ever, their depths swallowing him up like black water. He couldn't look away, couldn't move, couldn't speak. The world shrank, leaving only those bottomless eyes and the sharp-toothed smile. Then nothing.

Chapter 15

Friends and Foes

Gloucester didn't know where he was. He wasn't even sure if he was awake or dreaming. His surroundings, when he thought to take stock of them, seemed strangely vague. The more he tried to focus on them, the hazier the details became. Despite this oddity, a lightheartedness he hadn't felt in a long time abounded in him, dredging his spirits up from the dark water of reality like a buoy.

The more he gave into the happy feeling and let his mind relax, the more what surrounded him stabilized and grew clear. He was in a meadow, fresh with the scent of summer in the countryside. He knew this place, he realized, and a gentle feeling of joy pulled at his heart. It was just outside a small town south of Frettchen, near the coast. He'd come here a long time ago, on a date with Jeb. It was a fond memory, one of the happiest he had. It had been relatively early in their relationship, but he remembered sitting here together, laughing in the grass and the flowers and the sunshine, as the realization that he loved this man cemented itself in his mind. It wasn't the moment of saying so aloud, but rather the first time he remembered seriously thinking it. For once there hadn't been a question in Gloucester's mind or a puzzle to solve. Just the peaceful certainty that he was happy.

What was he doing here now? Even through the daze weighing down his thoughts like a warm blanket, the question wormed its way to the forefront of his mind, quiet but tenacious. This had been a long time ago, so why was he here now and how had he gotten here?

The louder the questions became, the dimmer the meadow grew. It faded like an old photograph or the remnants of a dream. Through it, he saw glimpses of other things. A hallway. He was walking, pulled along by someone else. A distant voice called out a name. His name. He started to turn, but a hand gripped his arm, and with the squeeze of fingers, the meadow became solid once more. The feeling of ease slithered back into his mind. Would it be so bad to forget the questions for a while? Surely he could set them aside, just for a bit. This was a beautiful place, a wonderful memory. Here he had Jeb, who was probably just out of sight. If he stayed here, they could be together again, here in this happier time and place. It was better to sit and remember and—

"Gloucester."

This time the voice was clear enough to cut through the haze of his memory, loud with impatience and fear. It was also accompanied by a shove that rattled the peaceful wandering of his thoughts. The meadow blinked out of existence.

Gloucester gasped, jerking upright. "What?"

The first thing he noticed was where he *wasn't*. He was no longer in the security agents' control room. He wasn't even in one of the corridors they'd passed through, nor the interrogation room he'd been stuck in before Denken showed up. In fact, beyond these observations, he had no idea *where* he was, only that he was slumped against a stone wall, dusty hardwood beneath him, in a room shrouded in shadows.

A familiar face stared back at him, however. Zane was crouched in front of him, worried eyes locked on his, and her hands clutching his shoulders.

"Gloucester. Can you hear me?" she asked, very loudly.

Gloucester flinched away, both from the shouting and the touch. His hands were still cuffed, he was annoyed to discover, though they were at least bound in front of him now. He nudged Zane back on her haunches as gently as he could. "Yeah, I can hear you. Don't shout."

Zane's expression was still wrought with worry, but her shoulders sagged noticeably in relief and she let out a long breath. "Well, that's a nice change of pace, then."

Gloucester blinked, baffled. "What do you mean?"

She shifted, curling her legs under her. "I mean you've spent the last two hours acting like some sort of bloody zombie! Like you were in a trance or something. Like you didn't hear me or even know I was there." She shivered. "It was bloody terrifying."

Gloucester gaped at her. "I—What? Two hours?"

"Near as I can guess," Zane said. She propped her chin on her hand, a glum line creasing the space between her brows. "I don't have a clock on me, which I guess is ironic. Those agent-people took everything in my pockets." She moved to sit next to Gloucester against the wall, scuffing her shoe moodily on the floor. "I don't know if we were worse off with them there or with Denken here. Denken cleaned up the worst of your cuts and bruises, but you still look like a mess. And I don't have any idea what he's planning to do with us."

Gloucester raised his cuffed hands to his face, feeling with tentative fingers as he did his best to take stock of his injuries. Though his face still felt tender and he winced at his own gentle touch, he was indeed feeling much better than before. He wondered what purpose healing him served Denken, what strange powers allowed him to do so, and whether he ought to be grateful or worried. He doubted Zane would know any better than he did, so he went with another of the questions teeming in his mind.

"Where is here?" Now that his head was clearing, he looked around again. They were in a small dark room, the only light provided by a pair of tiny windows high overhead and the crack under a door to his left. As far as he could tell, there wasn't anything in the way of furniture beyond a table pushed into one corner. What caught his eye wasn't the table, however, but the person sitting on it. In the low light, he could make out the short red hair and pale features of the younger Finch. The mysterious man wasn't looking at them. He sat hunched over, staring down at his hands, as he had in the interrogation room. Gloucester glanced back at Zane, nodding in Finch's direction with an unspoken question.

Zane shrugged. "Denken grabbed him after he got me. Put him in the same weird state you were in. I dunno why he took him."

"I told him to," Gloucester said quietly, watching Finch's motionless figure. The other man gave no sign he was listening to them in the slightest.

"What? Why?"

"I think he and his dad caught the Gambler. And if they can capture gods, they must know something about them. And how to find the Gambler."

Zane stared at Finch now too, her grimace somewhere between suspicious and pitying. "If he hurt the Gambler, I wouldn't want to be in his shoes right now. I don't even want to be in my *own* shoes right now, honestly."

"Wait, hold on," Gloucester said as a thought occurred. "How come Denken didn't use his mind magic on you?"

Zane dragged her gaze away from Finch with another shrug and, surprisingly, what looked like a tiny smile in the shadows. "Oh, he mentioned it. But I told him if he did that to me, he better make sure I never came out of it, 'cause I'd kick his bloody ass the moment I got my hands on him after waking up." Her mouth twisted into a grimace. "And I promised not to be trouble during the escape. Escape, hah! That's what he called it. Another bloody kidnapping, that's what it is."

Her amusement faded quickly from memory as her mood descended back into anger. "I just want to go home. Instead I'm shut in a closet who knows where with Young Bad Guy over there and *you*."

"And me?" said Gloucester, surprised by the sudden venom directed his way. The anger she'd spat at him in the car after the explosion was still fresh in his mind, but its abrupt resurgence now still caught him off-guard.

"Yeah, you." Zane's voice lowered to a hiss. Now that she'd found a victim to vent her temper on, she seemed all too keen on letting loose. Or perhaps her anger had never really abated, and she'd simply been keeping it in check until she knew he was all right. "They told me what your 'assignment' was. The one you said you were on before they brought you onto the whole assassination thing."

"Zane—"

"You were locked up! In prison! As some sort of . . . of traitor or something."

Gloucester's heart sank. Of course they would have told her about that. No doubt a nicely vilifying rendition of the whole ordeal. Divide and conquer. Enemies were all the weaker when they didn't trust each other.

"I know they probably said a lot of bad things about me," he said, forcing himself to meet Zane's eyes. "But I need you to believe me, I'm not a criminal, no matter what they said. I can explain—"

"Good. I want to hear your side of the story."

"They were trying to set you against me, and it was—What? Pardon?" Zane's words had taken a moment to travel from his ears to his brain.

"I want to hear your side of the story," Zane repeated with

exaggerated patience. She nudged him with her elbow. "You think it didn't cross my mind that they might be fudging the details of the story a bit? I don't know them. Don't know anything about the high minister save what we all see and hear in the news, and I don't especially like politicians. I mean, yeah, he's done a lot to help Frettchennian clock-workers like me, what with his whole push for less importing from the Nordlands, but it's not really a secret that he's way more of an elitist bastard than he likes to pretend with all his pretty speeches. And maybe I don't know you either, but I reckon I at least know you better than I do him and his lot, so you're owed a chance to tell your side of things."

Gloucester realized he was gaping at her and quickly snapped his mouth shut. "Oh," he said, at a loss for how else to respond. He had the strange urge to thank her.

"Something tells me no one's ever asked for your side of this particular tale," Zane mused, the fury finally fading out of her voice.

It was true, no one had. No one had ever even told him *their* side of the story.

"There isn't much to tell," he said, after a quick glance in Finch's direction. The other man still gave no sign he was paying them any attention. Turning his eyes back to Zane, Gloucester caught her dubious expression and added, "I can only tell you what I know, and that's not a lot."

Zane nodded slowly. "So what happened?"

Gloucester opened his mouth, then hesitated. Not because Zane didn't deserve answers. Not even because it was a story he'd never shared before and now he was about to tell it to two people he barely knew. He wasn't sure what gave him pause. Perhaps some lingering worry that she wouldn't believe him. Still, after everything that had happened, after every impossible thing they both now knew to be real, maybe that worry wasn't really due.

"I used to work as part of the high minister's security detail," he said, launching into his story. "Nothing really special. I didn't stand out. I didn't want to, really. But it was a good job and I was good at it. For two years after my training finished, everything was fine."

"What changed?"

"I wish I knew." Gloucester sighed. He'd been asking himself variations of that question for six months. "Half a year ago, I arrive at work like normal. Then next thing I know, I'm being arrested. I remember Mulligan yelling—he's the high minister's chief adviser—then I was dragged away and dropped in a cell."

Zane stared at him, wide-eyed. "Then what?"

"Then nothing. Just that cell. For months. It was maddening. No one came to question me, no one ever told me what I'd done. The only people were the guards, and they barely talked to me. Then one day they came to get me for this case. Because my incarceration was my alibi," he added, grimacing. "I couldn't have been involved because I'd spent so long locked up." Not that it had worked out in his favor in the end.

"But you must have *some* idea. Why they arrested you, what it was all for?"

Gloucester only shrugged. He felt a great pang of bitterness as he thought back on the lost months in that cell and the looming question mark of what had led to them. "No idea. That day is . . . blurry. And you would think I'd remember doing something that could get me thrown in prison."

"Or seeing."

The words, spoken neither by Gloucester nor Zane, made them both jump. They looked over at Finch in the corner. With his head raised, Gloucester could see the dim light from the window reflected in his eyes.

"What?" he said, eyeing Finch suspiciously.

"Remember doing or *seeing* something that'd get you locked up," drawled Finch. His lilting voice, which had been so cheery the night before, sounded quiet and resigned now. His tone wasn't what concerned Gloucester at the moment, though.

"Do you know something about it?" he asked. "If you know why I—"

"I'm just hypothesizing, mate." Finch's shoulders rose and fell in an uncaring shrug. "Don't know you. I'd never even heard of you until last night." He dropped his gaze back to his lap, apparently not inclined to continue the conversation.

Zane wasn't so easily deterred. "You know about the Gambler and Denken," she said, peering at Finch in the semi-darkness. "From the sound of your little meeting in that warehouse, the high minister was going to you and your dad for information about them. So what *do* you know? Who are you?"

The laugh that rang from Finch's lips held no amusement, a wry noise conveying little more than derision. "What's it to you?" he said, sparing her a dismissive glance. "I don't see how it's your business."

"Oh, don't you?"

Gloucester could practically see Zane's hackles rising.

"Looks to me like we're all in the same boat now. Or the same closet, as it were," she amended, gesturing around them. "If you know anything that might help, tell us now before I lose my bloody temper and *beat* it out of you."

"Zane." Gloucester held up a hand, the pacifying action hindered by his chains. Recounting his story to her had served as a brief distraction from their current predicament, but the reminder of Finch's presence there with them had dragged his thoughts back to more pressing matters than the months-old mystery of his incarceration.

Zane looked like she wanted to continue snapping at Finch, but she relented, settling for a glower in his direction. She paid little mind to the grateful look Gloucester offered her.

"So where *are* we now?" Gloucester asked, casting another glance around their dim surroundings in hopes of spotting some clue he might have overlooked.

Zane gave a hopeless shrug, but it was Finch who answered again, much to Gloucester's surprise. "Reckon we're in his

Pocket."

"His what?" asked Zane, at the same time that Gloucester said, "Whose pocket?"

He immediately felt stupid for asking, as Finch leveled a particularly judgmental look his way.

"Denken's Pocket," Finch said, speaking with overly careful enunciation that didn't so much border on condescending as fully embrace it. "His space. The little bit of the universe that belongs to him. His world."

"Yeah, obviously we should have gotten that from something as clear and explanatory as 'his Pocket,'" sneered Zane. She seemed to take offense at the look Finch had given him. Gloucester himself was less bothered by Finch's tone and demeanor, his incredulous reaction owed instead to the words themselves.

"We're in a different *world*?" This was a lot to swallow, even after a week of massive and world-altering revelations. "How—"

Finch waggled his fingers at him. "Magic," he said, now with so much condescension a deaf and blind person would have picked up on it. Possibly even from beyond the grave. Sour, Gloucester waggled one specific finger back at him.

"Wait," said Zane. "I remember hearing about something like that from—" She cut herself off, and Gloucester knew she was avoiding mentioning Antimony in front of Finch. "From somewhere," she finished, scarcely missing a beat. "The Gambler has a place like that too. The Crossroads. Is that where you reckon we are?"

Finch offered her a long look that was no longer patronizing but thoughtful. And perhaps even a touch surprised. Gloucester expected him to question her on where she'd gotten this knowledge, but he simply said, "No. Denken's is different. His is the Maze."

He tilted his head back and sighed up at the ceiling, then continued on, apparently deciding to be helpful after all. Perhaps Zane's point that they were all stuck in this mess together had actually struck a chord.

"Think of a room. In this room, nothing makes sense. Less and less the longer you look around it. Not the walls or the ceiling or the floor or the doors. It's too big and too small all at once. The walls are at the wrong angles. Stairs go to nowhere, or maybe to everywhere, and there are doors, thousands of doors, but you can't ever seem to reach them. That's the Maze, as I've heard it described."

He spoke with weary certainty. Gloucester stared up at him where he sat partially silhouetted in the meager light from the window, his red hair ringed in the faintest of glows, which extended around his form like a strange outline, rendering him like a drawing on an artist's page.

"Have you seen it before?" he asked. "If it's supposed to be like that, why are we shut away in a closet? How—"

The abrupt click of the door opening cut him off. Light spilled into the room, leaving the three prisoners squinting in the newfound brightness. A shadowy figure loomed over them.

"All good questions. Time for some answers."

Chapter 16

In the Shadows

"**Y**ou're shut away in here, Mik," came Denken's eerie yet charming tenor, "because I didn't want your little brains to explode from shock and awe. Remember what I said about being too much for some humans? Same goes for home sweet home."

Denken didn't sound much fazed by the notion of exploding brains. He stepped unconcernedly through the doorway and sank cross-legged to the floor in front of it. Light seeped in past him, bathing half the room in illumination, but not extending far enough to banish the shadows completely. Denken's own shadow was cast out in front of him, and out of the corner of his eye, Gloucester thought he saw it shift, though Denken hadn't made any significant movements since sitting down.

"And *he*," Denken continued, pointing at Finch, "hasn't ever been here before. *He* just knows things he shouldn't. Such a naughty boy." He was smiling, but something wild lurked beneath the friendly surface. "And a little bird tells me you know more than that, Mr. Finch. *Cassus.* I think it would be best for everyone if you shared those secrets, don't you?"

Finch's jaw twitched. He looked nervous, though Gloucester presumed he was doing his best to hide his fear.

"Everyone knows a little about something," he said with passably convincing nonchalance.

For a moment Gloucester thought Denken had leapt to his feet. He'd been looking at Finch, but movement, sudden and quick, in his peripheral vision caught his attention. Yet when he whipped his gaze back to Denken, the demigod was still sitting as before.

"True, true," Denken said, his voice a pleasant rumble, like the drone of bumblebees in a garden. It was difficult to resist. It made Gloucester want to close his eyes, relax his mind, and just listen—

He shook his head, trying to dislodge the effect. Denken had already been in his head more times than he cared for; he wasn't about to willingly let him back in again.

Right now, though, he wasn't in command of the demigod's interest. Denken's eyes were locked on Finch, glinting in the shadows of his face. The tattoo on his neck looked a little different from how Gloucester remembered it. Had it always traced up over his jaw and onto his face? Perhaps he was simply seeing things wrong in the uneven lighting.

"Everyone knows a little something, but I think you know a lot," Denken said. "About me and my brothers. It's rude to talk about people behind their backs, you know. Almost as rude as keeping secrets." He leaned forward and his shadow stretched further into the room, a phantom carpet rolling out in front of him, toward Finch.

Only it didn't stop moving when Denken did. Gloucester and Zane watched in horror as the shadow slid across the floor, lengthening and twisting into a shape all its own. It seemed to inhabit the air itself, almost corporeal. The room was scarcely big enough to contain the shape in its entirety, yet Gloucester could see hints of what it was. Triangular fins cut through light and lesser shadows like water, and a body like a torpedo, large enough to engulf them all, filled the space with such convincing menace that Gloucester looked around, half-expecting to find a creature swimming through the air above them. But the only source was Denken, smiling in the dark.

"Tell me everything that happened to the Gambler," he said. "Tell me what you know."

Gloucester and Zane pressed themselves back against the wall, dwarfed by the massive shark made of shadows. Finch, for all his grandstanding, quailed. When he spoke, his voice wavered and grew distant. He seemed to be speaking from the depths of a trance.

"My father discovered magic at a young age. I don't know how. From a book or a witch or maybe just by accident. He became obsessed with it. He traveled through the Lower Lands, searching out every story, every form of the supernatural he could find. It was his passion. From the mountains of the Nordlands and all the strange creatures that lurk in the woods there, to the hidden halls of magic along the southern coast, he became familiar with all of it.

"My mum was a hedge witch he met on his travels, living a quiet life on the southern edge of the Great Desert. Father always said she loved the adventure he brought her as much as she loved him. She was the first one to tell him tales of the Brothers, though they'd only ever been stories to her. Three demigods, personifying different aspects of sentience. I never knew if she believed the tales or not. She died when I was small. My father would tell me how she said one of the Brothers was the personification of Love and he had brought them together."

"I doubt it," said Denken.

Finch continued on as if he'd heard nothing. "After she died, Father's obsession only grew. He'd lost the only thing that could compete with magic for his passion and interest. I grew up on stories of the Brothers and other such things. Creatures of power that would make our human magic seem like nothing more than children's games. My bedtime tales were about dryads stalking hunters in the forests and sirens taunting sailors out at sea. But it always came back to you. The Brothers. We learned everything we could about you. All that was known of your powers, your influence. Your weaknesses."

Denken made an unhappy noise at the back of his throat, and his shadow managed somehow to loom even larger. "This is a fascinating story and all, but I want to know where my brother is *now*."

Finch was no longer fazed by Denken's impatience. He didn't appear to even notice it, staring into the fearsome shadows as if looking into the past. Gloucester supposed that was an apt description of what he was doing.

"A year and a half ago, the lord of the city-state approached my father. He'd heard about us, and about the Brothers, somehow. I don't know from whom. If my father knew, he never told me. I don't think he even cared. He'd been provided with the means to achieve something he'd wanted to do for as long as I can remember. Since before I was even born, I think."

"And what was that?" Denken pressed. Expectation in his voice hinted he knew the answer even as he asked. Maybe he just wanted to hear it admitted aloud.

"To capture one of you. To put all of his research, his life's work, to the test."

"But why?" asked Zane, sounding breathless. Gloucester reached down and found her hand, grasping it in his own. The contact was as much for his comfort as hers.

"His Lordship's power was slipping," Finch said. "There was talk of a political coup, he said. Whispers of violence. He's sacrificed a lot to get where he is, our high and mighty leader, and not often things that were his own to sacrifice. He was desperate to stay on top."

It didn't make sense. Gloucester had been working for the

high minister then. Surely he would have known if things were so bad.

Would he, though? Political instability was hardly something a glorified bodyguard could help with. The high minister always did like his secrets.

Denken was silent, his features no longer showing amusement, mockery, or even threatening violence. He looked like a statue, impossibly still in the light from the doorway. Gloucester and Zane shifted uncomfortable gazes back to Finch.

"The Gambler embodies Choice," Finch said, still staring into the depths of Denken's frightful shadow. The edges of the shadow had faded, its unnatural shape less distinct, but still it lingered, like the waning impression of light on your retinas after staring too long at the sun. Gloucester avoided looking at it.

"Imagine, His Lordship told us," Finch continued. "Imagine if you knew ahead of time what choices you would have to make. The big ones, the *important* ones. Imagine if you had some way of knowing which was the right choice to make. Which path at the crossroads to take."

"He's using him." Though quiet, Denken's voice was somehow more terrifying than anything else, even the spectral creature that lurked in his shadow. "That human is *using* my brother. For *politics*."

The air felt charged with electricity, making the hairs on the back of Gloucester's neck stand on end.

Finch nodded, apathetic. "That was the idea."

For a moment, Gloucester thought Denken's rage would be too much to contain, that the shadow shark would swallow Finch whole, and he and Zane along with him.

Instead, the shadow suddenly receded. Moving with the same unnatural agency that swept it into existence in the first place, it retreated back toward Denken, until it again appeared to be nothing more than a regular shadow, no different from any of the others populating every corner of the room.

Denken leapt to his feet, and just like that, his anger vanished. He grinned toothily down at them.

"Righty-o, then," he cried, arms akimbo. "Good to know." He was still blocking the doorway, looming over them like some surreal mockery of an overbearing mother. Like his shadow, Gloucester noticed Denken's tattoo had receded from his face again, stretching only along the length of his neck to his jawline, stopping before it crossed the skin of his face. Or had it always been that way? Gloucester wasn't sure he could trust anything about Denken, not even his appearance.

"So, um . . ." said Zane timidly. "What now?"

Past her shoulder, Gloucester watched Finch blink and shake his head, confused and groggy, like he'd just woken up from a deep sleep.

"Now, my dear, we—Oh. *Oh.* I know you!"

Denken's sudden outburst made Zane rear back in alarm. "Huh?" she said.

"I *knew* you looked familiar," Denken crowed. "You're one of Antimony's. How is the old bird?"

"Old?" Zane's shock dropped away in favor of bristling annoyance. "She's barely into her thirties. Who the *hell* are you to call her old? You're like eight billion years old."

Denken's laugh was strange, jarring, and pleasant all at once, and he held his hands up in surrender. The sound was such a distinct contrast to his recent dark anger that Gloucester only felt all the more uneasy. Still, that Zane could manage to hold onto her innate, well, *zaniness* despite everything that had happened to them was a comfort of sorts.

"Fine, fine, she's a young and beautiful flower. What's your name again?" asked Denken, considering Zane with amused interest.

She didn't look very appeased. "Zane. If you didn't even recognize me until now, why am I here?"

Denken pointed at Gloucester. "Grumpy here wouldn't leave without you. Made a big ol' fuss. Totally undignified. It was embarrassing."

"Hey!" In his indignation, Gloucester forgot that this was the same creature who had towered with such frightening menace only moments earlier. "I just said—"

"Yeah, yeah, Chatty." Denken cut him off with a dismissive wave, much to Gloucester's further vexation.

"I think the important thing's what he's planning on doing with us now," said Finch unexpectedly. He was more alert now, eyes sharp with anger and wariness.

Gloucester shut his mouth, the furious words he'd been about to hurl at Denken dying on his tongue. He blamed the fact that he'd let his focus slip so ridiculously on the stress of the last several hours. Finch was right. What was the point of arguing over stupid matters of pride when they weren't even sure they'd survive the night?

"It's not night," Denken said, staring directly at him.

"I—What?"

Leaning forward, Denken tapped a long finger against Gloucester's temple. Gloucester lurched back, smacking his elbow into the wall in his haste to get away from the touch.

"You were wondering if you'd make it through the night. It's not night. There's no night here. No time."

Gloucester stared. So many questions surged through him, but the only words that escaped were "Don't do that."

"Sorry," said Denken with a cheerful shrug. "Old habits, you know."

"Hey." Zane frowned. "If you can just read our thoughts—which is beyond creepy, by the way—why'd you have to go all mind control on him before?" She jabbed her thumb in Finch's direction.

Denken snorted. "Reading thoughts isn't a simple task, Zany. Unless I'm really trying, surface thoughts are about the most I can pick up. Some people have a lot of them"—he looked pointedly at Gloucester, who glowered back—"and some are sneaky bastards who know about my powers and are good at hiding what they're really thinking." His eyes turned toward Finch, narrowing.

"Sneaky bastard I may be, but my question still stands." Finch raised his chin stubbornly. "What now?"

"I think it should be pretty obvious," Denken said.

He stuck his hand out in front of Gloucester's face. After a moment, it clicked that he was being offered help to his feet. Suspicious of the demigod's intentions, he clambered to a stand by himself, as did Zane. Denken didn't seem to mind, face splitting into another wide grin as he said,

"You're going to come with me and help me get my brother back."

—

The moment they set foot outside the dark room of their temporary prison, Gloucester understood why Denken had thought it best to keep them there. He'd said it was to keep them from being overwhelmed, and as he looked around now at Denken's domain, he could see why that had been a concern. It *was* overwhelming.

In a strange, sneaking way. The room they stood in now was like a funhouse mirror, warped in a subtle way that crept up on you with its wrongness. Or an optical illusion that took you a moment to put your finger on just what wasn't making sense. Then once you saw the wrongness, you wondered how it had taken you so long to notice, and you couldn't *unsee* it.

Finch had called this place the Maze, and so Gloucester had drawn in his imagination an image of twisting passageways and branching paths, a labyrinth of stone. The truth of the Maze wasn't like that. The walls were indeed made of stone, or at least appeared to be, but that was the extent of the similarities it shared with what Gloucester had pictured. This was no ancient labyrinth or overgrown hedge maze. Not even Finch's description of the place did it justice, though he'd been correct about a few key elements:

One, there were doors everywhere, placed seemingly at random along the walls. There were even a few on the ceiling far above their heads and one Gloucester spotted on the floor, off in a corner.

Two, everything about the place was *off*. At first glance it appeared to be a large room, one that wouldn't look out of place in a castle, with flagstone floors and gray brick walls, each slab of stone massive. The longer he looked, however, the hazier the room became, the distance to the walls impossible to gauge and the walls themselves somehow leaning both inward and outward at once. Directly in front of him, though he couldn't fathom precisely how far, a staircase spiraled gracefully up a wall and to a landing on the ceiling, with no apparent respect for logic.

"Ugh," Zane said beside him. She too was eyeing the stairs, her head cocked at a dramatic angle as she took it all in. "Oh saints, I feel drunk."

On her other side, Finch's head was also tilted, tipped back to stare up at the ceiling and its inexplicable doors. What he thought of the sight was impossible to discern, his expression cryptic.

Denken stepped forward, a smug twinkle in his eye as he took in their reactions. "Pretty, isn't it? Welcome to my humble abode." He raised his arms and turned slowly on the spot.

"What now?" Finch asked, sounding like he was putting a lot of effort into seeming bored and unimpressed. Gloucester couldn't help but wonder what had happened to the cocksure man who so cheerfully held a gun to his head only hours earlier. Had he been that shaken by Denken's manipulations? Had his confidence only been for show? Or had the bizarre series of events since the warehouse simply been enough to shake his smirking attitude?

Denken sent Finch an exasperated look, but Gloucester cut in before he could say anything, deciding that whatever Finch's reason for his sober mood, it was well-earned. "How exactly do you plan on getting your brother back?" he asked.

Denken shrugged. "Not sure yet. I'll think of something. It's what I'm good at. At least I'm closer than I was. Now I know how the silly bastard got into this predicament, and I've got myself a jolly posse of sidekicks." He beamed at the others, none of whom looked jolly in the slightest.

"And if we don't want to be your sidekicks?" Finch asked sourly.

"*Well*," drawled Denken, tapping his chin in mock contemplation. "Then I guess I'd drop Mik here back with those cheerful fellows who were using his head as their personal punching bag, leave you in the Maze until you go insane or starve, and as for *you* . . ." He pointed at Zane, who stared back apprehensively. "Well, I've got nothing against you. I guess I'd drop you off with Antimony."

"Oh." Zane looked quite relieved. Then her eyes widened. "*Oh*. Why don't we start there? Not with the whole 'punching bag, insane, and starving to death' thing, but Antimony?"

Denken blinked at her. "What about her?"

"She's looking into the Gambler's disappearance too. She can help." She growled in frustration and threw her hands up when Denken scoffed. "Her place is somewhere safe to go, at least. To plan our next move."

Denken made a face, tilting his head this way and that as he made a show of thinking it over. "I guess," he said, a touch petulantly. "But she'll want to do everything all *nicely*." He grimaced, and though the look started out joking, it quickly darkened into something more genuine and dangerous. "I have no intention to be nice. Stupid *rules* might keep me from killing you humans myself, much as some of you deserve it, but that's not going to stop me from getting the Gambler back. Or from ending that little insect who calls himself High Minister. Just means I have to be creative." His eyes gleamed. "Which I'm good at."

"Right," said Zane, exchanging a worried look with

Gloucester. Clearly she wanted to avoid further argument, though, or risk losing the ground she had won for them. "Let's go to Antimony's, then. And fast—this place gives me the creeps."

"Excuse you," Denken snipped back, though his mood had lightened once more, and he sounded more pleased than bothered by this reaction to his domain. "Stop insulting my home and hold hands. It'll make transporting the lot of you easier."

"About that," Gloucester said. "Can I please get these off now?" The handcuffs gave a cheery clink as he held his bound hands aloft. "It's been a *really* long day."

Chapter 17

Back in the World

Mulligan flinched as a lamp crashed against an exquisitely carved mahogany bookcase, shattering on impact into a dozen shiny, jagged pieces that fell to the carpet in a shower of wrathful destruction. Beside him, Harrison remained stony-faced and silent.

"*How*?" the high minister seethed. "How did this happen? Three prisoners disappeared right out from under our noses. What the *hell* happened?"

"I—I don't know, sir," Mulligan stammered. He couldn't remember the last time he'd seen the minister this furious. "We were watching them. I'd been talking to Gloucester myself. He mentioned a name I didn't know, and I went to fetch you and—"

The minister's glare drove him into wretched silence.

"Something happened to the agents, sir," Harrison said. His grim calm was a stark contrast with the minister's wrath and Mulligan's dismay. "The whole lot of them who were on surveillance are still recovering from whatever it was. Hypnosis or something. Something got in their heads. Drugs, maybe, or—"

"Not drugs." This time it was the minister's words, not his anger, that interrupted his underling's explanation. "*It's him.*"

"But how, sir?" asked Mulligan timidly. "The Finches said he'd been contained, that his powers wouldn't be . . . And there hasn't been any trouble before now. Not in the entire year since he was brought in. Why would the—" He snapped his mouth shut at another sharp look from the minister.

"Harrison," the minister said. The security agent barely hesitated before nodding and leaving the room. The door clicked shut behind him. After a long moment of silence, the minister gestured for Mulligan to continue.

Apologetic, Mulligan ducked his head and then carried on. "Why would the Gambler start trouble now?"

The minister shrugged, face set in cold consideration in the wake of his waning outrage. "Opportunity, maybe. Perhaps it's taken him this long to work around the defenses. Maybe he's just grown bored. Or maybe he has outside help." He looked at Mulligan again, who was relieved to see the fire in his eyes had tempered. "What was the name Gloucester said?"

It was an odd one. Mulligan wasn't sure if it was even the name of a person at all. Perhaps it was a place or an object. "Denken," he said. "I think that's what it was. Do you think it's important?"

The minister was already heading for the door. "I don't know, but I'm going to find out."

—

The room was dark, lit by the faint flicker of candles spaced too far apart. Its walls, built of the carved stones of ancient cathedrals, yawned upward into the darkness, the ceiling hidden in shadow.

The high minister's footsteps echoed on the polished marble of the floor, like the solitary knocking of a drum. Or a heartbeat, he thought. One that beat more slowly and steadily than the anxious organ thrumming against his ribs.

No matter how often he came here, he could never quite banish the fear. It had lessened over time, of course, cooling from a raging boil into a simmering trepidation, only in danger of rising out of control if something provoked it. He remembered the first time he'd walked this long room, the way his heart had tried digging its way free of his chest, how his throat felt tight with terror in the face of the alien and unknown. He'd done his best to hide it, but the Finches, walking on either side of him, had surely sensed it. As had the creature.

Nothing moved in the center of the room, where the distant candles' light was replaced by a fainter glow with none of their earthliness. The minister had expected this stillness, but today it struck him as more worrisome. He wondered what the trapped creature was thinking. Did he know of the dangerous plots that revolved around him? Was he the one who had spun them? Whether or not he knew it, he was as tangled up in all this as he was in the complex prison that held him.

The cage was not made of steel bars or weathered stone. Stretching from the very center of the floor up into the dark abyss of the vaults above, a complicated net entangled a lone figure, his long limbs caught like fingers in a cat's cradle.

"You're sad today, Henry," the Gambler said when the high minister came to a halt several feet away, reluctant to move closer. "Or are you frightened?"

The Gambler's voice, amidst the creak of the ropes and the near-silent thrum of their magic, did nothing to ease the tightness in the high minister's chest. It was an impossible sound, quiet and echoing, imbued with a solemnity as deep as the oceans. It felt ironic to be accused of sadness by a being that spoke with the melody of ancient woes and the timbre of age-old tragedy. His voice sounded old, not through rasp or creak or murmured stutter, but something more subtle, some inflection that weighed on the souls of all who heard it.

In contrast, the Gambler looked anything but ancient. His face was smooth of wrinkles, with straight-edged features to which it was difficult to assign an age. The minister had always thought this fitting, given that any assumed age would be spectacularly inaccurate. The Gambler had pale blond hair that seemed almost washed out against the darker hues of his skin, and sometimes when he turned his head and the dim light caught it in just the right way, faint reds and blues shimmered among the strands like reflections.

It wasn't his ageless face nor his odd hair that caught one's attention, however. Nor was it even the slow *drip drip* of blood from his bare feet dangling a foot above the stone floor, forming a puddle that never grew in size. No, though the faint scent of copper wrinkled the minister's nose, it wasn't what frightened him most about the eerie creature caught in his trap.

Where the Gambler's eyes should have been, smooth skin stretched seamlessly over empty sockets. There were no scars to indicate eyes had ever resided in his face, but more hauntingly still, it never seemed like he *needed* them. As his solemn comment upon the high minister's arrival had proven, he was able to perceive the world around him through some fashion other than sight. The minister supposed it was a benefit of godliness, not needing eyes to see.

"Is there something you want, Henry?" the Gambler asked when the minister remained silent. He pursed his lips; he'd never told the creature his name.

"I have questions for you," he said finally, careful to keep his tone even. In the wake of the Gambler's powerful voice, he hated that his own sounded dull and weak.

The Gambler continued to watch him sightlessly, face implacable. "You always do."

He said nothing more, and for a moment they stood in tense silence. At least, it felt tense to the minister, who stared up at the unreadable face of his prisoner and wished he could see an answer or at least the hint of one in his features. The Gambler, for his part, showed no sign of tension. He was as frustratingly calm as ever. The minister couldn't help but feel relieved about this, though. He could only remember one time when the creature had been anything other than collected in his temper. It wasn't something he ever wished to witness again.

And yet, should the machinations unfolding around them come to pass, if this chaos was all part of some rescue plot or plan of escape . . . The minister shuddered to imagine the consequences. He suspected gods didn't take kindly to imprisonment.

"Who is Denken?" he asked.

Only to nearly leap back in alarm as the Gambler jolted, his tangled limbs shuddering as surprise shot through his expression. For a moment his mouth hung agape, a look so human that, were it not for his eyeless stare, the minister might almost have forgotten what he was.

"So you know the name, then," he said, halfway between smug and more worried than ever. "A friend of yours?"

"What has he done?" demanded the Gambler, his words carrying the distant rumble of an approaching storm. "Or is it you who has done something to him? Have your magicians set out to trap my brothers too?"

"It's him causing trouble, not me."

The Gambler's momentarily chinked armor seemed already mended. He offered a gentle shake of his head, sad smile pitying enough to raise the minister's hackles, as if his lapse into emotion had never even happened. "You humans have a saying about what happens when you sow the wind."

"He is not my whirlwind," the minister snapped. "He is a troublemaker and a . . . a trickster of some sort. He is, isn't he?" He recalled the odd look on Gloucester's face when he snatched up the gun in his office and the real confusion in his eyes when he refused to take the shot. He'd thought the man had lost it. Then he'd worried the Gambler's powers were more far-reaching than he'd known and somehow had something to do with it. Now he wasn't so sure. That name bounced around his skull, demanding its own importance. Denken. Somehow, he was the key.

"Trickster is a word for him, I suppose," the Gambler said amiably. "One many would apply to him. Including himself."

It was impossible to tell if he was trying to be funny. The minister had long since learned not to waste his time attempting to discern the Gambler's moods. "He's your brother, then?" he asked instead.

The Gambler made a small movement that the minister guessed would have been a shrug were he better able to move. The massive cat's cradle held him fast, not allowing any more movement than the nod of his head or the wiggle of his fingers and blood-stained toes. "Another word for him. There are those among you humans who call us the Brothers. In recent centuries, at least. Sometimes Sisters. Sometimes simply Siblings. We are family, much as any other."

The minister glowered at this enigmatic reply. This was the problem with the Gambler. He'd been indispensably useful since he'd come into the minister's possession, but the creature had a proclivity for non-answers and riddles that would wear on even the most slow-tempered of people. The minister liked to consider himself patient, but sometimes the Gambler made him doubt that.

Was it worth it to press the issue now, though? He decided it wasn't, at least for the moment. From what he gathered, the Gambler and this Denken were similar beasts, though possibly with different abilities. He spared a moment to curse the loss of the Finches, who likely could have shed some light on the matter with marginally more willing helpfulness than the Gambler. But the younger Finch had been whisked away with Gloucester and the Zephyr woman. And as for the elder Finch . . .

"Someone's trying their damnedest to kill me," he said, sneering. "Your brother seems the most likely candidate. Maybe 'puppet master' is a word for him too, eh? He's been using people to do his dirty work somehow."

"He is . . . influential," said the Gambler.

Influential, in the minister's ears, rang like *dangerous*. This Denken had already proven to be more than just an inconvenience. Not only had he swayed Mikalai Gloucester and who knew how many others to try to kill him, he'd just walked into a secure facility, bamboozled an entire team of trained security agents, and walked out with three important prisoners. Asking if he was powerful would be pointless.

"That day six months ago . . ." he started slowly. "Did you see this coming to pass then? Is that why you said we had to keep Gloucester alive? Did you want all of this to happen?"

The Gambler shook his head. "I wished only to spare an innocent man. A good man. And to save the lives and livelihoods of many. You may not see it, but things could be much worse. You are the leader of this city—surely you care to protect it?"

"Spare me the heroics and hypotheticals. If this Denken wants my head, why doesn't he just kill me himself? Nothing would stop him from waltzing into my office and getting the job done."

The Gambler nodded minutely, face set in stone. "Only rules."

"Rules?" the minister scoffed. "I would have thought you lot were above such things."

"There are some things none of us are above. He would not break them."

The minister stared up at the melancholy being caught in his net. "What would happen if he did?"

A shadow passed over the Gambler's strange face, the faintest hint of a shudder. "Consequences. As is always the case when rules are broken." His fingers twitched. "Allow me to see."

The minister hesitated. Normally he was eager to make use of the Gambler's abilities. Today, however, he couldn't help but wonder how much the leash was slipping.

"If you want a prediction, I need them," the Gambler said

patiently. He twisted his left hand, the magical cords biting into his wrist, his palm now facing the dark ceiling above, slender fingers splayed.

Giving in, the minister reached into his pocket. He drew forth a small wooden box, polished smooth but unadorned. He opened it and carefully placed the contents on the Gambler's waiting palm.

With a flick of his wrist, the Gambler rolled the dice. They rose high in the air, bone white in the shadows and pale light of magic. The minister's avid gaze followed their rise and fall, until they landed back in the Gambler's hand.

Two unblinking eyes, the color of amber, stared up at them.

"Snake eyes," the Gambler said, and smiled.

Chapter 18

A Meeting of the Minds

Antimony looked flabbergasted. Or at least, as much as Gloucester could recall—or indeed, imagine—her ever looking. Her normally hooded eyes widened slightly as they slid over each of them in turn, gaze questioning. They lingered longest on Finch and Denken, and though she didn't acknowledge the former beyond a stiff nod, her words were directed at the personification of Thought.

"I was not . . . expecting this," she said.

"I do love to be unexpected," Denken replied, beaming his sharp-toothed smile at her. "Your home is as lovely as ever."

They stood in the same sitting room Gloucester had waited in several days previously. They'd appeared out of thin air on Antimony's front step a few minutes before, reeling from the abrupt change in surroundings. If any passage of time was spent in transport, Gloucester hadn't been able to detect it. One moment Denken was ordering them all to shut their eyes, then the next a cool breeze was brushing his face, bringing with it the scents and sounds of Frettchen. Antimony appeared at the door a minute later, woken by Denken's impatient knocking, and ushered them into her house. She was dressed in a white night gown, her long hair woven into a braid and her eyes bleary with sleep. It was dark outside the window, and the clock on the wall declared it to be nearing four o'clock in the morning. As to what day it might be, Gloucester couldn't say. Nor did he really feel like taking the time to figure it out. There were more important problems to tackle first.

If only his body would cooperate with his mind. His racing thoughts and anxious ambition to end this madness made him eager to start working out their next move. Unfortunately, his aching body was less than keen on doing anything other than lie down and sleep for about a week straight. His head pounded, both from weariness and the beating he'd received, and he found his concentration wavering, no matter how important he told himself this all was. Whatever healing magic Denken used on him had banished the worst of the pain, but he still felt like he'd been put through the ringer.

Beside him, Zane looked equally weary, if distinctly less worse for wear. Gloucester hadn't had the chance to ask her how she was treated at the hands of the high minister's security team, but she appeared to be unharmed. As did Finch, though Gloucester was honestly unsure whether the mysterious man had been taken in as a prisoner or an ally.

That status was rather more clearly defined now.

"This lot are my prisoners," Denken was telling Antimony with the same cheery helpfulness one might employ to voice their opinion on the weather. "Well," he amended, smile dimming. "Not that one." He nodded toward Zane, who glared back at him. "You can have her."

"Not exactly how it works, Denken," Antimony scolded. Her expression softened when she turned her attention to Zane. "You had me worried. I went to your shop when I didn't hear from you, and there was no sign you'd been home since yesterday. I'm glad you're all right. Both of you," she added, looking at Gloucester. Her brows drew together after a beat. "Okay, maybe 'all right' is a bit of a stretch in your case. Sit down and I'll get the first aid kit." She gestured toward the sofa and chairs, before turning back to Denken with another hard look. "Try not to traumatize them in the few minutes I'm gone."

Denken only chuckled, plopping himself down on an armchair in one corner of the room. Zane moved to the sofa and sank down onto it with a tired sigh, leaving Gloucester and Finch standing awkwardly together in the middle of the room. After a moment, Finch crossed the small expanse of floor to join Zane on the sofa.

Gloucester dragged a weary hand over his face, wincing as the action aggravated the remaining bruises from his interrogation. He didn't want to know what he looked like right now. All he wanted was to find a bed and sleep away everything he'd seen and all that had happened. Exhaustion had drained away his fervor for answers, though he knew it would bubble back to the surface the moment the world no longer felt as if it was literally resting on his shoulders. Sadly, he had a feeling bed was still a long way off. All he could hope was that Antimony wouldn't take long to fetch the first aid kit.

Fortunately, she didn't, gliding back into the room a few minutes later with a large white crate in her arms. Ordering him to sit down on the coffee table, she set the crate on the floor, opened it, and promptly set about tending Gloucester's various cuts and bruises with a professional yet gentle touch.

"So, what's the plan, then, Denken?" she asked as she worked. "Or is it too optimistic of me to think that you might have one?"

"Well, I *had* a plan." Denken kicked his feet lazily against the side of the chair he was sprawled across. "I thought it was going just dandy, but then *some* people went and started making things difficult." He sent Gloucester, Zane, and Finch an exaggerated frown. The grimace quirked upward after a few seconds. "On the bright side, I now have useful people helping me."

"Prisoners," Antimony said, humming with distaste.

"The best kind of people to have around to help! Means they'll cooperate."

Antimony was unimpressed. "Hm. Yes. It's possible you've not paid much attention to how things generally work with taking people prisoner, Denken. Things tend not to be as easy as that. Imprisonment doesn't always breed helpfulness."

Denken scoffed. "These two are no problem," he said, gesturing at Finch and Gloucester. "Mik just wants this all to end as much as I do"—he ignored Gloucester's muttered protest at the name—"and Cassus . . . well, he owes me on account of the whole brother-kidnapping thing. Call it fixing past mistakes."

"I just want to sort out this mess," Finch said icily. "And don't call me that. We're not friends."

"On account of the whole brother-kidnapping thing," Denken repeated. Sharp, bitter tones seemed to have little effect on him.

"You want the high minister dead for whatever he's doing to your brother. This man caught the Gambler, him and his father," Gloucester said, his head half-obscured by Antimony's arms as she cleaned the various cuts on his face. His voice was strained from the sting of her ministrations, but his attention was on Denken. "Why don't you want them dead too?"

He was asking out of honest curiosity, and not until the words left his mouth did he realize how they probably sounded to the others, particularly Finch himself.

"Gee, thanks." Finch glared at him. "Don't talk about my dad."

"He's more useful alive," said Denken, speaking over him. "Even if he's a grouch. Don't mind him, he's just persnickety because his poor old pa got blown to bits."

Several things happened all at once. Zane cried out, "Wait,

what?" in a horrified voice, Antimony swore, and Finch, face livid with fury, launched himself from his seat toward Denken.

Gloucester lunged to his feet out of instinct more than anything, knocking Antimony's hands aside and surging forward to stop Finch. He latched onto the furious man's arms and pulled him back, struggling to keep his hold. Finch had a good several inches on him, plus he was being lent the adrenaline-fueled strength of rage.

Gloucester needn't have bothered with the effort. Denken vanished from the armchair in the blink of an eye. For a moment Gloucester thought he'd disappeared entirely, but then his voice rang out from the other side of the room.

"Struck a nerve, eh?" he said from where he now leaned against the door frame. His lighthearted tone had gained a chilly edge.

"I'll bloody kill you myself!" roared Finch, struggling even more ferociously to pull free of Gloucester's hold. "This is all on you, you bastard! He's dead because of you."

"No," said Denken. "He's dead *because of him*. Because of *you*. This is all on *you*."

The angry words of both Finch and Denken rang in Gloucester's ears. He hadn't considered the possibility that the elder Finch didn't survive the explosion. It hadn't even crossed his mind. He'd thought only of the high minister and Zane.

The odd old man with his carefree demeanor and smug tone had been an enemy, an unknown threat. Yet as Gloucester watched the wrath in Finch's face now, and the grief he knew lurked just beneath it, he was reminded that, whatever else the old man had been, he'd been somebody's father. He'd been loved and he'd been lost. And here Gloucester had dragged his reeling son into the fray, pushing Denken to take him for the usefulness he provided and leaving him no time to grieve.

"I'm sorry," he said quietly, his lips by Finch's ear as he continued to fight to hold him back. He wasn't sure Finch even heard him, the man's furious green eyes never leaving Denken's unsympathetic face, but after a moment, his struggles lessened. Just the same, Gloucester kept a careful grip on him.

"You want revenge," Denken said. "So do I. You and your dad got pulled into all this because of the high minister. Mik's—sorry, *Gloucester's*—life got torn apart because of the high minister. My brother, Antimony's friend, got kidnapped because of the high minister. I'm not the enemy here. *He is.*"

His voice was so sweet, so smooth, that Gloucester found himself nodding along without thinking about it. It sounded so right, so just. The high minister was the enemy, the only enemy—

He gasped, yanking himself from the descending veil of the trance. "Stop it!"

Over on the couch, Zane looked hazy and confused. Finch's arms, before so tense with anger, had relaxed in Gloucester's grip. Even Antimony looked like she'd been thrown for a loop.

She quickly regained her composure, however, eyes narrowing in disapproval. "Stop messing with our heads, Denken," she said, wagging an admonishing finger his way before packing up the first aid supplies. She'd mostly finished tending to Gloucester before he leapt to his feet minutes earlier. His head was now a mismatched array of band-aids and taped-on gauze, but he paid it little mind, focused on the situation at hand.

"You don't need to bloody hypnotize us to get us to think the high minister's a bastard," Zane said. She straightened up with a woozy grimace, one hand clutched to her head as if nursing a hangover. Clearly Denken's tricks still had her feeling off-balance. "You could have considered just *asking* for our help, you know."

"Would you have said yes?" Denken sneered. "I know the answer, so don't bother giving it. And I don't *want* anybody's help. If I could kill the high minister myself, I would. Painfully. I didn't want to have to involve a bunch of stupid humans in this. And I certainly didn't want *her* and her lot ruining my revenge." He pointed at Antimony, who eyed the accusatory finger impassively.

"There's no point in arguing," she said. "The important thing is rescuing the Gambler. We're all on the same page about that, yes?" She cast her gaze over all of them, pausing contemplatively when she reached Finch. Though his face was still surly and noncommittal, he nodded.

"Excellent." Antimony nodded in return, though the action on her part was less sullen. "You see, Denken? We can all work together on this. It's our best chance. *The Gambler's* best chance."

"Hm. For now."

The dark gleam was back in his eyes. Somehow Gloucester didn't think that boded well.

Whether Antimony noted it too was hard to say. She made no mention of it as she straightened to her feet, first aid kit in hand. Tossing her long hair over her shoulder, she regarded them all, a grimace settling over her features. She clicked her tongue in annoyance. "Oh, bloody hell, I'm going to have to make room for all of you here, aren't I? A few of you will be sleeping on floors and sofas, I'm sorry to say."

Gloucester blinked at her in surprise. The tone of her voice intimated that the conversation was drawing to a close for the night. "But shouldn't we—"

Antimony silenced him with a firm wave of her hand. "Never make important plans when you're sleepy," she said. "Besides the fact that you look like you're going to keel over dead at any moment, Zane and that Finch fellow both look exhausted. And might I remind you that you lot showed up at my door after three in the morning? You're all lucky that Murphy's out for the night, or we'd be having a hell of a time explaining things. I'm ready for bed, and if we make rescue plans now, the Gambler's going to spend the rest of his imprisonment with us idiots as his cellmates."

She spoke so matter-of-factly that Gloucester couldn't

argue, no matter how much he wanted to. And she had a point; Denken was the only one in the room not showing any signs of weariness. They needed clear heads to plan their next move.

"Now," said Antimony, hands on her hips. "Zane, you can sleep in the spare room, you remember where it is. Gloucester, you and Mr. Finch can sleep in here. Someone can take the couch and someone can take the floor. Polite thing to do would be to let the beaten one have the couch," she added, sending a pointed look at Finch, who only shrugged. "Denken, you can do whatever it is you do at night. Just don't mess around with anything in my house. Or any*one*."

Denken pouted. His face was cast in odd shadows from the lamp beside the door, making the comical reaction oddly unsettling. "Aw, fine. No fun."

—

The sitting room, which had seemed so cramped with everyone in it, felt overly large in contrast when it was only Gloucester and Finch. Perhaps it had been Denken's weighty presence that filled the space. The personification of Thought himself didn't cut a very large figure, but he still managed to take up as much space as he could wherever he happened to be, out of sheer force of personality.

Gloucester and Finch were silent as they set out the blankets and pillows Antimony had brought downstairs for them. Gloucester was glad for the quiet; his head still hurt, and besides, he wasn't really sure what to say to the other man. Hours earlier, Finch had been holding a gun to his temple. He'd had a hand in this whole mess that destroyed Gloucester's life. Yet for all that he wanted to hate him, he wasn't sure he could. Not right now, at least. Not when the grief and rage that had burned through Finch's voice was still fresh in Gloucester's memory.

"Leave me a blanket to sleep on, yeah?" said Finch, breaking the silence. "Make the floor a wee bit less hard."

"Yeah, 'course," Gloucester muttered. He bundled up one of

the blankets and tossed it to Finch, who caught it deftly and laid it out on the cleared space of floor.

"Not the worst place I've slept," Finch said a moment later, surveying his handiwork. The thickest of the blankets served as his mattress, with a thinner quilt over top and a couple of fat pillows at one end.

"Nor me." Gloucester sat on his makeshift bed. The couch was going to be slightly too short for him, he already knew, but it would be softer than the floor or the cot back in his cell.

Finch hummed in acknowledgment, shrugging out of his jacket and tossing it down on his blankets. Quiet fell over them again, and though all Gloucester wanted to do was lie back and give in to much-needed sleep, his brain couldn't settle, buzzing with thoughts that refused to be as silent as the room. He lay atop his blankets, staring up at the ceiling as Finch moved to the lamp by the chair and turned it off.

The ensuing darkness did nothing to soothe Gloucester's mind. He was brought back to the insomnia that plagued him the first couple months of his imprisonment, sleep always lurking at the unreachable edges of his thoughts. Back then, he'd longed for someone to talk with. Now he wasn't even sure how to.

"I'm sorry about your father," he said, voice tentative in the dark, unable to keep the words in any longer. He didn't take his eyes away from the fading details of the plaster overhead. For a moment, he wasn't even certain Finch had heard him.

Then, "You shouldn't be. You didn't know him. He wasn't anyone to you."

"Yeah, but he was someone to you. He was your dad." Gloucester blinked up at the ceiling. There was no longer any difference between what he saw when his eyes were open and when they were shut. The world had vanished, leaving only their murmurs in the dark. "And you lost him. I'm sorry."

A scoff reached his ears, but when Finch spoke next, his voice was surprisingly soft. "Thanks, then, I guess."

Silence reigned again. The noise in Gloucester's head had

dulled somewhat after he voiced some of what was bothering him, and the possibility of sleep edged closer.

Just as his eyes drifted closed and the weight of sleep began to settle over him, Finch's voice reached him again, chasing unconsciousness away. "All that stuff you told your friend Zane, was that true? How you got locked up and all that?"

Gloucester rolled his head on his pillow to stare sightlessly in Finch's direction. "Yeah. It was."

"That's messed up," Finch mused, not sounding overly concerned. So *unconcerned*, in fact, that Gloucester narrowed his eyes in the dark, wondering if the exaggerated apathy covered something else.

"It's my problem, I'll deal with it," he said, defensiveness raising his hackles, no matter how sleepy he was.

To his indignation, a laugh came from where Finch lay. "I'm sure you will."

Gloucester bit his tongue to keep from spitting a retort down at Finch in the blackness. He wasn't certain if the other man was trying to start an argument. Sure, Finch had laughed, but his words hadn't been derisive or sardonic, merely amused.

No explanation followed, though, and soon enough, faint snores reached Gloucester's ears.

The darkness loomed all around him, silence pressing down on him as if the very air had doubled in weight. He let it settle over him like another blanket, urging sleep to find him once more. Tomorrow was going to be a big day. Even if all they did was make plans, it would still be more steps forward than he'd managed so far.

Now if only I knew where I was going.

Chapter 19

Hiding Places

Despite his exhaustion the night before, Gloucester woke not long after daybreak, dawn's gentle light creeping through the window to bathe the side of his face in warmth. For a while he lay still, eyes closed, enjoying the calm before the storm that was full wakefulness. Shrouds of sleep still lingered, slowing his thoughts and keeping worries at bay.

It was a doomed peace, however, and soon reality began seeping in through the edges of his mind, like water leaking through cracks in a wall.

He opened his eyes slowly, half his vision obscured by the pillow and the rumpled bandages Antimony had applied. Even after more than a week out of his cell, waking was still an odd experience. Each time he awoke, he couldn't shake the expectation that the same plain white walls and cracked ceiling would greet him. Each time he opened his eyes to find this wasn't the case, a strange rush of emotion coursed through him, storming through his chest with a ferocity that chased his breath away. It was a mixture of overwhelming relief and something akin to unease. All these rooms—his room at the mansion, Zane's break room, Antimony's sitting room—seemed too big, too cluttered, with too much space and too many things.

It infuriated him to feel this way. Was he actually *missing* his prison? Had he really lost his mind that much? Did part of him want to go back?

No, he told himself firmly. *Never again.*

—

They convened in the kitchen an hour later, huddling around the countertop island amidst a quiet chorus of yawns and morning greetings. Finch shuffled into the room barefoot, a quilt wrapped around his shoulders like a cloak. Zane was bleary-eyed and nursing a large mug of tea. Antimony, wearing a long housecoat and her hair still tied back in a braid made loose and rough by sleep, brought Gloucester another set of clothes from the unexplained stash of menswear she possessed, so he excused himself to the bathroom down the hall to get changed out of the singed and blood-stained sweater and jeans. After donning in their place a plain black T-shirt and slacks, he glanced in the mirror and was surprised by the reflection staring back at him. His hair was an unruly mess and he desperately needed a shave, but the injuries Antimony had cleaned up the day before were noticeably improved. He touched his cheek tentatively and found it barely felt tender. Was there something more to the scientist's first aid kit than simple disinfectant and bandages?

If magic was involved, he wished Antimony could have used some to tweak the clothes she'd lent him. The pants were slightly too long, but complaining seemed ungrateful. He made do with rolling the hems up around his ankles and ignored Finch and Zane's amused smiles when he re-entered the kitchen a few minutes later.

The only one unaffected by the early hour was Denken.

Where he'd disappeared to the night before went unaddressed, but he was as chipper as ever. More so, in fact. He was dressed in the same dark shirt he'd worn the day before, but its sober color was now thrown into stark contrast with the rest of his outfit, which seemed to consist of the most garish hues he could lay his hands on. His pants were a vivid orange, the fabric loose around his legs before tapering to fit snugly a little past his knees. It was a style common in Frettchen, especially in the spring and summer, when winds from the east swept sand and dust from the desert into the city. Fashion made functional, as the trousers were designed to keep sand from getting into the wearer's shoes.

Popular as the style might be, it was strange to see it on someone as unearthly as Denken. He'd swathed his neck and shoulders in a long scarf, its shade of yellow as eye-searing as the trousers. Like Finch, he was barefoot. Propping his feet up on the counter as he leaned back on a chair, he grinned around at them all.

"Morning, lovelies." He beamed at Antimony and winked. "Glad to see you didn't let my prisoners sneak off in the middle of the night."

"Mhmm." Antimony sipped her tea, looking completely unimpressed. Gloucester suspected if either he or Finch had wanted to leave, she wouldn't have made the slightest move to stop them.

If Denken was thinking the same thing, it was impossible to tell. He merely winked the other eye and clapped his hands in gleeful anticipation. "All right. Time to plan some rescue and revenge."

"I'm honestly not sure which is more important to him," Zane whispered to Gloucester out of the corner of her mouth.

"I like to think they go hand-in-hand," said Denken, shooting her a cheeky wink. Gloucester made a mental note to suggest to Zane later that demigods might have better hearing than the average human.

"The question is, how do we go about either?" Antimony cut in, eyeing Denken sternly. "Where's the Gambler being held?"

"I can help with that," Finch said with a yawn, speaking for the first time since he'd wandered in from the sitting room. All eyes turned toward him. Like his father back in the warehouse, he didn't appear at all bothered to be the center of attention. Unlike the elder Finch, however, he didn't preen, only scratched his nose and frowned contemplatively. "I was there when we handed him over to His Lordship. Unless he moved him since then, the Gambler would still be in the last place I saw him. And trust me, I don't think he would have moved him. It would be too much work and plenty too dangerous. If the high minister was a bloke to take unnecessary risks, he wouldn't have demanded the Gambler in the first place."

Denken, who had snorted loudly at the words "trust me," leaned forward in his chair, dropping his feet from the countertop. "And where is that?"

Finch avoided Denken's gaze but showed no other outward sign that the demigod's presence fazed him. Gloucester had to admit it was admirable, considering all Denken had put him through.

"Dad and I were blindfolded to be brought there, but we heard one of the guards say a name. Some idiots will gossip about anything and everything. If you know to listen, you learn all sorts of things. Like that the Gambler's kept at the High Minister's Cathedral." He smiled crookedly. "Sounds fancy, eh? His Lordship's a smart man, but I don't think he could resist the poetry of it. In the heart of his seat of power, he's hiding the secret behind what's keeping him there."

Something stirred in Gloucester's mind, tickling the edges of half-formed thoughts, nagging like the vestiges of a forgotten dream. The feeling he was forgetting something niggled at him. Whatever it was, not only was it desperately important, it was so, *so* close. If only he could reach out a hand and snatch it back to the forefront of his brain, into the light of conscious thought where it could be illuminated in recollection.

But no dawning memory showed its face over the horizon of his mind. Frustrated, and not even sure why, he shook the feeling off as he refocused on the conversation.

"Cathedral? You mean the big one in the old part of the city?" Zane was asking.

Gloucester shook his head. "That's not his. Being high minister grants him religious leadership in the city, same way the title of lord of the city-state makes him leader of secular affairs, but the Old Cathedral's not his seat of power. Only the higher priests could claim to own it, and there hasn't been one of them in Frettchen for years. The High Minister's Cathedral is a nickname for the church he presides over, All Saints Shrine. It's not actually a proper cathedral."

Four pairs of eyes stared at him. Color rose in Gloucester's cheeks. "What? I used to work for him. I know some stuff, all right?"

"So where is this High Minister's Not-Actually-A-Cathedral, then?" asked Denken.

"Corner of Westmoreland and Park," Gloucester said. In his mind's eye, he could see the great stone building, its towers rising high over the surrounding architecture. Though it was dwarfed by Frettchen's true cathedral, All Saints Shrine was an impressive feat of masonry and stained glass, beautiful inside and out. Gloucester hadn't been raised to know much about religion, and certainly hadn't ever been a part of one, but he was assigned a few times to the detail that accompanied the high minister to his sermons and other duties at the church. More than the minister's eloquent words or the rapt faces of his followers, Gloucester remembered being impressed by the atmosphere of the place itself. Inside its walls, everything seemed perfect, muted and calm.

And apparently a kidnapped demigod was hidden somewhere in its depths.

"Westmoreland and Park." Antimony tapped a finger

against her lips, thoughtful. "That's on the other side of the city. And you know they'll be watching for us. They'll be expecting us. Or, well, you lot anyway." She nodded at Gloucester, Zane, and Finch.

"I do love to be unexpected," Denken said again, smirking.

"Why can't we just walk right in?" Gloucester asked him, his frown in contrast with Denken's jovial attitude. "I saw you hypnotize an entire room of agents. Can't you do that again?"

Denken's smile stayed in place, but it suddenly seemed frozen and false. After an uncomfortable moment, he shrugged, steepling his fingers and drumming their tips together. "It's a handy trick, isn't it? But it's not as effortless as I make it look. Focusing power on one person is easy, but a whole bunch is a different story." He paused, and for the first time Gloucester detected something akin to hesitance in his demeanor.

"I don't have the strength for it now," he said finally. "Not if I want to be of any use afterwards, anyway. I used it before because I thought it was important to be able to talk to you. Lucky for both of us, I was right." He winked at Gloucester, who narrowed his eyes in return.

On the one hand, Denken had gotten him out of the high minister's custody, had returned him and Zane to the safety of Antimony's home, and had gotten Gloucester more answers than he could ever have expected to find on his own.

On the other hand, Denken had manipulated him, *controlled* him on more than one occasion now. The demigod had a dangerous disregard for collateral damage. No matter their common goals, he couldn't be trusted. Even if he was admitting to an apparent limitation to his terrifying powers, they only had his word for it. And who knew what else he might be capable of, even if he did have some weaknesses? Though unable to kill humans himself, that didn't stop him from wreaking violent havoc. He'd nearly made Gloucester commit murder. He'd found vulnerable people and twisted their needs and—

"Who threw the grenade?"

He asked the question sharply, not unaware of the irony in repeating the question that had been thrown at him so many times the day before. Only after he'd voiced it did he think about how random it must sound to the others. Zane, Finch, and Antimony all looked confused, staring from Gloucester to Denken.

Denken's eyes widened in a show of innocence. His smile, so easily menacing, was now as small and mischievous as a child's. "Hm?"

"Whoever threw that grenade into the high minister's meeting with the Finches, I'm betting it was the same person who tried to kill him with the bomb in his car," Gloucester said, unmoved by Denken's clueless act. "Someone you manipulated, same way you tried to do with me. So who is he?"

Denken didn't answer right away, still looking so self-satisfied that Gloucester wanted to throw something at him. Finally, he shrugged and said, "Who is *she*?"

"What?"

Denken raised a finger, like a teacher pointing out a mistake on his pupil's grammar quiz. "Who is *she*. And the answer is Yvette Jacoby."

He still sounded completely unconcerned. Bored, even. Gloucester's chest constricted, not in fear but fury. How dare Denken care so little for the people he used? This Yvette Jacoby was as much a victim as Gloucester was, as much as Jeremy Wall. Their wills had been bent, twisted out of their grasp and manipulated by expert hands to make them something they might never have been if Denken had left them alone.

"The high minister approved the reconstruction of welfare laws in the city recently. She lost her income, her home, and her children. She was a bit angry with him." Denken scratched his chin. "Funny, though. She should have stopped after the first try."

Trepidation stirred in Gloucester's gut. He'd caught something in Denken's voice that wasn't there before, a curiosity that sounded almost like uncertainty.

"What do you mean?" he asked.

"The effect on her mind shouldn't have lasted for a second attempt," Denken explained, no longer bothering to be flippant. This struck Gloucester as all the more worrying.

"So, what, now she's just trying to kill him because she wants to?"

"She always wanted to. That was the point. That was why I picked her, like I picked you. The difference is now she's doing it all on her own."

"Great," grumbled Zane. "Just one more thing to worry about. Homicidal, revenge-driven bombers. Thanks, Denken, for loosing that one on us."

Denken made a face at her. "Oh, come on, she wasn't after *you*. Just don't stand within, oh you know, bombing distance of the high minister and you'll be fine." He laughed uproariously at his own joke, the raucous sound echoing throughout the house.

Gloucester thought he heard a sound from the floor below, as if something had been knocked over. The sudden laughter must have startled Antimony's cat.

"Setting that aside . . ." said Antimony. She, too, had glanced in the direction of the floor below, but she was quick to refocus her attention. "What we need to focus on is the Gambler. We can deal with the rest of this mess once he's safe."

"Well, we've got a place to start looking, at least," said Zane, setting her sarcasm aside as she turned away from Denken to address Antimony.

Finch made a quiet sound of derision. "And an army of five. Three of whom would be arrested on sight, one who doesn't want to tire himself out by actually using his powers to be useful, and one who looks like a light breeze would knock her over. No offense," he added to Antimony. "This is just destined for success."

Antimony sniffed. "That's hardly fair. It would take at least a stiff wind."

"And I didn't say I wouldn't be useful," Denken interjected, his smile vanishing in favor of the tiniest of frowns. "Just that I couldn't hypnotize them all. But I have an idea that should work . . ."

Chapter 20

The Calm Before

"This is a stupid idea," Zane said, chin propped morosely in her hands.

She, Gloucester, and Finch were the only ones left in Antimony's kitchen. Antimony herself had vanished downstairs "for work," presumably on whatever scientific breakthrough she was currently endeavoring to achieve. Perhaps she simply wanted to be alone. It would be hard to blame her, considering the conversation they'd just had and Denken's rather overwhelming presence.

Finch sighed. "Agreed." He still wore his blanket around his shoulders and was now nursing a steaming cup of coffee, apparently determined to cling to the early morning image, no matter the ticking passage of time carrying them ever closer to midday. "Alas, I don't think we get much of a choice in the matter. What do you think, agent-man?"

He quirked his brows at Gloucester, who shrugged. He stood

over the sink, elbow-deep in soapy water, the small collection of dirty dishes too distracting to ignore.

"Nothing I can think of is any better, honestly." He paused in his washing to look at the other two. Zane was tapping her fingers in quiet agitation on the countertop, and he couldn't help but follow the rhythmic action with his eyes. "Maybe it's the best chance we've got."

"Maybe it *isn't*," countered Zane. "Maybe if we're patient . . . maybe if we can convince Denken to wait—"

The two men shook their heads, both speaking at the same time. After a moment of confusion, Gloucester fell silent and indicated for Finch to speak first.

"I don't think we could convince Denken of something like patience anytime soon."

"And even if we could, we don't have the time," Gloucester added. "The high minister knows we're onto him. We know his secret. If we don't act now, he'll move the Gambler and change his defenses around. Even if we managed to evade capture, we'd never find the Gambler again."

Zane didn't look completely convinced, and she certainly wasn't pleased, but she gave a grudging nod. "So we strike now and hope for the best. Bloody hell, I wish I'd never met you, Gloucester." She winced the moment the words left her mouth. "Sorry, I didn't mean that. Or . . . I didn't mean it like that. It's just—"

Gloucester waved aside the stumbling apology, fingers flicking a small arc of suds through the air. "I understand," he said lightly, hoping the pang of hurt he felt wasn't obvious. He couldn't blame Zane for her misgivings. She was an innocent bystander, caught up in a storm for the simple fact that she'd offered to shelter him from it. She ought to be at her shop right now, with no greater worries than whatever clocks she had to repair that day. She'd joked earlier that she'd been thinking about taking some time off soon anyway, but the good humor hadn't been very convincing, and Gloucester had seen the fear lurking behind it.

Finch watched them both keenly but said nothing. In the light of day, he looked pale and drained, as if he hadn't slept well. Somehow, Gloucester suspected that had little to do with sleeping on the floor. His pallor made the dark smudges under his eyes stand out, along with a hearty sprinkling of freckles that dusted his nose and cheekbones. Despite his weariness, a fresh spark glinted in his eye. The meager night's sleep seemed to have refreshed his mind, if not his body.

Zane sighed, sinking low in her chair to rest her chin on the smooth surface of the counter. Her hair billowed around her in a cloud. "Ah, it's for the best, I guess. What with all this mess because of the Gambler. What would have happened if you hadn't come through my door, eh? If Antimony and I hadn't found out? How many people might've died while Denken sought his revenge? Or his rescue, whatever it is he's hoping to achieve."

"Revescue," Finch supplied helpfully. When both Zane and Gloucester turned to stare at him, he raised his shoulders in nonchalance, the shrug mostly hidden by the folds of the blanket pulled around him. "He wants both."

Zane eyed him sidelong. "*Riiiight*," she said. Huffing a breath, as if summoning strength, she got to her feet. "Well, on *that* note, I'm gonna go vent at Antimony for a while. She's a decent human being who won't go pointing out logical arguments that shoot down my complaints. Unlike *some* people." She offered Gloucester a cheeky look, inviting him to laugh. He suspected it was another, more subtle apology for her earlier comment.

He chuckled, and nodded in mock understanding. "Yours is a hard life, Zane Zephyr," he called after her as she left the room. It felt nice to laugh, a fleeting respite from the stress of everything else.

For a few minutes, the room was quiet. The loudest sounds were the clinks and splashes of the dishes in the sink as Gloucester washed them. A sunbeam was on his back, warming his skin through the fabric of his shirt, and he felt more at peace than he had in a long time. Perhaps it was the plan. It might be reckless, but at least it was something. A way forward. It might not have banished all his fears, but it gave him something to focus on other than questions and uncertainty. He let himself embrace the feeling while he could. Each clean dish he rinsed and set aside to dry felt like a burden he was washing away.

"Why are you doing that?" Finch asked suddenly.

It took a moment for Gloucester to realize he was talking about the dishes. "They needed to be done," he answered, scrubbing industriously at Zane's tea mug with a wash cloth.

"Yeah, but not by *you*. I watched you this morning. You didn't use any dishes. It's not your mess to clean up."

Gloucester paused, looking over his shoulder at Finch. The redhead looked like he wanted to say something more, but Gloucester wasn't sure what it would be. Why was he making such a big deal about a simple household chore? "I'm just doing what I can to help," he said, brows drawing together. "I don't like messes."

For a moment longer, Finch looked strangely contemplative. Then he laughed. "Heavens above, Mr. Gloucester, you must be a wonderful partner to have around."

"I had my moments, or so he told me," Gloucester quipped back. Though his tone was light enough to almost be jovial, caution drew up careful defenses behind his tiny smile. This wasn't territory he was happy to discuss with just anyone, and certainly not with a stranger tangled up in the high minister's intrigues, no matter how charming Finch's smile could be.

"Did he now?" Finch was still smiling, even wider now, but Gloucester wondered how genuine his good mood was. The man had just lost his father. Anyone would be reeling from that. He suspected the humor was a defense mechanism more than anything.

Don't be fooled, he told himself.

"So where's this very complimentary boyfriend now, then?"

Finch asked. Gloucester shrugged and returned to the dishes.

"Not on the run from supernatural creatures and power-mad politicians," he said. He set the clean mug aside and started in on a plate Denken had somehow managed to thoroughly coat in honey. Quietly, he added, "I imagine he thinks I'm long gone."

"That doesn't sound very optimistic. No plans to run into his arms when this is all done?"

Gloucester shook his head, still scrubbing away at the plate. The peacefulness of the chore was quickly fading.

"No," he said eventually. The word felt heavy on his tongue, but he knew it was the truth. "I don't . . . I don't think I can. Everything from before . . ." He searched for the words to explain how he felt when he thought of Jeb, of the life the high minister had snatched away. "Things are too different now. I'm too different. I don't think I'd be good for him."

Finch was silent for a long time after that, leading Gloucester to wish he'd just kept his mouth shut. He'd never been the best conversationalist, but after all those months of solitude, he fretted he'd lost what little skill he possessed.

"Sorry," he blurted out, at the same time Finch said exactly the same thing. Turning from the sink with dripping hands, Gloucester blinked in surprise at the other man, then huffed a laugh. Finch's grin was lopsided but amused.

"Maybe neither of us should be," Finch said, swirling an idle fingertip over the smooth surface of the counter.

"Maybe not."

The silence that rose up between them felt more comfortable this time. Gloucester finished the dishes and wiped down the counter with the wash cloth, before setting it aside and drying his hands on a towel. His mind, ever turning like clockwork, was mulling over something that had been bothering him since their group discussion earlier that morning. He came to stand on the opposite side of the island from Finch and regarded him seriously.

"Can I ask you something?"

"He asks," said Finch, humming with amusement. He turned his gaze away from the kitchen window to meet Gloucester's eyes. Outside, hummingbirds flitted past the glass, buzzing to and fro amidst the flowers of Antimony's garden. "But go ahead, ask away."

"If you caught the Gambler, how do you not know exactly where he's being kept? There must be some . . . some magic or something that keeps him from escaping. Wouldn't you have been involved in setting that up?" Gloucester was careful to keep any semblance of accusation out of his voice, coloring it only with curiosity. He wasn't sure he would be able to tell if Finch was lying, but he didn't want him thinking he was being doubted.

Luckily, Finch didn't seem offended by the questioning of his story. He shrugged his eyebrows and shoulders in unison, the tattoo on his forehead bouncing with the motion. "I'm what you call a magician, same as my dad, it's true. He taught me everything I know about magic." He held up a finger. "But not everything *he* knew. He set up the Gambler's prison, but he was sworn not to ever talk about it. Well, sworn's probably not the word for it. More like 'threatened.'"

"So he knew how the prison worked?"

"Yup." Finch gave a sharp little smile that quickly turned into a sour twist of his mouth. "The wrong one of us died."

Gloucester shook his head. "Don't say that." He wished he had any notion about how to talk to someone whose father had just been murdered. "No one should have died."

Finch wrinkled his nose, but Gloucester saw truer emotion than simple levity in his eyes. "You're not gonna say you're sorry again, are you? There was nothing you could have done. Nothing *I* could have done. I don't blame either of us."

"But you blame someone."

Finch set his mouth in a firm line, staring into the empty space over Gloucester's shoulder. "Doesn't matter."

Gloucester didn't push the issue, carefully choosing to

change the subject instead. "You know a lot about magic, then?" he asked.

His instincts proved to be right, and he watched in relief as Finch's expression relaxed.

"Oh, you know, this and that," he said, making a grand show of his nonchalance. Despite this, there was still the hint of a shadow in his eyes, but Gloucester knew that kind of anger and grief couldn't be turned on and off like a light switch. Expecting him to let go of it so easily and so soon wouldn't only be unrealistic, it would be unfair.

"I didn't even know magic existed until a few days ago," Gloucester admitted. He was trying to be conversational, but he got caught up in the thought. How weird to think that a couple of weeks ago magic had been nothing more to him than something from a fairy tale. Now here he was, chatting over the kitchen counter with a self-proclaimed magician.

"So I gathered," Finch said. "What, have you spent the last six months locked up in a cell or something? So behind on the times."

Gloucester snorted. It felt liberating to laugh about that, even wryly. "Cute."

"I hope so," he heard Finch mutter, but his face was innocent as he got to his feet, like he'd said nothing at all. "If we're gonna go through with this—which, I agree with Zane, is a *terrible* plan—I think I'm gonna get my rest while I can. I don't know about you, but the prospect of sleeping is a hell of a lot easier when the overbearing Thought-God isn't in the house."

Gloucester chuckled in agreement, giving a small wave as the other man left the room.

In his newfound solitude, Gloucester sat and thought. It wasn't exactly a surefire plan, it was true. It meant trusting each other, a ragtag group of strangers who, with the exception of Zane and Antimony, barely knew each other. And more than that, it meant putting faith in Denken. He'd gotten them out of the high minister's clutches in a timely if undignified jailbreak, and he'd stuck around for all the planning and discussions, but Gloucester couldn't shake the feeling that trusting the creature was a bad idea. Denken had manipulated and threatened his way through every situation he'd come up against since Gloucester met him. Since *before* he'd met him. He'd twisted people's thoughts to make them murderers. He'd ruined lives. And now they had no better plan than to put their own lives in his blood-stained hands. Was this Gambler really worth it? People had died because of Denken's actions. He felt like as much of an enemy as the high minister, albeit of a very different sort.

One thing at a time. Better to face one enemy with a plan than two on the fly. If they didn't save the Gambler, they would sacrifice this strange truce they'd forged with Denken. Without which, they would lose the advantage of his powers and maybe even end up having to go against him. Not a pleasant thought. Gloucester had little hope of dealing with all of this if it was just him and Zane.

And Finch, perhaps. He was another one Gloucester wasn't sure he ought to be trusting. What were his true motivations in all this? He'd just lost his father, a man killed in an explosion that only took place because of Denken's meddling. If Gloucester were in Finch's place, he would have revenge on his mind.

So who did that leave to trust? Antimony, he supposed. Yet he still knew next to nothing about her. Her motives seemed strictly in the interests of the Gambler's welfare, with no particular interest shown in anything related to the high minister himself. Whether that made her more trustworthy or less was difficult to say. She'd helped them, though, and housed them. This was certainly a kindness that ought not go overlooked.

Plus, Zane trusted her. Which counted for a lot because Gloucester knew that, whether or not it was wise, he trusted Zane. That was an undeniable fact, one against which his common sense raged. *Don't trust anyone,* he told himself over and over. *No one but myself.*

And certainly not someone he'd only known for a handful of

days, who claimed to be helping him out of nothing more than the kindness of her own heart. He ought to be scoffing at that, not buying into it.

Trust no one.

Yet the fact remained. He trusted her. More than that, part of him really *wanted* to trust her. Part of him cherished her friendship, new as it was. She believed him. She listened.

So what did he have, then? One sure ally, a maybe, and two wild cards. Not exactly the elite force he'd choose to take on an enemy like the high minister in his own house. And if the minister had employed magic to imprison the Gambler, who knew what else he might have up his sleeve?

What choice did they have, though? He hated to admit even to himself that the answer was *none*. No good choices, at least. He knew he'd even lost the chance to run. Denken would ensure neither he nor Finch made it far if they ran from saving his brother.

Hope for the best. He leaned against the countertop. The clean dishes drying in the rack shone in the sunlight from the window, the last vestiges of soap bubbles sparkling in the sink. *Hope for the best and prepare for the worst.*

Chapter 21

The High Minister's Cathedral

A warm wind swirled through the streets of Frettchen, chasing leaves and the occasional bit of trash along roads and sidewalks. Its invisible fingers spread down every path and avenue, rustling newspapers in stands and tousling pedestrians' hair. It carried with it the promise of warm months to come. Summers were hot in Frettchen, the snows of winter a distant memory as the air grew dry and dust filled the streets and parks. Springtime was more restrained, the temperatures reasonable and frequent rains keeping the trees green and lush. For now, the city rejoiced in this pleasant intermediate stage.

Gloucester climbed out of Antimony's car onto the sun-warmed sidewalk. After a day of hasty preparations, they now stood before the wide stone steps of All Saints Shrine on the corner of Westmoreland Street and Park Avenue. He paused for a moment to shrug into a plain black suit jacket over his pristine white shirt. The outfit was simple, but he felt odd to be wearing it again after everything that had happened. For so long, the security agent uniform was a mark of his work, but now it just felt like a costume. Which he supposed it was.

Odder still was seeing his companions in matching outfits. Somehow it was completely unsurprising that Denken pulled off the uncharacteristically sober look with breezy confidence. He fell into step beside Gloucester, hands in his pockets and head tilted back to enjoy the sunshine on his face. On his other side, Antimony looked even more enigmatic than usual, her eyes hidden behind dark sunglasses that gave the impression she was silently judging everything around her.

Finch and Zane walked on Antimony's other side. Finch's hair seemed redder than ever in contrast with the stark black and white of the suit, his freckles and tattoo standing out against his pale skin. He, too, looked at ease, though something guarded in his eyes made his gaze as unreadable as Antimony's, even without the aid of dark sunglasses.

Zane, meanwhile, just looked uncomfortable.

"I can't believe this," she said out of the corner of her mouth, tugging at the sleeves of her jacket. "I can't believe the plan is 'just walk straight in.' This is a *terrible* idea."

"Calm down," Denken told her cheerfully. The request wasn't overtly demanding, yet it halted Zane's nervous complaints in their tracks. Glancing at her, Gloucester guessed from her indignant expression that she hadn't actually intended to stop talking, but had rather fallen prey to the demigod's hard-to-resist charms. Annoyance sparked through him, and he flashed a warning look at Denken.

"Stop it," he said. Denken smirked but didn't argue, shrugging as if nothing had happened.

The church that people called the High Minister's Cathedral shone in the sunlight ahead. Built of white stone, it stood immaculate and beautiful among the newer buildings surrounding it, a remnant of a different time. Its spires, though indeed shorter than those of Frettchen's Old Cathedral, still reached majestically skyward. The bells in the tallest tower rang twice a day, at midnight and noon. Gloucester remembered the first time he'd heard the sound up close, from within the walls and not just from a distance as it rang out across the city. Standing guard for the high minister as he tended his flock, Gloucester had jumped when the bells began to toll, rich and full, echoing through the halls of the church and filling the nave with their call. He remembered feeling the vibrations in his chest and finding himself strangely moved, despite not sharing the faith of those who prayed there.

He'd liked those shifts at the church. Not for the sermons his employer gave, full of charisma and passion, but for the beauty of the place itself. He liked the echo of his footsteps on marble and the way the air seemed still and frozen in time, light from the stained glass windows shining with dust motes.

A beautiful place with darkness at its heart. Somewhere in that church hid the Gambler's prison, sealed with magic and guarded by who knew what else.

Nothing is ever what it seems. The last week had certainly taught him that.

In many respects, Zane made a very good point. They were headed into enemy territory, an enemy who would surely be expecting them. And they were *just walking right in.* It really did feel foolhardy. Doomed, even.

But Denken had said "Trust me," and it was difficult not to. So they'd agreed with vague nods, then felt the worry slowly build back up until here they were now, wondering just what the hell they were thinking, doing what they were about to do.

"We're gonna be the best dressed prisoners ever," Zane grumbled, her eyes flickering in Denken's direction.

"Or the best dressed corpses," said Finch. Both Zane and Gloucester cast him scandalized looks.

"Yeah, thanks for that." Zane tugged still more nervously on her sleeves.

"You're sure they won't see us?" Gloucester asked Denken,

raising his voice just enough to let his companions know he didn't have the patience for their bickering.

"Oh, they'll see us," Denken said. "Handsome bunch that we are. But they won't think anything of it. Just another few of you security people, that's all. And if they try to think back on our faces, they'll find themselves a bit fuzzy on the details. It's easier to work with props," he added, adjusting his lapels with careless grace. "Takes less concentration to work the illusion."

Gloucester held in a sigh. "As long as it works."

At least it was a Saturday, when the church would be less crowded. It was rarely empty, unfortunately, but they wouldn't have to sneak past a packed service.

The sooner this is over, the better.

"Of course it'll work," Denken said, exuding such confidence that it was suffocatingly difficult to believe anything else.

"I'm going to have the worst headache by the end of this," Zane muttered.

They all paused at the top of the steps, looking up almost in unison at the building's intricate facade. Besides the main double doors in front of them, two smaller entrances were located some three meters away on either side, closer to the corner buttresses that rose up in support of the tall structure. Unlike the Old Cathedral, there were no flying buttresses to grant the church greater height and larger windows, but the architecture was still impressive. Its stained glass looked dark and colorless, but Gloucester knew that, from within, each window was vibrant and detailed, telling the city's history in pictures and light.

From the outside, its stonework displayed the greatest beauty. Some long-forgotten artist had carved high relief depictions of the Holy Order along the walls, the revered saints after whom All Saints Shrine had been named. Followers of the church worshipped them almost as devoutly as the God who had bestowed His grace upon them. Their many faces stared down at all who entered, features worn from centuries of rain and sand and wind. Over their weathered heads, carvings of vines and flowers interlaced, the great stone bricks textured with their design. Gloucester had always preferred the carved plants to the stone people, whose unblinking gazes he avoided as he stepped away from the main doors and toward the smaller, less impressive entrance on the right.

"Where are you going?" Antimony asked. Gloucester glanced back at her and the others, all of whom were staring at him.

"Security staff doesn't use the main doors," he explained. "That's just for people coming to pray or who have business with the high minister."

"I'd say we qualify for the latter," Denken said, laughing lightly. "But I see your point. I concede to the expert." He gave Gloucester a mock bow, then followed him to the smaller door. The other three trailed in his wake like tall, well-dressed ducklings.

The door swung open silently, its hinges well-oiled. Gloucester led the way inside, expecting a trap to befall them at any moment. Under normal circumstances, the high minister often visited the church on Saturdays to meet with other priests or coordinate with the religious community. Was he still operating under lockdown? It seemed unlikely that he would have resumed his normal schedule. But what if he was waiting for them? Did he know they would be coming here? He supposed it depended on whether the minister knew Finch had overheard about the place. Even if he didn't, it seemed likely he would take precautions anyway.

Yet no alarms sounded upon their entrance. No guards surrounded them, and no one was shouting for their arrest. Though Gloucester allowed himself to breathe again, his whole body still felt taut, like a string pulled tight on an instrument.

The inside of the church was quiet. The vaulted ceiling looked down on them, carved with more faces that stared at the group with cold eyes, as if they saw past their disguises and knew they were here for trouble.

It was as he remembered it: the same ceiling, the same

windows, the same candles burning, filling the air with a hint of scented wax. Even the parishioners seemed familiar, though more so in the way they moved through the nave and pews with quiet respect than any faces in particular.

Gloucester wondered what he and his companions looked like to them. He really wasn't sure how Denken's trick was supposed to work. Did they appear unlike themselves in the eyes of anyone who glanced their way? Or was it a more subtle illusion, where they still looked like themselves, but Denken got into their onlookers' heads to convince them they were supposed to be there?

He didn't know. What *was* clear was that no one felt alarmed by their arrival. One or two people in the pews looked over at them, but they soon returned to their business, apparently not seeing anything amiss.

"Where to now?" whispered Zane. "I've never been here before. Where d'you think he'd keep the Gambler? Are there, I dunno, crypts or something?"

"There's a basement, but I don't think it's extensive enough to call 'crypts.' Plus, no dead people, as far as I know. Just utilities and the vault," Gloucester muttered back.

"Let's start there," Finch said. "Good a place as any. His Lordship would want him where no one could stumble upon him by accident, so we're looking for someplace off-limits to his flock."

"No one's allowed in the basement except the high minister and his priests," Gloucester confirmed. "Even we . . . Even the security agents are only allowed down there if they're accompanying an official with permission."

It did make the most sense. The basement was quiet, secluded, and restricted: the ideal place to keep a secret prisoner.

They made their way toward the far end of the nave, led by Gloucester. He'd only been in the basement once before, when the high minister had business in the vault, but he remembered clearly how to get down there.

Halfway toward the altar, an old wooden door was set into the stone wall, discreet in color and decoration. It wasn't a door designed to draw attention, but rather the kind intended to blend into the background, maintaining its purpose without getting in the way of the decor. Directly across the nave from this door, its twin led to some small rooms for the priests to use, but the basement door stood for the most part ignored. It was opened only once or twice a week, for the priests to check on the furnace or, more rarely still, to access the vault. Once, this had been where the high minister kept donations made to the church. Since rising to greater power as lord of the city-state, he'd relocated much of the riches to his mansion, something Gloucester suspected his religious followers might not be very pleased to discover.

As they reached it, Gloucester and the others slowed their steps, eyeing the door.

"If I were holding a powerful supernatural creature prisoner for a prolonged time, I'd put some protections in place," Finch said with false lightness. "Be on the lookout for anything amiss. If our illustrious leader wants to go first?" He gestured at Denken. From the smile playing on his lips, it seemed meant to be taken as lighthearted teasing, but the warmth didn't reach Finch's eyes.

Denken shook his head, grinning back at the magician. Finch's chilly smile had nothing on Denken's, whose dauntingly sharp teeth made any competition a bit uneven. "I'll be right behind you. Don't be scared, Cassus."

It was strange to hear Finch called by his first name, and judging from the look on his face, the familiarity was unwelcome. Finch spun away. Gloucester, standing beside him, saw that his mouth was set in a grim line, eyes narrowed.

Finch squared his shoulders and raised a hand toward the door. He didn't reach for the handle, however, instead holding his arm straight out in front of him, palm outward and fingers splayed. The inch of empty air between his hand and the door thrummed with energy. A low hum, in tune with the vibration, emitted from Finch's lips. No words were discernible, but the hairs on the back of Gloucester's neck stood on end, and he knew this was magic. And to think, he'd once believed magic a thing of fantasy.

What did it feel like, he wondered, to have power literally at your fingertips? Did it drain you, wear you out like energy draining out of a battery? Or was it electricity in your blood, fire that burned through you, making you stronger? Was it frightening? Addictive?

Whatever it was, a moment later it was gone. The humming stopped, and with it the buzzing of power. Finch dropped his hand back to his side and shook his head. "There's no trap or ward. Not my father's magic or anyone else's. If this door's protected, it isn't with spells." After a moment's pause, he widened his eyes expectantly. "What, no applause? No thank yous? No proclamations of adoration? That wasn't as easy as it looked, you know."

Zane scoffed, Denken gave a very ungodly snort, and Antimony smiled wryly and tapped her hands together in a tiny, silent round of applause. Gloucester, for his part, offered what he meant to be a flat, disapproving stare, but his nerves were thrumming as much as Finch's spell, running his emotions ragged, and some unbidden amusement leaked through, granting him a tiny smile as he reached past Finch to pull on the door.

Cold air washed over them, but it brought nothing more than dust motes with it. Still no alarm echoed through the church halls. No guards ran toward them up the staircase. All that greeted them was chilly air, dust, and darkness.

"Come on," Gloucester said, leading the way again. He tried to convince himself that the feeling hanging over them as they stepped through the doorway was one of luck and not foreboding.

As they descended into the gloom, he wished he'd thought

to bring a flashlight, but soon he found it wouldn't have been necessary; the light from the nave followed them down the stairs just enough to illuminate a light switch on the wall at the bottom. Gloucester's hand hovered over it, and after only a brief pause, he turned it on. Any enemies who might be lurking in the dark would've already seen them anyway.

Light flooded the basement. Not a bright light, but the dim yellow was still an abrupt contrast to the darkness. They stood blinking for a moment as they waited for their eyes to adjust.

They weren't in a room, but rather a corridor lined in rough-hewn walls and flagstone floors. This would be the oldest part of the church, its air quiet and heavy with history.

"Keep your eyes peeled for anything that seems amiss," Antimony whispered. Gloucester looked over his shoulder to find her tucking her sunglasses into her jacket pocket. He nodded his understanding.

Antimony opting to come with them had surprised him. She'd struck him as the type who dealt in information, not action. Yet here she was, expression unreadable but certainly not fearful. Short of Denken, she appeared to be the least fazed, inspecting the basement with something more akin to curiosity than worry. It made him wonder what was going on inside her head. This question stirred quite often when he looked at other people, always had. He spent so much of his life watching, thinking, asking questions, yet he'd never figured out if it was comforting or intimidating to remember that everyone else was doing it too. Behind every pair of eyes was a mind staring back out at him.

Whatever Antimony's mind was thinking, Gloucester had seen fire in her eyes when she spoke of saving the Gambler, and he knew simple curiosity wasn't what had brought her here.

Up ahead, the hallway came to an apparent end. They moved down it anyway, pausing at doors to edge them open and peek inside at deserted rooms filled with unused furniture, the furnace, and cobwebs. When they reached the wall at the end of the corridor, they discovered the dead end was in fact nothing of the sort. Instead, their corridor met one that ran perpendicular, disappearing into shadows in either direction. Though the stone bricks of the walls were ancient, little in the way of dust coated them. This was not some long-forgotten catacomb.

"How far do you think it goes?" Zane asked in a hushed voice.

Finch leaned past the rest of them, his shoulder brushing Gloucester's in a way that seemed intentional as he peered down the new hallway, first one way and then the other. "Hard to say. Old place like this, could be like an iceberg. What's above's only the tip." He nodded upward in indication of the church a floor above their heads. "Now, let's see . . ."

He shrugged off his jacket and tossed it aside, then pushed his sleeves to his elbows. The hint of another tattoo peeked out from under the fabric on his left arm, trailing lines that looked like the ends of tentacles curling down around his elbow. Finch stepped forward into the intersection of the two corridors. Again he held his hand aloft, palm outward. He stood very still, only the faint quiver of his outstretched arm ruining what would otherwise have been a very good impression of a statue. No hum left his lips this time, but the vibration of a spell rose through the air, buzzing in Gloucester's ears. The spell up in the nave had been steady, like the flow of electricity. This one was different, a pulse whispering through it, as if the magic had a heartbeat.

"Someone went that way. Recently," Finch said, his hand falling back to his side. He nodded down the path to the left.

"A guard?" asked Gloucester. As soon as the question left his lips, he scolded himself. How was Finch supposed to know that, even with a handy spell? It seemed like some sort of magical echolocation more than anything.

Which just went to show how little he knew of such things. He'd expected another patronizing stare from Finch, but instead the magician shook his head.

"If they are, something's dead wrong. Their emotions are

running hotter than a summer in the South Cities. Fear and anger, and plenty of both."

Gloucester stared into the curtain of darkness that hung before them, concealing the path. Fear and anger didn't sound much like the high minister. Anger maybe, but fear? The lord of the city-state surely got scared sometimes, but it was hard to picture him out of control of any of his emotions. Even his anger tended to run cold rather than hot, all ice and terrible calm. If it was him down there, then something was seriously wrong.

"Could it be the Gambler?" he said hopefully, lowering his voice. They weren't alone down here.

He was met with the exact same reaction four times over. Antimony, Zane, Finch, and Denken all shook their heads.

"Trust me," Antimony said. "If anger and fear were coming off the Gambler enough to be picked up by a location spell, there'd be a hell of a lot more fear floating about. And very little of it would be his."

Beside her, Denken smirked.

"The question then is, who is it?" Zane asked. Like Gloucester, she was staring down the dark hallway, her nerves obvious as she picked at the hem of her sleeve and worried at her lip. Gloucester knew how she felt, his own trepidation clawing at the shield of his training. It beat in time with his heart and filled his lungs with every breath. He'd long ago learned to push it away, though, to lock it behind walls in his mind, always there but under control.

He thought unexpectedly of something his mother once said to him, long before he'd ever entered into any training program:

"*No one's afraid of the dark, Mikalai,*" she'd said, her hand on his then-tiny shoulder. She was speaking in Nordish, as she always did with him, the language more fluid and musical than the Frettchennian he spoke with his father. "*We're afraid of what might be waiting in it. What we can't see. Fear of the unknown. If you can face that fear, if you can turn on the light, you just might find that there's nothing there to fear at all.*"

"*But what if there is, Mama?*" he asked, staring up into her round face. Her eyes, the same dark shade as his own, were sympathetic. "*What if there's a monster?*"

"*Then you face it,*" she said simply. "*Face it and find out that you're braver than you thought.*"

Now, as he stood between Finch and Zane, staring into the dark, he wondered: Was there a monster down that pathway? Was he brave enough to face it?

He'd just have to find out the answer to both questions himself. Taking as surreptitious a deep breath as he could, he stepped forward in the direction of the mysterious presence.

"Come on," he said. "Let's go say hello."

Chapter 22

In the Basement

For several long minutes that stretched into hours in Gloucester's mind, there was nothing but the quiet sound of their footsteps as the group made their way down the dark corridor. Antimony had been quick to locate another light switch, but the bulbs that came to life when she flicked it on were few and far between, leaving large pools of inky shadows spotting their path. The people who came down here on a regular basis must have brought flashlights or lamps with them.

They passed a few rooms, but none of them, locked or otherwise, contained any sign of the Gambler. The locks were mundane in their mechanisms and no obstacle to Denken's eerie ability to move past boundaries that ought to have been solid, nor to Finch's whispered spells, but every opened door revealed only dark, empty rooms. Even the vault, when they reached it, was no trouble to get into, and it too contained only disappointment. It was stripped nearly bare, its wealth now almost entirely stowed away at the high minister's mansion. And still no hint of a kidnapped god.

Nor was there any sign of the person Finch had sensed through his spell. No echo of footsteps or whisper of movement in the dark. Gloucester kept expecting whoever it was to burst out at them from each new patch of shadows they approached, yet again and again, they found nothing but more empty corridor. He wasn't sure if he was relieved or disappointed.

Every now and then, Finch would lift his hand out in front of him, murmuring under his breath. So quiet were his words that Gloucester couldn't tell if he was speaking in Frettchennian or not. Whatever he sensed, if he sensed anything at all, he didn't share it with the rest of them. Until:

"I think we're being had."

The other four stopped in their tracks and stared over at the magician, each with varying degrees of concern. Though Finch's red hair looked dark in the shadows, his eyes were bright as ever. Further down the corridor was another pool of light, but between there and where they stood, it was as if the world simply ceased to be, fading into a void of black. Gloucester schooled his features into a stoic expression to conceal his misgivings.

"Because we're going in a circle?" he said.

Indeed, they'd made two turns since setting off down the second hallway, both times to the left. Two more like that and they'd end up right back where they started.

"If the basement's just a big loop, what's their game?" Finch grumbled.

"They could be leading us into a trap." Antimony squinted through clear spectacles that had taken the place of her sunglasses, as if she might spot the trap being laid out ahead of them.

"Or to the slaughter," added Denken, cheerfully ignoring Gloucester's and Zane's unimpressed glowers.

"How comforting," Zane said.

"So, what, we turn back?" Even as Gloucester made the

suggestion, he knew that none of them, himself included, would agree to it. They'd come too far.

"Mayhaps just be on our guard," Finch replied. "Be ready for anything."

Yet as they progressed deeper into the gloomy passage, the way ahead remained deserted. Tense apprehension buzzed in Gloucester's ears like flies, his eyes straining for any sign of lurking danger. Were they being led astray?

After several long minutes, Gloucester counting the seconds by the loud beat of his heart, they came upon another branch in the path. The corridor continued along straight ahead of them, but a second corridor peeled away from it, opening to the left. They all stopped, staring in nervous silence down its length as far as they could see. It wasn't very far at all. The corridor was narrower than the one they stood in, its walls and floor vanishing into the black, with no lights to illuminate where it might lead. Looking at it, Gloucester thought it must be a mirror layout to the path they'd initially followed from the bottom of the stairs. The other one had led up to the main floor of the church, so where might this one take them?

"Is there anyone down there?" he asked Finch. Before the magician could raise his hand to check with another of his spells, Denken answered instead.

"Nope," he said brightly, though even in the imperfect lighting Gloucester could see the good cheer no longer reached his eyes. "Not unless they have no thoughts at all. And even an idiot or a fool has thoughts. There's no escaping your own mind."

Gloucester looked back down the new corridor, nodding in acceptance of this explanation. Then something caught his eye and he froze. "Someone *was* here," he whispered, pointing down at the floor. The off-shooting pathway was clearly less used than their current one; a thick layer of dust coated the flagstones. And in that dust trailed a path of footprints.

Gloucester sank into a crouch. "Small feet." His tone was

clipped, professional, as he fell back on his training to ignore the renewed stirrings of trepidation. "What size are your feet, Zane? Antimony?"

He half-expected a snarky response, especially from Zane. However, neither woman argued the question.

"Nine," said Zane.

"Eight and a half," said Antimony.

"These don't look bigger than a lady's eight," Gloucester estimated, leaning forward to measure the nearest footprint against the length of his forearm. "Probably a woman." A discomfiting notion took form in his mind as he stared down at the tracks. "These footprints go in *and* out. She went down there and then came back out. We must have missed her by minutes."

The dusty passage stretched out before him, sinking into shadowy mystery. He was beginning to suspect what might be down there. He just hoped he was wrong.

He straightened up again and started down the new path. "Come on."

"No one's down there," Denken said. Gloucester wasn't sure if the words were a protest or a warning. They somehow sounded like both. "Not the Gambler, not the high minister. I don't care about some random woman. If the Gambler's not down there, we move on."

A wave of fierce annoyance swept through Gloucester at the words "*I don't care about some random woman.*" Of course he didn't. She was only a human, viewed at best as nothing more than a cog in his machinations, only as valuable as she was useful. If she was who Gloucester suspected, she'd already been used by Denken. When she'd failed him, he moved on, abandoning her with a mind twisted by magic and a trail of destruction in her wake.

The shadows grew deeper as Gloucester strayed from the dim lights lining the main corridor. His footsteps were muffled by the dust, which shifted and stirred beneath the soles of his shoes, erasing the footprints he was following.

"Stop." Denken didn't shout, but the word was impossible to ignore. Gloucester's feet faltered, and he nearly fell as he stumbled.

"No," he ground out. "Something's wrong."

"A lot's wrong," Denken said. "We're here to right the wrong against my brother. Now come here."

Gloucester's feet started to turn. He braced a hand against the cold stone of the wall, rough beneath his fingers and palm. He shook his head jerkily, as if the voice overpowering his thoughts could be shaken off like a bothersome insect.

"Denken, enough." Antimony was nearly drowned out in Gloucester's ears, but he heard the sharpness in her words. "Leave him alone."

For a moment longer, Gloucester's own mind fought against him. He *wanted* to turn around, to stand by Denken's side, obedient. Or rather, he *thought* he wanted that. Another corner of his mind raged against it. Something was at the end of this passageway, *he knew it*. They couldn't just walk away from that. Conflicting thoughts, some his own and others imposters, warred a pitched battle behind his eyes. Vestiges of the dire headache that nearly drove him to murder stirred at the edges of his skull, closing in—

And then Denken relinquished his hold, and Gloucester reeled in the absence of the invisible grip on his thoughts. He was glad for his steadying hand against the wall; it was the only thing keeping him upright as his head spun, seemingly in competition with his stomach for who was the better acrobat.

"We're wasting time," Denken said, his voice no longer layered in power. Instead it was chilly and flat.

Gloucester gasped for breath, still struggling to regain his bearings. He shook his head. "I don't think so. Someone was down here, and she was here for a reason." He swept a pointed gaze over at the others, though the look was somewhat marred by the way he swayed on the spot as he pushed himself to stand straight. "Can you think of anyone, any woman, who might have a reason to be lurking around, afraid and angry, where the high minister is often found to be?"

Antimony nodded somberly. "Yvette Jacoby. Bomber extraordinaire."

"Well, then," Denken said. "Best find the Gambler as soon as we can, shouldn't we?"

"This church is full of innocent people," said Gloucester. "If there's—"

"*Fine.*" Denken's snarl was so ferocious that Gloucester flinched back despite the meters of space between them. "Go and have a look. But waste more than two minutes of my time, of my brother's time, and I'll have you screaming."

A shiver ran down Gloucester's spine, and like an animal scenting danger in the air, his instincts urged him to run.

No more running.

With an uneven nod, he turned on his heel and strode down the dark corridor. His hand still trailed over the bricks of the wall as he walked, his fingertips seeking a light switch. It wouldn't do much good to reach the end of the passage and whatever waited for him there, only to be unable to see anything.

Footsteps hurried behind him, and for a panicked moment he thought Denken had changed his mind and was in pursuit to drag him back to the others. His heart stuttered in his chest as he looked over his shoulder.

In time to see Zane and Finch go from silhouettes to clear-featured as several flickering lamps flared to life and lit up the corridor.

"I found the switch." Zane pointed at the wall beside her with forced good cheer. "It was on the other wall from you."

"You two don't have to come," Gloucester said. He didn't want anyone else to risk Denken's wrath. Any more than they already were, at least.

For having only met a short while ago, Zane and Finch did an admirably synchronized shrug.

"I think you're right," Zane said. "I want to help."

"And I keep remembering that you've spent half a year in a windowless room," added Finch. "Don't want you wandering off and getting lost in the big wide world, eh?"

"I'm sure Antimony would come too, but I think it's best she hangs back with Denken. Out of all of us, she has the best chance of keeping him from getting impatient and causing trouble." Zane fell into step beside Gloucester. Finch, longer-legged than either of them, strode a few steps ahead. Gloucester stared at his back for a moment, then slid an appreciative look at Zane.

"Thanks," he said quietly.

"Hey now, I'm just as determined as you are not to get myself or innocent people killed, you know?" Zane smiled back at him, though Gloucester could still see the fear in her eyes. She nodded up at the ceiling. "Far as we know, the most wrong any of those people up there have done is choose the wrong church to pray in."

"There's something up ahead," Finch called over his shoulder. "I see a light. Not the proverbial kind at the end of a tunnel either. A little blinky one."

Gloucester's heart sank. He'd wanted to be wrong. He would have been able to live with Denken's annoyance if only it meant he was mistaken.

But he wasn't. They were coming to the end of the hallway. Gloucester estimated that the entrance to the basement and the staircase they'd descended were only a few meters ahead of them, on the other side of the dead end wall. That would place them squarely underneath the nave of the church. Not far over their heads, parishioners wandered through the light-filled hall, ignorant of the danger lurking below.

A danger that sat right in front of Gloucester, Zane, and Finch. Set against the base of the wall rested a deceptively small device, an elegant little collection of wires and metal.

Zane made a sound that was both humorless laugh and moan of dismay. "So, who here knows how to disarm a bomb?"

Chapter 23

Tick Tick

It didn't look like a terrible thing. No bigger than a briefcase, it sat innocently against the wall, a small red light on its side flicking on and off like a winking eye.

"I'm no expert," Finch said, "but it definitely looks bomb-like to me. Definitely bomb-ish. We should really be going."

In contrast to his earlier lead, he now stood several meters back behind Zane and Gloucester, and looked like he was keen on putting much more space between himself and the device. Zane looked like she, too, was itching to be elsewhere. Gloucester couldn't blame either of them.

"It has no external timer," he said. "Clever, that. Doesn't give us an indication of how long we have."

"Could be an hour, could be thirty seconds," Zane whispered, as if afraid a raised voice would hasten the impending explosion. "Maybe Finch is right. Maybe we should just run."

"We don't know how powerful it is. It could take out the

whole church. Or maybe it would destroy the entire street. How many people could be in the blast radius?"

"Not us, if we leave now," Finch said. "Come on, you daft bastards! I'm not going to die like this. Not like—" He bit off the sentence before he finished, but Gloucester could guess where it had been heading.

"Go back to the others, Finch," he said, looking over his shoulder to meet the man's eyes. "Find Antimony and Denken and try to get as many people out of the church as you can. I doubt Denken will help you, but Antimony will. You can get out of here. You don't have to risk your life for this."

The bomb called for his attention, each flash of its blinking light in his peripheral vision tightening his chest with worry, but Finch held his gaze for a long moment, and Gloucester couldn't bring himself to look away first. A storm of emotions raged behind Finch's green eyes, impossible to read.

Then, much to Gloucester's surprise, he stepped closer and crouched down beside them. "So what can we do? How do we stop it?"

"It doesn't look booby-trapped," Zane said, eyes nervous but focused as she took a deep breath and leaned closer to inspect the device herself.

"Chances are Jacoby didn't expect anyone to find it in time. Or maybe she just didn't know how to rig it with one." Gloucester squinted at Zane. "How do *you* know, though?"

"Bombs are all about small and tinker-y parts. I like small and tinker-y parts." She caught the look on his face and huffed. "It's not like I've built any in my basement. I've just studied them a bit, okay? We don't have time for this."

She was right. Each passing second was another one they couldn't spare. Gloucester pushed aside his incredulity and nodded.

"I trained in bomb defusing, but it's been a while," he said.

They both crouched over the bomb, muttering to each other and trying not to acknowledge the fact that each wink of the light might be the last one before it blew.

"As far as I can tell, there's nothing stopping us from removing this panel and—Ah! Look!" Zane pulled a compact case out of her pocket, which contained a neat assortment of small screwdrivers. Gloucester didn't waste time asking her about it, watching with bated breath as she pried open one panel of the device's metal siding to reveal a little screen displaying digital numbers. An internal count-down clock. Just under four minutes remained. Gloucester's stomach clenched as Zane said, "At least now we know how much time we have."

Not a lot.

"Not enough to get away," said Finch, echoing Gloucester's thoughts. "Is it enough to stop it?"

Grim-faced, Gloucester replied, "It'll have to be."

"Gloucester, look." Zane pulled his attention back to the task at hand. "This wire display is familiar. Do you know it? I'm thinking if she didn't rig for booby-traps, she may have forgone anything to prevent tampering, but if I'm wrong . . ."

"Don't be wrong." Gloucester regarded the bundle of wiring within the exposed side of the bomb and pointed out a pair of curling wires. "We can rule out these two. Cutting them would either do nothing to stop it or nix the countdown and blow the damned thing up now. But these three here, provided there's no trick . . ."

"I think you're right," Zane agreed. Gloucester could hear the shaking of her voice. She was terrified. He couldn't bring himself to tell her that he was too.

"Do you have anything to cut them with?" he asked instead, nodding at the mini tool kit. "Denken hasn't let me touch anything with an edge since he pulled us from the high minister's custody."

Zane shook her head. "I don't have anything better than a screwdriver right now. I grabbed a set from Antimony's, just to have *something*. I usually have a pocketknife, but those security agents took it along with everything else I had in my pockets."

The timer read two minutes. Gloucester cast about for something, *anything*, that would work. "The flathead screwdriver, maybe," he said, sweat prickling his brow. "Or a sharp bit of stone?"

One minute, thirty seconds.

"Here."

He couldn't help but flinch as something small and metallic was held out to him. It was a knife, leather-sheathed with a delicately carved bone handle. Gloucester blinked at it, then looked up at Finch.

"Where in the world—"

"I'm not so easily disarmed," Finch said. The smug twinkling in his eye was reminiscent of his father. "Even by mad demigods with a grudge."

The rather intriguing question of where he'd been keeping the blade whispered in Gloucester's mind, but the exposed timer on the bomb read one minute and fifteen seconds, and he knew now wasn't the time.

"Thanks." He took the knife and spared Finch a hurried smile before turning back to Zane and the bomb. If he was right—*gods, he hoped he was*—then cutting through those wires would be all that was needed. And if he was wrong . . . Well, it wasn't like any of them would live to know, right? Knife in hand, he tugged as gently as he could on the wires, so that he would be able to get the blade behind them to sever—

"Wait!"

Finch's urgent hiss made his heart jump into his throat, and for a moment he thought he might just cough it up. He shot a distinctly less kind look at the other man.

"*What*?"

Unbelievably, Finch was smiling. It was an odd expression, crooked and grim, but with an edge of mischief that had Gloucester wondering if he'd somehow lost his senses. A suspicion that only grew stronger when Finch said, "This is the part with a kiss."

Gloucester stared. "What?" he asked, this time with less exasperation and more honest confusion in the question.

Finch pointed at the bomb. One minute left. "In films. In stories. This is the part where there's a kiss." He spoke very quickly. "Everything on the line, now or never, no time to waste, all sealed in that last-minute kiss."

Gloucester exchanged an incredulous look with Zane.

"There is a *bomb*," she said, pointing at it as well. "Now is *not* the time."

Gloucester passed her Finch's knife. "We're a bit busy here, Finch," he said. Forty-five seconds. Zane worked at getting the blade of the knife behind the bundle of wires, her fingers nimble and delicate. Delicate, but quick. Finch was right about one thing: there was no time to waste.

"These might be your last moments," Finch said quietly. Against his better judgment, Gloucester looked back at him. Finch still wore his smile, but something else shone in his eyes, an emotion hard to place. "Come on. One kiss to do the thing right."

Thirty seconds.

"Oh, for pity's sake," growled Gloucester. "Here, for your bloody cliché." Rising to his feet, he looked down at Zane, then over at Finch. In two paces, he closed the distance between them. A silent plea that he wasn't wrong, along with everything else he was hoping in that moment, and then his lips were pressed against Finch's, the kiss fierce with the commotion of fear and adrenaline.

Finch's hands gripped Gloucester's arms, and for an instant he expected to be shoved back, thought he'd been mistaken, that he was squandering precious seconds for nothing at all—

Then the hands pulled him closer—embracing, not balking. Finch's mouth moved against his lips, returning the kiss with the same intensity. For a heartbeat, the world was narrow, two people and shared breath. No bomb, no plots, no magic or mayhem.

Zane cleared her throat. "Did it," she said loudly.

Gloucester broke away from the kiss. "What?" He wished he could think of something more intelligent to say, if he was destined to sound like a broken record.

Zane pointed at the bomb. Cut wires spilled from its dismantled side like an automaton's innards, and no more lights blinked, the screen that had been counting down the seconds now dark. "Yay," she said, waving her hands in a subdued gesture of celebration.

"Oh . . . er . . . thanks . . . er . . . sorry," stammered Gloucester, his face hot. Behind him, he heard something that sounded infuriatingly like a chuckle from Finch. When he flashed an indignant look the other man's way, however, his face betrayed nothing more than open relief. Gloucester chewed on his lip, feeling like a complete idiot. "You didn't have to—"

"I sort of did," Zane said, cutting off his contrite words. She laid a hand on his arm as she rose to her feet, and her smile, though shaky, was surprisingly soft. "You pointed out what to do. It was only a matter of me cutting the wires."

"I wasn't sure," Gloucester admitted. "I shouldn't have . . . I should have focused on the bomb."

Zane pulled back her foot to kick the disarmed device, then seemed to think better of it and meekly nudged it with her toe instead. "Eh, seems you were right, so I think we're probably fine. And anyway, if you had been wrong and I blew us all to smithereens, it's nice to think you two would have died enjoying yourselves."

Gloucester stared down at his feet. He was caught between feeling so mortified that he wondered if the bomb would have been preferable, and thinking about the lingering taste of Finch's kiss on his lips and the crooked smile the man now wore as he leaned back against the wall.

"Well, that was invigorating," Finch said, more animated than Gloucester had heard him since his father's death. "Let's go find us a demigod! Dunno about you two, but I'm feeling like things are looking up."

—

Denken and Antimony were arguing when they caught up with them further down the main passageway. Sharp whispers like the hissing of angry snakes echoed faintly off the surrounding stone, reaching the trio's ears long before they came into view up ahead. Apparently having tired of waiting for their companions to return, Denken and Antimony were striding along in the direction they'd all been headed, heads bent close together as they spoke. It wasn't until Gloucester, Zane, and Finch were almost upon them that their words became discernible beyond mere noise.

" . . . not the way to do it," Antimony was whispering urgently. Despite the uneven light of the far-flung lamps, her cross expression was blatant to Gloucester. "If we did this carefully . . . thought this through—"

"Don't talk to me of thought," Denken growled back. For Antimony he bore no false mask of joviality, his face set in grim determination, a fire burning in his eyes. "Don't you dare accuse me of not *thinking*. This is who I am. This is *what* I am."

Antimony opened her mouth to argue, then caught sight of the others as they approached. "Find anything?" she asked, the anger in her own eyes cooling, though her shoulders were still taut with tension. It was the most agitation Gloucester had yet to see from the stoic scientist.

"Boy, did we," Zane replied with a nervous chuckle. As the minutes ticked by, realization of just how close they'd been to death was probably dawning on his friend. "There was a bomb. I disarmed it."

Gloucester couldn't help but smile at the well-earned pride coloring her tone. Antimony was so surprised that she forgot to look collected and enigmatic.

"You disarmed a bomb?"

"Well, Gloucester and I sort of worked it out together,"

said Zane. "And I cut the wires while he, um . . ." She trailed off, glancing sideways at Gloucester, who wished the shadows surrounding them would literally swallow him whole, and Finch, who looked very pleased with himself. Zane cleared her throat. "We worked it out together," she said again.

Gloucester gave a stilted nod, uncomfortably aware of the knowing smile blossoming across Denken's face. He hurriedly tried to think of anything other than what had transpired down the side passage while the clock counted down its final seconds.

"Nice try," said Denken, the ferocity of moments earlier forgotten. Or at least skillfully hidden away once more.

"Let's move on," Gloucester said, very firmly. "We still have to find the Gambler. We're no closer to that than we were when we came down here."

"Well," said Antimony, "I for one appreciate not being blown up, so I'd say it was a worthwhile detour."

"Yeah, we're all very appreciative of each other," Denken agreed, eyeing Finch and Gloucester with mischievous glee. His mood had shifted so quickly that it felt odd to think they'd interrupted an argument.

"It's looking more and more like the Gambler is somewhere else. The presence Finch sensed must have been the bomber." Gloucester skirted around Antimony and led the way down the corridor in the direction she and Denken had already been heading. The others followed after him.

"It could be that the place is cloaked, wherever it is they're keeping him," Finch suggested. "My father was a master of illusions and cloaking magic. His Lordship would want to hide the Gambler away from any prying eyes. Could be he's down here and we just don't know it."

"So we could have walked right by him already," Zane said, disheartened.

Finch shook his head. "Cloaks and illusions aren't the same. Illusions take more power on the part of the caster. You've gotta maintain the visual magic, even if it's unconsciously. If there was an illusion hiding the Gambler's cage, it would have died . . ." He wavered, then cleared his throat. "It would have died with my father."

"But not the cloaking spell, if there is one?" Gloucester asked, hoping that staying on topic could help them figure things out more quickly, but also perhaps distract Finch from his grief.

"Oh, there definitely is one. I helped set it up. From the inside," he added when Zane looked like she wanted to say something. "I know what the prison looks like from inside its doors, but not its actual location. Considering the amount of magic that went into the place, it could be anywhere. And yeah, the cloak should still be in place. They're not so fragile as illusions. Normally I'd be able to trace a spell I participated in the casting of—you get a feel for your own magic, you see—but cloaking spells are engineered to be extra tricky."

"What does a cloaking spell do?" Gloucester asked. No one else looked confused, which was a stark reminder that he was the only one here with no magical experience. It left him feeling ignorant and childish, though he did his best to hide it. "What does it do that's different from an illusion spell?"

"Illusions are visual," Finch explained, not sounding bothered in the slightest by the questions. Again he seemed like his father, appreciative of the attention he was being given—even if it was only from Gloucester and Zane, while Denken and Antimony passed them to walk a few steps ahead, their attention on the surrounding darkness, not the brief lesson in magic. "They hide things from sight. Another term for them is a glamour. They can change the appearance of things or hide something from view. A room containing an imprisoned demigod, for example. Cloaking spells aren't about seeing, they're about all the other senses and about magic. Like I said, the Gambler could be down here somewhere and my spells wouldn't locate him. Nor would we hear him if he cried out.

"And it doesn't just keep my magic out," he added, shaking his head. "There's more than just a simple cloak on that prison.

There's an enchantment to keep the Gambler's magic *in*. That more than anything was why we were tasked with spelling the place. You've seen what *he's* capable of." He nodded at Denken's back. Gloucester could picture the grin on Denken's face, knowing they were talking about him. "His brother is just as powerful. Just . . . different. We set up the wards to contain him. His magic's caught in that room same as he is, and even then, the spells dampen them to the bare minimum. In there, he doesn't have the influence to do the things Denken can do."

"The Gambler can't do the things I do anyway," Denken called back over his shoulder. "Not that he's ever pretended to want to, boring bastard."

"The Gambler's powerful," Zane said, sounding defensive. Gloucester glanced at her in surprise, before remembering she had met the Gambler before. Out of the odd group he'd gotten tangled up with, she always seemed the most grounded, so it was strange to remind himself that she had been the one to first lead him into the world of magic he'd never realized existed right under his nose.

"I never said he wasn't," Denken replied, turning to face her without ever stopping or even slowing his pace, walking backward with ease. "Just that he's boring. He's forgotten how to have fun. Bloody ironic, considering he spends the most time out of all of us here amongst you humans. Well, out of the three of us, at least."

He turned back around before Gloucester could ask what three he was talking about. They made another left turn, the stone walls offering them no other options. Mapping out their path in his head, Gloucester surmised they were well over halfway through what was indeed looking to be a large underground loop. Every now and then, they came upon a door, but like all the others they'd poked their heads through, the rooms beyond were deserted and filled with mundane things to be expected in a church basement. At this rate, they'd end up right back where they started, and regardless of what Finch said about cloaking spells, Gloucester was doubting more and more that the Gambler was anywhere close by.

He picked up his stride. He couldn't shake the feeling that one of Zane's clocks was hidden in his brain, counting down the time they had left. It was surely only a matter of time before they stumbled upon someone who knew they weren't just another group of security agents, even with Denken's mind magic backing them up. Or what if the high minister planned on moving the Gambler? What if he had a trap in place, an ambush waiting for them? With each step, more questions whispered and the ticking clock grew louder.

Another corner came and went with still no sign of anything out of the ordinary. Zane trailed a hand along the wall as she walked, perhaps in hopes of activating a secret latch or button that would reveal something they couldn't see; alas, her fingertips found nothing but rough stone.

"Waste of time," Denken muttered.

"*Bomb*," Antimony said pointedly in return.

Chapter 24

Fraying Tempers

Finally they saw light ahead, brighter than the lamps staggered along their path. As they drew closer, the source was revealed: it spilled forth from a more evenly lit corridor leading away to their left. The same passage they'd walked along when they first descended into the basement. They were back where they'd started.

Disappointment laid a heavy hand on Gloucester's shoulders, pressing down relentlessly, though he did his best to ignore it.

Easier said than done with Denken around. He spun toward the rest of them. "He's not down here. There had better be somewhere else in this stupid church where he could be, or we've gotten nowhere, and that is *not* acceptable."

"There are plenty of rooms upstairs." Gloucester pretended not to notice the wave of fear that swept through him in the face of the demigod's simmering displeasure. "And if magic's involved . . . they could hide him almost anywhere, right?"

Okay, Gloucester, not exactly stellar comforting skills right there. "We just have to trust that he's still here somewhere. You make it sound like it's quite the setup," he said to Finch. "Even if the high minister is planning on moving the Gambler to be safe, it'll take him a while to get everything moved, right?"

"Right," Finch agreed, rubbing his chin. "Should do. The amount of magic we used on the place, they could be keeping him in a confessional and it'd still look like a castle from the inside. He'd need another magician to dismantle it all, and there aren't that many of us around. Not ones powerful enough to manage that level of spellwork, at least."

"'Course, this is all riding on Red here being right about something he overheard from some nobody guard." Denken gave Finch a snide look. "For all we know, we're searching the wrong place entirely."

"Do you have a better suggestion?" Gloucester retorted, nettled by the description of security agents as "nobody guards." No matter what he thought of the high minister, he'd been on his security team long enough to have respect for his fellow agents. He'd made friends at that job, had seen people risk their lives for their duty without a second thought about their own safety. He was also growing increasingly short-tempered with the demigod. Though, he regretted his nettled tone when Denken gave him a look so cold he could almost feel its touch like frost on his skin.

"No, I don't," Denken said. "Come on." He waved them all forward, ushering them into the better-lit hallway and toward the stairs at the end of it. "We're gonna search this place top to bottom, even if we have to dismantle every brick and beam."

—

After the inconsistent and often dim lighting down in the basement, the sun-filled hall of the church seemed overly bright, making them all squint and blink as they emerged from the door at the top of the stairs. It was a beautiful day outside, and the many stained glass windows cascaded colorful patterns of light across the floor and walls. Dust shimmered in the air like mist, lending to the ethereal feel of the place.

They had little time to appreciate the beauty of their surroundings, however, as Denken scarcely paused to look around before striding purposefully across the nave and throwing open the door on the opposite side from the basement entrance. His companions didn't need to see his face to know the disappointment he felt when the action revealed nothing more than a modest office and one very surprised priest. They could *feel* it, weighing on their minds like a silent lament. Gloucester doubted that Denken had intended for this particular effect of his powers to be known. It was a rare instance of vulnerability, in its own way. Gloucester didn't think he was even aware of exuding the thoughts of wordless anguish creeping into all of their minds. Several pews away, a woman stopped her prayers with a sob, looking confused.

"Where else in this place could they be hiding him?" said Denken, deceptively calm.

After a moment of thought, Gloucester pointed around the corner to their left. "There are private chambers in the north wing. Not as deserted as the basement, but still restricted from the public."

Denken started in the indicated direction. The other four hurried to keep up with him.

"So, um, is anyone else worried about the *bomber* that could still be hanging around?" Zane asked, casting nervous glances around at the seemingly innocent people dotted about the church interior.

It was a good point, one that had amazingly almost fled Gloucester's mind. He was finding it difficult to keep his head on straight as their mission teetered between the narrowly escaped bomb and their search for the Gambler. For so long, he'd had nothing but boredom and four walls to think about. Now the world was overly complicated, filled with magic and mayhem, and a moment of distraction could get him and who knew how many others killed. And yet distractions plagued him. Noise and movement and people all whirled around him, each calling for attention. Even in moments of relative calm, his own thoughts gave him little reprieve, gnawing away at the mysteries he'd been presented like a dog with a bone.

It was Finch who replied to Zane's question, waving a hand through the air in a subtle yet complicated gesture. To an onlooker, it might appear as if he were swatting at an irritating fly, but Gloucester knew he was casting another of his odd, wordless spells.

"If she's here, she's calmed down remarkably," he told them, dropping his hand to his side. "All that fear and anger from before is gone. She might be nearby, but if she's still feeling that, she's not in the building anymore."

"She still feels like that," Gloucester said. "That kind of emotion doesn't just go away. Not in a matter of minutes."

Finch nodded. "I know."

"She's probably out on the lawn, staring at her watch and wondering why this place isn't sky-high right now," said Zane. To Gloucester's surprise, she smiled grimly. "Ha, take that, bomb lady."

"She probably got as far from here as she could, as fast as she could," Gloucester said, sweeping his distracted gaze over their surroundings as they walked. They were attracting more attention now, the eyes of passersby lingering on them as they made their way toward the north end of the church. Whether due to Denken's own distraction making him lose focus on the illusion—or was it a cloaking spell, Gloucester wondered—or the minister's flock being familiar enough with security agents to notice when they were acting oddly, people were beginning to notice them. They needed to hurry.

"Do you think she'll come back?" Zane asked, pulling him out of his fretful thoughts and back into their whispered conversation. "When she realizes the bomb didn't go off?"

"I doubt it," Gloucester said. "If all these bombs are the same person, this Yvette woman, then she seems to be trying something new each time—car bomb, grenade, now one with a timer. She's attacking from a new angle each time, and I think she's getting desperate. The high minister isn't even here today. His schedule has been so out of sorts since the first attack that she probably had no idea how to predict where he would be. This church is easier to access than his mansion, so she likely just took a chance." He grimaced at the thought. What had Jacoby become, if she didn't even care about the collateral damage her rash assassination attempts might cause? "In any case, I can't see her taking the risk to come back here today when she could start working out the details for her next attempt."

"How new of an angle can it be when they're all types of bombs." Finch sneered, his mouth a taut line, his eyes cold. There was no forgetting what he had lost in the warehouse explosion. Yvette Jacoby had better hope she never crossed paths with the young magician again.

"She's dealt with for now, at least," Gloucester said quickly.

"Provided there wasn't a second bomb," muttered Zane. Her worry held none of Finch's snideness; she wasn't being argumentative, simply voicing her thoughts aloud. Gloucester couldn't fault her for that, not when the same concerns whispered in his own mind. "And we all might explode at any moment."

"Probably best not to think about it," said Antimony over her shoulder. Once again, they had fallen behind Antimony and Denken, whose longer strides weren't hindered by distraction. "Nothing we can do about it, except move as quickly as we can."

This last part was said rather pointedly, and the three of them picked up their pace in order to fall into step with her and Denken. The demigod ignored them, his gaze still fixed on the hall ahead.

At the end of the room stood a series of doors, the entrances to the north wing. As they neared them, Gloucester caught the eye of an old woman, who watched them curiously as they passed where she stood watering plants in one of the windows.

"We're starting to attract attention," he whispered to Denken, striding alongside him now.

"Take it as motivation to move faster." After a moment, Denken rolled his eyes and added, "I'll work on it."

Gloucester wasn't sure what this meant, but when he glanced back at the old woman, he saw that, whatever he was doing, it was working. The woman blinked at him in apparent confusion, then an absent expression stole over her face and she looked away, returning her attention to her plants as if she'd noticed nothing amiss at all.

Gloucester turned to Denken, a *thank you* on his lips, then hesitated. What gratitude did he owe him? They were pawns, all of them, in Denken's manipulations as much as the high minister's. "*Thank you for playing your part in the half-baked plan into which I was blackmailed and forced to partake*"?

Again, Gloucester couldn't help but consider how drastically his world had changed since his release. Since his arrest, really. It was easy to get whirled away in the madness. Or, in attempts to prevent that, get so caught up in little details that the big picture became unclear. Little details were easy: was the plan running smoothly, would they get caught, where might the Gambler be hidden? The big picture was what made things confusing: that he was walking side by side with the personification of Thought; that magic existed, and mind control, and different dimensions. It was too much to take in. He wasn't about to let himself thank one of the people responsible for getting him caught up in it all.

"The door on the left leads to the dormitories," he said instead, pointing at the first of the closed doors ahead of them. "The one on the right leads to the tower and the bells. Middle's the high minister's private chambers."

All Saints Shrine was set up for the purpose of not only being the holy leader's house of worship but also his or her home. Were it not for his other position as lord of the city-state, the high minister would live there, as he had prior to the election. Instead, his secular title now allowed him to flout the tradition, living instead at the lord's mansion. Yet the private chambers there in the church were still respected as out of bounds to anyone who had not been given permission to be there. No one went in or out without the high minister's say-so.

Another perfect place to hide a magical prison. And hopefully a more successful place to search.

"Doubtful he'll be in the bell tower, considering it gets used," Antimony said. "Dorms are unlikely too, unless they're abandoned?"

Gloucester shook his head. "The high minister doesn't sleep here, but the friars and some of the minor ministers do. Someone would have noticed something amiss if they were living every day with the Gambler right under their noses, surely? Even with spells to hide him."

"Hard to say," was Finch's unhelpful contribution. He eyed the doors in a thoughtful manner, head tilted to the side, as if a change in perspective might allow him to see through the solid wood.

"The high minister's private chambers are the best bet, though," Gloucester said, nodding at the door straight ahead of them. "Almost no one ever goes in there, and those that do are right in his inner circle. I've guarded this door before, but I've never been inside."

Part of him was curious, wondering if the room would be similar to the minister's quarters in his mansion, or if the man had left nothing personal behind when he took the role and abode of the lord of the city-state.

Would the door open to reveal the Gambler in his prison? Was it too much to hope it would be so easy? Probably. Yet it was the nature of hope to crop up where it had no right to be, steering the heart away from the clear logic of the head.

"I'd suggest we split up to be sure," Antimony drawled. "But, well, we all know how well that tends to turn out in the stories, eh? I don't really fancy being drawn away from the herd to have my throat slit."

"Charming as ever," Denken said with a sly glance at the blonde. "I bow to your stolid advice."

Antimony managed to convey in expression alone just what Denken could do with his "stolid advice" nonsense. Denken beamed.

"Middle door it is, then," Zane said.

"Take two." Denken's inhuman voice now nearly crackled with seething impatience. Trepidation prickled along Gloucester's spine as he watched the demigod move to pull open the door.

To all of their surprise, it opened without resistance. The unease brewing in Gloucester's mind mounted. Denken didn't seem to care or even notice, striding through without a second thought.

Funny that such a dangerous creature could look so innocuous. Denken wasn't much taller than Gloucester himself, and yet he carried in him a silent menace. Gloucester remembered his looming shadow, as daunting as it should have been impossible, filling the room with unmistakable threat. For all he looked human, Denken was anything but.

No time now to be fretting about that. Trying his hardest to push his misgivings to the back of his mind, Gloucester followed the others through the door, casting a final glance over his shoulder to make sure no one was watching. The woman tending the plants hummed quietly to herself, still ignoring them.

Any hopes that they would immediately be greeted by the Gambler in his prison were dashed as they entered the room on the other side of the door. It was, in fact, not a room at all, but rather a short hallway. A window high above cast light down on them, the glass in its frame a melee of vibrant hues making up a floral pattern. Tapestries covered the walls on either side of the passage, depicting scenes from the holy books. On the left, the Banishment of Great Evil was portrayed as two figures, the saints Marianne and Tomas, raising their hands against an army of mysterious robed figures. Foreign invaders of a time long past. On the other side of the hallway, a colorful forest scene showed the story of a saint Gloucester didn't recognize, surrounded by animals and adoring worshippers.

At the end of the hallway, some five or six meters from where they were gathered, stood another pair of doors. One opened up on the right, the other at the very end of the hall. Both were crafted of dark, heavy wood, carved with images as detailed and ornate as those on the tapestries.

A strange feeling stole over Gloucester, twisting through him like a vine and making the hairs on the back of his neck rise with unease. There was something hauntingly familiar about this place. He was certain he'd never been past the first door—in fact, had distinct memories of being told not to enter. So why did he feel like this wasn't the first time he'd stood here, staring at these tapestries?

He tried to shake off the sense of déjà vu, raking his hands through his hair as he followed Denken down the hallway. Unexpectedly, a hand on his arm stopped him short. Finch stepped up beside him, staring at the doors ahead with narrowed eyes.

"I feel magic," he said. As statements went, this was still a strange one to hear. The Mikalai Gloucester of two weeks ago would have scoffed at such a seemingly silly announcement. It would have sounded like something better suited coming from the mouth of a child. Finch sounded dead serious, though, and had dropped his voice, as if something dangerous was waiting on the other side of the doors.

And isn't there? If their hunch was right and the Gambler was close at hand, then danger most definitely lurked nearby. What was the Gambler like, he wondered, uneasy curiosity tingling over his skin like an electric charge. Was he as mad as his so-called brother? As powerful?

What if he was more so, on both counts? It was a frightening thought. Perhaps the Gambler was locked up for more reason than the high minister's need to combat political unrest.

Or maybe he was locked up for no reason at all. I know what that's like.

"Can you tell which one?" he asked. Finch didn't spare him a glance, his eyes focused ahead. Gloucester imagined he was reaching out with his senses, though he had no idea how his magic worked. Amidst the foreboding and brewing anticipation, a part of Gloucester's mind strayed, thinking back to the passageway in the basement, the air charged with fear as the bomb's timer ticked down and the warmth of Finch's mouth against his own.

He pushed the thought away. Now wasn't the time for dwelling on such things, on whether it was nothing but the whims of adrenaline or the potential of something more. He mentally shook himself. Finch was clearly having no trouble prioritizing, and Gloucester ought to follow suit. There would be time later to figure himself out, provided any of them got out of this with their freedom or their life intact.

"The door straight ahead," Finch said, nodding at the intricately carved door at the end of the hallway. Gloucester wasn't sure what type of wood it was: something solid and darker than mahogany, polished with a lacquer that made it look almost like stone, were it not for the lined texture of the grain.

"It feels familiar here," Finch said. "I was blindfolded before entering or leaving the room, but this . . . this feels right."

"Nothing about this feels right," Denken said scathingly.

"What about wards?" Antimony asked, stepping between the demigod and the current target of his displeasure.

Her question brought a satisfied smirk to Finch's face. "None I can't handle."

"Which is good." The discomfort in Denken's voice made Gloucester's gaze snap over at him. It was a new thing to hear from the demigod. "Something is blocking my powers."

Standing beside Finch, Gloucester felt more than saw him twitch at the words. Without thinking, he raised a hand to silently warn him away from acting on the demigod's admitted weakness; ill-conceived revenge now would just get them all in more trouble than they could handle. He surprised himself with the physical contact, though, just as he had down in the basement with the kiss. He yanked his hand away, ducking his head and pretending not to see the look Finch turned toward him.

"It must be what keeps the Gambler from escaping," he said, perhaps a little too quickly.

Finch was still looking at him, the emotions in his eyes too conflicting to decipher. "Yeah. The wards. They're cast to minimize all magic but that of the casters. Means the Gambler can't work his magic to get out, and his brothers or anyone like them can't use their own to break him free. Not as long as the ward's in place."

"Can you take it down?" Antimony asked. "You said you cast it with your father, so can you undo it without him?"

Finch's face hardened. "I'll have to, won't I? But not yet."

"What?" snapped Denken. Not having control of his powers, even as briefly as this, was clearly taking a toll on his already severely frayed mood. His eyes were darker than ever, the whites receding until only the barest hint of them could be seen around the ebony expanse of his irises. It made his eyes look empty, like endless tunnels haunted by anger.

"I won't lower it yet," Finch said firmly. "Not until I know what we're dealing with. Even if the Gambler's right on the other side of this door, I want to be sure you don't snatch him up first chance you get and abandon the rest of us here. Or kill us all the moment you have the chance."

"He wouldn't do that," Antimony said, now glaring Finch's

way. "He *can't*. It's not a matter of what he wants, but what he's capable of. Demigods cannot kill humans, simple as that."

"I don't know that for certain. And sorry, lady, but I can't just take your word for it." Finch shook his head. "There are other spells to take down first anyway, if we even want to get the door open. It's got a safehouse spell on it, for one. It'll only let past certain people—or person, rather—as long as it's in place. He had us add that months after the fact. Give me a minute."

Not waiting for a response from any of them, he closed his eyes and raised his hands. This time they didn't remain still, as they had when he'd cast the location spells before. Now they ducked and weaved, the hands of a conductor directing music. Again the vibrations of magic brushed across Gloucester's skin, audible only in the odd sensation-based way of powerful background noise. It made his ears itch, crawling into his brain until he was tempted to put his hands over them to block it out.

As quickly as the spell started, it stopped, dying away with a faint sigh. The ringing stillness and silence in the aftermath was a breath of fresh air. Gloucester shook his head slowly from side to side, staring down at his feet as he regained his composure. A step behind him, he could hear Zane muttering in displeasure.

A hand on his shoulder surprised him, and he raised his head so sharply that dizziness spun through it. The hand, pale and freckled, belonged to Finch. His fingers felt hot, even through the fabric of Gloucester's shirt and jacket, but the touch was gentle, a gesture of comfort as much as his own had been moments earlier. Gloucester blinked down at it, unsure what to think. After a moment, Finch pulled it away without a word.

"Can we go in now?" Denken asked curtly.

Finch looked unabashedly smug, much more like the man Gloucester and Zane first encountered in the warehouse. "Should be fine. Though," he said, holding up a dramatic hand, "anything could be waiting for us on the other side of this door. So just, you know, try not to die, everyone."

His mouth twisted into a grimace as his gaze landed on

Denken. Gloucester doubted he had much desire to see Denken unharmed.

"Let me guess, you want me to give you and Gloucester your guns back," Denken said with a snort.

"I dunno." Finch abandoned all pretense of humor, coldness flashing through his eyes. "You're the mind-reader."

Denken held his gaze for a too-long moment, then rolled his eyes with a level of melodrama to match Finch's. "Fine! Fine. But if you try anything, I guarantee you'll regret it."

He raised his hands, and with a flick of his wrists, they were no longer empty. Each of them held a weapon. One Gloucester recognized as the gun he had taken from the minister's mansion, the other equally recognizable as the one Finch had held to his head the night they met. Not an experience he was going to forget any time soon. With another warning look, Denken held them out to him and Finch.

The gun felt reassuringly solid in his grasp, an accustomed weight. "Right." He checked the gun was properly loaded before pointing it safely at the floor as he moved forward. "We should—"

His unfinished advice fell on deaf ears as Denken turned his back on the rest of them and swung the door open.

"—be careful," Gloucester finished, rolling his eyes skyward.

"This is it, I know it," Denken said, words filled with desperate eagerness. "Lower the last ward, Finch."

Finch shook his head. "That one I've gotta do from the inside. It's not cast on the door. It lines the walls themselves."

Denken made a harsh noise but didn't waste time arguing. Squaring his narrow shoulders, he didn't even glance back before stepping through the doorway and disappearing into the shadows.

Antimony sighed, then followed in the demigod's wake. "Here we go."

Though she held no weapon and commanded no known magical powers, the quiet confidence about her as she stood tall and strode toward the door made it feel like she was going for a stroll in the park, not walking into the danger of the unknown. Zane followed after her. Finch went next.

"See you on the other side," he quipped, before taking his turn.

Gloucester, last in the corridor, stepped forward on Finch's heels. He could see the rest of them through the doorway. They stood in a large stone hall, draped in shadows. He caught a quick glimpse of something glowing faintly deeper in the room.

Then a voice rang out, not in his ears but in his mind. The world spun, jolting him in surprise and pain. Gloucester clutched his head and stumbled, fighting the rising darkness that had come out of nowhere.

The last thing he heard was someone calling his name, and then the world blinked away into darkness.

Chapter 25

The Missing Day

*T*he church bells were ringing. Their sound echoed through the halls of All Saints Shrine like some ancient beast's melodious call. Gloucester held in a wince, tempted to cover his ears.

"Oh, come on, it's not that bad."

Erikkson chortled at him from his post on the other side of the doorway. His partner for this shift was a cheerful fellow. He'd been at the job longer than Gloucester and had an older brother air about him, teasing and supportive in equal measure. "Trust me, Gloucester," he continued, eyes twinkling in amusement. "You'll get used to the bells one of these days."

"They're just loud." Gloucester sighed. Even to his own ears it sounded a bit unnecessarily plaintive. He shrugged, trying to tune out the noise without further sign of discomfort.

"Well, they are supposed to be heard throughout all of the city. Remind everyone how important this place is and all."

Erikkson gestured at their impressive surroundings; but Gloucester wasn't terribly impressed. He'd been inside the church enough times now for the initial awe to wear thin. While he still enjoyed the beauty and calm of the place, the religious significance of the building meant little to him.

He narrowed his eyes, surveying the high stone walls and ornate stained glass windows with a critical gaze. "I thought the Old Cathedral was the important one."

Erikkson laughed. "I always forget you're not from here originally. Still, though, you've been in the city for how many years now? You know how it works. It's not about how big you are, it's about who owns you. And compared to this place, the Old Cathedral might as well be a pile of rubble."

"I think there are a lot of people who wouldn't like the sound of that."

"People not liking things isn't anything new. And it doesn't change the way things are." He took on a more serious look. "You want to be careful saying stuff like that, mate. His Lordship takes loyalty seriously."

"I didn't mean anything by it," Gloucester said, rolling his eyes. "I was just—Oh, look sharp."

A brown-clad priest approached them from the nave, his face stern. Erikkson stepped forward as the priest drew near.

"Can we help you, Father?" he asked.

The priest's stoic look eased into a more kindly smile. "A word with the high minister, young man, if he has a moment."

"Of course."

Moving back to the door, Erikkson rapped twice on the smooth wooden surface. They waited in silence for a moment, then the door opened to reveal the high minister. In contrast with his priest, the sternness on his face didn't change upon sight of his agents.

"Yes?" he asked, impatience lacing his words. Behind him, Gloucester caught a glimpse of an intricate tapestry.

"One of the priests would like a word with you, sir,"

Erikkson told him.

"What's that?" asked the high minister, voice still sharp with annoyance. He looked from Erikkson to the priest, ignoring Gloucester.

"Delegates are here from the Blue Church in the Nordlands," the priest said, ducking his head to the minister. "The priestess wants to speak with you as soon as possible. She is . . . insistent."

The high minister grimaced, glancing over his shoulder. "Can it wait?"

"Um . . ." said the priest. A smile fought to show itself on Erikkson's face, though he did an admirable job hiding it. "I don't think so, my lord. The folk who follow the sky gods are . . . not patient people."

The high minister hesitated a moment longer, glancing behind him again, then sighed loudly. "Fine, fine, let's see what they want. Gloucester, stay at your post. Erikkson, with me." He strode through the door, shutting it quickly behind him and beckoning Erikkson to follow. As they walked away, Gloucester heard the minister add, "I hope it's a different priestess from the last time. What a nightmare that was."

They soon rounded the corner into the main hall of the church, leaving Gloucester alone outside the door. The bells had stopped their tolling while he'd been distracted, and now that he had the opportunity to notice, a profound silence reigned. He didn't mind. Moments like these were what he enjoyed most in his job; when he could stand at the sidelines and simply bask in the peace and quiet. He stood on the edge of someone else's life and was content to stay there.

It was a dangerous thing to think, being precisely the breed of contemplation that tempts the universe to be ironic.

The silence of the church was broken, not by the sound of bells or voices but rather, impossibly, by a stirring in the back of Gloucester's mind. He flinched at the invasion, staggering where he stood.

"I—What?" he gasped, pressing his hands against his

temples.

Whatever it was, it pulled at his thoughts, not words or even a voice, but a feeling. Breathing in uneven jolts, Gloucester turned to look at the door he was guarding. The high minister, in his haste, hadn't stopped to check that it latched properly before he hurried away with the others. It swung ajar, just enough to reveal a thin sliver of the corridor on the other side. Somehow, Gloucester knew the source of the strange feeling lay beyond it.

They weren't allowed past the door, though. He knew that; every security agent did. You went where His Lordship told you to and you did what he ordered. You certainly didn't go poking around in places you had been specifically told to stay out of.

Yet when he laid his eyes on the door, the emotion pulling at him leapt to new heights. It wasn't painful, but it still somehow hurt, so desperate was the feeling of despair sweeping through him. Unthinkingly, he took a step closer. Beneath the despair, something brighter emerged, like a sun trying to shine past the clouds. Hope.

The door was right in front of him now, the doorknob in his hand. He didn't remember taking the final few steps toward it, nor did he recall actively choosing to investigate.

He pushed the door open. It swung inward on well-maintained hinges, making no noise to betray Gloucester's trespassing. He knew he wasn't supposed to go past the door, but all the same, he knew that he had to. He just didn't know why.

Beyond lay a short passage, and at its end stood two more doors. Gloucester's head rang like the church bells up in the tower, and he knew as if guided by an invisible hand which door he needed to go through. The feeling in his mind grew stronger, coalescing into an almost tangible force, pulling him ever closer.

He stood in front of the furthest door, staring at the solid wood, his mind so filled with the invading emotion that there was little room for his own thoughts. Sweat trickled down his brow and his hand shook as he reached forward and pushed this door open too.

The mental hold on his brain relinquished, and he stumbled forward in relief. It took several long moments to regain his composure enough to look up.

He stared in shock, gaping at his new surroundings. The room was bigger than he would have expected, the walls hidden in shadow save for the small and distant patches of illuminated stone where candles glowed in lonely sconces. The ceiling arched high above his head, taller than ought to be possible. Thinking of the exterior layout of the building, he had no idea how this place even fit.

Yet the bizarre dimensions of the room were far from its most intriguing feature. In the center stood a strange structure, stretching up from the floor toward the ceiling like a massive tower of twisting vines. They were ropes, Gloucester realized. Ropes that glowed faintly blue in the darkness, interlacing and as thick as his fingers.

And in their tangling hold was a person, caught like a fish in a net.

"Hello?" he called out. Though his voice wasn't raised much beyond a whisper, it echoed in the grand expanse of the room, bouncing off the shadowed walls. The figure suspended in the netted tower of ropes didn't move. Heart thudding in his chest, Gloucester stepped closer. "Who are you?"

Again no response came, the strangely hollow click of his shoes on the polished floor the only sound as he approached. The air in the room felt charged, and he half-expected to see sparks of static electricity chase across his feet as he walked. As he got closer to the tangle at the center of the room, its motionless inhabitant was revealed to be a young man, tall and lean of build, with brown skin and fair hair. He was dressed plainly in a white button-down and torn jeans.

He raised his head as Gloucester drew near. Gloucester was relieved to see the simple action, the first sign that he was even alive.

His relief was short-lived. Gloucester stopped short a few feet away from the hanging man, transfixed in horror. The man had no eyes. He stared back at Gloucester, as if he could see despite the empty skin stretched over his sockets.

A quiet drip drip pulled at Gloucester's attention, and after a moment he forced himself to look for the source of the sound.

Blood. It pooled beneath the man's feet, which hung several inches above the ground, crimson and wet. Swearing under his breath, Gloucester raised his gaze again, eyes wide as he traced the blood up the man's legs to his knees. The denim was sodden, nearly black in the dim light the ropes emitted. Unlike the long-healed skin of his mutilated face, these were clearly fresh wounds. The high minister was torturing people? Why?

"Who are you?" he whispered. "Can you hear me?" Warring emotions raged inside him as he stared up at the prisoner, urging him at once to step closer and to run. "What are you doing here?"

"A lot of questions."

The man's voice made Gloucester stagger back a step. It wasn't loud, nor particularly fearsome, yet something about it overwhelmed the senses. In that moment, Gloucester knew this was the person who had drawn him into this room. But how? And why?

Well, the latter struck him as more obvious. If he'd been strung up, blinded, and tortured, he'd be keen to bring in whatever help he could too.

"I'm—"

"Mikalai Gloucester," the strange voice cut him off. "Bodyguard to the high minister and lord of the city-state. One of many. Yet here you stand. Alone."

"I heard you." Gloucester stared up at the eyeless face. "In my head. But it wasn't your . . . your voice. Not really. How did *you do that? And how do you know me?"*

"So many questions, Mikalai." The blind man looked serene, despite his circumstances. An air of sadness hung over him, clinging with the same tenacity as the ropes that bound his limbs. "All your life. Asking questions, seeking answers. Do you find them, I wonder?"

"Who are you?" Gloucester demanded again, unwilling to waste time with mind games. The high minister could return at any moment, and he didn't know what would happen if he was found here, but he knew it wouldn't be good.

"I've outlived many names," the man told him. Though he didn't look much older than Gloucester, a strange echo in his heavy voice lent the statement gravity. Whoever the man was, he was more than just that, a man.

"Now they call me the Gambler," he said. "I would shake your hand, Mikalai Gloucester, but . . ." He waggled his restrained hands as much as the ropes would allow and gave a tiny movement that might have been a shrug.

Gloucester scarcely noticed the attempt at dry humor. Thinking quickly, or perhaps not thinking at all, he glanced once over his shoulder, checking for any approaching intruders, then turned back to the Gambler. "There will be time for that once we get you out of here," he said. In the back of his mind, he knew what he was about to do was rash and quite possibly a terrible decision. But it didn't feel like the wrong choice. He tore his eyes away from the strange man to examine the glowing cords that bound him. "Now how do I get you down? This rope . . . how does it work?" He peered more closely, trying to discern the source of the glow, but it really did emanate from the ropes themselves.

"Magic," said the Gambler.

Gloucester waited a moment, but no punchline or further explanation followed. The Gambler was simply looking down at him.

"Magic," Gloucester repeated. The Gambler nodded.

"You're . . . you're not joking?"

A shake of the head.

Gloucester stared at the ropes again. It felt stupid even considering the possibility. Magic didn't exist. It belonged only in fairy stories and children's tales.

Or did it? He'd followed an intangible pull into this room, with its too-high ceiling and impossible floorspace. And he'd found this man, this Gambler, who was definitely no mere human, bound by ropes with an unnatural luminescence.

Was magic so impossible?

Later he could ponder in awe how much bigger and stranger the world might be than he'd ever thought, digest it all when there wasn't a trussed-up eyeless man awaiting rescue and an angry high minister who could return at any moment.

"Magic, yes, but not unbreakable. At least, not to you," the Gambler said. "The rope's spell is designed to keep me powerless and contained. But those who cast it are human, and it was made with their own and the high minister's needs in mind. He needed to be able to undo it if the occasion ever arose."

"Occasion? What—No, never mind. There isn't time." *Gloucester checked over his shoulder again, but the open door into the corridor still showed no one. The coast remained clear for the time being. "How do I undo it?"*

"There's a single knot at the bottom, beneath my feet. Pierce it with anything, steel or scissors or even just untie it, and the ropes will come apart. Even if I could reach it, I wouldn't be able to touch it. Human hands only."

Gloucester crouched in front of the Gambler's feet, avoiding as best he could the sizable puddle of blood that soaked the stone. About six inches above the ground, five of the glowing cords came together and tangled into a knot he didn't recognize. It was complex, a bundle of intertwining ropes like a hibernaculum of pale snakes.

"I don't think I can untie this," he whispered. He hurriedly patted down his pockets for something with a sharp enough

edge to cut through the strands.

The search proved fruitful, and he made a quiet sound of victory as he produced a pocketknife from the inside pocket of his jacket. His heart was beating very fast, but his hands were steady as he flicked the blade out and set to work sawing through the knot.

He half-expected it to burn or hurt him somehow when he set the knife to it, some sort of protective mechanism magically infused in the cords. Or maybe it would be spelled to be unbreakable after all.

Instead, the steel bit into the rope as it would any other, the glowing light and almost inaudible thrum of power the only things marking these restraints as anything special. Whatever they were made out of was tough, though, and the going was slow and laborious.

"What are you?" Gloucester asked as he worked away at the knot. It was an impertinent question, but with his head still reeling from the force that had drawn him there and his eyes straying up to the Gambler's empty sockets, which had no scars, the question escaped unbidden past his lips.

Luckily, the Gambler wasn't offended. He broke into laughter. In it Gloucester could hear the crackle of fire, the murmuration of a thousand whispers, the echo of screams. He caught strains of tears and joy, of love and sorrow. It wasn't a sound so much as another wave of emotion, tumbling out of the Gambler's lungs to fill the empty air. Gloucester flinched, resisting the urge to flee.

"A fair question," said the Gambler. "Forgive me, it has been a while since I've had anyone nice to talk to. I am Choice. Or the personification of it, at least."

Gloucester paused in his slow battle with the ropes, sitting back on his haunches to get a better look at the madman hanging above him, the urgency of the situation momentarily forgotten.

But was the so-called Gambler mad? Logic demanded such

as the explanation. It certainly made the most sense.

Except the Gambler hadn't made sense right from the get-go. Not in words, nor in appearance, nor in whatever magic he'd worked to draw Gloucester into the room.

"Choice?" he repeated uncertainly. "A personification? Like . . . like Death?"

"Less macabre, perhaps, but it is a fair comparison," the Gambler said, his hushed tone doing little to downplay the unearthliness of his voice. It lingered in Gloucester's ears even after he finished speaking, like the last haunting strains of an echo.

The existence of such a strange creature was a lot to take in. Part of Gloucester still wanted to run, to find somewhere safe and sit down with his head in his hands and sort things out, try to separate fact from fiction.

But another part of him—most of him, really—wanted answers. Right here and now. Questions boiled in his mind, thousands of them, all hissing and crying out, demanding to be asked. Without knowing which of the countless queries would burst forth, Gloucester opened his mouth again.

"What are you doing here?" he asked.

That one seemed apt as any.

The Gambler sighed. "There are those who believe their bad choices can be fixed through trickery and clever cheating. I confess myself to be both a victim and a pawn in this matter."

Gloucester turned this over in his mind. "You're a prisoner," he said slowly.

That much was stating the obvious, what with the half-cut ropes and the dark room steeped in secrecy. The Gambler nodded, ever patient.

"But why?" Gloucester stared up at him, pondering the odd face gazing back. "He . . . The high minister wants to use your power to—What is your power? What can a personification of Choice do?"

"Many things, same as any other creature. What your high

minister desires is only one facet of my abilities. I can see the futures."

"The futures? Wait, more than one?"

The Gambler smiled. The glow from the ropes binding him cast his skin in a pale blue light, highlighting the angular planes of his face. "It would be a mighty power to be able to see with certainty only what will occur. Mighty and impossible. I don't know of anyone, human or otherwise, in all of history who has possessed such an ability. There are those who catch glimpses, but it comes to them in riddles and it can take them a lifetime to decipher. I see what could be, countless possibilities stemming from the choices you all make. Some are more likely than others, and I see the odds."

"Hence 'the Gambler,'" Gloucester muttered, pushing his hair back from his furrowed brow, before resuming his work on the knot. It was proving to be more challenging than he'd hoped, but he was making progress. He still half-expected to wake up and find this was all a strange dream and nothing more. But it felt real, the cool air on his skin and the faint buzz of the ropes under the blade of his pocketknife. "He's holding you here to tell him his future? Futures? Why?"

"Why do you think the high minister is as powerful as he is?" said the Gambler, parrying the questions with one of his own.

"I—" Gloucester hesitated. He didn't understand a lot about what was being revealed in this eerie hall, but the Gambler's words echoed in his thoughts, prying open doors to unforeseen notions. "How long have you been here?"

The Gambler's smile was lopsided, an intimately human expression. "He was already high minister and lord of the city-state when he took interest in the stories of my powers. His own power was beginning to slip through his fingers, something he refused to allow. Faced with a city full of enemies and rivals, his stratagems for maintaining his lofty position delved into . . . unexpected territory."

It was quite the story, one Gloucester was having a hard time swallowing. He realized his hands had slowed again, as his thoughts struggled to wrap themselves around this impossible situation. He'd always thought the high minister powerful, but to find out just the sort of power he was commanding . . . Gods and magic and predicting the future . . .

In the back of his mind, an urgent voice whispered, constant as the ticking of a clock: he didn't have much time; he shouldn't be here; if the high minister returned—

But he couldn't turn away from this. There were too many questions. Too many impossibilities. And at the center of it, one person—some kind of god or not—who was strung up against his will, apparently for no better reason than the selfish agenda of another. Gloucester knew it was none of his business, but he couldn't just ignore it.

"If you're so powerful, how did he catch you?" he asked, the question fleeing his lips more swiftly than the others, as the warning voice in his thoughts grew louder. He forced himself to get back to work, sawing through the knot. A few of the tangled cords gave way.

"No matter how powerful we are, everyone makes mistakes," the Gambler said ruefully. "There are magics in the world, and people who wield them, who can trick even someone like myself." There was a wry twist to his lips. "Age doesn't always denote wisdom, it would seem."

"Did he hurt you?" Gloucester's eyes lingered on the blood staining the Gambler's knees. He glanced up at the blank, eyeless gaze, then dropped his eyes away again, uncomfortable.

The Gambler chuckled. Evidently his lack of vision didn't make him blind. "I am a strange sight, I know. My appearance is not the doing of any one human." His face hardened. "But I am imprisoned. Forced to do my captor's bidding. Treated as a thing, a tool, a resource to use in times of need and ignored whenever else. So yes, he has hurt me."

The Gambler fell quiet. The silence stretched out so long that

Gloucester looked up from the knot, concerned. The Gambler was watching him sightlessly, his head tilted to one side.

"What?"

"You really would rescue me," the Gambler said.

Gloucester wasn't sure if this was a question or not.

"Bit late in the game to ask that, isn't it? Anyway, couldn't you see that coming?" he asked, anxious impatience sharpening his tone. Another cord snapped away from the knot. He was almost through it.

"This place limits my power," the Gambler answered, and to his credit, he didn't sound offended at being called into question. "To be used at my jailor's discretion. And it is less a question than it is . . . surprise, I suppose. You are more impressive than you think yourself, Mikalai Gloucester."

"If you say so," muttered Gloucester. He was trying very hard not to think too much about what he was doing, for fear of what might happen when it properly registered just how stupid this was.

"I do," said the Gambler. "And I am sorry."

Before Gloucester could ask what for, the knife sliced through the last of the knot with a loud snap like the string of a harp breaking. A pressure Gloucester hadn't even consciously noticed before vanished, leaving him feeling strangely light.

The Gambler wasted no time in pulling at the ropes holding him, now that they were no longer secure. Gloucester hurried to lend a hand. Once the Gambler was free of the ropes and standing unsteadily on his own two feet, Gloucester looked toward the door again. It was innocuous in its emptiness, and yet he couldn't shake a sense of impending danger.

"We need to get you out of here as soon as possible. I don't know how we're going to get you through the church itself without being seen. I don't suppose you can, I don't know, turn invisible or something?"

"Not here." The Gambler rubbed his wrists where the cords had twisted around them. His voice sounded almost as shaky *as his footing. Did gods get emotions? If this one was anything to go by, it certainly seemed like it. Gloucester wondered how long it had been since the Gambler felt the ground beneath his feet. Had he been bound like that the entire time he'd been the high minister's prisoner?*

"There is magic in this room," the Gambler said, squaring his shoulders. "More than just the ropes. Magic that nullifies much of my own. Once we are away, my full powers should return."

"Should" struck Gloucester as a worrying term, but he didn't question it. All in all, he was still trying his hardest not to think too much about everything that was happening and whatever consequences might lie in wait just around the corner.

"Come on, then," he said, keeping his pocketknife in hand as he beckoned the Gambler to follow him. He didn't know what use it might be, but it felt reassuring to have a weapon in hand. They weren't allowed firearms in the church, even if he suspected the high minister himself probably wouldn't enforce that if not for the other priests. Not that Gloucester had any idea who he would be aiming at if he did have a gun. The high minister? Turn on his boss just like that, the man his entire job was dedicated to protecting?

My boss keeps people tied up in secret rooms, he reminded himself.

Even in the privacy of his own thoughts, it sounded bizarre. He couldn't help but wonder what the minister would do if he caught him.

He pushed the door open the rest of the way and led them out of the dark room and into the corridor. The Gambler's footfalls behind him were near-silent. After the echoes of the large room, the corridor seemed notably muted. It was a short matter of strides to reach the door at the other end of the hallway.

He paused. How to do this? Step out on his own first, to make sure the coast was clear for the Gambler? Except it would still be him, a security agent exiting a room he was forbidden to enter. He might as well burst out in a rush with the Gambler at his side. Either way, if they were spotted, it was all over.

Still, he'd always had a difficult time not going the route of caution. Glancing back at the Gambler, he held a finger to his lips and silently swung the door open—

Only to reveal the cold face of the high minister glaring back at him.

He wasn't alone. A stricken Erikkson was being shoved out of sight by Mulligan, the high minister's chief adviser. They were both shouting, but their voices blended into cacophonous nonsense, falling into the background as Gloucester stared at the high minister. The older man wore an expression he'd never seen on him before, some mix of fear and fury, a silent crescendo of tension building up to an explosion.

So engrossed in the minister's face, it took Gloucester a moment too long to realize he wasn't empty-handed. Sunlight through the high windows glinted off metal as the high minister's arm rose; Erikkson was gone now, shepherded away in confused protest; Mulligan was still shouting, striding to the minister's side; Gloucester stared down the barrel of the gun—

"STOP."

The command boomed through the hall like a clap of thunder right overhead, reverberating through their bones and stealing their breath away. Gloucester staggered, but so too did the high minister and his aide, the gun wavering in its aim.

"Silence," the high minister snapped, but his normally authoritative voice sounded pitiful and weak in comparison to the Gambler's. He must have heard it too, for when he spoke next, the forcefulness in his tone was stronger than ever. "Don't you dare try anything."

Was that fear in his voice? Gloucester didn't think he'd ever heard the man afraid.

"My intentions are noble," the Gambler said. "I merely want to spare us all a terrible fate."

Gloucester risked taking his eyes off the barrel of the gun in order to toss a sidelong look at the god. Did he actually have a plan? Or was he just extremely talented in the art of bullshitting?

"Oh really?" the high minister said with a sneer, sounding much more put-together now, unlike Mulligan, who had fallen silent as he visibly struggled against the effects of the Gambler's voice. "And what terrible fate would that be?"

"Look," said the Gambler. "See."

The world shifted, reality swirling off-kilter like a train jumping its tracks. A gasp tore its way through the air, and Gloucester didn't know if it had escaped his lungs or those of someone else. Were the others still there? He couldn't see, couldn't hear, could only feel the rush of wind in his ears, wind that roared through his thoughts, through his bones—

A gunshot rang out—a flash of light and the smell of copper. There was no pain, beyond the strange cold that stung for the barest of instants.

And Mikalai Gloucester died.

—

What he found rather curious was the way things kept happening after. He'd never put much thought into life after death, but he'd never imagined that, should it exist, it would happen the way events were unfolding now. More oddly still, he found he was only mildly miffed about his own untimely demise. His attention was not on his very recent death, but rather on its aftermath.

There was something strange about the way this aftermath was shaping out. He watched, invisible, as the high minister and Mulligan stared down at his body. Then people were shouting, other security agents storming into their midst, no doubt attracted by the sound of the gunshot. The minister barked orders, which were echoed by Mulligan. Gloucester's body was dragged away. A pair of men, one old and the other redheaded and smirking, arrived to lead the Gambler away, both laughing and confident. The Gambler's face was unreadable.

And then, in the blink of an eye, the High Minister's Cathedral was gone. Gloucester stood amidst smoke and flames, watching the burning wreck of a car cough up billows of ash.

He stood in the high minister's study, and again a metallic tang laced the air. The minister's body lay lifeless in front of the shattered window, blood spattered across the floorboards.

He stood at the edge of the city, listening to the riots, watching the flags of Frettchen descend, replaced by those of the Nordlands.

His head hurt. He didn't even know how that was possible, as he didn't seem *to* have *a* head *anymore. Yet pain lanced through him, uncaring that he was without form, without life, scorching a trail of agony through his consciousness, until he couldn't stand it any longer—*

He gasped, the air in his very real, solid chest burning like fire.

He was back in the church, the unspent gun still in the minister's hand but pointed harmlessly at the floor, the fingers gripping it white-knuckled. The minister stared past him, as did Mulligan at his side. The Gambler, Gloucester thought dazedly. *They're looking at the Gambler.*

"What—" he started, but the ragged question was overtaken by retching. Bent double, he coughed, every muscle in his body twitching and sore, his stomach heaving.

What just happened? His thoughts, barely more coherent than his words, nonetheless had more luck in articulating the question, even if it was only himself hearing it. Had the others seen what he had seen? Had they felt what he'd felt?

From the panic in Mulligan's face, Gloucester knew the

answer was yes. The adviser was shouting again, snarling and fearful as a cornered animal. Gloucester couldn't hear the words past the rushing in his ears. The high minister was speaking too, but Gloucester couldn't hear his commands any more than Mulligan's vitriol.

Rough hands pulled at his arms and he gasped in shock, but even that sound evaded him. He hadn't noticed the arrival of the other security agents, but now they swarmed the room, a crowd of black suits and silent shouts.

Gloucester struggled, instinct taking over. An arm snaked around his neck from behind, cutting off his air and pulling his head back. He thought he was yelling, but wasn't sure. The hall and all its chaos slipped away, the chokehold around his neck sending darkness in from the edges of his vision, the rushing of blood in his ears only growing louder and more overwhelming.

The last thing he saw was Mulligan. The chief adviser looked furious and frightened, his eyes shining in the quickly encroaching blackness.

—

He awoke in another's arms, but no longer were they clutching at him violently. These hands were gentle, though after a blinking moment of confusion, he realized they were shaking him, as a voice overhead called his name in an urgent whisper. Gloucester gasped a breath and struggled to sit up.

"I remember."

Chapter 26

The Gambler

"You know," said Finch, his arms still bracing Gloucester's shoulders and back. "The whole swooning into my arms thing is pretty adorable, but maybe now's not the best time, aye?"

Gloucester ignored him, staring past his freckled face into the dark room that surrounded them. "I remember," he repeated. He was having a difficult time catching his breath, as if he'd just run a very long distance.

Finch's brow knitted, wrinkling the sun tattooed on his forehead. "Brilliant. Remember what?"

"This!" Gloucester shrugged away Finch's hands and clambered unsteadily to his feet. "I've—I've been here before. I saw—"

"*Quiet.*"

The command in Denken's voice was irresistible, and Gloucester fell silent with a flinch, whirling to face the demigod.

But Denken wasn't looking at him. He was staring deeper into the room, at the glow of a faint light and the figure it illuminated. It struck Gloucester that only instants must have passed since he'd stepped through the doorway.

The room was exactly as his returned memories painted it: the walls, too tall and too far away to be physically possible, shrouded in shadows and disappearing up to a ceiling hidden in darkness; candles in sconces dotting the lower edges of the walls, too sparse to do much more than create spots of pale yellow, like stars in the ebony expanse of space.

And at the center of it all, the Gambler. He hung limp and lifeless in the gentle light cast by his netted prison. He gave no sign he registered the arrival of his rescue party.

"What in the world?" Zane gaped at the sight. Beside her, Antimony was equally expressive for once, slack-jawed, her eyes locked on the imprisoned demigod. For a long moment, they all stood frozen.

All except Denken. He moved through the space between the door and the center of the room so quickly it was as if he didn't move at all, merely disappeared from one spot and reappeared next to his brother. At least some of his inhuman power clearly remained, despite the Finches' spells.

"Gambler." He cradled the other god's face. "Joujou, talk to me."

Gloucester approached slowly, watching the two gods. He still felt shaky on his feet, and in the wake of what he'd just remembered, the prospect of getting too close to the eyeless man in the cat's cradle was not a welcoming one.

"Let's just hurry up and get him out of here."

Gloucester jumped at Zane's voice in his ear. He hadn't even noticed her walking a step behind him. She hastened forward to match his stride, squinting in the dark at the Gambler.

"He's alive, isn't he?" she muttered. "He's got to be. Is he okay?"

"Gambler," Denken urged, the same question evidently on

his mind too. "Wake up. Come on, *wake up*." The demigod's obvious distress made him sound almost human. Curiously, the wave of emotion Gloucester expected to roll off of him and crash over the rest of them never came. That, then, would be the effect of the wards.

At long last, the Gambler stirred. There were no eyelids to flutter open in groggy awakening, nor to blink in confusion at the sight of his motley band of rescuers. Instead, a shudder coursed through his whole body, from his pale-haired head to his bare, dripping toes. "Denken," he breathed.

The single word carried in the grandiose space of the room, and Gloucester shivered. While Denken's voice was rich with charm and warm persuasion, the Gambler's was deep and heavy, melancholy without sounding glum, and as aged as the stones around them. It evoked an involuntary and implacable wistfulness, as if its owner had seen the best and worst of humanity, had loved and lost a thousand times over. Perhaps he had.

The emotional weight was lost on Denken. "Hey!" he said, miraculously remembering to keep his voice down, but sounding delighted nonetheless. "We're here to bring you home."

"Hey," Finch whispered from Gloucester's other side, close enough that only he could hear him. "This is too easy."

Dragging his eyes away from the reunited brothers, Gloucester exchanged a look with the other man. A dark foreboding swept over him. Finch was right. They'd come here today expecting the worst. With magic on his side, surely the high minister would employ dangerous tricks and safeguards to protect his secret weapon. And yet, they'd been able to walk right in with no more trouble than a few sealed doors that were easily taken care of with Finch's spells. It shouldn't have been this simple.

Which, in his experience, generally meant it wasn't.

"I've been here before," he whispered back. "The day I was locked up. *This* is what I saw, why they put me in that cell. I saw the Gambler. I tried to save him."

Finch stared at him for a moment, but it was impossible to tell what he was thinking.

"My point is," Gloucester hurried on, feeling self-conscious and furious at himself for being so at a time like this, "I was *caught* then. When no one was probably even worried about him being found. No one was expecting a rescue attempt."

Finch nodded. "So how come there's no one catching us now, when His Lordship should be on high alert?"

How come indeed.

"Are you all right?" Denken asked the Gambler. "What has he done to you? Are you hurt?" The questions shot from him like arrows from a bow, only to be met by a slow shake of the Gambler's head.

"It doesn't matter now," he said in a murmur that filled the room. "Denken, something is coming. I rolled Snake Eyes."

The statement meant nothing to Gloucester, but Denken stared agape at his brother, eyes even bigger than usual.

Equally worrying was Finch's reaction. The magician turned his attention swiftly away from Gloucester, a barely audible curse carried on his breath as he too stared at the Gambler. Antimony strode forward to stand at Denken's side and said, "Are you sure?" in a troubled voice.

The only other person who seemed to have no idea what this meant was Zane, who exchanged a confused look with Gloucester. "Um," she said to the room at large, clearing her throat. "What's Snake Eyes? And is it a bad thing? It sounds like a bad thing. You've all got, uh, bad thing sort of faces on."

Antimony put a hand on the Gambler's arm, her skin ghostly pale in the reflected light of the magical bindings. "It's an omen. He's a Seer, he can predict things, especially with the help of his dice. Snake Eyes is a dangerous roll," she explained, while beside her Denken ignored everyone other than his brother. Antimony grimaced. "It's a prediction of the worst manner of things."

Gloucester found this anything but comforting. In his mind, the shape of the situation was beginning to form, revealing disturbing possibilities. The feeling of "this is too easy" was a dangerous thing to mix with news as ominous as "something is coming."

"We've found the Gambler, so let's just free him and get out of here, all right?" said Zane. "Before our luck runs out and whatever this 'something' that's coming arrives. I don't know about the rest of you, but I'd kind of like to be away from here when that happens."

Denken stepped back from his brother, face pinched in frustration. "I can't touch the ropes. They're spelled to nix my control of my powers, same as they do for the Gambler. Finch, get over here and—"

"The knot."

Gloucester found himself the focus of all eyes and gazes in the room. It was even more off-putting than usual, as these two things ought to, but did not, mean the same thing in this case. He cleared his throat and pointed at the base of the web of ropes, where the knot from his memory held it all together. They must have redone the entire unique prison after he'd been dragged away. He wondered if it was Finch's father who did it. Had Finch known? A sideways glance at the magician revealed nothing. The list of immediate things to worry about already weighed heavily on Gloucester's mind, however, and he knew adding more concerns to it wouldn't help anything. There would be time later to question Finch's honesty and loyalty, provided they made it out of here in one piece.

"Cut the knot beneath his feet. It'll unravel the net," he said. They all continued to stare, and impatience rose in him, born of both urgency and discomfort. "Now!"

"You remember," said the Gambler, as Denken growled for someone to find a knife and Antimony obligingly—and somewhat alarmingly—pulled one from the inside pocket of her jacket. The Gambler ignored the harried actions of his brother and friend, regarding Gloucester with a look that managed to convey deep regret even with no eyes. "I am so sorry, Mikalai Gloucester. It is a terrible thing to see yourself die. It is a testament to you that you recovered at all after such an experience."

There were a hundred different things Gloucester wanted to say in reply. Angry, incredulous, apologetic things. He wanted to quip that there hadn't been much else to do in solitary confinement. That it was easy to recover when his memories weren't there. That he didn't understand. That he was sorry he hadn't rescued him.

Frustratingly, the eloquence to form any coherent reply wasn't coming to mind. Words surged like crashing waves against the inside of his skull, rolling in a storm of raw emotion too-long bottled up to easily sort through. Instead, he cleared his throat again and said, "We need to get out of here, now."

"No."

Like all of their hushed words and whispered conversations, the monosyllabic denial was strangely loud in the room, despite a lack of volume on the speaker's part.

But it was the speaker himself who froze the room with his presence. Gloucester knew that voice without needing to turn around. It had haunted nightmares and revenge fantasies alike for months and had been the embodiment of authority before that.

The high minister.

They all turned toward the doorway as one. It was no longer empty. A dozen figures filled the space now, spilling into the room from the corridor beyond. The hallway lamps cast them in shadow as the light filtered past their backs, but Gloucester spotted familiar faces nonetheless.

The high minister stood at the forefront, Mulligan by his side. Behind them was Harrison, looming over both even from a few steps back. Gloucester also recognized the two women who had stood guard at his door during his stay at the minister's mansion, Jess and Amelia. A few others looked familiar in the vague way of people he'd seen before but never spoken to.

"Clearly powerful doesn't necessarily mean smart," the minister said, stepping forward. Gloucester tensed, though the older man appeared unarmed, hands empty. His own gun was a very solid presence in his hand, but he dared not raise it. He wouldn't even have time to aim before he was taken down by the very much armed security agents facing them. They all had weapons drawn, but seemed to be waiting for a signal from the high minister.

Harrison stepped forward, his own weapon pointed at Gloucester's chest. Gloucester crouched down slowly, and carefully set his gun on the floor.

"Clearly," growled Denken, sidestepping to stand between his brother and the newcomers. Risking a look over his shoulder as he straightened up again, Gloucester could see Antimony crouched behind the slim demigod, the only one in the room with her back to the minister. Instead, she was facing the Gambler's feet.

"You must be Denken," the minister said. "You don't look much like your 'brother.'" He took another step forward. Gloucester took an involuntary step back, his free hand blindly reaching out to find Zane's arm. When his fingers closed around her sleeve, he pulled her behind him. He felt like they were all watching two wild beasts circle each other, waiting to see which one would lunge first.

"Well, we can't all be as handsome as I am," Denken shot back, teeth and eyes glinting in the light from the doorway. "Wouldn't be fair to the world."

"Funny that you should bring up fairness." The high minister smiled coldly. "I'm sure you've noticed that the magic of this room puts us all on more . . . even ground, shall we say?"

This was a bit rich coming from a man surrounded by armed henchmen. Gloucester glanced at Finch, the only other person in their number currently armed with anything more than a pocketknife. He also hadn't been quick enough to raise his gun when the minister's men stormed the room, and had been wordlessly ordered to drop it. Like Gloucester's weapon, it was cast aside on the floor, useless. Would his magic, uninhibited by the enchantments in the room, be of any more use? Gloucester hoped to catch his eye, but Finch ignored him, his attention locked on the exchange going on in front of them, as everyone else's was. Everyone except Antimony, her slight form inconspicuous where she crouched behind Denken.

Not inconspicuous enough. "What are you doing back there?" the minister snapped, his gaze moving from Denken to the scientist and a good deal of his smug composure slipping away. "Get back from there!"

Antimony complied, hands raised in a placating gesture. But too late.

With a violent snap, the cords binding the Gambler were broken. He stumbled as he fell the short distance between his previously dangling feet and the floor. Blood splattered across the stone. Gloucester was momentarily overwhelmed by déjà vu, and with it the recollection of the forced vision from that day six months before.

Though he swayed on his feet like a sailor fresh on shore leave, the Gambler stood on his own, silent and somehow watchful in spite of his appearance.

"I'm taking my brother and leaving," Denken said. His voice was always alluring, but now it held a different power, something more overtly dangerous. It was the darkness lingering in all human minds, the tiny whispering voice, curious and frightful, urging the leap from rooftops or the step into traffic. It was the voice in the void murmuring *What if?* and daring you to follow, even when you knew it wasn't a rabbit hole you were being led down, but an abyss. Impulse given sound and inflection and life.

Yet the expected impact was lacking. Gloucester could feel it, the compulsion, gnawing at the edges of his will, but it wasn't overwhelming—an itch he found he could scratch with conscious will.

The high minister's smile was back in place. "Like I said, you have no power here."

A reckless, idiotic part of Gloucester wanted to snap, "*What are you gonna do, kill all of us?*" Besides the fact that this would be an embarrassingly cliché thing to shout, though, the most probable response was "*Yes, precisely that.*"

Still, he *was* angry. More and more so, as he realized the pounding of his heart wasn't just in anxious anticipation of a fight but a *desire for it*. Gathered in this room were both of the people who had stolen his life from him, and as they prepared to go head-to-head, he didn't think he wanted either of them to triumph. He wanted to strike them both down, to see the smugness disappear from their faces as they begged for the chance to apologize—

Focus.

The thought was grounding, a single word to cut through the cacophony of righteous anger, calm and clear.

And not his own.

He looked at Denken and wasn't the least bit surprised to be met with dark eyes staring back at him. After a mere couple of seconds, Denken swept his gaze away, but Gloucester knew it hadn't been an idle crossing of their eye lines.

He risked a sidelong look at Zane and Finch. If they had also received the message, they showed no signs of it. Nor did Antimony, still standing with her hands raised, a few steps away from the Gambler. Her own eyes kept flicking to the eyeless demigod, a worry line digging into the skin between her brows.

I need your help, Gloucester.

Denken's voice was so clear in his thoughts he may as well have been whispering in Gloucester's ear. Clearly his powers weren't as impeded as the high minister believed.

Gloucester didn't want to help him. Denken was as guilty as the high minister, in his own way. He hadn't locked Gloucester up, but he'd played with his life, and the lives of others, like they were pieces on a chessboard, his own to manipulate and sacrifice. He was no better than—

I know what you think of me. There will be time for that later. Now, focus.

On what? thought Gloucester as waspishly as he could manage. He wasn't used to holding conversations in his head, at least not with other people involved, and the task of proper psychic emoting was a tricky one.

You're unarmed in a room full of people holding weapons. Arm yourself.

The sensation of Denken's thoughts in his head was uncomfortable. It felt like an invasion, a vivid reminder of the demigod's previous trespasses.

A couple of security agents stood within feet of him. And beside them, Mulligan. Perhaps uncomfortable being unarmed in such dangerous company, the minister's adviser had snatched up the gun Gloucester had relinquished. He held it awkwardly, as if it were too heavy in his hands, but his face was set in determination. He, like the agents around him, watched the high minister and his confrontation with Denken. Gloucester would have to be quick.

"Don't do this."

The Gambler's order felt carved in stone, centuries old and immovable. The minister fell silent at his statement, then immediately looked annoyed at himself for being so affected.

"I rolled Snake Eyes. You know what this means, Henry," the demigod said.

For a wild moment, Gloucester was distracted from his scrutiny of Mulligan and the guards, wondering who the Gambler was talking to, before realizing it was still the high minister. Henry. It was strange to be reminded he had a first name, like a normal person.

"I know what you told me, yes," said the high minister. "Words to shake me. To scare me into letting you go. As if I would last an hour if you were free." He jerked his chin at Denken. "Your rabid brother would have me dead by sundown."

"Henry, you must listen—"

The high minister cut him off with another angry rebuke, but Gloucester stopped listening. *Focus.* As the argument between gods and men heated up, the security agents were wavering. This wasn't anything they were trained for. It wasn't something they had ever been meant to see. They stood uncertainly, stances more defensive than prepared now, many of the guns that had been pointed at Gloucester and his companions half-lowered. The high minister hadn't told them what to do, and more likely than not hadn't given them any idea what to expect. Even as he prepared himself for what he had to do, Gloucester felt a pang of sympathy for them. What would become of them if the high minister walked away from this victorious? *He'd* been locked away in isolation after his encounter with the Gambler. Was that what would be waiting for the black-suited men and women that filled the room, gaping at the strange scene unfolding in front of them? Opponents or not, it wasn't a pleasant thought.

He took his chance when the nearest agent, a brawny man in his forties, flinched at the sound of Denken's raised voice, which boomed as he leveled another threat at the high minister. Gloucester didn't waste time pondering if the boost of volume was an intentional distraction for his benefit, instead springing into action.

He launched himself past the agent, giving him a hard shove to knock him off balance and out of the way. The man fell, alarm scrawled across his features, but he wasn't Gloucester's target.

Instead he latched onto Mulligan's shoulder, pulling him around and delivering a swift punch to the adviser's gut. Mulligan gave a breathless grunt of pain, raising the gun in his hand, but the element of surprise and his lack of combat training worked in Gloucester's favor. The scuffle was over almost before it began, and after a moment he managed to wrest the weapon from Mulligan's hand, his other arm looped around the man's neck in a chokehold. Mulligan was taller than Gloucester, but it wasn't his physical bulk that made for an effective shield between himself and the guns of the security agents swinging to point his way. It was who he was. Perhaps the only person in the world that the high minister might hesitate to sacrifice. All too well, Gloucester knew the value placed on the lives of the minister's guards. If he grabbed one of them, he wasn't sure the minister would care. They were expendable. Mulligan wasn't. He hoped.

To his relief, his instincts were proven correct and the high minister gave no order for his agents to shoot. Gloucester ignored Mulligan's cursing in his ear and aimed the gun over the adviser's shoulder, at the one other person in the room who actually mattered to the high minister.

"You wouldn't dare," the minister said, glaring at the gun pointed at his chest as every agent in the room looked from him to Gloucester, waiting for orders. "We've been here before, remember? You don't have it in you."

"Things change," Gloucester said. Though his mind whirled as he wondered what the *hell* he was doing, his voice was as steady as his hand, the barrel of the gun never wavering. He could feel his hostage's breathing against his chest, uneven with strain and emotion. "I'm making my own choices now." He wished that were true, but it had been a long time since he'd felt in control of his own life.

The high minister snorted. "Are you, Gloucester? Or are you just a puppet again? Acting on the whims of monsters? Drop the gun and you don't have to end this day a corpse."

"Just a prisoner?" Gloucester retorted. Even if he surrendered, he doubted he'd be seeing the outside of this room ever again. Something told him the minister had learned his lesson about keeping unnecessary threats alive. What it came down to was simple. Not gods or magic or power, just a simple matter of life or death: stand his ground or die here.

"Should we see how many times I can shoot you before they kill me, then?" he asked. A deadly calm descended over the whispering panic in his mind, the cacophony of thought fading back until all that existed was the moment, the *now*. All eyes were on him, something he normally hated and now scarcely noticed. His finger brushed the trigger. He could see, almost *feel*, the breath catch in the high minister's chest as an order rose to his tongue, Gloucester's fate about to be put into words.

"Made you look," Denken sing-songed in the high minister's ear.

Gloucester felt a sudden shortage of air in the room, as if the collective gasp of everyone present had dragged the oxygen away. The spells to dampen the Brothers' powers hadn't been a match for Denken's uncanny ability to move in the blink of an eye. Or perhaps they weren't designed to combat it. The demigod had moved like a slim shadow, flitting across the floor before anyone could react, until suddenly he stood at the high minister's back.

Time slowed as Denken's hands wound almost lovingly around the minister's neck, fingers slender and strong as jungle vines. Teeth glinted in the semi-dark, sharp and merciless, the smile not reaching eyes too big and too black to be human. They were bottomless, tunnels into something angry and lost.

A shout filled the air, unlike anything Gloucester had ever heard before, and though he couldn't tear his eyes away from Denken's hands around the high minister's neck, he knew it was the Gambler. No human throat could produce such a sound. It was a dirge call, a harbinger, a Valkyrie's song.

In that moment, Gloucester knew it was too late to stop what was about to happen.

Denken's hands barely moved, his fingers tightening, wrists twisting in a simple fluid motion. The *crack* that rent the air echoed off the far walls, and Gloucester's stomach twisted.

The body of the high minister, lord of the city-state, crumpled twitching to the floor. He gave a final gurgling gasp, then stilled.

"Denken," whispered the Gambler in the thundering

silence. "What have you done?"

Denken smiled, shark teeth stretched too widely across his face and victory shining in obsidian eyes. "What I needed to."

Chapter 27

The Magician and the Shark

Silence held sway in the wake of Denken's declaration for several seconds, each passing beat heavier with tension than the last, as if electricity were building in the air. Until finally lightning struck, in the form of Harrison. Pulling himself from his shock, the towering man roared as he swept his gun around to point at the grinning demigod. A gunshot echoed, the flash of the muzzle blinding in the gloom.

In the split seconds that followed, the other agents followed suit, their shots loud as cannon blasts. Gunfire filled the air. Gloucester shoved Mulligan to the ground and threw himself down after, scrabbling for the meager cover of the floor. Out of the corner of his eye, he could see Zane doing the same. Antimony and the Gambler were both shouting, but their words were lost in the cacophony.

Unlike Mulligan's horrified wail. The minister's chief adviser crawled on his hands and knees to the body of his employer, his face a rictus of misery and disbelief. He seemed to be in a tragic world all his own, oblivious to the bullets flying past over his head.

And then it stopped. Silence rose up again like an overtaking wave, marked only by the quiet clicks of guns now empty, as the agents wielding them kept squeezing the triggers convulsively.

In the center of the room, alone save the crumpled figure at his feet and Mulligan who cowered beside it, Denken patted down his shirt as if the bullets were dust bunnies to be swept away with a careless hand. The fabric was riddled with holes, but he appeared uninjured. Denken's smile stretched wider, an ivory crescent slicing from ear to ear. The whites of his eyes, nearly invisible, sparked amidst the endless black depths of pupil and iris alike, like those of a great ocean beast.

"Bad luck, ladies and gents. Looks like some things aren't as restricted by those pesky little spells as we all thought, eh? Lucky me." His lips twitched as the agents stared at him in horror. "Less lucky you lot."

"Denken, stop!"

The Gambler's cry crashed like cymbals in their ears. Tears pricked the corners of Gloucester's eyes; he thought he might go deaf if either god kept this up.

"Hush, Joujou," Denken cooed, bottomless eyes never wavering from the agents. "You're injured. I'll take care of this. Antimony, help him."

The magic of the room might temper his powers, but the strained look on Antimony's face made it clear she was still feeling the effects, even if they were weakened.

"I thought they couldn't kill," moaned Zane, as she crawled to Gloucester's side. "They're not supposed to be able to kill humans." In her eyes was the same terror that the stricken agents wore openly on their faces. The same fear that pressed on his own heart and mind. With his free hand, he found one of hers and took it, interlacing their fingers.

"They can't, they can't, they can't," Zane muttered under

her breath.

"That's most people's mistake," said a voice above them, lacking Zane's quiet fear or the gods' inhuman charisma. "Mixing up 'couldn't' with 'shouldn't.'"

A black-booted foot stepped past Gloucester's head, and he looked up to see Finch. Unlike his companions, he wasn't ducking in precaution, nor was he gaping like the agents. He stood tall, back straight and face set.

Denken turned to face him. Though he still bore a human form, little about him seemed human beyond the bare essentials. His eyes, huge and black, and his too-wide, razor-toothed mouth were those of a creature, not a man. The air around him hummed with power, as if the room's restrictions were causing his magic to be pent up inside of him instead. Gloucester thought suddenly of the bomb they'd disarmed down in the basement. Denken had no countdown clock, but if he did, Gloucester had a feeling it would be nearing zero.

"Someone's feeling brave," Denken said, eerily sweet. "The little orphan boy, out for revenge."

"Doesn't it bother you?" Finch held a gun in his hand, the one Denken had returned to him before they'd entered the room. He must have taken the chance to retrieve it in all the confusion. Looking from him to Denken, Gloucester sat up slowly. Like everyone else in the room, he felt almost paralyzed, breathless as he watched the man and the god face each other.

Finch was smiling. "Doesn't it *bother* you that you didn't see this coming?"

Holding the gun between his palms, he murmured a string of words Gloucester didn't catch. They didn't sound like a sentence or even how he imagined a magical incantation to sound. It was halfway between music and laughter, almost buzzing, as if an insect caught in Finch's throat were making the sound in his place. The gun glowed brightly golden for a moment. Finch's smile widened. He didn't look happy, just relieved. At peace.

"See what coming?" Denken sounded unimpressed, but

his eyes were on the gun. It had ceased glowing, save for inscriptions Gloucester had never noticed before. They looked like some intricate form of writing carved into the metal, which shimmered in a light that came from the weapon itself. "A petty magic-monger trying to attack me with a little gun? You think I didn't expect your pathetic attempt at revenge?"

Finch's laugh was empty. "You expected it, yeah. But you didn't *know* it." He tapped the index finger of his free hand against his temple. "Doesn't it bother you?"

Denken's grin shrank. Yet in unnatural contrast, the rest of him seemed to do the opposite. Gloucester disentangled his hand from Zane's and rubbed his eyes, staring. It wasn't Denken's physical size that was expanding, but rather the space consumed by his very presence. In the shadows around him, something stirred. Fins in the murk.

"The room is—" Denken began, smile no longer on his face, but Finch cut him off before he could finish the sentence.

"The room is impeding your powers *now*, but I've been counting on this opportunity since we got here. Since you made this plan." While Denken's grin had withered away, Finch's had only spread, and now it cut across his face, a merciless imitation of happiness. "I know something you don't know."

Denken took a step toward him, his shadow crossing over the still body of the high minister. Mulligan, on his knees beside it, shuddered at the passage of the shadow.

"I knew what this room would do to you," Finch said. "I knew it would make you weak."

"Ask *him* how weak I am." Denken looked less human than ever as he gestured at the minister's body, his fingertips lengthened and sharpened into long claws, edged like razors.

"You did what any strong enough human could do," Finch said with a scoff. The safety on his gun clicked off. For such a quiet, simple sound, it rang in Gloucester's ears like a bell. "And now you get to do what any human would do when shot with this gun." He raised the gun to point at Denken's narrow chest.

Antimony and the Gambler began shouting again. The security agents stood frozen, unsure what to do in the face of the impossible. Zane's hand, which had found its way to Gloucester's shoulder, slipped away as Gloucester got to his feet without consciously telling himself to rise.

"Finch." He reached for the magician's arm as shadows shifted and twisted before them, coalescing into the unnatural creature that dwelled behind Denken's human mask. "Don't—Ah!"

The jab of Finch's elbow caught him square on the jaw, knocking his head back with unexpected force and sending him reeling. Blood filled his mouth from where his teeth had cut his bottom lip. Finch's hand swung toward him again, and though this time it didn't touch him, *something* did, a concussive force of air colliding with his chest like a battering ram. He went down with a cry. Zane was yelling now too, but her words clamored meaninglessly in his ringing ears as he stared up at the distant, hidden ceiling, stunned and gasping for breath.

"Don't get in my way," Finch said. His cold indifference was a painful contrast to the humor and emotion that usually colored his voice. Gloucester wondered in a daze which one was the facade.

He struggled to sit up, wheezing as he braced himself on his elbows. Zane appeared in his field of vision, and though her hand was back on his shoulder, her eyes were not on him; she was glaring up at Finch. But as Gloucester followed her gaze, it wasn't the magician that caught his attention, but Denken. He was taken aback to see the demigod staring back at him, inky eyes piercing. They widened with bitter realization.

"The kiss. You were distracting me."

"Best way to hide a plan from a mind-reader. Give him lots of surface thoughts to read. Juicy ones to play with."

Denken smiled again, all teeth and no mirth. "How clever. Clever and cruel. You didn't tell him." He nodded at Gloucester, who looked from him to Finch, nonplussed. Finch didn't return the glance. His gaze never left Denken, nor did the gun waver from its target.

"You said it yourself, he's easy to read. And this has nothing to do with him. Just you and me. And my father."

"A petty old man who interfered with things he shouldn't have," spat Denken. "A cunning criminal who played with magic like a child with his parent's gun. He was greedy and foolish. Do you think anyone but you will mourn his death?"

"No," said Finch simply.

He pulled the trigger.

Chapter 28

Creatures of Violence

The shot rang clear, surrounded by silence almost as loud. Everyone stood frozen, staring, as the muzzle of the gun flashed.

The gun kicked in Finch's grip, his arm jerking to allow the motion without injuring his wrist. His expression didn't change, didn't twitch. He'd fired this gun before.

Denken dodged.

It wasn't a showy action. He didn't throw himself out of the way, nor perform elaborate feats of acrobatics to evade the bullet flying toward him. Perhaps he didn't have enough time to move or maybe he was simply so accustomed to bullets being harmless that he'd forgotten what to do when faced with ones that could actually do him damage.

Either way, his dodge was slight; he pivoted on the spot, turning side-face. Yet for once, not quickly enough. The shot meant for his heart struck his shoulder instead, and he staggered back a step with a growl. It was the first time Gloucester had seen Denken anything short of graceful.

Denken gnashed his teeth. "Is that the best you can do?"

It is widely accepted that a statement like this is best avoided in times of conflict, seen as a taunt too tempting to resist, not only by one's enemies but by the universe as a whole. It's the sort of unwise verbal jab that comes prepackaged with an assortment of other equally ill-conceived commentary, ranging from the foreshadowing "Pick on someone your own size" to the always ironic "At least it can't get any worse."

But in Denken's case, he seemed to be more than up to the task of standing behind the challenge he'd issued. Not only was he still on his feet after the gunshot, he was already regaining the steps he'd retreated and then some, prowling—albeit a little unsteadily—forward.

Finch fired again. This time there was no dodge, no stagger back. The bullet hit Denken in the chest but didn't cause the demigod more than a brief pause as he looked down at the wound. Something too black to be blood seeped from it, as if he were bleeding ink or shadows. He looked up again, opened his mouth, and laughed.

Since their first encounter, Gloucester had heard Denken laugh many times: giggles, chuckles, snickers, and snorts. He'd heard him laugh snidely, jokingly, and in honest amusement.

None of those laughs had sounded like this.

The noise Denken made was guttural, slinking through the air and into their ears like a whispered lie, full of danger and ill-portent. Gloucester could hear in it the growl of the dog about to bite, the whistle of the approaching train, the creak of the ice underfoot. More than that, he *felt* the laugh.

Shadows gathered around Denken and shrouded him like a living cloak. For, indeed, they seemed alive, twisting themselves again into the shape of the massive shark that had loomed across the room in the Maze and in Gloucester's nightmares since. Independent of the scant light binding the rest of their shadows to their places, it swam through darkness and light alike as it continued to grow.

He's going to swallow Finch whole. Gloucester's mind felt slower than usual, as if his thoughts were running through thick mud. He stared from the creature of shadow and malice to Finch, who looked tiny in comparison. *The gun won't work. He's going to die.*

Like his thoughts, the world had slowed, seconds stretching into lifetimes as Finch's doom closed in. Only two people existed now: man and god. The others in the room were forgotten. The security agents, frozen as statues; Mulligan, sobbing over the high minister's body; Antimony and the Gambler, their pleas falling on deaf ears. Even Zane, so close by, her hand on his shoulder, faded into the background.

He's going to kill him.

Either one.

One way or the other.

The shadow beast surged forward. Its wide gaping maw descended upon Finch, and he disappeared in the living darkness. Gloucester opened his mouth, but he wasn't sure if he was shouting or even breathing at all. His heart thundered in his ears. This couldn't be happening. They were surely all next. This was how it was all going to end. How could any of them fight a creature immune even to a magician's spells—

"Not gonna work here, bastard."

Finch's voice was muffled by the shadow surrounding him, but he sounded very much alive. The darkness began to dissipate like morning mist in the sun. Denken howled in anger as the shadows fell away to reveal Finch unscathed. He was very pale, but furious victory laced every word he spoke.

"You're just an illusionist here, mate," he said, tone miraculously level for someone just eaten by a demon shark. "You can create pretty pictures and light shows, that's all. As long as you're in this room, the only way you're getting to me is if you're brave enough to get close. And . . ." He hefted the gun in his hand, angling it to aim between Denken's eyes. "I dare you to try."

"We won't be in this room forever." Denken sounded nothing like the cheerful being Gloucester had met a day or so earlier. His voice was low, layered and ugly. Gloucester's skin crawled with every syllable.

"You will," Finch said. His finger squeezed the trigger and another shot splintered the air.

The bullet ricocheted off one arching stone of the vaulted ceiling and buried itself in another, raining down a small shower of rubble onto the floor. Its clatter was lost in the echo of the gunshot and Finch's shout of infuriated alarm as he was bowled over. Gloucester had thrown himself to his feet with the unthinking strength of desperation and tackled the magician, sending them both flying into a heap on the marble.

Finch writhed beneath him, roaring in rage as he fought to throw him off. Gloucester clung on doggedly, grappling for the gun in the other man's hand.

"*Get off.*" Finch's free hand shoved against Gloucester's chin. His fingers chased along Gloucester's jaw before tightening around his throat. Gloucester choked, dragging in a breath that couldn't make it past the squeezing hold, but he didn't let go. His hand felt the twisting skin of Finch's wrist, struggling madly, and the pivoting bone beneath it, then the hard metal of the pistol grip. He tried to wrench it out of Finch's hand. Finch spat a curse, his hand tightening further around Gloucester's neck. Lights danced in his vision. His fingertips could still feel metal for a moment longer, then it was jerked away, only to return in force.

The butt of the gun smashed into his face. With a crunch and an explosion of pain, warm blood filled his nose and mouth. It slid down his throat and he choked on it, already struggling for every breath. His hands lost their grip on Finch as darkness closed in. He needed air—

He was suddenly wrenched away, the crushing hold on his

neck removed, leaving him sputtering and gasping for air. Blood splattered from his nose and lips, sticking to his face. He didn't know what was happening, only that he could *breathe* again. His gasps were loud and rattling, rough with coughs and wet with blood.

"That wasn't very nice." Even half-conscious, Gloucester knew the voice was Denken's. The demigod sounded close by, almost on top of him, and he wondered if he'd been the one to pull Finch off of him. "He'll think you don't care."

He was answered with gunfire. It, too, sounded right overhead. Gloucester realized dimly that he was lying facedown on the marble floor, blood pooling beneath his face. The gunshot echoed in his ears, and he moaned in pain.

"I don't," Finch said from further away. He'd used the gunshot to buy himself the time to retreat a good distance. "All I care about is setting things right."

"Me too."

The voice was unfamiliar, new amongst all those that had been shouting back and forth. It was a feminine voice, deep, melodious, and shaking with emotion. Gloucester forced himself to look up through eyes streaming with tears, his broken nose still gushing blood and throbbing in agony.

He almost forgot about the pain as he clumsily pushed himself into a half-sitting position and bore witness to the unfolding scene.

The security agents had retreated to the edges of the room. Harrison stood next to an empty-faced Mulligan, presumably having helped drag the high minister's body out of the fray. It lay at their feet like a broken doll. Zane, Antimony, and the Gambler were out of Gloucester's field of vision, gathered somewhere behind where he lay. Denken, as he'd suspected, stood over him. Finch, gun raised and face haggard, stood closer to the door and the corridor beyond. All eyes were locked on the newcomer who stood in the open doorway.

She was a striking woman, smooth-skinned despite the gray

in her hair, her hooded eyes calm. Though her oval-shaped face and neck were both slender, her torso was strangely bulky. The reason for this became apparent as she took a step further into the room and the light that had been throwing her back-lit torso into shadow illuminated the vest she wore. Wires were strung around her like tinsel on a tree.

"I wondered why my bomb didn't work," she said. "But it's okay, I had a Plan B."

Denken laughed his terrible laugh again. "Yvette Jacoby, as I live and breathe."

Looking up at Yvette Jacoby, Gloucester wondered if this was how he had appeared, back at the minister's mansion when he'd leveled a gun at the man's head and almost pulled the trigger. Jacoby's face was void of emotion, showing only a vague sort of calm. Gloucester hadn't felt calm at the time. Was it different for her, or was the torment the same and he just hadn't been aware of how little he'd shown it?

They were questions to which he doubted he'd get answers. Everyone in the room watched Jacoby as she strode in, a predator arriving at the watering hole. In the semi-dark of the room, the blinking light strapped to her chest was all too obvious.

"I keep making mistakes," she said hollowly. "No more. This time it ends."

"It's already ended, you mad bitch!" Mulligan cried. He glared at Jacoby. "His Lordship's dead." His voice cracked over the word like dry bone. "Your job's done for you."

Jacoby stared down at the high minister's body, seemingly uncomprehending. Gloucester looked from her to Denken. How was she this affected by the demigod's power? When he'd failed to take the high minister's life, Denken's hold over his mind had broken. Why wasn't that the case with Jacoby?

Denken looked as confused as the rest of them, his huge black eyes narrowed as he regarded her in the half-light. Like he was trying to figure out an impossible puzzle. Maybe that's what she was to him.

Sensing his eyes on her, Jacoby turned and met Denken's gaze. A flicker of emotion passed over her face, and she gave a shuddering gasp.

"I know you," she said, raising a hand to point at him.

Something was gripped in her fingers. The *detonator*.

"Oh, Yvette." Denken sighed. "It's a mess in there, isn't it?"

"You did that," Finch accused. His gun was still pointed at Denken. "You got inside her head like a burglar sneaking into a house. And you broke things."

Yvette didn't react to his words. Gloucester wasn't even sure she knew any of them were there, other than the dead high minister and Denken.

"It can happen," Denken said with a cold indifference. "If a mind is too fragile."

"I bet it didn't even occur to you as a risk," Finch said, disgusted. "She was just an opportunity to you. A weapon ready to be armed. Any of the other people you assaulted could have been broken too." His finger jabbed in Gloucester's direction, who flinched involuntarily. "What about *his* brain? Did it ever cross your mind when you were digging around in his, that you might be doing damage?"

Denken sniggered, though his eyes barely spent an instant on Finch before flicking back to Jacoby. She still stood motionless, detonator raised as she regarded him coolly. "Bit rich, that concern. Seeing as it's the same brain you nearly bashed in just now."

"Don't talk about me like I'm not here!"

Gloucester's outburst surprised no one more than himself. Zane whispered a warning, reaching to pull him back, but he shook her off and climbed unsteadily to his feet. "Just shut up, the pair of you."

"I've met you before," Jacoby said, still staring at Denken, deaf and blind to everyone else. "You spoke in my ear." Her face twitched and she made a harsh hissing noise. "In my ear," she repeated.

In the ringing silence that fell upon the room, Gloucester thought he could hear all of their heartbeats, like the chorus of clocks that filled Zane's shop.

The silence stretched on a moment too long, and in the space between breaths, Gloucester knew Jacoby had reached a decision.

"You did this," she said, calm as the still air of the church. Her hand moved.

Another gunshot shattered the air. Jacoby crumpled, boneless, to the floor, her head knocked back by the impact of the bullet buried in her forehead. In the instant before she fell, Gloucester saw her face as the light left her eyes.

She looked relieved.

Finch's expression, in contrast, conveyed no semblance of peace. His breaths were halting and uneven, loud in the resounding silence that followed the shot, save for the faint echoes of the blast bouncing off the far walls. A quiet click followed. He'd squeezed the trigger again, perhaps convulsively, but the gun was out of ammunition.

Gloucester dashed toward Jacoby's body, his bleary eyes on the device in her hand. In death, her fingers had tightened around the bomb's detonator. A tiny muscle spasm that saved all of their lives. Barely daring to breathe, he swiped his sleeve across his eyes to clear away the lingering tears clinging to his lashes. The cloth came away bloody, but he paid it no mind, reaching forward to carefully extricate the device from Jacoby's stiffening grip.

He hesitated before he touched it, staring at the bomb itself. More exposed than the tidy little device they'd disarmed in the basement, its wires twined around the dead woman's vest. Whether it was desperation or confidence or simply the ache in his head obliterating logical thought, Gloucester threw caution to the winds and didn't waste any more time second-guessing which wires were right or wrong. Instead, he went with instinct and the recollection of old training, tugging a pair of identical wires free of the main body of the bomb simultaneously. The lights stopped flashing, dying as surely as the woman whose corpse they decorated.

The silence returned, like water seeping up around them no matter how often they bailed it out. Yet it felt somehow lighter now.

"Is it safe?" Zane asked.

Gloucester nodded dumbly. His head hurt. His thoughts spun in a confusing kaleidoscope of emotion, quickly losing focus now that Jacoby was no longer a threat. He had the sudden and almost overwhelming desire to sleep, to lay down right then and there on the cold stone floor, wet with blood and stinking of death. To close his eyes and wait for it all to go away.

But the fight wasn't over. He raised his head, which felt several times heavier than usual, and though he saw that most eyes were still on him, his own tired gaze went straight to the only two people whose attentions were elsewhere.

Finch stood in a daze, his gun pointed harmlessly at the floor. Though his back was still stiff with anger, he looked tired, his face gray. Denken, too, was no longer brimming with furious energy. He looked uncharacteristically hesitant and uncomfortable. They both seemed wary, unsure of the next move to make. Gloucester noticed that Denken's hands, still monstrously elongated with claws, were shaking badly.

"Denken, listen to me," said the Gambler, speaking for the first time in several action-packed minutes. "You've broken the rules. The consequences—"

"I know," snapped Denken. "I don't . . . I don't care."

But that didn't seem to be the case. He had an odd look in his eyes, one that had been building for a while, and Gloucester recognized it in that moment as fear.

"You need to get out of here," said the Gambler. He was leaning heavily on Antimony, his face bloodless and gaunt with fear of his own. "*Now.*"

Denken opened his mouth and looked for a moment like

he wanted to argue. Then he nodded jerkily and drew in a long shuddering breath. As he sucked in air, he pulled in the supernatural shadows he'd exuded as well, the gloom retreating back into him like a bad aura. Gloucester was surprised to see how much of the room's darkness had been the demigod's angry presence.

"No!" Finch threw the empty gun aside, his eyes wild as he cast about for another weapon.

There wouldn't be time. By the time Finch got his hands on another gun, Denken would be gone.

Finch seemed to realize this too. With an animal roar of last-ditch rage, he threw himself at Denken, unarmed. The demigod's inhuman hand moved through the air as a blur, and then he was clutching Finch by the throat, the magician's feet barely touching the floor.

Denken's hand shook so much that Finch's whole body looked like it was shivering. He struggled, choking and red-faced, but his eyes were bright with fury. Denken's eyes just looked dead.

"You would do it again?"

The Gambler's simple question conveyed such sober horror and bitter disappointment that Denken flinched. His fingers released Finch, who fell to his knees, gasping for breath. Denken stared down at him, then turned wide eyes on his brother. Fear that wasn't entirely his own washed through Gloucester, unstoppable as water through a broken dam.

And then Denken was gone.

Chapter 29

Consequences

"What the *hell* just happened?"

Harrison broke the silence in the wake of Denken's departure. The brawny agent stared at the spot where the demigod had been standing before he vanished. Gloucester wondered with hazy dispassion whether Denken really could disappear or if he was simply able to move so quickly it seemed that way. Regardless, it was obviously another power that hadn't been as dampened by the Finches' ward as they'd all been led to believe.

Really ought to have a word with Finch about that. Struggling to stand, he coughed and spat out another mouthful of blood. His face felt swollen, his vision pinched as his broken nose caused the skin around his eyes to become puffy. He was sure he looked as bad as he felt. Finch had more than a few things to answer for.

The magician apparently had no intention of humoring

them, however. Ignoring Harrison's question, he avoided all of their eyes and turned toward the doorway.

"Stop!"

For a moment, Gloucester thought he was the one who had called out the protest. He was baffled by how different a broken nose made him sound, before realizing it was Harrison who had spoken again, merely voicing Gloucester's thoughts aloud.

"You're not going anywhere," the agent said heatedly. "None of you." The shock of the situation was waning. Gloucester was suddenly once again intensely aware of the fact that they were a group of wanted fugitives in a room filled with very angry, very confused security agents.

And one dead high minister.

"Who the hell was that?" Harrison demanded. Now that he'd found his voice again, he seemed intent on using it. "He killed the . . . He . . . The high minister is dead!" Amidst all of his professional outrage, he still looked terrified. "What *was* he?"

"Something you were never meant to know about."

In contrast to Harrison's agitation, Mulligan sounded drained. He was kneeling down again, the minister's body pulled halfway onto his lap. He looked lost. "It was the secret. No one was supposed to know. The Gambler—"

"The Gambler didn't do this," Antimony said. "Killing the high minister wasn't the plan. It was *never* the plan."

Gently, Mulligan disentangled himself from the high minister's still form and got to his feet. "It was all going well. All until you." His eyes cleared, and his bewildered grief hardened into fury as he turned to the group of fugitives. "You ruined it all."

"No," said Antimony. "He did that himself, messing with magic. He thought he could *tame* it, use it for his own ends. He was damned the day he told the Finches to catch him the Gambler. We were just here to witness the inevitable."

Harrison stared at her in open and angry bafflement. "Why should we trust you on any of this? Who *are* you?"

Much to all of their surprise, it was Mulligan who answered. "It's a long story, Harrison. One too long to tell now." Though Gloucester knew the chief adviser wasn't past his mid-forties, he looked significantly older now, as if the death of his employer had aged him. He knuckled his brow, then aimed a look Antimony's way. A more pragmatic expression settled onto his face. "Though," he said, "I have to agree with Mr. Harrison. I don't know who *you* are."

Antimony wasn't cowed by his scrutiny. "Someone you'll probably need the help of soon enough, so mind your manners and listen here. What Denken did just now, that was bad. For everyone," she added, sweeping a warning look around the room before anyone could claim this to be obvious. "And I'm not just talking about the leader of Frettchen getting murdered. I mean because of who murdered him. Because of *what* murdered him."

"She's right," said the Gambler, stepping forward. He was steadier on his feet now, though his eerie face was still pinched with strain. If the assembled agents had given Antimony baffled looks, it was nothing compared to how they regarded the Gambler. Somewhere in the city was a therapist who was soon to be very busy and very bemused. "My brother made a grave mistake, one I know he will regret. But his regret is not enough to undo the damage. He broke the rules. We do not kill, not without consequences."

From the looks of it, there was no end to the questions Harrison and Mulligan wanted to ask. They gawped like floundering fish for several seconds, while behind them the rest of the agents looked from them to the Gambler, blatantly lost.

Finally, Mulligan said, "What do you mean, consequences? For him or for us?"

"For everyone. The universe holds us in check. It has rules to prevent our power from . . . affecting us. Changing us. Too much power can make a monster of anyone, but in our case it is dangerously literal. They are rules that should not be flouted, for the sake of our own well-being as much as for that of the world."

"I always thought that it was '*couldn't* be flouted,'" said Zane shakily. With a gentle hand, she pulled Gloucester away from the crumpled body of Yvette Jacoby, shuddering as she averted her eyes.

The Gambler's face was grim. "We have always been trusted to know better."

Antimony laid a hand on his shoulder again. "He was desperate."

"He was foolish. And now it is not just him who will pay the price."

"You keep saying that," snapped Harrison. He took a furious step toward the Gambler, though his bravery faltered when the demigod turned his face in his direction. He stopped in his tracks, but otherwise held his ground. "But what does that *mean?*"

All eyes went back to the Gambler, everyone in the room holding their breath in anticipation of his answer.

The Gambler shrugged away from Antimony's hand and walked toward the high minister's body. His feet made quiet slapping noises as he moved, leaving red footprints behind him. Mulligan made a strangled sound that might have been the beginnings of a protest, but he quickly swallowed the noise, as if afraid to break the silence.

Unlike Jacoby, no blood surrounded the high minister's corpse. Were it not for the unnatural turn of his head, he might have been sleeping. Mulligan had pressed his eyelids closed, making him look more peaceful than his demise had actually been. The Gambler crouched beside him. The lines of his face didn't betray any pleasure at the sight of his captor's fate. Gloucester wondered how the strange creature felt, looking down at the man who had held him prisoner for so long. He wondered how *he* felt. The high minister had been his captor too. Looking at him now, though, he couldn't sort through his emotions to determine what he felt about the man's death.

Maybe he didn't feel anything. Maybe it would hit him later, reality dawning slowly over the horizon of his mind. All he felt now was tired and sore.

Still, curiosity fought its way through the fog of his mind as he watched the Gambler rummage through the high minister's pockets. This desecration proved to be too much for Mulligan, who squawked a proper protest this time, only to be shushed, unexpectedly, by Harrison.

The Gambler played dumb to both of them. He continued his search until he produced a small box from the minister's inner jacket pocket. Then he smiled faintly. He opened the box and tipped its contents onto his palm.

It was a pair of dice, carved of white bone or perhaps stone or ivory. In the dim light, Gloucester couldn't tell for sure. The Gambler looked down at them, then closed his hands around the dice, as if he were cupping a tiny creature. Gloucester felt the barest hint of magic, a gentle sigh against his skin, then the Gambler opened his fingers once more.

Something flew from them. Two somethings.

At first, Gloucester assumed they were the dice. All considered, that would be practically mundane at this point. The objects were roughly the same size, and with the way they whizzed around the Gambler's head, it was difficult to get a good look at them. Once he did, his stomach twisted. Behind him, a few of the agents muttered in disgust.

They were eyes. They orbited the Gambler's head like tiny enthusiastic moons, spinning this way and that as they flew. The Gambler got to his feet, his sad smile still in place. Before Gloucester could ask why the high minister would keep such things in his jacket pocket, the Gambler spoke.

"Now we will see."

He was met with silence. Gloucester, wondering if that had been meant as a joke, realized belatedly that the demigod was answering the question Harrison had posed to him.

"You don't even *know*?" Harrison seethed. "We're just

supposed to wait around for some sort of, of demon to rain terror down on us all?"

For the first time, something like impatience sparked in the Gambler's demeanor. His free-flying eyes whirled out of sight, and the corners of his mouth twisted downward before his face smoothed once more. "Not ideally," was his terse reply.

"Look." Antimony strode forward with her hands raised placatingly. "We can stand here bickering or we can actually try to do something about it. We need more information. There are people we can go to—"

"Oh no. No, no, no." Mulligan waved his hands in a far more open show of his displeasure than the Gambler. "The only place any of you people are going to is a cell. You'll be lucky if it's not a firing squad."

"Mulligan! Shut up!"

The voice roared through the chief adviser's ire, and it wasn't until all eyes turned on him that Gloucester registered it was his own. He'd been doing that a lot today.

A lead weight settled in his stomach. The ache in his head had become a hard-to-ignore pounding, but not only with pain. Looking down at his hands, he saw that he'd balled them into white-knuckled fists. He raised his eyes back to Mulligan and felt his anger rise as well, hot and fast as a sun flare.

"Stop talking for once and listen to what people are saying. We're not your bloody enemies. We didn't want the high minister dead, and we certainly didn't want to unleash an angry god on the world, but these people?" He jabbed a finger at Antimony and the Gambler. "They are the *only* people I know of who might be able to stop this before things get worse. So shut up and let them help!"

He was panting by the end of his tirade, chest rising and falling with each sharp breath. Everyone stared at him, and he dropped his glare down to his feet, furious and self-conscious in equal parts.

"Thank you," said Antimony. Gloucester risked glancing

up at her and read the gratefulness in her eyes. He nodded his understanding and his own gratitude.

"Mr. Gloucester is right," the Gambler said. "We are all going to need each other for what is coming." He looked at Mulligan, and even without eyes, his sympathy was clear. "The death of the high minister and lord of the city-state was brought upon him by his own actions"—he ignored the chief adviser's indignant scoff—"but it is a dangerous thing. With no leader, the church and the city-state will be in chaos both."

His eyeballs flitted back into view to stare at Mulligan from over each of the Gambler's shoulders. They were the color of amber, unlike any eye color Gloucester had seen before.

"Unless you act quickly," he finished.

"Me?" blustered Mulligan. "How—"

Harrison placed a massive hand on his shoulder. "It's right, sir," he said, paying no attention to the Gambler's frown at being referred to as "it." "We need to get this under control before anyone else finds out he's dead. There are other priests, trustworthy ones, we can choose from for the high minister post. As for the Lordship title, we can—"

"How can you talk like that?" Mulligan's demand was shrill and shaking with grief. "He's dead! Fuck's sake, Harrison. His body's not . . . not even cold yet."

"I know, sir. I know. But we have to do what we can to keep things under control. It's what he would want."

"He'd want not to be dead," Mulligan retorted, with something that sounded suspiciously like a sniffle. "He wouldn't care at all about what happened after he was gone." He said this with a miserable admiration, as if he couldn't think of a more impressive show of moral fortitude.

"Well," said Harrison with the hint of a sad smile, "that still leaves the rest of us to care, then."

Mulligan took a deep breath, while Gloucester held his, waiting to see if what followed was an agreement or just further argument.

"We have a lot of work to do," Mulligan muttered at last.

"And a lot of explaining," Harrison said. Mulligan looked up at him, then nodded, though from the look on his face it was only with the greatest reluctance.

"I suppose that too." He turned his gaze to Gloucester and the others. Any warmth in it disappeared. "Don't think I'll forget what happened here. We're not friends, and you're not forgiven of your crimes. If you can't hold up your end of the bargain, if you can't prove yourselves to be useful, we'll be coming for you."

Gloucester nodded once, but it was Antimony who answered, "We're the least of each other's problems. You just try to keep the city afloat, and we'll deal with Denken."

Mulligan offered a curt nod of his own. "You'd better. Now get out of here. I have your mess to clean up and . . . and arrangements to make."

Sensing that he was dangerously close to changing his mind, Gloucester and the others wasted little time in filing out the door, leaving the stunned agents and mourning chief adviser behind.

After the dimness of the Gambler's prison, the corridor outside felt too bright, as the nave had when they'd left the basement. They all squinted around at each other, save the Gambler, who fell into step beside Gloucester.

"Thank you," he said as they stepped through the second door and out into the wider hall of the church. He smiled down at him, and Gloucester was taken aback by the warmth that flooded through him at the sight. The Gambler's emotions were like Denken's, infectious and a little overwhelming.

"Hey," Zane called out. "Where's Finch?"

Gloucester used the open space and good lighting of the nave to take a proper look around them. The magician had disappeared. He stopped in his tracks, glancing back the way they'd come. "He must have . . . must have slipped away when we were all distracted," he said. In the aftermath of Jacoby's death and Denken's departure, he'd been so caught up in what was happening that he hadn't paid the other man any mind.

"Do you think he went after Denken?" he asked, raising a hand to his face and brushing his fingers gingerly over his broken nose.

"Went to lick his wounds, probably," said Antimony. "I reckon he knows better than to go after Denken when he's not in a room that minimizes his powers. Especially now." She gestured for them all to keep walking, tugging distractedly on a loose strand of hair that had strayed from her bun. "My question is, will Denken be going after *him?*"

The Gambler let out a long breath. Now that they had left his prison behind, he was much steadier on his feet. "Denken has bigger things to worry about at the moment. But yes, I think eventually we will all have his wrath to contend with."

Hardly the words of comfort Gloucester had been hoping for. He bit his lip, immediately regretting the nervous action as it aggravated the split there, and cleared his throat. "Do you think that we . . . Will we . . ." He wasn't even sure what he wanted to ask, the question jumbling up on his tongue without bothering to first pass his brain's inspection.

The Gambler seemed to know, though. Kindly, he said, "We will see Cassus Finch again."

"Oh," Gloucester said, feeling both relieved and incredibly stupid for some reason. "Oh. Good. I, uh, I want an apology. For my face." He gestured at his throbbing nose.

The others didn't look completely convinced, but they didn't argue. Zane gave him a tired smile as she came over to sling her arm around his shoulders.

"Of course," she said, with a laugh that was more of a sigh. "Speaking of which, we should probably get that sorted out. Don't want to face the Denken-pocalypse with your nose on sideways."

Gloucester's laugh wasn't much more enthusiastic than Zane's, but there was a touch of honesty in it. "Absolutely not," he agreed.

—

Though the fresh air outside All Saints Shrine came on the wings of a spring breeze that had turned chilly while they'd been inside, Gloucester breathed it in gratefully. Only then did relief really set in, pulling some of the tension away from his shoulders and allowing him to feel like he was once again free.

He knew not to be fooled by the fleeting feeling. They'd accomplished their mission, they'd saved the Gambler, but at a cost none of them had expected. As good as the open air felt, it was the calm before a whole new storm.

The Gambler vanished as they left the church. Unlike his brother and Finch, he offered a farewell.

"We will face this together, all of us," he told them, smiling faintly. "Antimony, you know what to do."

And with that, he was gone. No sound accompanied the disappearance, nor did he fade slowly like a photograph aging in the sun. One moment he was there and the next he was gone, as if he had never been.

The remaining three clambered into Antimony's car where they'd parked it on the street. A ticket was on the windshield, which prompted a strangled sound from Antimony that might have been a laugh. Zane climbed into the passenger seat and Gloucester took the back, resisting the temptation to lie down across the seat and fall asleep.

"What now?" he asked as they pulled away from the curb. He didn't expect the other two to have an answer, but still the question came. *Always asking questions.*

Both women were quiet, their eyes on the road ahead. Finally, Zane said, "Let's go home."

Gloucester looked out the window at the city streets. His reflection on the glass imposed itself over the passing scenery like a ghost. "I don't know where that is," he admitted.

Zane turned in her seat, smiling back at him.

"We'll figure it out," she said. "Together."

Epilogue

Back at the Crossroads

Clouds build and gather and fall away to nothing, like the rise and fall of empires. The sky overhead of the Crossroads, roiling for so long now with the army of an oncoming storm, gives way to the course of nature: for the first time in a thousand years, it rains there. Drops fall fat and heavy, soaking the ground in minutes, in hours, instantly. In some respects, it has always been raining and always will be, just as when it stops, it will never have happened. Such is the nature of timeless places, something better left uncontemplated. It is a land of ever-present.

The Gambler walks among the raindrops, home once more. Like the rain, now that he's here, he always has been, always will be. The rain runs down over his face, blond hair slicked back and trailing clear water. Soon the storm will pass and the sun will return, blue skies eternal.

—

Somewhere else, as unreachable as the Crossroads, the Maze stands abandoned. Its stone walls echo with distant laughter, mad and desperate, and the ebbing traces of footsteps. One by one, the impossible, twisting staircases begin to fall, their stones crumbling. And in a rush of wind hot as the breath of a dragon, the countless doors swing open.

This is the home of a god. And he is *angry*.

The end.

And so the clock is wound, and all the little pieces start their moving and ticking.

Acknowledgments

There are so many people who helped and encouraged me, without whom this book could not exist. I owe you all the greatest of thanks.

To my first readers: Kate, Mum, Dad, Mackenzie, and Cindy. Your interest, time, and feedback meant everything to me.

To my family and friends, for their enthusiasm and support.

To Susan Brooks and Literary Wanderlust, for taking a chance on my book and seeing something in it worthy of your name.

To Jennica Dotson, my editor, whose kind words, encouragement, creativity, and keen eye have made my book so much more than it was. Your enthusiasm for the story and your love for the characters means more than I can say.

And to my readers, past, present, and future, for whom this book was written. I hope you found something to love in its pages.

About the Author

Ali Ives is a writer, artist, and daydreamer. She grew up with a love for reading, art, and creativity that hasn't waned with adulthood. Working in a small indie bookshop near where she lives in rural Ontario has only made her love and appreciate the world of books all the more. When she isn't writing or surrounded by books, you're likely to find her drawing, wandering around her property with her dog, or covered in dirt and grass-stains from her other part-time work as a lily gardener. The story that would eventually develop into her first novel started taking form all the way back in her teen years, with the characters filling up many a sketchbook and doodled on the edges of her schoolwork.

Instagram: https://www.instagram.com/aliiveswrites/
Tumblr: https://aliiveswrites.tumblr.com/